# I Saw Her First

## JEN MORRIS

*I Saw Her First* Copyright © 2024 by Jen Morris

All rights reserved. No part of this book may be reproduced or used in any manner without written permission of the copyright owner except for the use of brief quotations in a book review. For more information, contact at: www.jenmorrisauthor.com.

First edition October 2024

Epub ISBN: 978-1-7386153-2-2

Paperback ISBN: 978-1-7386153-3-9

Cover illustration by Elle Maxwell www.ellemaxwelldesign.com

*For anyone who's lost someone they love. I hope you can find happiness again. You deserve it.*

The heart that grieves is the heart that heals.

# AUTHOR'S NOTE

Please note: this book contains cursing and on-page sex, including dirty talk. The hero is a widower, therefore the story contains discussions of grief, and there is on-page marijuana use (once, by a side character). Additionally, the heroine is a virgin, and there is an age gap of eighteen-nineteen years between the characters, with an older man/younger woman dynamic (the heroine is 25, the hero 43-44).

I hope I have treated the topics in this story with the care they deserve. If these are delicate issues for you, please read with care.

# 1

## DAISY

You know something isn't quite right when a cupcake makes you question everything about your life.

It's not a bad cupcake by any means; red velvet, with that decadent cream cheese frosting that melts on your tongue. I know because we've sold them here at Joe's Coffee for years, and I've eaten more than a few. Usually, I savor one with a chai latte on my break, but today this particular cupcake seems to do nothing more than make me wonder how I got here.

"Seven years." My boss, Dave, beams at me. "You're the longest-running employee here at Joe's, Daisy."

I stare at the cupcake in his hands, into which he's jammed a slightly askew birthday candle. The tiny flame flickers, waiting for me to blow it out. Two of my co-workers loiter nearby because Dave forced them to be here, not because they're interested.

In fact, to my left, Celine mutters, "Seven years? Fuck, if I'd been here that long I'd kill myself."

I glance from the candle to where she's scrolling, half

asleep, through her phone. She seems to sense it because her gaze flicks up.

"No offense," she adds in that way people do that seems to somehow add *more* offense to the original statement. She runs her silver tongue-piercing along her bottom lip, a habit she's had the entire four months she's worked here, then drops her gaze again with a yawn. She's not used to being here so early—it's usually only me opening up at six in the morning—but Dave insisted we all gather before opening, "for the occasion."

"Hey, come on now," he says, throwing Celine a look of disapproval she misses because she's once again engrossed in her phone. "It's great. I hope you're all still here when I celebrate my seventh year."

To my right, Jaya snorts, and I don't have to look to know she's sharing an eye-roll with Brett. We all know Dave would die here, given half the chance. He's like a labradoodle: perky and easily excitable, and loyal to a fault. Until it closed, he used to manage a Starbucks in the West Village, and he'd been there for over a decade. He only started here eight months ago after our last manager quit, and already he's got a ten-year plan, most of which involves "fun work-place incentives" to "boost morale."

It's not like Joe's Coffee is an especially bad place to work. The shop itself has a great vibe. Set in an old building on Fruit Street in the historic district of Brooklyn Heights, it's got exposed brick walls painted a clean white, an old-fashioned tin ceiling, and double bay windows facing the quiet, residential street. Black and white photos detailing the area's history cover the walls, small cast iron tables scatter across the bare wood floor, and the marble counter nestles at the rear.

I've always loved the atmosphere in here. That's not the

issue. The issue is, well, being a barista was never my long-term plan.

Still, life never really goes according to plan, does it?

I clear my throat. "Er, thanks, Dave." Pushing my mouth into a smile, I blow out the candle and take the cupcake from him. Celine announces she's going to go sleep in her car until her shift starts at ten, Brett mutters that he's going to Trader Joe's, and Jaya hoists her yoga mat onto her shoulder before sauntering out for her early class. Dave heads out the back to do paperwork, leaving me with my cupcake in the empty coffee shop. I watch the thin thread of smoke rise from the cooling candle, wondering how I ended up here; stuck in a job I'd never intended to be in long term, and still a virgin.

Oh, did I not mention that?

Yeah, I'm a virgin. And I'm beginning to think I might die a virgin.

Okay, I know that's dramatic. I'm only twenty-five, and it's not like my doctor diagnosed me with a life-threatening illness or anything, but when you get to this age and you *still* haven't had sex, things feel a little bleak.

High school was... complicated, to say the least, so I never had the chance to lose my virginity like most of the people I knew. It seemed to just get harder after that. Don't get me wrong, I've dated, but it's never gotten to the point where I wanted to take it further with any of them.

In reality, I know that "virginity" is only a social construct created by men to keep women pure, and if we're getting really technical, my hymen was no doubt broken by horse-riding as a teenager, or using tampons, or my vibrator. I'm not from the Dark Ages.

But also... there's no denying that people still view those with less experience—those like me—as different. Whenever I've told guys, they've always been surprised, if not a little judgmental. (One particular guy told me it was "whack" that I hadn't had sex and that he could "definitely help me out with that issue." Gross.)

At my age, it feels like some kind of mark against me. The older I get, the less I feel like telling the guys I date—and the less I feel like sleeping with any of them. Maybe I keep choosing immature men, I don't know, but the thought of sleeping with a guy my age has almost zero appeal. I haven't gone on a date in forever because, honestly? I'm sick of wasting my time.

So, here I am. A twenty-five-year-old virgin with no career prospects.

An uneasy feeling rises inside me as I glance at the cupcake in my hand. I try not to think about this stuff too much, but it's hard to avoid when someone waves it under your nose like this. I didn't even realize I'd been here that long, but it didn't get past Dave. He never misses an opportunity to celebrate, and despite my usual cheery outlook, celebrating is the last thing I feel like doing right now.

A suffocating feeling claws its way across my chest as I stare at the cupcake, trying to pinpoint what the sensation is. It's the feeling of being stuck; being stuck in my life and not knowing how to fix it.

The door to the coffee shop opens behind me, and I set the cupcake on the back counter with a sigh. I'll have to deal with this quarter-life crisis later. I flick the espresso machine on and, in spite of everything, a smile tugs at my lips because even without looking, I know who walked through the door.

Weston.

He's always the first here, and lately, he's become the best thing about working at Joe's. It's not only his good looks: salt-and-pepper hair that leans more toward salt than pepper, three-day scruff on his square jaw, and a sparkle in his blue eyes.

Well, maybe it's a *little* of that. I'm only human.

But there's more to Weston than a pretty face. He's been my secret project for the past year. Which isn't as creepy as it sounds, I swear.

My only goal was to make him smile.

It took far longer than I could have imagined. For the first month, he wouldn't even make eye contact, which made things tricky. Then one morning I tried something new: I created my first piece of latte art. It wasn't much—only a cresting ocean wave swirled into the milk of his coffee, but it made him pause when I set his cup down in front of him. Finally, *finally*, instead of muttering a simple *thanks*, he glanced up.

Is it too ridiculous to say that the minute his ocean-blue eyes met mine, I fell in love a little?

Probably, so I'll keep that tidbit to myself.

Anyway, he didn't smile, more like gave me a searching look before mumbling his usual *thanks*, but it felt like progress, and I accepted the challenge. I took every opportunity to practice my latte art, and I've developed quite the talent for it, if I may say so myself.

It was the morning I handed him a sunrise, with caramel syrup rays of sunlight—a gamble because he's never asked for syrup in his coffee before—that his gaze lingered on mine before his mouth tilted into a tired smile, and this time it wasn't his usual thanks. Instead, he glanced at my nametag before looking back at my face, saying, "Thank you, Daisy."

I was a goner.

Seven years in this place and not one guy who's made my heart leap from a single smile.

Until Weston.

"Good morning," I call, finally glancing up from the coffee machine. My gaze lands on the handsome older man, dressed in his usual wool coat over a navy-blue suit and tie, hair styled with just the right amount of product. My belly does a little flip when he sends a warm smile my way. In the time he's been coming here, he's graduated from reluctant smiles and single-word responses to actually making small talk. I know it's silly, but I always look forward to chatting with him each day.

"Morning," he replies in a voice still a little rough from sleep. He rubs his hands, cupping them together and warming them with his breath. "Cold out there."

"It sure is." I'd had the same thought when I stepped off the subway this morning. "So much for spring."

Weston hums in agreement as he shrugs off his coat. He bumps the noticeboard by the door as he does so, sending a sheet of paper fluttering to the ground. It's a flier for a local Thai restaurant that opened up down the block a few months back. I should make Weston's coffee, but I can't take my eyes off the way his six-foot-something frame bends to retrieve the flier. His suit fits him so perfectly it must be custom-made, the dark navy fabric complemented by the brown Italian leather loafers on his large feet. I'm so mesmerized by his movements that he straightens and glances over to catch me staring.

Shit.

"It's good," I blurt, ignoring the heat I can feel on my neck. "The Thai place, I mean." I gesture to the flier. "The ginger duck is my favorite."

Weston scrapes a palm across his stubble as he examines the flier, before pinning it back on the noticeboard. I motion for him to take a seat at his usual table in the window, where I've already laid out the newspaper I know he likes to read, then force myself to focus on the coffee machine. Today I'm experimenting with a new design in his latte: a musical note. It takes a few moments of concentration to get it right—which has nothing to do with Weston's presence distracting me—but finally the image takes shape. Perfect.

I step from behind the counter and wander to his table with a smile. The subtle but spicy scent of his cologne hits the minute I'm in his orbit, rich and warm with hints of bergamot, and I can't help but inhale a deep lungful.

He is so gorgeous. A thick head of hair that would have once been chestnut brown but is now dappled with silver, broad shoulders that fill out his suit jacket, tiny creases fanning out from his blue eyes as he glances up from his paper. I don't know a single person who still reads an actual newspaper, but I love that about him. It makes him seem like he's from another time.

Which he kind of is, I guess. I don't know his exact age, but probably early-to-mid forties. In other words, almost two decades older than me.

I swallow, setting his coffee down. This is exactly why I need to get on with it and lose my virginity. It's making me do absurd things, like develop a crush on one of our regulars who is, technically, old enough to be my dad.

"Thanks, Daisy." His eyes shimmer with a smile as he takes in the musical note I've carefully crafted into the foam of his drink. "You're quite the artist."

Before I can stop myself, my gaze strays to the black and white photographs hanging on the wall of Joe's. They're artsy shots of Brooklyn Heights taken by a local artist, and every time I look at them I feel a tiny tug in my heart; one I've gotten very good at ignoring. They're a painful reminder that once upon a time I was an artist who'd planned to pursue a career in photography.

But that was a different life.

Weston cradles the latte in his hands. I haven't felt the urge to express myself in any form for a long time, but finding new ways to make Weston smile through the simple act of creating these tiny scenes in his coffee has re-ignited that spark. I find myself scouring Pinterest after work for latte art ideas, and coming in early each morning to practice. I might be unable to pick up a camera, but playing with art in this way feels doable. It feels safe.

"Thanks," I murmur in response, but instead of being able to bask in the usual glow I get from our conversations, that tiny tendril of stuckness weaves through me again. My gaze moves from the image swirled in the milk to the gold band on Weston's left hand, and my heart clenches in the way it always does when I force myself to acknowledge it.

Of all the men in the city, why did my heart choose *him*? Someone who is so utterly, completely, unavailable?

I give Weston a faint smile and head back to the counter. My celebration cupcake is still sitting there taunting me, and I glare at it. I'm suddenly overcome with the urge to do something drastic and life-changing.

But what?

I guess I could quit, but like everyone else, I have bills to pay. Besides, it's not like I hate my job, and I don't know what else I would do. I've worked at Joe's since I moved to the city, and I don't have any other plans.

I snatch the cupcake off the counter with a frown, knowing I could find some random guy and have sex—hell, I could probably accomplish that one tonight, if I tried—but what would that achieve, really? Somehow, that doesn't feel like enough, and it's not sex I want, it's love. I want to fall in love—with a man who *isn't* married—but that's not something you can make happen just because you want it.

I swipe my finger through the frosting and bring it to my lips with a shake of my head. Seven years in the city and my life hasn't changed since the day I moved here. The thought makes me cringe.

I don't know what, but something has to change, and soon.

## WESTON

The stack of Thai takeout containers wobbles precariously in my arms as I step through the front door of my house on Fruit Street, Brooklyn Heights. Sneakers litter the entranceway, and the unexpected minefield causes me to stumble.

I set the takeout on the hall table and sweep the sneakers to one side with my foot before toeing off my loafers. Three years ago, coming home to a mess like this would have made me furious. Now, I can't help but smile as I survey the pile of shoes by the door.

It means my son is home.

"Jesse?" I call, closing the heavy oak door behind me.

Usually, I hit the pool after work and swim laps—anything to delay coming home to an empty house—but this evening I came straight back, hoping Jesse would've finished moving his stuff in and, if I'm lucky, be ready to eat.

"Jess?" I call again. "I got dinner." My voice echoes through the silent house, and disappointment washes over me. He probably dumped his stuff and went out with friends.

I sigh, taking the food through to the kitchen and dropping it onto the marble countertop. It's been less than twenty-four hours and he's already avoiding me. Great.

But the sound of footsteps on the stairs makes my heart lift hopefully. Jesse ambles into the kitchen with his headphones clamped to his ears, and I give a small chuckle.

Of course. What did I think, that he was just sitting up there in silence? That's a skill his generation doesn't seem to have.

He notices me and tugs his headphones off. He's wearing my old New York Yankees hoodie, probably because he hasn't done a load of laundry in months. His gaze lands on the food and a frown pinches his brow, but he doesn't say a word.

"I thought we could have some dinner and see what's on," I say, motioning vaguely to the living room. I know if I appear too eager, he'll bolt. My son is as disinterested in hanging out with his old man as any other twenty-three-year-old.

But that's not the real problem. The real problem is that he can't stand me.

I loosen the tie around my neck before reaching into the drawer to grab two forks. When I set them on the counter, Jess is still surveying the food, and it occurs to me that there's a chance he might actually join me. If he's desperate enough.

"You hungry?" I ask, casually taking the food from the bag and popping off the lid. The smell of Pad Thai wafts from the tray—my son's favorite meal. At least, it was when he was last speaking to me.

Jesse swallows, and I can practically see the saliva pooling in his mouth. I know I'm playing dirty, but I'll do anything to get my son to stay in the room with me for longer than two seconds. You'd think giving him a place to live would help, but I sense he's planning to hole up in his old room and pretend I don't exist.

Still, a man's gotta eat.

I nudge the Pad Thai container closer to Jesse, then pull two bottles of Miller High Life from the fridge before popping the tops and handing him one. I grab my own food and head into the living room, plopping nonchalantly onto the huge leather sectional as if I couldn't care whether he follows, but I'd be hurt if he took his food and left. I'm desperate to heal this rift between us, even if I did nothing wrong in the first place. Even if he blames me for something that was never my fault.

Jesse's sigh reaches me from the kitchen, then he reluctantly enters the living room and settles at the other end of the sofa, taking a long swig from his beer. Reaching for the remote, I fight the urge to grin as I flick through the channels, stumbling across a rerun of *Seinfeld*, which we used to watch together back in the day. I grew up on this show, so it's nostalgic for me, but Jesse watches it to laugh at the anachronisms, such as adults calling each other on landlines because they don't have cell phones, which he finds hilarious. I'm forty-three, and this kid makes me feel old as fuck.

I glance at Jess, wondering if I'm being too heavy-handed by choosing a show we once enjoyed together, then decide to leave it on. He's tucking into his Pad Thai with gusto, and I doubt he'd leave because of *Seinfeld*. In fact, he's probably forgotten we even watched it.

I take a sip from my beer, pretending to watch the show, but it's hard to relax when this is the first time my son has sat down to eat with me in three years. His eyes stay glued to the screen, and I steal a glance his way.

"Get all your stuff moved in okay?" I ask when there's a lull in the show.

He nods, shoveling food into his mouth. At the rate he's going, he'll be done soon and this whole evening will be over. I have to move quickly.

"I could have sent a moving company," I add, and he shrugs. All I want is one sentence from him. Just one. "Must be weird being back in your old room," I try again.

He freezes, his fork halfway to his mouth.

Fuck. Why the hell did I say that? He doesn't need to be reminded of what his life was like when he was last here. He doesn't need to remember what we all went through.

He swallows, slowly lowering his fork. I wait for him to storm out of the room, maybe tell me again how much he hates me, but instead, he finally meets my gaze.

"Yeah," he mutters, poking at his food. "It's weird." Then he stuffs another forkful of noodles into his mouth. It's barely a full sentence, yet it feels as if he's reached across the sofa and wrapped me in a hug.

My throat thickens as I reach for my own food.

Three years. Three years with barely a word from him, except to say how much he can't stand me, until two days ago. A desperate phone call while I was at work, at four in the afternoon. He'd lost his job and was way behind in his rent, and his roommate—who I assume had been carrying him for the past few months—gave him an ultimatum to pay up or leave. Jesse might have blamed me for his mother's death, but that didn't stop him from turning to me when he needed help, and nothing would have prevented me from being there for my kid when he needed me. I haven't touched his room since he took off the day after Lydia's funeral, and I told him he was welcome to stay for as long as he needed. That this would always be his home. I know he only came to me because he had no other choice, but I'm grateful to be given another chance with him. A chance to mend the rift that never should have formed. A chance to start over.

I push the thoughts away as I pop the top off my takeout. The zingy, fragrant smell of ginger rises from the container, and I almost moan as I take a mouthful of tender duck and vegetables.

Fuck, Daisy was right. This is delicious.

The image of the brunette barista from Joe's Coffee fills my head as I eat. I don't know what it is about her, but ever since my old coffee place down the street closed and I started going to Joe's, my world feels a little less gray. Maybe it's the way she's always so bubbly, greeting me with a smile and making conversation about any and everything as if somehow she knows it's not the words that matter, it's the connection with another human being I need when I feel so alone in the world. Maybe it's the way she puts so much effort into her coffee, creating the most original and artistic images in the foam. Or maybe it's her delicate beauty; the soft smattering of freckles on her alabaster skin, the warm walnut brown of her eyes, and the way her long, dark-choco-late hair falls in loose tendrils around her pretty face when she pins it back.

Maybe it's the fact that she's the first woman I've found myself thinking about since my wife died.

I reach for another long pull of my beer with a deep sigh. Because part of me wishes I hadn't developed a thing for the woman who makes my coffee—especially since she can't be much older than my son.

Still. No harm in looking, right? Things in my life were fucking bleak for a while, when I lost not only my wife but my son in the process. Sure, I could haul myself out of bed and still make it to work, even if shaving and eating were beyond the scope of what I could manage. Lydia's best friend, Pauline, did everything in her power to help me. She made sure I kept showing up at the office—it's my ad agency, after all—and brought me food as often as she could. I spent two years in a haze of grief, numb and barely existing.

Then one day, I met a barista who went out of her way to get me to smile. Somehow, she cut through the fog, and in the simplest of ways, cleared a path for me. Suddenly, I woke with a smile, knowing she was the first person I'd see that morning, knowing she'd always be there, waiting to greet me, making the world a little better with her warm energy and her beautiful coffee. I'm sure to her I'm nothing more than one random guy in a long line of customers she serves, but she became the highlight of my day. She pulled me out of my misery and back into the world, back into myself, and I'll be forever grateful for that. For her.

Jesse polishes off his food and deposits the container on the coffee table, reaching again for his beer. I'm so buoyed by our meal together that I can't help but push for more.

"Want to find a movie or something?" I ask, finishing up as well.

*Damn, Daisy, that was so good.* I can't believe that restaurant has been two blocks from my house for months and I haven't ordered from there. It might be my new go-to place.

Jesse takes a long swallow from his beer. "Nah," he says at last. "I'm gonna see what Rex is up to." He pulls out his phone, fingers flying across the screen.

I frown into a sip of beer. Fuck, Rex is the worst and I don't know why Jess insists on hanging out with him. He's nothing but trouble. Arrested at least twice that I know of, and ever since Jesse started spending more time with him after Lydia died, he's been on a dangerous path. He and Rex spend their time smoking weed and playing *Call of Duty*. I'm all for blowing off a little steam, but this isn't the life I imagined for my son. I was married with a kid at his age, working my way up to a corner office. Why doesn't he care about making more of himself?

I can't say anything though because he's barely started talking to me, and complaining about his best friend is hardly going to help me mend the gap between us.

"Okay," I mutter, trying not to let the disapproval into my voice, but Jess picks up on it all the same.

He rolls his eyes. "Gotta problem with that?"

I lift my hands in defense. "I didn't say a word."

"I don't know why you hate him so much. He was actually *there* for me after everything happened."

I open my mouth to protest because I'd wanted nothing more than to be there for my son after his mother died. *He's* the one who pushed *me* away. But we've had this argument more than once, and I know better than to go down that road right now.

"You don't have to stay friends with him just because of that," I murmur.

Wrong move.

"What do you know about having friends?" Jess laughs bitterly. "You spend all your time alone in this big house. Thanks, but I don't think I need to take advice from *you*."

My jaw tenses, and I set my beer down. Part of me is pissed that he's so damn ungrateful, that he thinks it's okay to speak to me like that, but a bigger part of me is glad he's speaking to me at all, because if he's speaking to me, then he might *listen*.

"I don't hate Rex," I say evenly, though it's far from the truth. I can't stand the little shit. "I just don't want him getting you into trouble."

Jesse snorts. "I'm twenty-three, Dad, not thirteen. I think I can handle myself."

I twist to face him. "Exactly. You're twenty-three. What are you doing with your life?"

"Jesus fucking Christ," Jesse mutters under his breath. "I've only just lost my job, and you're giving me a hard time already?" He shakes his head, shoving to his feet. "I don't need this shit." With that, he stalks from the room, and a second later the front door slams shut. I stare after him for a moment, exhaling slowly.

Well, I fucked that up, didn't I? I know I didn't help my case by jumping all over him about his life choices, but like every parent, I worry about my kid. Ever since Lydia died, he's become a different person, and the more he pushes me away, the more I worry.

My chest aches as I think about Lydia, wishing I wasn't doing this alone. She'd never let him talk to me like that. Hell, if she was here, we wouldn't be in this situation at all. Her naturally calm, positive energy always created harmony between people. This house was so much warmer when she was here.

And that's why I can't give up. I need to fix things with Jess, not just for us, but for Lydia. For the sake of what's left of our family.

# 3

## DAISY

The sun casts a copper glow across the historic townhouses of Brooklyn Heights as I lock up Joe's and step into the cool evening air. I rarely work such long hours, but Celine decided to call in sick with a migraine at eight-thirty this morning, most likely to get back at me after Dave made her come in so early for my seven-year anniversary thing. Anyway, Dave had to go see his daughter's play, so he asked me to work a double shift. As usual, I had nothing else planned—and I hated to leave him stranded—so I agreed.

My feet regret that now, though.

I should head straight for the subway, but I've been craving ginger duck from that Thai place since I mentioned it to Weston this morning. My plan is to grab some and head home, where I'll spend the next few hours vegging in front of Netflix.

I frown to myself as I trudge along Fruit Street. It was only this morning that I promised myself my life would change, and what am I doing? My usual act of scurrying home after work to retreat from the world. I should be out partying, like other people my age. I should be meeting up with someone off Tinder, or whatever the latest dating app is.

But I'm so *tired*.

I sigh as I spot the Thai place up ahead. All I want is ginger duck and to pour myself a glass of wine at home. Honestly, sometimes I think I'm a middle-aged woman trapped in a young woman's body, which is exactly why I struggle to date guys my age.

*What about Weston?* my brain suggests, which is hardly fair, knowing that will never happen.

I allow myself exactly ten seconds to slip into the fantasy I've indulged in many times before.

I'm in the coffee shop, in the early morning, and Weston enters, no longer wearing his wedding ring. I make a heart shape in the foam of his coffee and he looks at me with longing in his eyes—

*Right. That's enough.* This *is why you're stuck.*

I shake the image from my head with a frustrated exhale. I'm nearly at the Thai restaurant when I hear a door slam to my right, and a male voice spits furious words.

"*Fuck you.*"

My eyes widen and I freeze, glancing to find a guy thundering down his front steps, angry gaze intent on me.

What the hell? I know this is New York, but jeez.

He slows his steps, blinking as if suddenly noticing I'm there. "Shit, sorry. That wasn't directed at you."

I glance around the street, searching for whoever he *was* speaking to, only to see we're alone.

He shakes his head. "No, it was—" He rubs his hands down his face in agitation, before motioning back toward the house. "My dad... never mind."

Oh, right.

I look from the house back to him, and my heart squeezes a little when I notice his frustrated expression and slumped shoulders. If anyone knows anything about not getting along with their folks, it's me.

"I get it," I murmur, and he gives me an odd look as he pulls a cigarette and lighter from his pocket.

"Get what?" The anger drains from his eyes and he cocks his head curiously. Meanwhile, my feet groan in protest at me standing here, talking to a random guy when I could be eating Thai food on my sofa. This is the problem with spending all day making conversation with strangers. Sometimes I forget I don't have to do that when I'm not on the clock.

"Nothing," I mumble, turning to go.

"Wait." He lights up and takes a deep drag. The smell of weed wafts toward me and I realize it's not a cigarette. "What did you mean, that you get it?"

I shrug, turning back. "Just that I argue with my dad too. With both my parents."

He nods, flicking the ash off the end of his joint, which glows in the fading evening light. It's definitely working its magic because he's now studying me with a relaxed air of interest.

For reasons I can't quite pinpoint, I find myself studying him back. He's tall; six-foot, I'd say, with a lean, athletic build. Up close his ice-blue eyes gleam with mischief, and a smile plays on his full lips as he pushes his wavy chestnut hair back from his forehead. He's around my age, and even though I have no explanation as to why, there's something vaguely familiar about him. Maybe I've seen him at Joe's.

Silence settles between us, but it's not uncomfortable. He leans on the railing of the stoop, watching me as he smokes.

"What do you argue about?"

I lift a shoulder. "How much time do you have?" I joke, but it's not funny. I don't argue with my folks anymore. Not since I cut off contact with them when I moved to the city years ago.

The stranger grunts a laugh of recognition. His gaze drifts over me, from my messy bun all the way down to the aching, tired feet in my Keds. His eyes spark when they meet mine again.

"I could make the time."

Whoa. *Is he flirting with me?*

The minute the thought crosses my mind, heat rises to my cheeks. This is the problem with having a pale, freckled complexion like mine. My emotions are transparent.

He notices, and a grin curls along his lips, but it's not a mean or mocking grin; rather, it seems like he's appreciating my reaction.

"Maybe I could take you out sometime," he adds, offering me a cocky smile.

Okay, so he *is* flirting with me. More than that, he's asking me out.

An excuse rises to my lips, but I swallow it back. Wasn't I *just* thinking that I wanted to get out of my rut? It's like the universe heard me and intervened.

And he is kind of cute.

I run my gaze across his navy-blue Yankees hoodie and ripped jeans. He carries himself with a casual, confident air, although that could be because of the weed. The smoking would usually put me off, but it feels like everyone in the city smokes weed. I smell it everywhere in Brooklyn. It's legal, after all, and he's had a fight with his father, so I can't blame him for wanting to unwind. Besides, I was about to switch off in front of the TV for the rest of the night because I don't feel like dealing with my own feelings right now. At the end of the day, these are all simply different methods of accomplishing the same thing: escape.

Again, I think of Weston, the way his gold wedding band glinted under the bright lights of Joe's this morning, and make a decision. It's time to break the pattern I've been stuck in for way too long.

It's time to get unstuck.

"Maybe you could," I reply, and my belly flips when his mouth tugs wider in response. I can't explain why, but something compels me toward him. I feel like I know him from somewhere.

"Have we met before?"

He cocks his head, studying me as stamps out his joint. "I don't think so. I'm sure I'd remember you."

My cheeks warm again at the compliment, but I can't shake the familiarity of him, the nagging feeling that we've crossed paths before.

"I work at Joe's." I motion down the street. "Do you go there?"

He gives a slow shake of his head. "Never heard of it. I only moved into the neighborhood today."

Huh.

"I'm Jesse. Jesse Abbott."

"Daisy Griffin," I reply.

He pulls his phone from his pocket and hands it to me. "Give me your number, and I'll text you." His mouth hitches up on one side into a grin. "After all, it sounds like you had a pretty juicy story to tell me about your folks."

I scrunch my nose. *We will not be talking about that, thank you very much.*

He notices and gives an easy laugh. "Right, I get it. How

about this—no family stuff. Let's keep it light and have a good time, yeah?"

"Okay." I relax, examining his face. I feel like I've gazed into those clear blue eyes before, and more than anything, the need to figure out where I know him from has me entering my number into his phone. He texts me so I have his number too. I stare at the message from him—*Are you free tomorrow night?*—and my heart gives a little kick of anticipation.

I have a date for the first time in months. Or is it years?

I smile and text him back: *Yes.*

His mouth curls back into that grin. A car's horn honking behind us makes us turn to the street.

"I'd love to stay and chat," he says, pocketing his phone, "but my ride is here. I'll text you later."

I nod, watching as he climbs into a heavily modified Dodge Challenger. The tinted windows obscure any view of the driver, and the car is so low it barely clears the ground. My stomach falls at seeing him climb into such a ridiculous car. Part of me had thought he was different from guys my age, but that car is all I need to know I was wrong.

―――――

By THE TIME I get home, I've all but convinced myself to cancel plans with... what was his name? Jesse. What was I thinking, agreeing to go out with a total stranger? Sure, he was cute, but is he really the kind of guy I want? Someone who smokes weed, who gets around in a car that looks like something off the set of *The Fast and the Furious*?

Besides, is my life really so bad as it is?

After letting myself into the apartment I share with Denise in Bed-Stuy, Brooklyn, I set the Thai takeout down on the kitchen counter and open the fridge, looking for something to drink. Hundreds of pink Post-Its assault my vision, each with a huge letter 'D' on them, and I roll my eyes. "Oh, for fuck's sa—"

"Good, you're home."

I snap my mouth shut, turning to see my roommate standing behind me, blond hair pulled back in a tight ponytail, one manicured hand resting on her hip. I know what this pose means; she's pissed about something I've done, even though I tread very carefully around our apartment.

"Hey," I say warily, grabbing a bottle of water from the door of the fridge. It's one of the few items without a Post-It on it, because it belongs to me.

"You ate my yogurt again." Denise's eyes follow the water bottle as I carry it to the living room with my dinner, no doubt checking it's mine.

The tiredness from the day finally catches up with me, and I sink onto the sofa. "I didn't eat your yogurt. I ate the yogurt *I* bought. It was on my shelf."

At least twice a week we have this conversation. It's exhausting.

"You can't sit out here," she says, gesturing for me to move. "I've got the girls coming over for the final of *The Bachelor*."

I press my eyes shut for a beat, summoning patience. It's never worth fighting with Denise, because it makes life in this apartment extremely unpleasant.

"Fine." I rise to my feet, grabbing my dinner and bottled water. At least she's forgotten about the yogurt. "I'll eat in my room."

The word "room" is way too generous, though; it's more like an alcove off the living room with nothing but a curtain separating it from the rest of the apartment, which is why I can afford to live in this neighborhood on a barista's income. I think it was once the dining room in the original layout of the house before someone broke it into apartments, but I can't be sure. Either way, it gives me the space I need for a twin bed, dresser, and an armchair with a view overlooking the street, but it has almost no privacy. Usually, Denise goes out with "the girls," but it seems tonight I'll be subjected to them tearing apart the women of *The Bachelor*.

As Denise's friends arrive, I pull the curtain to my room shut, shoving my noise-canceling headphones onto my ears. Then I settle into my armchair and kick my feet up onto the windowsill, looking out across the street as I eat. The food is as good as last time, and I try not to feel guilty about spending what little extra cash I have on takeout, instead of cooking. I used to love cooking, but it's hard when I share a kitchen with Denise. The shrieks from the living room cut through my headphones, and I fight the urge to hurl myself out the window. I've been unhappy in this apartment for some time now, but the thought of trying to find a new place to live is overwhelming. Denise usually calms down after a while, and I usually convince myself everything is fine.

Though as I sit here, thinking back over my day, everything feels far from fine. I've spent seven years in a job I only ever intended to be short-term. I'm still a virgin who's never been in love. And my living situation makes me want to tear my hair out.

But tonight, something different happened. Tonight, I got asked out by a cute guy.

I reach for my phone to reread our brief text exchange, as if to reassure myself that it was real and I didn't imagine the whole thing. And there on the screen is a text from him.

**Jesse: It was nice to meet you tonight. Unexpected and really nice.**

With a smile I set my food down, responding.

**Daisy: It was nice to meet you too.**

I know the standard thing for guys is to play it cool and not text back immediately, so I probably won't hear from him again tonight, and that's—

My phone buzzes in my hands. I stare in surprise at the reply he's sent.

**Jesse: I'm looking forward to tomorrow night. What kind of food do you like?**

I glance at the Thai food and grin, replying. And to my amazement, he replies immediately again. I ask his age: twenty-three. He's younger than I'd hoped, but the way he texts back in such a timely manner—and doesn't ask me to send nudes—gives me hope.

Maybe I misread him earlier.

We chat while I finish up my food and get ready for bed. Denise's friends are still here, so I climb under the comforter, my noise-canceling headphones still in place, and when I tell Jesse I'm going to bed, he sends me a kiss. It's sweet, if not a little premature.

I think again about his cute, mischievous smile, and snuggle under my comforter, trying to ignore the raucous laughter of Denise's friends that cuts through my head-phones. I want to get out of my rut, and going out with Jesse is a good first step. I can't help but smile as I close my eyes, and for the first time in months, I drift off thinking of someone other than Weston.

## 4

## WESTON

Early morning darkness covers me like a cloak as I roll over and hit my alarm clock with a yawn. Instinctively, I reach a hand out to Lydia's side of the bed. The familiar ache stirs in my chest when I find it empty, but it's fainter now. It doesn't take my breath away like it once did. Still, after more than two decades together, it takes time to get used to waking up alone.

On autopilot, I shower and dress for work before heading downstairs. Jess came in late last night, and he's left a pile of dirty clothes by the washer. I step over them as I head to the kitchen, trying to ignore the irritation that fizzles in my gut. As desperate as I am to mend the rift between us, I'm getting sick of his lack of respect. I don't want to pull the whole "as long as you're living under my roof, you'll obey my rules" shit with him—I mean, he's not a child, and he wouldn't respond well to that anyway—but I'm also not running a damn hotel. When he first moved back in I went easy on him, but it's been over a month of playing video games all day in his underwear, then staying out at all hours. I might be trying to fix things between us, but I'm also his father, and it's my job to provide boundaries and guidance whether he likes that or not.

I pour bran flakes into a bowl and add milk, thinking about my son. I think he's started dating someone, but given he hardly grunts two words in my direction, it's hard to know. The only clue is the goofy look on his face when he picks up his phone, and that I've caught him heading out more than once in the evenings in a cloud of cologne, his hair styled neatly. Last time I checked, he doesn't make that kind of effort for Rex.

The sound of footsteps on the stairs makes me pause, and I nearly drop my spoon when Jesse walks into the kitchen. It's ten to six in the morning. The only time I've ever seen him awake so early is when he's getting in from a wild night out.

"What are you doing up?" I ask as Jess sticks his head into the pantry.

There's a long pause, and for a second I think he's going to straight-up ignore me, but finally he answers, "I have a job interview downtown."

I try not to balk. "For real?"

He turns from the pantry to stick two Pop-Tarts into the toaster before glancing back at me. "You don't have to sound so surprised."

I quickly school my features. "I just... wasn't aware you'd been looking for a job."

He casts his cool gaze over me. "There's a lot you're not aware of."

This fucking kid. Honestly.

I grit my teeth, about to finally give him a talking to, when he says, "My girlfriend set it up."

I snap my mouth shut. *Girlfriend*? I figured he was seeing

someone, but didn't know it was that serious. Whoever this mystery woman is, she's obviously good for him.

I hide a smile behind my hand. "Girlfriend, huh?"

Back when we were close, we'd talk like this all the time. Jess had a long-term girlfriend of two and a half years before his mom died, and I'd assumed those two were going to settle down for good, like Lydia and I did at that age. But after his mom's death, everything changed.

Jesse contemplates me as if he's considering sharing more. I'd give anything to have him slide onto the stool at the island beside me and tell me about this girlfriend, like the old days.

Instead, he turns back to the fridge and pulls out the orange juice, pouring himself a glass, saying nothing.

"Well, I think it's great you're going for an interview." I run my gaze over his jeans and plain tee, wondering if I should suggest he change. Surely he shouldn't be dressed so casually?

But before I can say anything, the toaster pops. He drains his juice and grabs his breakfast, turning on his heel.

"Good luck," I call as he leaves the kitchen, but either he doesn't hear me, or simply chooses not to respond.

My money's on the latter.

I finish my bowl of cereal with a sigh. What's it going to take for Jess to start talking to me again? I've given him somewhere to live. I feed him. Hell, most of the time I even do his laundry. He's not a kid anymore, but I'm doing this because I love him, and I want him to see I'm trying. I want him to see I still care, despite everything.

I glance at my watch and realize I need to get moving, especially if I want time to enjoy the quiet at Joe's before the day starts. Dumping my bowl in the sink, I decide I'll load the dishwasher and do the laundry later. Then I grab my wallet and keys and head out into the fresh morning air.

Joe's is only a few blocks from my townhouse on Fruit Street, and it's a pretty walk. Brooklyn Heights is a designated historic district, lined with four and five-story townhouses and brownstones. The oak trees are a vibrant green in spring, but the short walk doesn't have its usual invigorating effect. All I can think about, as I push open the glass front door of the coffee shop, is the chasm between me and Jess.

"Good morning," Daisy chirps from behind the counter.

"Morning." I sink into my usual seat in the window, where the newspaper waits for me. She always leaves it here, knowing I'll want to flip through it while I drink my coffee. As the hum of the espresso machine fills the air, I wonder who else she does that for.

"You okay?"

I glance up in surprise. Daisy appears at the table with my latte, and I realize I've been staring into space, lost in thought.

"Sorry. Yes." I glance into her rich brown eyes. Today they're subtly ringed with eyeliner, highlighting her natural beauty, and she's woven her long hair into a braid that snakes over her right shoulder. Out of nowhere, I have an image of that braid wrapped around my fist as she straddles my lap. Heat pools in my abdomen at the thought, and I suck in a breath, glancing away. I haven't felt such a sharp, visceral sensation of lust like that since...

Well, for a very, very long time.

She hovers by my table, looking uncertain. "You sure you're okay?"

I swallow, pushing the image away. When I glance back at Daisy, her eyes swim with concern, and something breaks a little in my chest. She doesn't realize it, but she's become the one constant in my life. The one good thing.

"My son won't talk to me." The words slip from my mouth without my permission. She's not my therapist. She's only the local barista, trying to go about her day. But compassion knits across Daisy's brow, and she lowers herself into the chair opposite me.

"What happened?"

"He…" I blow out a long breath. "It's complicated."

"Right." She smooths a hand over the table, apparently unbothered by my vague answer. "Is there anything you can do?"

I shake my head. "I've tried everything. The harder I try, the more it feels like he pulls away."

"That's rough." She's quiet for a moment, then gives a small, humorless laugh. "It seems like everyone I know is arguing with their parents lately."

A smile whispers across my lips. "I guess some things never change."

"Yeah." Daisy studies me, her gaze warm and reassuring. "Well, whatever it is, I'm sure he'll come around. Maybe he just needs time."

I nod, wishing it were that simple. "I hope you're right," I murmur, looking down at the coffee in front of me. When I see the Ghostbusters symbol she's crafted into the foam, my heart lightens. "Another masterpiece," I say with a chuckle.

She laughs too. "Glad you like it. I've been practicing that one."

"I love it." I lift my gaze to hers again. "It's one of my favorite movies."

"Mine too. At least, the original is." She wrinkles her nose. "None of the new movies compare."

"Couldn't agree more," I murmur, surprised that a

woman so young would love an eighties film. Her answering grin is pure delight, and warmth suffuses my chest. "You always know how to make me smile, Daisy."

A blush touches her freckled cheeks as her gaze sears into mine. Her breathing becomes unsteady and she swallows. "You make me smile, too."

My gaze falls to her full mouth, and for the first time since Lydia died, I contemplate what it would be like to kiss someone else. To wake up beside someone else. To share my life with someone else. Is it too absurd to think that someone could be Daisy? Sure, she's young, and it would be unconventional to date a woman her age, but I've never played by other people's rules. Everyone said I was crazy to marry Lydia at nineteen and start a family at twenty. Everyone laughed when I quit my stable job to start my own ad agency at twenty-five. I didn't listen, because I'm a man who's always known what he wants.

And looking at Daisy, I know what I want.

I gaze at the pretty brunette in front of me, thinking about the way she lays the newspaper out for me, the way she tries to make me smile with her coffee, the way she always stops to talk to me.

She feels this too. I know she does.

When her lips curve into a soft smile just for me, I decide that sometime, when the moment feels right, I'm going to ask her out.

Daisy rises from the table, brushing past my shoulder as she returns to the counter. My skin tingles from her brief touch, warming me through, and when I head off to work, I'm smiling again.

Smiling at the thought of new possibilities.

# 5

# DAISY

I press the doorbell with a nervous flutter in my belly. I've been seeing Jesse for a while now, and we became exclusive a couple months back. I'd helped him get an interview with a friend of Dave's who runs a coffee shop on the Lower East Side, and when we met up after and he told me he'd gotten the job, he surprised me by asking me to be his girlfriend. He's surprised me in so many ways since I met him, but the biggest surprise of all has to be the way he responded when I told him I was a virgin.

We had the conversation on our first date. He'd taken me to a fancy restaurant I hadn't expected, and when I asked him how he knew about the place, he told me his mom had recommended it. True to his word, we kept things light, and talked about movies and work and our favorite places in the city. By the end of the evening, I knew I wanted to see him again, and decided to come clean about my lack of experience. I thought he'd be shocked, but he took it in stride, telling me he wasn't in any rush. He said he'd done the casual thing and was interested in something more. It was refreshing, to say the least.

That was three months ago, and while I've had fun hanging out with him, part of me feels there's so much more to Jesse than he lets on. But how well can you know someone after such a short period of time? That's the point of committing—to see where it could go. And since we've started dating, that stuck feeling has gotten quieter. It's not gone completely, but it's easier to ignore. So it's worth sticking around to see what this thing with Jesse could become.

And he's letting me in more. At least, it seems like he wants to. He invited me to come to his place tonight, which I think means meeting his parents. I mean, I know he lives with his folks, so it's likely they'll be here.

The door swings open and Jesse stands there in his Yankees hoodie, a grin on his mouth. "Hey." He leans in to peck me on the cheek before stepping aside, and I enter the foyer of the townhouse with wide eyes.

Holy crap, this place is *nice*. I should have known that, given the red brick façade and beautiful tree-lined street, but inside it's like another level. The historic building has been completely redone, the interior clean and modern, with bright white walls and dark stained floors. I follow Jesse through to an immaculate kitchen, lined with glossy white cabinets, and a huge marble island in the center. I think of the barely one-and-a-half-bedroom apartment Denise and I share, and grimace, knowing I'll never take Jesse there as *this* is where he comes from.

"Nice place," I murmur.

He shrugs. "It's okay. My mom redecorated it before..." he trails off and shoves his head into the fridge, then retreats, brandishing two beer bottles. "This okay? Or there's probably some wine somewhere. I know my dad drinks it."

"This is great, thanks."

He pops the tops off the beer and hands a bottle to me, then motions for me to follow him into the next room. It's a living room with a huge black leather sectional facing a giant flat-screen TV.

"Whoa, that's massive," I say, and Jesse shrugs again.

"I don't spend much time down here. Usually, my dad is home, getting on my case about something, so I go to my room. I have the whole top floor to myself."

I glance around the quiet house. "Where's your dad now?" I must admit, I'm relieved his parents don't seem to be home. Meeting the folks is a big step, and if I'm honest, I'm not sure I'm ready for that yet, especially since Jesse has made it clear he doesn't get along with his father.

"He's got a late meeting," Jesse assures me. I'm about to ask where his mom is when he adds, "We'll have the place to ourselves for a few hours. I figured that would be better."

That same nervous sensation ripples through me and I swallow, unsure what he's expecting tonight. Hesitation tugs at me when I think about sleeping with him. I know we've been dating for three months, but shouldn't I be feeling something... more? Excitement, maybe? Or love? Is it ridiculous to admit that I'd like to fall in love before having sex? It feels so old-fashioned, but as Jesse takes my hand and leads me to the sofa, I realize that I'm not prepared to do this with just any cute guy. I've waited this long, and that makes it feel even more important.

Jesse places his beer on a side table and turns to me with a smile. Is he someone I could fall in love with?

I shake the thought off, irritated with myself. It's only been a few months, for God's sake. Maybe I'm not in love with him now, but if I give it time, I'm sure I could be. He's sweet and cute and funny, and he's been nothing but a gentleman since I told him how inexperienced I am. What more could I ask for? I simply need to be honest with him.

I take a sip from my beer and set it carefully on a coaster on the coffee table. "So, listen. I'm not ready to have sex tonight."

"Oh." Jesse's brow dips. "Right, of course." He slides closer to me on the couch, smiling gently. "I guess I can wait some more."

I tilt my head. "You're okay with that?"

"I... yeah." He lifts my hand to his mouth, brushing a kiss across the back of it. "I like you, Daisy. A lot. I think this could really go somewhere."

Whoa. Okay.

*See?* I reassure myself. *You've made a good choice with this one.*

"I'm glad," I whisper, sliding closer still. Then I lean in and press my mouth to his. He responds by wrapping an arm around my back and tugging me into him, and I raise a hand to touch his cheek.

The sound of a throat clearing behind us makes me jump, and I lurch away from Jesse, spinning around to see who's there.

My gaze lands on a tall man with salt-and-pepper hair and three-day scruff on his sharp jaw. When his ocean-blue eyes lock with mine, my stomach falls through the floor.

*Weston?*

I spring up from the sofa, confused. "Hi," I say, wiping a hand across my mouth. Heat sears my cheeks. "What... what are you doing here?"

"I live here." His gaze moves from me to Jesse, then back again. "And you must be..."

Beside me, Jesse rises to his feet with a sigh of resignation. "This is my girlfriend, Daisy."

A muscle tics in Weston's jaw.

"Daisy, this is my dad."

Oh, *no*. Weston is Jesse's *dad*? *Jesse* is the son Weston was talking about?

I look between the two of them, cataloging the similarities. Both tall. Same cool blue eyes. Same chestnut hair, even though Weston's is laced with silver.

God, *Weston is Jesse's dad*. That makes him... *Weston Abbott*. I think back to how familiar Jesse seemed when I first met him. It's no wonder I was attracted to him. He must have, on some level, reminded me of the guy from work I have a crush on.

I mean, had. *Had* a crush on. I'm not crushing on him anymore, now that I have a boyfriend. And I'm *certainly* not crushing on him now that I know he's my boyfriend's dad. That would be all kinds of wrong. Much like the things I've done while thinking of him, alone in the bathtub. I shudder at the thought.

"I..." I smooth my skirt, cringing. I can't believe Weston just caught me making out with his son on his sofa.

"We know each other," Weston says after what feels like an eternity.

Jesse's expression darkens. "How?"

"Your dad comes into my work every day," I explain, deciding to leave out the part about how he's my favorite customer, how I've spent every day of the past year trying to make him smile. "We... chat sometimes."

Weston's gaze bores into mine for a long moment, and I shift my weight. We both know that's a very simplified version of things, especially lately. Because lately, I've felt a shift between us that I haven't been able to put my finger on. We've gone from talking about benign things like the weather, to asking how the other is, and answering more and more honestly. But, I'm ashamed to admit, we've both left out important parts of our lives. I never talked about Jesse, and he never spoke of his wife.

Well, that's going to have to change now, isn't it?

"I thought you were working late?" Jesse grumbles.

Weston lets out a long breath, tearing his gaze from mine as he loosens his tie. "My meeting finished early. I should be allowed to come home to my own house, Jess."

Just like that, the tension between them pulls taut. I let out a faint laugh, desperate to lighten the mood.

"Of course you are," I say, nudging Jesse. "Right?"

Jesse glances at me sullenly. "Right," he mutters.

I turn back to Weston, forcing a bright smile. "Is your wife working late too?"

An icy chill falls over the room, and Jesse stiffens beside me. Weston gives me an odd look before glancing at his son in disbelief. Finally, he turns back to me and sighs.

"My wife... Jesse's mom... died three years ago."

She *what*? I look at Jesse in shock. His jaw is hard as he stares at the floor, refusing to meet my gaze. His mom *died*? How could he not tell me that?

But... No, he said his mom recommended the restaurant he took me to on our first date, and he said other things about her, too. Though it's only just occurring to me now that they were things that happened in the past. He never spoke of her in the past tense, though. Almost like...

Like he didn't want to admit she was gone.

I take in Jesse's slumped shoulders, think of the trouble he's had getting along with his father—with Weston—and yet he's been able to laugh and be so sweet with me. My heart squeezes.

"I... I'm so sorry to hear that," I murmur at last.

I turn back to Weston, and before I can stop it, my gaze

falls to the ring on his left hand. I think of how different he was when he first started coming to Joe's last year, how he never smiled. How it took me ages to get him to even make eye contact with me, how over the past year he's been slowly warming up and laughing more until it felt like he almost came back to life. I don't know what I'd been assuming. That maybe he'd been in a bad marriage? That he was unhappy at home? Whatever it was, I was way off the mark.

Because he's not married, I realize. He's grieving for his wife.

I thought I knew both men, albeit under totally different circumstances, but now I wonder what it was I thought I knew. Why does Jesse hate his dad so much? I can't fathom how the sweet man who chats with me every morning could possibly be as terrible as Jesse makes him out to be, but what do I know about him really? What do I know about either of them?

I back away, shaking my head. It suddenly feels like I'm intruding on an extremely personal family moment, and I'd rather be anywhere but here.

"I should... I should go."

"What?" Jesse glances at me before shooting an angry look at his dad.

"No, Daisy." Weston heaves a weary sigh. "You don't have to leave."

"Yeah, no..." My head is reeling with this new information. It's too much to take in. Weston is Jesse's father. His wife—Jesse's mom—passed away not that long ago. And these two, for reasons I don't understand, can't seem to stand each other.

"I need to go," I say again, turning for the kitchen and snatching my bag off the counter. Jesse appears at my side as I reach the front door.

"I'm sorry I didn't tell you." His blue eyes are ringed with misery, and I lift a hand to his face.

I can't be mad at him. Do I wish he'd told me? Yes, but this isn't about me. I'm not the one who had to deal with something so painful. He obviously didn't feel comfortable enough to bring it up, and I need to respect that.

Besides, I didn't tell him about my parents, or that I don't even speak to them anymore. In fact, the few times he's asked, I've deliberately changed the subject. Because Jesse isn't the only one who's hiding. I'm hiding too. Not just from him—from myself. I have been for years. And I can't face that any more than he can face the death of his mom. So I can hardly blame him for keeping this from me.

"That's okay," I say, softly stroking his cheek. "It's your business, Jesse."

"Then why are you leaving?"

How do I explain the awkwardness I feel about Weston being his dad? The shock about learning what he's—what they've *both*—been through?

I shake my head, rising on my toes to peck him on the lips. "It's just... a lot. I'll text you, okay?"

Jesse gives a reluctant nod, then opens the door for me. I step out into the night air and walk to the subway, my head spinning.

And all I can think about is if I'll be able to face Weston in the morning.

## 6

## WESTON

For the first time in a year, I don't go to Joe's for my morning coffee. I know it's cowardly, but I can't imagine seeing Daisy after last night. I need a day to get my head on straight.

I can't believe I was going to ask her out. Mortification floods me at the thought. Here I was thinking there was a connection between us, and all the while she was dating my son. My twenty-three-year-old son.

I shake my head as I climb into my Audi and pull out onto the quiet morning street. I'll get my coffee in the city today.

What was I thinking, that a woman her age could be into a guy like me? I must be twenty years older than her. Sure, I'm in great shape, thanks to swimming laps after work most nights, but I don't have the energy of a twenty-something, and I come with so much fucking baggage it's not funny.

Of course, Jess comes with baggage too. I'm shocked to learn that even after seeing Daisy for several months, he didn't tell her about his mom's death. It's the most significant thing that's ever happened to him. If they've never spoken about that, what *do* they talk about?

Unless they spend very little time talking at all.

My stomach churns with unease at the thought, but I push it away. It's none of my business. So I know her from the local coffee shop—that means nothing. She works a job that relies on tips; is it any surprise she's been so nice to me? She's probably nice to everyone. Her livelihood depends on it.

I can't shake the thought that there was more to it than that, though. And that makes me feel like a bit of a creep—that I'm still convinced she was into me. That I went to that coffee shop early, every day, just so I could see her. What the fuck have I been thinking?

I tighten my hands on the steering wheel and my wedding band catches my eye. Of course she thought I was married. How did I not consider that? I haven't taken my ring off since Lydia died. It's a part of me. It never occurred to me that Daisy would notice it.

And that's how I know this entire thing has been in my head. I've been going there to enjoy her company, thinking we had a connection. Meanwhile, she's been serving me coffee, going out of her way to get a generous tip from the married guy who comes in every day.

I feel so fucking stupid, I want to bash my head on the steering wheel. And now she's dating my son, and I'm going to have to see her with him. I could stop going to Joe's, that's easy enough, but Jesse might want to bring her home again, and how would I explain the fact that I'm avoiding the coffee shop?

Besides, I like going there. I like this routine I've built for myself, and I'm not sure what my life would be like without it. I'm not sure who *I'd* be without it, and I don't want to find out. I can enjoy Daisy's company without being weird about it, right? That's what I've been doing for most of the past year anyway. It's only recently that I've realized I want more from her. A few months, tops. And that's nothing—I can switch that off.

I have to. My relationship with my son depends on it.

Somehow, things with Jesse have gotten even worse. After Daisy left in shock last night—for which I can hardly blame her—Jess and I had a huge blowout. He yelled at me for ruining his night and freaking out his girlfriend, and when I asked him why he hadn't told her about his mom, he stormed out of the room. Just when I thought things with him were improving, we're back to square one.

I need to repair this. I need to show Jesse I'm willing to make things better, and I need to make sure Daisy feels comfortable in our house. Comfortable around me. Not just so I can keep going to Joe's. I need to do it for my son.

———

IT'S POURING out when the doorbell rings at 7 p.m. I hurried home from the office so I could be here, but Jesse hasn't made it home yet. That means I'll have to man up and face Daisy alone, whether I like it or not.

I called Jesse from work this morning and told him I wanted to have Daisy over for dinner, so we could sit down and get to know each other properly. He fought me at first, but when I pointed out that we hadn't made a great impression together last night, I was surprised to hear him agree with me. One hour is all I asked him for, then they're free to do whatever they want. I said I'd provide the food, and he agreed to text her.

But I didn't count on Daisy arriving first.

The doorbell rings again and I press my eyes shut. Oh well, here goes.

I pad to the front door and swing it open with a smile. "Hi, Daisy."

"Hi." She's standing on the stoop under the torrential rain, and I quickly usher her inside.

"Shit, you're soaked." I dash into the laundry to grab a towel and spy my Yankees hoodie waiting to be folded after I washed it this morning. I snatch that up too and head back to the entry hall. "Here. Dry yourself off and put on something dry."

"Thanks." She won't meet my eye as she takes the towel and hoodie from me. "Are you sure Jesse won't mind me wearing his sweatshirt?"

*His* sweatshirt? True, he's stolen it from me a handful of times, but that hoodie is mine and always has been. I've worn that thing over the years until the cotton became softer than silk. On more than one occasion Lydia tried to give it away to Goodwill, but I always caught her before she could get it out the door. The memory makes me smile.

"Sure," I say, side-stepping the question of sweatshirt ownership. I shouldn't be offering Daisy my clothing to wear, but it's too late. "Bathroom is down there." I motion along the hall, and she scuttles off to change as I step back into the kitchen.

I place my hands on the cool marble countertop and take a slow, deep breath. Jesse shouldn't be too long. I need to act normal until then. I've spoken to her hundreds of times—this doesn't need to be any different. It's not like I ever made any of my feelings toward her obvious, because I was downplaying them until I was ready to make a move. Thank God for that. In fact, she most likely has no idea. I'm just the guy who comes in to get coffee every morning.

Daisy enters the kitchen quietly, her dark hair swept over one shoulder, my hoodie falling to mid-thigh of her damp jeans. I wrench my gaze away.

"Jesse's running late," I say, my voice suddenly rough. I clear my throat. "Can I get you something to drink?"

"Yes, please. Whatever you've got is fine."

I glance back to find her fiddling anxiously with her cuff. She still won't look at me, and I realize it's up to me to break the tension here. I need to confront this head-on, or tonight will get us nowhere.

"So... this is a little awkward," I begin, leaning against the kitchen island and folding my arms. "When Jess told me he had a girlfriend, it never crossed my mind it could be you."

She emits an uncomfortable laugh. "Yeah, well, it didn't click for me either. What are the odds, anyway?"

"Pretty low, I'd expect." I shift my weight. "But, you know, I'm glad. I couldn't imagine anyone better for him."

"Thanks." A rosy color dusts her cheekbones, but she doesn't look up, and I sense she's waiting for me to say something more.

"And things between us don't need to change," I add. "You're still my go-to barista."

She nibbles on her bottom lip. "Then why..." Her words trail off and she gives a shake of her head. I know what she's asking, and there's a tiny tug in my chest at the way she seems hurt by it.

"I had an early meeting today," I lie, "so that I could be free tonight. I'll be back tomorrow."

"I thought maybe... I don't know. You felt too weird about it, or something."

"Not at all," I lie again. The lies are starting to pile up, but I need to do this. For Jesse.

Finally, she lifts her gaze to mine. Her eyes search my face as if looking for the answer to something, then she nods, letting her mouth tilt into a smile.

"Okay, well, I'm glad."

The tension in my stomach eases a little, and I return her smile. "Now, what can I get you to drink? And don't say 'whatever I have,' because you make me the perfect coffee every single day. It's my turn to make you something you'd like."

"Okay." Her eyes shimmer. "I'll have a Cuban Breeze."

Oh, shit. Do I have everything I need for that? What does a Cuban Breeze even contain? Rum, maybe? I glance at my drinks cabinet, and she laughs.

"I'm kidding. If you've got red wine, that would be nice."

I exhale a laugh. "*That* I can do." I reach for a bottle of merlot from the wine rack and fish the corkscrew out of the drawer. The cork makes a pleasing pop as it releases, and I pour the wine into my decanter. "I should let that breathe for a few minutes, if that's okay? That way you'll get the best flavor."

She lifts her eyebrows, possibly impressed, but I can't be certain. "Sure."

I grab a can of seltzer and pour it over ice for her to drink while she waits.

"So you know about wine, then?" she asks.

"A little. I've done some work for a couple different wineries here and there. You pick up a few things."

Daisy sips her seltzer. "I've always wondered what it is you do."

"I'm in advertising," I say, motioning for Daisy to follow me into the living room as I crack open my own can. It feels awkward standing in the kitchen, but as I lead her to the sofa to take a seat, I realize this might be more awkward. It's where I caught her with Jess last night. I'm not sure if she's thinking the same thing, but she hovers to one side, casting her gaze over the bookshelves. They house my books on advertising and graphic design, plus a few photography books I've never gotten around to reading. There's also an antique globe, a few knick-knacks from my travels, and an old Nikon SLR film camera I've had for decades. They used to hold Lydia's art books, but I put them into storage not long after she died because looking at them all the time was too painful. Looking at any of her stuff was too painful.

"Wow," Daisy murmurs. She places her seltzer on a coaster and reaches for the Nikon, then hesitates. "May I?"

Her politeness makes me smile. "Of course." I join her as she picks up the old camera and turns it over in her hands, face alight.

"I haven't seen one of these in years."

"I'm surprised you even know what that is," I tease. She's young enough that she may never have actually used a film camera, for all I know.

She laughs. "Of course I do. I'm not *that* young."

*You're young enough.*

"Well, I haven't used it for a long time," I admit. "It's far too easy to take pictures with my phone."

She nods in understanding, glancing at me over the camera. "It's not the same, though, is it?"

I shrug. "It means I don't have to find a place to develop film. Do they even still do that?"

Her gaze sparkles with amusement. "Yes. Or you could develop it yourself, if you know how."

There's a reverence to her voice that makes me pause. She's so creative with her coffee, and I've always sensed she has an artistic side. Was I right?

"Do *you* know how?" I ask, intrigued.

"I..." She swallows, her face shuttering. "I did. A long time ago." She sets the Nikon down and turns away, indicating the conversation is over, but all I want to do is ask her more questions.

There's a sound at the door as Jesse tumbles in out of the rain, cursing to himself. Daisy and I enter the hallway to find him peeling off his soaking jacket.

"Hey," he says, noticing Daisy. His gaze travels the length of my Yankees hoodie, and he frowns.

"I hope it's okay I put this on," she says, motioning to herself. "I got soaked on the walk over."

Jesse's gaze swings to me, then back to Daisy. "Yep." He rakes a hand through his damp hair. "Sorry I'm late. There was a delay on the train." His apology is not directed at me. It's directed at Daisy, who he pulls close and kisses. I look away.

The doorbell rings and I'm relieved to excuse myself, going to fetch the takeout I ordered. I got Thai, knowing it was a safe bet with Daisy. Though as I tip the delivery guy, I wonder if she might find it strange that I remembered. Why didn't I think of that?

I carry the food into the kitchen and unload it onto the counter, setting us up to eat at the island. I haven't entertained in years, and usually, I'd use the dining room where there's more space and it feels more formal, but I want tonight to feel easy and casual, so we'll eat in here. I pour two glasses of wine from the decanter and grab a beer from the fridge for Jess. He and Daisy are still in the hall talking, so I slide onto a stool, take a sip of the merlot, and wait.

"Come on," I hear Daisy say, and she pulls Jesse into the room by the hand. Her gaze lands on the ginger duck I've served on a plate, and her eyes light up. "Oh, yay! I've been craving this." She glances up at me, grinning. "I can't believe you remembered."

I wave a hand as if it's no big deal, secretly pleased by her reaction. Jesse shoots me an odd look, then perches on a stool in front of his Pad Thai, his brow low.

"How was work?" I ask him as I bite into my own ginger duck.

He lifts one shoulder, scooping up a large forkful of noodles. I swear, it's like he's regressed into a moody teenager all over again. I thought we were long past this.

Daisy nudges him with her elbow, and he glances up to find her giving him a look. With an exaggerated eye-roll, Jesse says, "Work was good." He looks back at Daisy as if to say, *Happy now?* but she rolls her hand, gesturing for him to elaborate. "Busy," he adds.

I glance at Daisy. "I've been meaning to thank you for that, by the way—getting him a job."

Daisy's cheeks color. "Oh, well—"

Jesse glares at me. "She didn't get me a job; she set up an interview."

I sigh. It's such a minefield around Jess. "That's what I meant. Thanks for setting up an interview."

She smiles. "Of course. He completely charmed them."

Ha. Now *that* I'd like to see.

"I didn't even know you knew how to make coffee," I add. His last job was in retail, I think, but he changes jobs so frequently that I can't keep up. That, plus he hates talking to me.

Jesse shovels a forkful of food into his mouth, shrugging.

"They train you," Daisy says, taking a delicate bite of her ginger duck and swallowing. "That's why I thought it could be a good position. You get barista training you can use anywhere."

I nod appreciatively. Jesse is lucky he met someone with connections like this.

"I hope you thanked Daisy," I say.

He shoots me a murderous look, then glances at Daisy. Mischief morphs his expression. "Oh, I thanked her."

My stomach lurches at the implication. "Alright, we're eating," I say with an uneasy laugh.

Daisy drops her gaze to her food, her face crimson.

*God, Jesse. Way to make her feel uncomfortable.*

I nudge the conversation back on track. "Who knows, maybe you'll end up running your own coffee shop one day."

Jesse huffs incredulously, slamming his fork down. "Right. Because being a barista isn't good enough for you, is it?"

My mouth pops open in shock. I hadn't meant that at all —I'd just been trying to encourage him.

He shoves to his feet, pushing his half-finished meal away. "Not all of us can run our own company, Dad. Not all of us want to."

Daisy stares at Jesse in surprise, reaching for his arm. "Jess—"

But Jesse yanks his arm away. "I'm not hungry anymore. I'll be upstairs when you're finished." And with that, he stalks from the room.

I blow out a long, tired exhale when he's gone. I guess I'd expected with Daisy here he might behave himself, but no chance of that, obviously.

"Sorry about him," I mutter, raking a hand through my hair.

"It's okay." She takes a long sip of her wine as I poke at my food, wondering if I should continue or go and talk to Jess.

"Believe it or not, this is the most he's spoken to me since he's been home."

Daisy cocks her head, brown-eyed gaze moving across my face. "Can I ask... what happened between you two?"

I open my mouth, contemplating what to say, then snap it shut. It's not my place to tell Jesse's girlfriend why he hates me. "You'll have to ask him."

She twists her lips to one side. "I have, but he wasn't very forthcoming." Pushing her plate away, she sighs. "Thanks for the food. That was delicious." She motions to my meal. "It's good, right?"

Despite the somber mood, I smile. "So good."

Her smile doesn't quite reach her eyes. "Guess I should go see if he's okay. He's on the top floor?"

I nod.

She starts to leave the room, then turns back uncertainly. "Thanks, Weston. For trying. With the dinner, and... with Jess. Don't give up on him, okay?"

My chest fills with an unusual cocktail of emotions. Jesse behaved like an asshole tonight, but she still cares about him. She wants him to be happy, like I do. At least we can agree on that.

He's a lucky guy.

"I won't," I say, my voice hoarse.

She slips from the room and I drop my head into my hands, trying to make sense of the sensations swirling through me. Of the fact that the woman I was intending to make mine—as recently as a few days ago—has gone upstairs to do God knows what with my son, instead.

Then I hate myself for even having that thought. She's good for Jesse. I mean, of course she is—she'd be good for anyone. She's a fucking ray of sunshine. And my son needs that more than I do right now. I'm glad he has that.

Even if it means I won't get it for myself.

# 7

# DAISY

"Jess?" At the top of the stairs I give a tentative knock on what I assume to be Jesse's door. "It's me. Can I come in?"

The door opens, and he pulls me into his arms, sighing. "I'm sorry you had to see that," he murmurs into the top of my head, kicking the door shut behind me. "My dad drives me crazy." He flops down onto his huge king-sized bed, sitting in the middle of the spacious room. There's a sofa along one wall, a desk, and a large TV with three different video game consoles plugged in. The roof slopes down as it leads to the bathroom at the rear, and I imagine Jesse has to duck when he crosses to that side of the room.

I perch on the edge of his bed, trying to be diplomatic. "I think he worries about you."

Jess shakes his head, his anger gathering momentum again. "He completely infantilizes me. *Did you thank Daisy?*," he mimics, raising his eyes to the ceiling. "I'm not a fucking child."

For the first time since we started dating, I feel a stab of irritation toward Jesse. He might not be a child, but he's sure acting like one.

I take a deep breath, choosing my words carefully. "You're not a child, no, but he's your dad. He's always going to want to look out for you. That's his job."

Jesse's jaw is hard as he gazes at me, but he lets his breath out slowly and softens, reaching for me. I let him tug me down into his arms.

"I'm glad you're here," he murmurs, brushing his lips over my forehead. "I like having you close."

I press my nose to his shirt. I might be physically close, but it's beginning to feel like the more time I spend with Jesse, the less close we are. We know so little about each other—about the things that really matter.

And if this is going to become something real, that needs to change.

"You're lucky your dad cares so much," I say quietly. "I don't even speak to my parents anymore." He leans away to gaze at me. "It's complicated, but... we've never really gotten along. They want me to be someone I'm not, and they were cruel and hurtful when I was at my lowest point. I cut off contact with them, and I hardly ever see my brother, either."

Jesse's brows dip in concern. "I had no idea."

"I know." I push the hair back from his forehead. "Just like I had no idea about your mom."

He lets his gaze fall to his hand, stroking a gentle pattern across my arm.

"I get why you didn't tell me," I add gently. "I know what it's like to lose someone you love."

He glances up. "You do?"

I nod. "I lost my best friend when I was seventeen."

He sucks in a shocked breath. I don't talk about this, ever. It changed the trajectory of my life in unimagined ways, and I'll never forgive my parents for the way they handled the most traumatic event of my life.

I take Jesse's hand and squeeze. "If we're going to be together, we should tell each other this stuff. We can't get to know each other if we don't."

He nods slowly. "You're right. I'm sorry I didn't tell you sooner."

"Me too." I pause, wanting to ask more about his relationship with his dad, but sensing now is not the right time to push him.

Instead, I lean in and brush my mouth across his. What starts as a chaste kiss builds in intensity, but when Jesse's hand strays to my breast, I draw back.

"We shouldn't..." I grimace. I don't know how to tell him I'm still not ready for sex, even after he's been so patient, so I say the only thing I can think of. "Your dad's home. It feels weird to do anything with him here."

Jess gives a resigned sigh, nodding. "I don't love living here either," he mutters, adjusting the front of his jeans. "I will find a place of my own, I promise. I have some debts to pay, and then I need to save a little, but after that, I'll be free."

I'm surprised to feel relief trickle through me, knowing that will probably take a few months. A few months to decide if he's really the right guy to do this with. To see if we might just happen to fall in love.

"It's okay," I reassure him. "But we could cuddle?"

He slips his arms around me and tucks me into his side. We lie like that for a long time, until I feel Jesse's soft, rhythmic breathing fan over the shell of my ear. Outside his window, the rain has stopped, and I disentangle myself from his arms and slip from the bed, careful not to disturb him. I stand for a moment and gaze at him, his massive frame sprawled on the bed, his wavy hair across his forehead. He really is cute.

Unbidden, Weston flashes into my mind. I can see so much of Weston in Jesse, and I can almost imagine what he would have looked like at this age.

I catch myself, pushing the thoughts from my head. It's no longer appropriate to think about Weston, for many reasons, and I need to sort my shit out.

On Jesse's desk, I spy a notepad, and scribble a little note of goodbye, then tuck it onto his nightstand. I have an early start at Joe's, and I'm longing for a shower and my own bed, even if it is half the size of this one.

Padding from the room, I pull the door shut quietly and tiptoe down the stairs. Weston must have gone to bed too, as the house is dark. I'll have to thank him tomorrow at Joe's for dinner—if he shows up. There's a momentary flicker of uncertainty in my chest, but it passes. After our conversation in the kitchen earlier, I know he'll be back.

I slip into the downstairs bathroom and change back into my top, which is mostly dry. In the kitchen, I fold Jesse's sweatshirt carefully and place it on the marble island. I turn to go, but movement from the corner of my eye makes me pause. In the living room under a lone reading lamp, fiddling with the Nikon camera, I notice Weston. A half-empty glass of red wine sits on the coffee table, and something about the entire scene makes my heart clench with loneliness. I imagine him sitting there with his wife, two glasses of wine on the table. There was probably chatting and laughter, and so much love. But this scene before me just feels so... desolate. Before I know what I'm doing, I cross the kitchen into the living room to be closer to him. So he doesn't have to be so alone.

He hears me and glances up, his face in shadow. He looks tired and lost, like the man I first saw at Joe's last year.

"I've had this since I was a kid," Weston murmurs, turning the camera in his hand. "I used to love shooting pictures on it."

"Maybe you should try doing that again," I suggest, knowing damn well it's the advice I need to give to myself.

He lifts a shoulder. "I don't even know what I'd shoot now."

I nod, because I know exactly what he means. Where do you start after having not done something for so long? What if you've forgotten how to do it? What if it doesn't make you feel as good as you'd hoped? Or worse—what if it does?

He sets the camera on the coffee table with a sigh. "Are you heading off?"

"I have an early start tomorrow."

Weston's eyes meet mine, ringed with exhaustion and something else I can't quite pinpoint. Sorrow, maybe?

"Of course. So do I." He rises to his feet, pushing his mouth into a smile. "Let me call you an Uber."

"It's okay, I was going to take the subway from Clarke Street."

His eyebrows draw together. "No, I'll call you an Uber. I don't want you on the subway alone at this time of night."

I want to tell him I'm always on the subway alone at this time of night, but there's something about the concern in his voice that I relent.

"Okay, if you're sure."

"I'm sure." He pulls his phone from his pocket and taps at the screen. "Two minutes. I'll walk you out."

"Thanks." We shuffle through the kitchen and I motion to the Yankees hoodie in passing. "I've left that here for Jess. Please thank him for me."

Weston's eyes move over the sweatshirt and he gives a single nod, saying nothing.

At the front door, I thank him again for dinner.

"You're welcome, Daisy, and I want you to know you're welcome here, any time. I know things are tense between me and Jess, but I'll stay out of your way."

I open my mouth to say that's not necessary—that's not what I want—then close it again. Maybe that would be easiest, after all.

My ride pulls up and Weston gives me a tired smile as I retreat down the steps. "See you at Joe's in a few hours."

# 8

# DAISY

I glance at my duffel bag sitting behind the counter at Joe's. Jesse is supposed to be here soon to take me to Greenport, an idea he had after the dinner at his dad's went south last week. I said yes at the time, because who *wouldn't* say yes to a week's free vacation on the beach? But during the past few days, I've been wondering if I should cancel. Ever since I found out that Weston is Jesse's dad, I've been rethinking our relationship. The fact that he's the son of the guy I've been crushing on for the past year feels weird. And when I think of the way he behaved at dinner last week... I don't know. It's hard to see Jesse in the same way.

The door to Joe's swings open, and two of my regulars step inside. Actually, they're more like friends now. Violet and Kyle run a restoration company that specializes in historical houses, and they live in the neighborhood. I got to know them last year when they started coming to Joe's and needed a little nudge to get together. They're an unlikely pair—she's around my age and he's in his forties—but they're perfect together. Just goes to show that age doesn't really matter if you're a good match.

"Hi," Violet says, smiling as she approaches the counter.

"Hey, guys. The usual?"

She nods, running a hand through her blond hair. Kyle steps up behind her, slipping his arms around her waist.

"Make hers a single shot," he tells me. "She's already had two today."

"Hey," Violet protests, but he squeezes her and she relents. "Fine. A single shot." She lifts her gaze to the ceiling. "Like, what even is the point?"

I laugh as I go to the espresso machine. "He drinks decaf," I point out, referring to Kyle's usual order of a decaf cappuccino.

Violet wrinkles her nose. "I know, and I'll never understand it."

Kyle strokes his beard, looking at his girlfriend with love. "You don't need to understand it. Just trust me when I say you don't want to see me on caffeine."

She gazes up at him, rising on her toes to press her lips to his. I focus on the coffee, attempting to ignore them, but it's hard when they're like this. My heart tightens as I watch him brush a few strands of hair from her eyes and press his lips to her forehead. He adores her—it was clear from the minute I saw them together last year—and every time I see him be sweet with her, my chest hollows with longing. I want someone to be sweet with me like that. I want a man to look at me the way Kyle looks at Violet, to treat me like I'm the best thing to ever happen to him.

I hand over the coffees and watch Violet and Kyle leave, thinking about Jesse. I *have* a boyfriend, yet here I am acting like I've got no one. Maybe I should go to Greenport with him, regardless of my reservations. In fact, maybe getting away—from Joe's, from Weston's house—is *exactly* what we need. It will give me a chance to figure out how I feel about him, without his dad around. I know Weston said I was welcome at his house, but I feel uncomfortable there. It's not only the tension between him and Jess, it's the way I keep thinking of Weston, sitting alone in the living room, playing with the Nikon. The way my chest ached at the sight of him. I don't want to feel that again.

Besides, some time away at the beach will be good for me. I haven't taken a proper vacation in years. It's no wonder I've been feeling stuck. A little sun, sand, surf—and maybe sex—could be exactly what the doctor ordered. It's not like I have to marry Jesse, for Christ's sake. We could just go and have a fun week. Why not?

Celine pushes through the door to cover my shift, clearly thrilled to be working when the weather is far more suited for an afternoon by the pool. I haul my duffel bag onto my shoulder as she picks up a rag to wipe the counter.

"Thanks, Celine. See you in a week."

Her mouth pulls into a sardonic smile. "Have a blast. I'm not jealous *at all*." She rolls her eyes, turning back to the counter with a huff.

I snort a laugh as I step out onto the hot street. Summer in New York can be unbearable, and I'm relieved to get a break from the suffocating heat of the city. Now that I've made up my mind, excitement ripples through me at the idea of spending the week at the beach. I could use some peace and quiet. Denise has been in rare form the past few days, working from home so I never get a moment to myself, and I need to not be around her right now.

I glance along Fruit Street looking for Jess. I'm not entirely sure how we're getting to Greenport—it's two hours away, in the North Fork of Long Island—but he said he'd organize a ride for us. Maybe he's hired a car, or—

My thoughts grind to a halt when I hear the obnoxiously loud rumble of a modified car, and a moment later, the Dodge Challenger belonging to Jess's friend Rex rolls into view.

Oh, God. Did he really borrow Rex's car to drive us there?

My stomach bottoms out when the driver's-side window rolls down, and I find myself wishing Jesse *had* borrowed the car from his friend.

"Hey, hey, pretty lady," Rex drawls, shooting me a cocky grin. "Heard you need a ride."

I grind my teeth. I've met Rex several times, and he is the absolute epitome of everything I hate about guys his age: loud, arrogant, immature, and always ready to party. I don't know why Jess is friends with him, but it seems a little too early in the relationship to question his friendships.

Jesse leans across from the passenger side to wave out Rex's window. "Hey, babe. Rex is giving us a ride."

I pause for a second, considering my options. Do I really want to spend the next two hours in the car with Rex? No. But do I want to give up my week at the beach? Jess said the place we're staying is on the water, and I'm looking forward to sitting back with a book and forgetting about real life for a while.

Besides, do I want to walk back into Joe's and tell Celine I'm not going after all? More to the point: do I want to go home and deal with Denise tonight?

Hell no.

I sigh. I guess if Rex is only giving us a ride, that's not so bad.

With a tight-lipped smile, I stuff my duffel into the trunk

beside two huge boxes of beer, then squeeze behind Jesse's seat into the cramped back of the car.

"Thanks, man," Jess says to Rex, popping the top off a bottle of beer. "You're a good friend."

Rex nods. "I wouldn't do this for just anyone." He pulls out into the street, turning the stereo up. Limp Bizkit blares from the speakers, and I slump against the backseat with a sigh, counting the minutes until the car ride is over.

———

JESS SPENDS MOST of the ride drinking beer and laughing with Rex, who, thankfully, is not drinking. It's nice to see Jess relaxing, especially after how tense he's been around his dad, and it's no surprise when we have to stop halfway for him to pee. Rex pulls off the Long Island Expressway to find a gas station, while we wait in the car.

"I'm worried about him," Rex murmurs out of nowhere, watching through the front windshield as Jess walks to the restroom.

"Really?" I ask. "Why?"

Rex lifts a shoulder. "I think he parties too hard." He glances at me over his shoulder, his brow dipping with an unfamiliar expression. It takes me a moment to realize it's concern, and my mouth pops open in surprise.

Rex is worried about *Jess* partying too hard? Shouldn't it be the other way around?

"It was fun for a while," he adds, heaving a weary exhale. "I want to be there for him, but... fuck, I don't want to lose my job."

I blink in shock, drawing breath to respond, when Jess returns to the car. The concern vanishes from Rex's face, morphing back into that cocky grin as he starts the engine.

"Ready, bro?" he asks, and Jess nods.

We peel out onto the highway again with Limp Bizkit blasting, as if the conversation never happened, and I stare out the window, frowning as I consider Rex's words. They're a little ironic coming from him, but I push them from my mind as I watch the scenery roll by.

My legs are cramping by the time we finally pull up at the place we're staying, and it really is on the beach; a huge house with weathered cedar siding, bathed in the golden light of the evening sun. I don't know how Jess can afford this place—or why he got somewhere so huge—but I'm not complaining. This is the beach house of my dreams.

I unfurl myself from the backseat and stretch my stiff legs. Rex and Jesse spent the rest of the drive singing along to the mind-numbing lyrics of Limp Bizkit as if I wasn't even there, which was incredibly annoying, especially after Rex seemed to transform into a different person while Jess was in the restroom. Why did he return to his usual obnoxious self the moment Jess appeared again? And why did he say—

Wait, is that a pool? It is! To the side of the house, behind a glass fence, I notice a freaking swimming pool. Even with the beach this close! Okay, that's awesome. Any irritation I feel melts away at the thought of relaxing here for the next week, and I turn to Rex with a genuine smile.

"Thanks for the ride, Rex." A couple hours in his company was a small price to pay for this vacation.

"You're welcome." He rakes a hand through his auburn hair. "Will we see you tonight?"

I glance at Jesse in confusion. His gaze lingers on me for a moment, then swings to Rex.

"Nah. Maybe tomorrow night."

Rex nods, his gaze cutting to me. There's something in his expression I can't quite read, like what I saw at the gas station, then he slips back into the car. The Challenger roars away, and I follow Jesse up the front path, relieved. He sets our bags down and fumbles in his pocket for the keys.

"Thanks for putting up with him," he murmurs. "I know he's a lot."

*He's confusing, that's for sure.*

"No problem," I say, eying the swimming pool again. "What's happening tomorrow?"

"The guys are having a few drinks."

I turn to him. "The guys?" I knew Rex was up here, but I figured he might be with his family or something.

"Yeah. They're in New Suffolk for the week. That's why I thought I'd bring you up."

Huh. Here I was thinking this was Jesse's idea of a romantic getaway, but clearly I was wrong. Instead, he wanted to find a way to fit me in with his friends.

I think again of how I wasn't going to come, and glance back down the driveway. Guess I'm stuck here now.

Still, at least we've got our own place, and let's face it, staying here won't be a hardship. He can see the boys whenever he wants, and I can sit by the pool with my book. A thrill runs up my spine at the thought, because I literally cannot remember the last time I did that. If ever.

Jess finds the key on his keychain and slides it into the lock. He jiggles it left, right, left again, and the door pops open. "It sticks a bit with the salt air," he explains, carrying our bags into the foyer.

"Have you been here before?" I ask, and he gives me an odd look.

"This is our place."

"Yours?"

He nods. "Well, it belongs to my parents. They got it

when I was a kid, but dad is the only one who comes here now."

Oh.

I glance around, seeing the house anew with this knowledge. This isn't some random Airbnb he found online—I almost laugh at the thought now, because no *way* could he afford this—it's his family's. Now, his dad's. This is Weston's beach house.

*So much for escaping him.*

I sigh, wandering into the spacious entry hall that leads to a large, open-concept kitchen, dining room, and living room with stained oak floors and white-washed pine walls, reaching to a high vaulted ceiling that frames a view of the undulating sand dunes and water beyond. A huge beige linen sectional sofa dominates the space, soaking up the sea views, with a battered wooden coffee table in the center. The kitchen boasts white wooden cabinetry, and a large center island like the one at Weston's house on Fruit Street. Padded bamboo stools nestle under it and rattan light fixtures hang from the ceiling above. Everything feels fresh and bright and beautiful. There's a hallway to my right and one to my left, as well as stairs leading to some sort of basement. I turn back to Jesse in shock.

"How many bedrooms does this place have?"

"Six."

*Six.* Six bedrooms in a freaking beach house.

"And bathrooms?" I ask.

"Uh... three. No—four. There's one downstairs."

Jesus. This is insane. I think I might have underestimated just how wealthy Weston is. What did he say he did again, advertising? I need a career change, pronto.

"It's... very nice," I say inadequately, and Jesse shrugs

again. I guess when you grow up with these things, they don't seem like such a big deal.

"Come on, I'll show you to my room."

I hesitate. Shit, I didn't think this part through. Do I want to stay in his room? I mean, I should, right? It'd be weird if I didn't, wouldn't it? But what if I would rather...

"Are you coming?"

I clear my throat, scuttling after him before I lose him in this gigantic house. We round a corner and head along a hall with several doors leading off, and Jess shows me into a large, airy room with a view of the sea. I'm not entirely sure if I'm comfortable staying in his bed, but that view is to die for.

He dumps the bags on the floor and turns to me with a grin. The beer has made him loose and relaxed, and as he takes me into his arms, I let myself soften against him. Now that we're alone, and he finally seems to be at ease, I decide to broach the subject I've been wondering about for so long.

"Jess... why do you hate your dad so much?"

His brows slash together. "Seriously? You want to talk about that now? When we've come all this way to get away from him?"

I sigh. I guess he has a point there.

"No, sorry." I try to shove down the frustration rising inside me. "Forget I said anything."

He frowns at me for a beat longer, then releases his breath slowly, letting that grin return. "I want to focus on being here with you," he says, taking my hand and leading me to the bed. "Alone." When his gaze roves over me with intent, a rock forms in my gut.

*Come on*, I berate myself, shaking it off. *You're in the perfect location with a cute guy. Lighten up.*

I let him tug me down onto the mattress and meet his

lips with mine. He's not a bad kisser, although it'd been so long before Jess that I can hardly compare. And I'm not sure I've ever been kissed properly, by someone who knows what they're doing.

But it's probably me. I'm so in my head about this, and I don't know why. Maybe because I've waited too long. I mean, I'm twenty-five and so inexperienced it's embarrassing. Yes, I've made out with guys. Yes, I've had a few guys grope around, but it's been so unbelievably awkward and underwhelming that I've hardly been begging for more. And now, when I finally have the chance to move past that, I'm freezing up.

Jesse's hands roam my back as his tongue darts in and out of my mouth. I try to match his enthusiasm, but he tastes like beer and my neck is at a weird angle. I'm tired from work and the car ride, and, if I'm being completely honest, I just wish he'd stop.

I draw away with an awkward laugh, but Jesse isn't amused.

"What's wrong?"

"Nothing." *Liar.* "I just... I'm tired."

He blows out a heavy, irritated breath. "Come on. We finally get the chance to do this, and *now* you're tired?"

I swallow. "It's been a long day." I rub my face as guilt weaves through me. He's been very patient; some guys barely last a week. What is wrong with me? Why don't I want to do this with him yet? We've never had a more perfect opportunity than right now, but the thought of sleeping with him makes me feel anxious more than anything. Is it just nerves, or something more?

I like him, at least I think I do.

But maybe that's the problem. I only *like* him. And I really want to feel more, especially when it comes to having sex, but I'm beginning to wonder if that's unrealistic.

"I—" A sound from somewhere in the house makes me stop. "What was that?"

Jess gives a sullen shrug. It reminds me of the way he acts with his dad, and irritation flares in my chest. With a roll of my eyes, I push to my feet and go to investigate. It was probably nothing, but I'm desperate for a moment to myself. I wander toward the kitchen, planning to get a glass of water and stare out at the sea as I get my thoughts in order, but when I round the corner, I crash into a solid wall of man. Strong hands steady me, and I glance up into Weston's ocean-blue eyes, my heart catapulting into my throat.

"Daisy?" Weston blinks down at me in surprise. "What..." He loosens his grip on my arms, stepping back, and my skin burns from his touch.

I take a deep breath to steady my runaway heart. "Jesse brought me here. We got a ride with Rex."

"Ah." Weston nods, scrubbing his palm over his stubbly chin. He's in his navy suit, tie loosened around his neck, eyes tired from what I assume has been a long day. "Well, that backfired didn't it?"

"What?"

He sighs, gesturing to his bags at the front door. "I took a few vacation days from work. Thought I'd come up here to give you guys space at home. I didn't realize..."

"Oh." I breathe out a laugh. "Didn't Jess tell you we were coming?" Weston shakes his head, and I frown. How rude of Jesse to not even tell his dad that A) we're using his beach house and B) he wouldn't be home for a week.

There's a sound behind me, and I turn to see Jess round the corner with a thunderous expression aimed at his father. "You've got to be fucking kidding me."

"*Jess.*" I shoot him a shocked look. Honestly, the entitlement with this one.

"It's fine." Weston heaves a sigh. "I'll go."

"No."

I whip back to Weston before I even realize I've said it. Both he and Jess say "What?" at the same time, and it would be comical if not for the tension between them.

"I mean... it's *your* house, Weston. We can't kick you out after you drove two hours to be here because you felt as though you couldn't be in your own home in the city."

I glance at Jesse, who has his arms folded across his chest as he glowers at me, and I can't explain why, but suddenly I feel the need to make sure Weston stays. The relief at seeing him is palpable, and if having Weston here means I get to delay things with Jesse for a bit, then I'm taking that opportunity.

Even if I can't understand why I need it so badly.

I look back at Weston. "We're all adults. The weather is beautiful. You shouldn't miss out on that because of us. This is a huge house; I'm sure we can stay out of each other's way."

Weston glances between me and Jess, and for a second I think he's going to insist on leaving again, but after a moment of studying my face, he nods.

"Okay. I'll stay."

My shoulders sag with relief, and I send him a grateful smile.

Behind me, Jesse throws his hands up and turns back down the hall. "Fucking great."

# 9

# WESTON

Daisy sighs wearily as Jess retreats. "Well, he's going to be fun to share a room with."

My stomach wrenches at the mention of her sharing a room—and no doubt a bed—with my son. But what did I expect?

For fuck's sake. This is exactly what I came here to avoid.

"You could sleep in one of the guest rooms if you'd prefer."

What? What am I saying right now?

I expect her to politely decline, but I'm surprised to see something akin to relief in her eyes.

"Would... would that be okay?"

"Of course, Daisy. There are plenty of rooms. If you'd be more comfortable with your own space, please take one of the other rooms." I busy myself with my bags so she can't see my expression, which no doubt gives away how relieved *I* am she doesn't want to share a room with Jess.

I'm an asshole.

"Okay." She exhales, smiling. "Thank you."

"You're welcome." I straighten up with my bags and

return her smile. She's wearing a sundress I've never seen, in an olive green that suits her alabaster complexion. I never knew she had freckles on her shoulders, and it's an effort to keep my eyes from trailing over her exposed skin.

Fuck. I need to lock myself in my room and never come out.

"Well, goodnight," I grit out, even though it's only 8 p.m. I wrestle my gaze away and turn to pass through the kitchen to the master suite on the other side of the house. The further I am away from her, the better. I should get back in my car and leave them to it—that's why I left the city, after all. Jesse's clearly livid that I'm here, and I can't blame him for that.

But there was something in the way Daisy pleaded with me to stay, a kind of desperation in her eyes that made me cave, against my better judgment. I might not know why, but she wants me to be here.

I set my bags on the king-sized bed and stride to the large picture window to stare at the sea. It's shimmering with golden light in the late evening sun, and I'm itching to dive into the water, to take my mind off whatever it is I've walked into.

I strip from my work clothes, having driven from the office, and into swimming trunks. I pause as I gaze at Lydia's dresser, standing next to mine, empty now apart from a few framed photos of us scattered along the top. There's that familiar ache at her absence, and I press a kiss to my finger-tips before touching them to her picture. God, what would she think of me being in this situation?

*There is no situation*, I tell myself firmly, tying the draw-string on my trunks. I grab a towel and head onto the deck, following the path down through the dunes. The sand is warm on my feet after a day in full sun, the air balmy. We used to come here every summer, the three of us. Jesse would build sandcastles and Lydia would lie on the lounger with a book on her stomach, always intending to read but usually dozing off the minute she was in the sun. She worked long hours at the gallery, and family vacations were her only time to relax.

It's good to be back again, even if it's not quite what I'd imagined with Jess and Daisy here too. But maybe this is a good thing, I think as I wade into the sea, bracing myself against the cool water. Maybe being here together, which Jess and I haven't done since Lydia passed, will help us reconnect. Maybe Jess will remember the good times we had here over the years, and let his anger toward me fade. God knows, that's the least I deserve.

I take a deep breath and dive into the surf, praying it will be that easy.

———

I turn the Nikon in my hand, looking for the tiny catch on the back to release the door that opens for the film. Ever since Daisy picked it up off my shelf, her eyes bright as she talked about shooting with a real camera, I haven't stopped thinking about it. I sourced some film from a shop in Williamsburg, hoping I could shoot a few rolls while I was away. I won't be able to develop them myself, like Daisy suggested, but that's okay. I only wanted something to take my mind off everything.

For the life of me I can't figure out how to load the film. It's been... shit, it's been decades since I used this thing.

"Need some help?"

I glance up to find Daisy padding into the dark kitchen. She's in a yellow tank top with matching pajama bottoms, her long hair piled in a messy tangle on her head. When she steps into the pool of warm light coming from the rattan light fixture above, I read the text on her tank: "Good Vibes Only." It makes me smile, because that's how I think of Daisy—a sunny person who radiates positivity.

Then I remember I'm wearing nothing but a T-shirt and boxer shorts, and I shuffle further under the island. What the hell was I thinking, coming out here in my freaking underwear?

"What are you doing up?" I ask. I'm aiming for gruff, maybe a little harsh, to scare her back to her room, but it comes out as an invitation.

She shrugs. "Couldn't sleep." Her gaze moves from me to the camera as she slides onto the stool beside me. "You brought the Nikon."

I swallow, forcing myself to keep my eyes on her face and not her bare legs. "Yeah. Got some film for it, too." I try to shuffle away from her but I'm at the end of the island. "Figured I could shoot the beach, or something."

There's a light in her eyes when they come back to mine, an upturn at the corner of her mouth. "I'm jealous."

My eyebrows pop up, and I nudge the camera toward her. "You can use it, if you like. I don't even know what I'm doing."

"Oh." Her gaze drops to the counter. "I can't, but thank you." She continues before I can ask what this means. "I can help you load the film though, if you need." Taking the film canister, she expertly pops the back of the camera open and positions the film into place, before snapping it shut. "See? Easy."

I marvel at the way she handles the camera like it's an extension of her, like she's done this a million times before. But her hands shake when she sets it on the counter, and her breathing has become uneven. Concern needles my insides.

"Are you okay?"

She takes a second to compose herself, then lifts her gaze to mine. "Yeah. Sorry, I haven't done that in..." She shakes her head. "A really long time."

"You're a natural."

An unsteady laugh slides from her lips. "I was. Once."

I want to ask what she means, why putting film into a camera has caused such a strong reaction, but I sense she doesn't want to talk about it. Instead, I decide to make her laugh. I wind the film on ready for the first photo and raise the viewfinder to my eye.

"Say cheese."

Daisy hesitates. I steel myself because this could go one of two ways, but my chest fills with utter delight when she laughs, poking her tongue out in the most childlike way, and I press the shutter.

I stare at the camera, missing the instant gratification that comes with using my phone for pictures. I can't see how the image will turn out until the film is developed, and that's okay.

Some things are worth waiting for.

I think of how long it's taken for me to finally feel okay after losing Lydia. How many months I woke in the dark searching for her beside me, then sobbing into my pillow when I remembered she wasn't there. I never thought I'd make my peace with that, but slowly I'm learning that my life will go on—that it *is* going on—without her.

Then I think of my son, who refuses to talk to me. Who still blames me for everything, three years later.

"Is Jess okay?" I ask quietly.

Daisy huffs a laugh. "I don't know. He went out."

"He what?" I stare at her in disbelief. Jesse brought Daisy all the way up here, then he went out *without* her?

"Yeah." She traces a pattern on the marble countertop. "I don't think he was in the mood to hang out."

"Right," I say, narrowing my eyes. "And where did he go, exactly?"

"Rex and the boys are having a party or something."

I try to hide my eye-roll. Fucking Rex again.

"I don't like him either," Daisy mutters, and I exhale a grim laugh.

"You caught that, did you?"

"I did." She's quiet for a moment, staring at the counter, and I become acutely aware of how close we're sitting. I've never been this close to her, and every cell in my body is hyper-aware. I smell the sweet, citrusy scent she wears, feel the heat from her exposed legs next to mine.

I shake my head, looking away. How the hell could Jess go out tonight when he's got Daisy at home waiting for him? If she were mine, I wouldn't be able to keep my hands to myself, let alone leave her behind.

And then a second, much worse thought hits me—that she deserves better. I hate to think that about my own son, but Daisy *does* deserve better than this. Better than the way he behaved in front of her at dinner last week, better than him storming off whenever he's pissed. She deserves a man who treats her like she's the best thing that ever happened to him—because she *is* the best thing to ever happen to Jess, and he doesn't have a damn clue.

"I'm sorry about Jess," I mutter. "He can be temperamental, but you need to know, it's not about you."

"I'm not so sure about that," she mumbles.

"You're good for him, Daisy. He won't talk to me, and his

friends are more or less losers, but with you he has a stable, caring relationship. He needs that."

I don't miss the way she shrinks at this, staring at her hands.

"And you helped get him a job—" I pause here as something occurs to me. "Wait, how has he managed to get a week of vacation when he's started a new job?"

Daisy's brow sinks. "Actually, I don't know."

We stare at each other for a beat, and I wonder if we're thinking the same thing—that he got fired. We both look away at the same moment, and this time I know she's feeling the same guilt as I am. I shouldn't think the worst of my own son, but it's hard not to, given the past couple of years. Jess has had plenty of time to get his life sorted. I know losing his mom was hard on him—it was hard on me, too—but it would have been so much easier for both of us if he'd only let me in. Since he won't let me help him, he has to take responsibility for his life on his own, or it will never change.

But instead of growing up, he's out partying with Rex, leaving his girlfriend here alone.

Daisy rises from her stool with a yawn. "I should get to bed."

"Yeah, me too. Thanks for the help," I add, motioning to the camera.

She pushes her mouth into a smile, but I know it's not genuine. I know her smiles, and I know when she means them and when she doesn't. I shouldn't know that, but I do.

And with my son out doing God knows what, with God knows who, I feel a little less guilty about that knowledge.

## 10

### DAISY

I stretch out on the soft cotton sheets, yawning. I hardly slept at all, and with the bright rays of the early morning sun streaking across my ceiling, I know I won't get any more sleep.

Sitting up, I press my ear to the wall beside me. After Weston arrived last night, Jesse was in a foul mood. I tried to talk to him and calm him down, but he announced that he couldn't be in the house with his dad, and that he was going to Rex's. I know he was pissed at me for asking Weston to stay, but I meant what I said—it's his beach house, and he'd driven two hours to be here. I'm not rude enough to kick him out, and he shouldn't let Jess push him around like that. I know he's trying to repair things with Jess, but he lets him get away with too much.

But what do I know? I'm hardly an expert on parent-child relationships.

There's no sound through the wall, and I flop back onto my pillow with a sigh. I set up in the guest room beside Jesse's room, mainly because I didn't want to be disturbed when Jesse got in late. At least, that's what I told myself, and what I plan to tell him if he asks. That's justifiable, right?

Except, Jesse didn't come in late. In fact, I don't think he came in at all.

I tried to sleep, but every noise made me start, every time I thought I heard him. That, and the irritation I felt toward him. It's not like I wanted to go and party with his friends—not even a little bit—but it would have been nice to be invited.

Instead, Jess stormed out like a teenager. The more I see this side of him—the way he acts around Weston—the less attracted I am to him. On our first date, he took me by surprise with his maturity, with his understanding about my inexperience and wanting to take things slow, and in the months following, he continued to surprise me. But the more time I spend with him around his father, the more immature he seems. He says he wants a relationship, but it's hard to believe he's ready for something so grown up.

It doesn't help that I don't know why he hates Weston so much. Family relationships are complicated—hell, I know better than most—but I struggle to see how Weston could have done something so unforgivable. From what I see, he's a father who cares deeply about his son and wants nothing more than to repair their relationship, even at great cost to himself.

I'd give anything to have parents like that.

The sound of footsteps in the hallway breaks my train of thought, and I hear the door to Jess's room open and close. There's rustling, then a moment later I hear the sound of creaking bedsprings as he collapses onto the bed. I check the time on my phone and frown. It's 7 a.m.

I should be relieved, but all I feel is anger burning hot in my chest. He's out all fucking night, without me—without even texting to let me know where he is or when he might return. He might be annoyed with his dad, he might be frustrated that I haven't put out yet, but I deserve a little more respect than that.

I haul myself from the bed with an irritated grunt and pad out to the kitchen. I'll let him sleep now, but later he needs to make things right. With me, *and* with his dad.

There's cereal in the pantry and milk in the fridge. I hesitate. I don't think Weston is up yet, otherwise I'd ask before helping myself, but I can only imagine he'd say yes. I pour a small bowl and wander over to look out at the sea as I eat. The morning sun glitters on the waves, rolling gently and steadily into the shore. Beyond them, a figure swims laps, back and forth across the bay, their path so precise it's as if there are lanes painted on the ocean floor. I watch them, mesmerized, thinking about how soothing that must feel. Suspended in the cool water with the azure sky above. I don't spend enough time in nature, I think, as I chew my breakfast. It's hard in the city, but I don't even visit the parks much. I spend almost all my time on the subway, in the coffee shop, and in my apartment. But taking in the expanse of sand and sea and sky, I realize how much I miss being outdoors. I spent forever playing in the yard as a kid, and that part of me is still alive somewhere, deep down inside.

I polish off my cereal and am about to turn and deposit my bowl in the dishwasher when the figure in the sea swims ashore. They step from the surf, and I realize it's a man, with a lean and well-defined torso, chest covered with a fine layer of hair, biceps firm and strong. He comes closer, crossing the dunes, and that's when I realize who I'm looking at.

Holy shit. That's *Weston*.

My mouth dries at the sight of him, wet and glistening from the sea, abs flexing as he navigates the undulating sand, hair wet and curling slightly at the tips, dripping water onto his broad shoulders. I should look away, but I'm riveted. I knew he was attractive, but the body he hides under those suits? Holy hell. I press my legs together at the sight of him, feeling restless. I recognize this sensation running through me, hot and urgent.

It's arousal.

I mean, just because I haven't had sex doesn't mean I'm not sexual. I have urges and needs, like everyone else. It's just that I usually have to take care of them myself, and there have been many occasions where I've done exactly that, picturing the man on the dunes in front of me. I haven't done that since meeting Jess, of course, but seeing Weston now, seeing his *body*—the urge strikes me again, and I swallow hard, wetting my lips.

He glances up at the house as he approaches, and his eyes meet mine through the glass sliding door.

*Fuck.*

I break from my trance and stumble away from the door, heart racing. What the hell am I doing, perving on my boyfriend's dad in his bathing suit?

I shove my bowl into the dishwasher with shaking hands and scurry to my room before Weston enters the house.

Before he can ask me why I'm watching him, half naked on the beach, while his son sleeps in the next room.

———

I DON'T SEE Jesse for the entire day. I'm not surprised; if he was partying all night, and no doubt drinking too, he'll be sleeping off a major hangover. Yet another reason I'm glad I didn't join him. You know, if he'd asked me. Hangovers are the biggest waste of time on the planet. I've had exactly two in my life, and neither was worth it.

I spend my day by the pool, reading. Or trying to, anyway. I can't get the image of Weston out of my head, despite the guilt I feel every time I let myself think about it. I've seen Jess without his shirt on, and while he's lean and athletic, he doesn't have the same muscle definition as Weston. He's not as strong, as broad. He doesn't—

Fuck, I need to stop. I shake my head, closing my book and staring up at the cloudless sky. I might have had a crush on Weston when he was the guy who came to Joe's, but now he's the father of my boyfriend, and not only is that wholly inappropriate, it's just plain weird. I'm dating his son. I'm kissing his son. I'm... well, I'm *considering* sleeping with his son.

Am I, though? We've been dating for over three months now, and any time it gets to the point where things could go further, I freeze. I pull away. I thought maybe I simply needed more time, but that's not helping at all. If anything, it's having the opposite effect. Maybe it's time to face the fact that this relationship isn't going to be the one.

My mind flashes again to Weston emerging from the surf this morning. The way my body felt so achy at the sight of him. The way I felt so... needy. That's the only word for it. I felt a primal, desperate *need* for him, and that's a feeling I've never had for Jess, even in our best moments. It's a feeling I've never had for anyone.

I really wanted to make things work with Jess, but the truth is, I've never gotten over my feelings for Weston. It was fine when I didn't know he was Jesse's dad, when I thought he was married, and I only ever saw him at work, but after spending time with him away from Joe's, my feelings have only gotten stronger, no matter how much I deny them. He's gorgeous, yes, but he's also kind. He cares so much for his son, and he's gone out of his way to make me feel welcome. When we talk, it feels like we really connect. It's always felt that way. It's like I don't have to hide around him—like he sees parts of me I don't even see myself.

And this only came about because I spent more time with him through Jess. The irony is not lost on me. Maybe if I'd known Weston was single sooner... I don't know. Would I really have made a move on him? Probably not. I would've been too worried he'd see me as young and inexperienced.

Because I am.

I've put the final nail in the coffin by dating Jess because now Weston will only ever see me as Jesse's girlfriend. No good man goes after his son's girlfriend.

And if there's one thing I know about Weston, it's that he's a really good man.

"Hey."

I glance up to see Jesse, hair disheveled, eyes bloodshot and lined with dark circles.

"Hey." I slide my sunglasses back onto my nose, turning to look at the pool. I've had the entire thing to myself today, which has been nice, actually. Peaceful.

Jess lowers himself onto the lounger beside me, raking a hand through his chestnut hair.

"How's the head?" I ask coolly. He must know I'm annoyed after last night, but he's not giving anything away.

He shrugs. "It's fine."

Right.

I blow out a long breath and reach for my book again, trying to figure out what to do now. Do I just end things with him? That feels harsh, especially when he's brought me up here. And how would I get back to the city?

"So..." Jess's voice interrupts my thoughts, and when I

glance over at him, he's rubbing the back of his neck in thought. "I shouldn't have left like that last night."

I give a slow nod.

"And I probably should have let you know I'd be out so late."

"Probably." But the thing is—I wasn't actually worried. I was angry, sure, but I wasn't worried about who he was with, or what was happening. Even now I don't really care. And shouldn't I?

"It's just..." Jesse slumps back on the lounger, shielding his eyes from the late afternoon sun. "When my dad arrived, I got so mad. I came here to get away from him, you know?"

I twist to face Jesse properly. "I *don't* know, Jess, because you won't tell me what he's done."

Jesse rolls his head to the side to meet my gaze. He eyes me for a moment, then swallows. I think he's going to look away and change the subject, but something in him opens, just a little, and he takes a deep breath.

"My mom got really sick a few years ago. Breast cancer."
Oh. Wow.

I reach for his arm. "I'm so sorry."

Jess flinches under my touch, his jaw hard as he stares at the pool. "And she... Dad..." His voice cracks and he stops, shaking his head. "I'm sorry. I can't."

"I know it's hard," I begin, stroking his forearm gently. "But—"

"No, Daisy. I can't talk about this, okay?" He yanks his arm away from my touch and rises to his feet. "I have to go."

I look up at his tall figure. "Go? Where?"

"Rex is having drinks again tonight. I wasn't going to go but..." He lifts a shoulder. "I think I will." He glances down at me, but his eyes are distant, like he's already left. "Are you coming or what?"

I blink. He can't be serious.

Why did I push things by asking about his dad again? I know he doesn't like to talk about that, but...

I rub my arm, shaking my head to myself. How can he expect me to be with him, to understand him, if he won't share what is clearly causing him pain? If he won't open up to me?

"I, uh... no, thanks." I rub my temples, searching for an excuse. "I've got a headache after being in the sun all day. I think I'll get an early night. I'll sleep in the guest room again."

I expect some pushback on this, but Jess shrugs. "Whatever." Then he turns on his heel and stalks off, leaving me alone by the pool. The relief I feel at him leaving tells me all I need to know.

It's time to end things with him.

But... I think of what Weston said to me in the kitchen last night, how I'm good for his son. He'll be so disappointed when I break up with Jess, and I can't stand the thought of that.

I chew on a nail, anxiety twisting my insides. I don't want to hurt Jesse, but it's not fair to string him along when I already know in my heart it's not going anywhere.

When I have feelings for his father.

It doesn't matter if Weston will be disappointed, if it might cut our vacation short. I need to do the right thing the next time I see Jesse.

## 11

## WESTON

I hesitate before knocking on the door to Daisy's room. She's avoided me today, and I'm not sure why. I saw her watching me on the beach this morning, but when I went inside to say hello, she was gone. She spent the day out by the pool, and I'm sure she skipped lunch. I considered taking some out to her, but decided that was too much. She knows where the kitchen is, and if she's in the mood to be alone, I want to respect that.

Besides, one glimpse of her in the white string bikini she wore by the pool was all I needed to tell me to stay away. I know better than to tempt fate.

Still, it's been a whole day, and I know she hasn't eaten. I won't let the woman starve.

I raise my hand and knock. There's a rustle inside, then the door swings open. Daisy stands there in a cornflower-blue sundress, her hair tumbling loose over one shoulder. I swallow, keeping my eyes locked on hers.

"I'm cooking dinner, if you're hungry," I say matter-of-factly.

She twists her lips to one side in thought, then nods. "Yeah, actually. I'm starving."

"Do you like steak?"

"I do." Her lips curve in a hesitant smile, and she rubs her elbow, shifting her weight. Something in her body language tells me she's uncomfortable, so I step back.

"I'll leave some on the counter for you. You can eat in here, if you'd like."

"Oh." Her brows dart together, and I feel like a jerk.

"I mean, you don't have to," I add quickly. "I wasn't sure if you wanted to be alone, or..." I know that Jess has gone out again because I saw Rex's car pull up a few hours ago, but I doubt she wants me to dwell on that. "Or... you could join me."

Her warm brown gaze moves over my face for a beat, and on instinct I straighten up and offer her a smile. It's not until she nods her agreement that I realize I've been holding my breath.

"Sounds good." She pulls the door to her room shut and follows me down the hall to the kitchen.

"Wine?" I ask, hoping it might help us both relax a little.

"Sure."

She hops onto a stool at the kitchen island, and I pop the top on the cabernet franc—a bottle from a winery local to the area. I decant it to breathe while I season the steak, Daisy sitting quietly. It's so silent in here that I'm aware of every sound I make, every time Daisy clears her throat.

We need a distraction, like, now.

"Do you want to put on some music?"

"Uh, sure." Daisy slides from the stool. "Do you have a Bluetooth speaker?"

I wash and dry my hands, leading Daisy into the living room. "I don't, but I have a record player."

God, all this does is make me appear ancient. My dad gave me his record collection when he and my mom moved to Florida a few years back, and sitting with a glass of wine while listening to his records has been one of my favorite ways to pass the time here since Lydia died.

I pick up the crate of records and lift the lid from the record player. "I know it's old-fashioned, but—"

"I love it." Daisy dives on the records, flicking through them with delight. "Ooh, how about this?" She holds up Steely Dan's *Gaucho* with a grin, and I blink in surprise.

"You know Steely Dan?"

She gives me a strange look. "Of course."

"Alright." I chuckle, lifting the needle on the record player. "So, you put the record here, and—"

She laughs, a light, musical sound that instantly puts me at ease. "I know how a record player works, Weston. Step aside."

I can't help but laugh in response, and I raise my hands, taking a step back. I watch, impressed, as she places the record on the turntable and positions the needle with expert precision. The opening track starts, and after a few chords, Donald Fagen's voice fills the room.

"You can call me Wes, you know."

She lifts her gaze from the vinyl to me. "Wes," she repeats, the lightest hint of a blush on her cheeks. "Okay."

I turn back to the kitchen, forcing myself to ignore the way her voice sounds like a soft purr as she says my name.

I pour the wine and hand Daisy a glass, then busy myself taking the steak out to the grill on the deck. Music wafts through the open sliding door, but doesn't drown out the sound of surf crashing onto the beach. The sky is apricot and pink as the sun inches toward the horizon, and the smell of sizzling steak mingles with the salty ocean air.

Through the glass door I see Daisy on the sofa, glass of wine in her hand, eyes closed and foot tapping as she listens to the music, and for the first time since I can remember, my heart feels light. I let myself imagine, just for a moment, that this is my life.

Guilt engulfs me, and I tear my gaze away from the woman inside.

*She's your son's girlfriend*, I remind myself, fists tightening at my side. What is wrong with me? Why do I keep forgetting that?

I shake my head, turning the steak on the grill. I'm lonely, that's all. It's been three years since Lydia died—three years since I've felt the touch of a woman. Daisy is the woman I've most consistently spent time with over the past year—seeing her almost daily—so it's natural that she'd take on that role in my head, but it's inappropriate. Even if Jess decided he didn't like her anymore, I could never be with her. She'd always be my son's ex-girlfriend.

Even if I saw her first.

I push the thought from my head and shut off the grill, taking the steak inside to let it rest while I throw together a quick salad.

"Do you need help with anything?" Daisy offers, entering the kitchen. Just having her in the room shifts the energy, and I suddenly wish she'd declined my offer to eat together. This was a terrible idea.

"I've got it," I mutter. "Thanks."

I serve up our meal and consider taking my plate to my room, but that would be rude. I invited her to eat with me, and it's not like she knows what I'm thinking. I just need to rein in my imagination and behave like an adult.

We sit on the stools and eat, the sounds of Steely Dan's *Hey Nineteen* playing in the background. It's not lost on me that the song is about an older man who's interested in a much younger woman, and I silently pray Daisy isn't listening to the lyrics as she eats. Although, given her unexpected love of the music, she probably knows all the words.

"I'm surprised you like the music," I say around a bite of steak.

She gives me a faint smile. "I've always loved this music."

"Are your folks into it?"

Her face darkens. "No." Her lips close around her fork and she chews slowly, as if in thought. After swallowing, she adds, "My friend Beth and I used to listen to it. Her mom and dad were into music from the seventies and eighties. They were cool. *She* was cool."

I pause. I don't miss the way she uses the past tense, but that could simply be because they've lost touch over the years.

"She died when I was seventeen," Daisy says, so quiet I almost don't hear her. She's stopped eating, instead pushing her food around her plate. "When *she* was seventeen."

There's a tight squeeze in my chest. "Oh, Daisy..." I set my fork down and reach out to touch her arm, then withdraw my hand, letting it hover. "That's... I'm sorry."

"She was my best friend. We'd known each other since elementary school, and we did everything together. She was the only person who truly knew me, you know? She liked me for who I was. I felt invincible with her. She was more like a sister than a friend. I didn't know who I was without her. Then one day... she was gone."

This time I let my hand land on Daisy's arm, and squeeze. "I'm so sorry."

Daisy shakes her head, as if snapping out of it, and glances up at me. "No, *I'm* sorry. I shouldn't be talking about this. Not when..." she trails off and reaches for her wine with another firm shake of her head.

"It's okay." I give her arm another squeeze and remove my hand.

"No." Daisy sets her glass down, her mouth in a thin line. "This happened eight years ago. That's ages, nothing compared to..." She looks at me, waiting.

"Lydia," I say softly.

"Lydia. I'm sorry, Weston."

"Wes," I correct, and she chuffs a grim laugh.

"*Wes*. I'm sorry. The music just took me right back there." She inhales a shaky breath, then picks up her wine again.

"It doesn't matter how much time has passed. Grief is like that. You think you're doing fine, then it comes out of nowhere and completely blindsides you."

She takes a sip of wine, her eyes sad. I've never seen her sad before, and it pierces something deep in my chest. Something I try to ignore.

"I don't think about it often," she murmurs, "but you're right. Sometimes it hits me out of nowhere."

I reach for my fork, thinking about the strong reaction she had to loading the film into my Nikon last night. "Does this have something to do with why you won't use my camera?"

Daisy meets my gaze and nods. She doesn't elaborate, and I don't push her. The record stops and I rise from my stool to change it.

"Should I put something different on?" I ask, and Daisy gives me a melancholy smile.

"No, it's nice. Do you have *Aja*?"

I nod, slipping the next Steely Dan album from its sleeve and putting it on. Music fills the air, and with a deep sigh,

Daisy returns to her food. I return to my stool and join her, thinking about what she shared about her friend Beth. It doesn't surprise me. If anything, it explains more about Daisy. She's always come across as more mature and worldly than her age—which I've now deduced is twenty-five. Grief will do that to you, especially if you experience it at a young age. It forces you to grow up, matures you beyond your years.

Unless you're my son, of course. I don't know what will get Jesse to grow up. I'm astounded that he went out without Daisy again, and thinking about that, I feel a sudden surge of indignation on her behalf.

"I'm sorry that Jess hasn't been in a great mood," I say. "He shouldn't be out without you."

Daisy lifts a shoulder. "He invited me. I just..." she trails off, poking at her food.

"Didn't want to be around Rex?"

She emits an awkward laugh. "Yes, actually. I know it's awful of me, but..." She grimaces. "I'm not sure about that guy."

I give her a wry smile over my wineglass. "You and me both."

"Jess is like a different person around him." Daisy looks up as I nod. "And... you," she adds, her cheeks coloring slightly. "He's different around you."

I twist my glass, letting my breath out in a long stream. "Believe it or not, Jesse and I used to be close."

Daisy studies me. "Before his mom... Lydia... died?"

I swallow. "Yes."

She rubs her forehead, confusion etched into her features.

"He still hasn't told you, has he?"

Daisy shakes her head. "I've tried to talk to him, but he's

a closed book. Every time I bring it up, he gets angry." She lifts her hands helplessly.

I stare down into my wine, contemplating her words. Poor Daisy. Jess isn't making this easy on her, and it's not fair.

"Jesse blames me for his mother's death," I say simply.

Daisy's mouth pops open. "But... why?"

I rub my jaw, not wanting to paint Jess in a bad light, but wanting to be honest. "Lydia had stage four breast cancer. She was in and out of treatment for months, but it left her very unwell. Eventually, she decided to stop the treatment and make the most of her time left. It wasn't long, but it meant she could enjoy every moment without being so ill. But Jess..." I let out a long breath, draining my wineglass and swallowing hard. "Jesse blamed me for not forcing her to continue treatment. I wanted to respect Lydia's wishes, but he didn't see it that way. He saw it as me giving up."

"Oh, Wes." Daisy's eyes are moist and she reaches out to take my hand, squeezing. It mirrors the squeezing in my chest. I haven't said these words out loud since I started therapy two years ago, and they're making me feel raw.

"It's hard enough watching someone you love go through that," she murmurs, her face lined with compassion. "But to lose the support of your son... to have him blame you..."

I nod, looking down at her hand over mine. I don't know what I was expecting when I told her, but it wasn't this. This compassion, this empathy. As if she can feel the pain I've experienced the past three years, carrying the burden of my son's blame on top of losing Lydia.

"You know it's not your fault, right?" Her voice is barely above a whisper.

"I do," I say, my throat tight. "I just wish Jess would see it that way."

She gently withdraws her hand. "I wish there was something I could do."

"So do I." I give her a rueful smile, reaching for her empty plate. I stack it on top of mine and take them to the sink, rinsing them absently. Daisy is quiet while I load the plates into the dishwasher, then I pour myself another glass of wine and top off her glass. I lean against the counter opposite her, and we both sip our wine, listening to the music.

"You should take my Nikon and go shoot something," I say at last.

Daisy glances up at me in surprise. "What? Why?"

I shrug. "I just... have this feeling you'll feel better."

She huffs a laugh, glancing down at her hands. "I want to. Really, I do. But... I don't know."

"There are some beautiful places around here that would be perfect."

Daisy opens and closes her mouth, and I decide not to push her. Not now.

"There's no pressure," I add. "But it's there if you want to use it. I hope you'll consider it."

Her gaze sparkles as it moves over my face. "Okay," she says, pulling her long hair over one shoulder. "I'll think about it."

Just hearing her say that makes me smile. Her lips curve in return, and we gaze at each other across the kitchen island, the soft sound of Steely Dan's *Home at Last* playing in the background. An unfamiliar sensation warms me from head to toe, and it takes me a good ten seconds to realize what it is.

I'm *happy*.

Shit, I haven't felt that in years. I've wanted to, but it's eluded me, blocked out by the dark clouds of grief. The only time those clouds have parted, and only briefly, is when I've seen Daisy smiling at me over her coffee creations at Joe's. But even then, I wasn't happy. I was just... less sad. Less numb.

But sitting here with Daisy, listening to this music after sharing a meal—and, it feels, sharing *ourselves*—has my heart feeling light and peaceful in a way I'd almost forgotten was possible.

God, I wish she were mine. I wish I could do this with her every night.

But the moment I have the thought, Jesse's face appears in my mind and guilt slices through me. Because it doesn't matter how much I enjoy her company. She's not mine, and she never will be. I need to find my happiness elsewhere.

I clear my throat, setting my glass of wine down. "Well, I should get to bed."

"Oh." Daisy rises from the stool, dropping her gaze. "Yeah, I should..." She heads for the door without looking at me, then at the last moment seems to reconsider, turning back. "Thanks for dinner, Wes. And the music, and... you know. Talking."

Warmth spills through my chest, but I smother the sensation, turning away. "No problem." I listen as she leaves, letting my breath out slowly.

I can't keep doing this. I can't keep hanging out with Daisy just because Jess can't get his shit together. It's not fair to Jesse, and it's not fair to me. It's not fair to my confused heart.

I turn off the music and kitchen lights, wandering to my room with a weight in my chest. It's this time of night, when I have to turn in alone, when the bed feels so big, that I miss

Lydia the most. She wasn't only my wife and the mother of my child, she was my best friend. The person who understood me like no one else, who laughed at my shitty jokes, who didn't mind spending hours together doing nothing. I miss having that.

I gaze at Lydia's picture on the dresser. It's been three years since she died, and I'm finally, *finally* starting to feel like myself again. And there's only one reason for that.

Daisy Griffin. The one woman I'm not allowed to have.

I scrub my hands down my face, trying to see the positive. Maybe I'll never be able to have Daisy, but I do know I'm ready to move on. Grieving Lydia was the hardest thing I've ever had to do, and I'll always love her, but I can't stay in limbo forever. She'd want me to be happy with someone else again, and for the first time since she died, I can imagine that happening.

I press a kiss to Lydia's picture, feeling more hopeful than I have in a long time. And with a deep breath, I slip the ring from my left hand and place it on the dresser.

## 12

## WESTON

The sea is cold when I plunge into it in the early glow of morning. After last night—after removing my wedding band for the first time since Lydia died—it feels like a rebirth. And while that thought scares me, it also excites me.

I swim with more energy than usual, plowing through the salt water with renewed vigor, preferring the freedom and wildness of the ocean to the pool. I swim in city pools every day, so when I get the chance to swim in the ocean I take it. The sea below me, the sky above... I feel alive here.

Inside my room I shower and dress, then wander into the kitchen to brew coffee. It's still early, and I don't expect the others will be up for a while. Daisy no doubt forgave Jess for going out and spent the night with him, because she's not the kind of person to hold a grudge. She's too sweet for that.

I pour cream into my espresso and slide onto a stool at the breakfast bar, wishing I was having one of Daisy's beautiful creations at Joe's. Raising the cup for my first sip, I hear Jesse's low voice in the hall.

"Just go, okay?"

I frown, setting my coffee down. Why would he ask Daisy to leave?

"Come on, Jess," an unfamiliar voice purrs.

I rise from my stool before I even know what I'm doing. When I round the corner into the hall, I find Jesse ushering a half-dressed blond out the front door, and my jaw falls open in shock.

"What the—"

"Bye!" Jess shoves the door shut and spins around, wide-eyed. "Morning, Dad."

I stare at him in disbelief. "Who was that?"

He swallows audibly, glancing past me down the hall, and I grind my molars, hands clenching into fists at my side. He'd better have a damn good explanation for why I've caught him saying goodbye to a woman other than Daisy this morning.

"If you don't tell me who the fuck that was *right now*, Jess, I swear to God—"

"Okay, okay." He motions for me to keep my voice down, glancing past me again. "She was some chick I met last night, okay? Nothing happened, we just—"

"You've got to be fucking kidding me." I drag a hand down my face, rage flaring in my veins. What is *wrong* with my son? How could he do that to Daisy?

"Nothing happened," Jesse repeats, wringing his hands.

"Then why was she here?" I explode.

He looks past me down the hallway in panic, then steps forward, trying to calm me down.

"That doesn't even matter, Jess." I shake my head, nostrils flaring as I stare him down. "You crossed a line, big time." And I'm not even sure I believe him. No twenty-three-year-old guy brings home a half-dressed blond just to chat.

"Please don't tell Daisy," Jesse pleads, and I scoff in utter disbelief.

"Of course I won't." Relief washes across his features, and I shake my head again, clarifying. "*You're* going to tell her."

The blood drains from his face. "You can't be serious."

I growl and step forward, vibrating with fury. I thought I'd raised my son better than this. "I'm dead serious. That's the least she deserves."

"What's going on?"

I spin around to find Daisy behind me, rubbing her eyes. She's in her yellow pajama tank with the matching bottoms, dark hair in long messy waves over her shoulders. She's never looked more angelic, and I turn back to my son in disgust. How could he do something so hurtful? Even more baffling, how could he risk losing her? What man in their right mind would do that?

"Either you tell her," I grit out, "or I will."

The fear and guilt on Jesse's face gives way to anger as his eyes darken. "Fine." He leans past me to glare at Daisy. "I met someone last night." He shoots me a defiant look. "Happy?"

I give a slow, furious shake of my head. "Tell her what you did."

Jesse rolls his eyes, glancing back at Daisy. "I brought her home, because *you* refuse to—"

"I'm sorry, Jess." Daisy cuts him off with a muttered apology that has me stepping back in disbelief.

"Why are *you* apologizing? Jess is the one in the wrong."

She shrivels, her face pink as she examines the floor.

"I can't believe you, Jess." I stare at my son. "Daisy has been nothing but good to you. She even got you a job, for Christ's sake."

Jess grimaces, and an icy feeling washes over me.

"Don't tell me. You fucked that up, too?"

His chest rises and falls with his heavy breathing. "It wasn't working out, okay?"

"Jesus." I raise a hand to my face, shock and disappointment a heavy knot in my chest. "You're twenty-three, Jess. It's time for you to grow up, and—"

"You know what?" he spits in rage, his gaze moving swiftly between me and Daisy. "I'm so sick of this. Sick of you trying to run my life. Sick of you, Miss Uptight, who only wants to fucking talk all the time instead of actually fuck. I don't need this. Rex will drive me back to the city, away from both of you." He looks from me to Daisy, his expression dark. "We're done." Then he storms past us to his room.

When I look back at Daisy, she's shaking. Her cheeks are streaked with crimson, her eyes fixed on the floor.

"Shit, Daisy, I'm so sorry." It takes all my strength not to reach for her, to soothe the hurt my son has caused. "I can't believe he did that."

"No, it's..." She swallows, backing away from me. She almost crashes into Jess as he rounds the corner again, his duffel bag over one shoulder. He doesn't say anything as he pushes past us, slamming the front door behind him. The sound reverberates through the house, and for the first time ever, I'm glad to see the back of my son.

## 13

## DAISY

My face is on fire as I close the door to my room. I can't believe Jesse brought someone home while I slept only a few feet from him. What the hell was he thinking?

I lower myself onto the bed, trying to untangle the cyclone of emotions whirling through me. There's hurt there, of course, that Jesse cared so little for me after the time we've spent together. There's relief too, that I don't have to end it with him, because he did a magnificent job of blowing things up all on his own.

But the main thing I feel, if I'm completely honest, is humiliation. I'm utterly humiliated that Weston saw the way Jesse treated me, that he heard him call me *Miss Uptight*, and worse, that he heard Jesse say I wouldn't sleep with him. I had zero intention of revealing my inexperience to Weston —why would I?—but that secret has been taken out of my hands and placed into Weston's. God knows what he must think of me.

My hands shake, and I press my eyes closed, mortification washing through me. I can't face Weston, not after that.

I'll have to quit my job, maybe leave the city. My stomach quivers at the idea, because where would I go? What would I do?

And then there's the very pressing issue of how I'll get home from the beach house. My palms sweat as I realize I'm well and truly screwed.

*Okay, calm down*, the rational part of my brain says. I force myself to take slow, deep breaths, and my heart settles. I don't need to figure anything out right now. All I need is to keep breathing.

A knock on the door puts a stop to that and has me shriveling into myself, like a turtle that's lost its shell. I don't answer, and the knock comes again, softly.

"Daisy?" Weston murmurs through the door. "Are you okay?"

*No.*

Tears press at my eyes as I burrow into the mattress. I'm so furious with Jess for his thoughtless actions, for putting me in this position.

The door creaks open a fraction, and Weston's head peeks in. "I'll leave you alone if you want, but I needed to make sure you're okay." His gaze lands on me, curled into a ball on the mattress, and his face crumbles. "Oh, shit." He strides into the room, crossing to the bed and lowering himself beside me. I want to crawl under the bed and hide, but as his hand gently brushes my arm, my body uncoils against my will, ever so slightly.

"My son is a grade-A asshole," he whispers. "You didn't deserve that."

I swallow against the lump in my throat, twisting to look up at Wes. Concern pools in his blue eyes, but the tension in his jaw tells me of the fury he feels toward Jess for his actions.

"He was lucky to have you, Daisy. He shouldn't have let you go."

My pulse tumbles over itself at Weston's words, but before I can let myself consider what they mean, another feeling lashes through me: guilt. Because what Wes doesn't know is that I was about to end things with Jesse. If anything, Jess saved me the trouble, and now I don't have to be the bad guy. Yes, he went about it in a shitty way, but I can't deny the relief I feel at him being gone. At the pressure to sleep with him being lifted from me. He shouldn't have brought someone else home, but I also can't blame him for being frustrated with me for not having sex with him. I can't even understand why I held out so long myself.

I take in the indignation on Weston's face and pull away. He believes I've played no part in things falling apart with Jess, and that's also not fair. I can't stand the guilt that claws at me, and I push up to stand on shaky legs.

"I should head back to the city," I say, grabbing my bag and stuffing my things inside. "Can you take me to the Jitney?" I rub my forehead, reaching for my phone to check the schedule. I can only hope I won't have to wait too long.

"Wait." Wes rises from the bed, gently taking my phone from my fumbling hands and setting it back onto the nightstand. "I can drive you back."

I feel awful for the inconvenience this causes him, but I'm too frazzled to say anything other than "Thank you."

"Please don't feel you have to leave, Daisy. You're more than welcome to stay."

I force myself to meet his gaze. "What?"

He lifts a shoulder. "You don't have to cut your vacation short just because Jess doesn't know how to behave like a decent human being."

My mouth opens, then closes, as I absorb his words. He's asking me to stay?

"I'll drive you back if that's what you want," he adds quickly. "Of course I will, I don't mind. But..." he pauses as if weighing his words carefully. "If any part of you wants to stay, please feel welcome. You must have taken time off from work, right?"

I nod silently.

"And as you said, the weather is great. I have this huge house and no one to share it with." He falters at this, shaking his head. "I mean, there's plenty of space here, and it's wasted on one person."

I tilt my head, noting the way the olive skin of his cheekbones tinges with pink. He hasn't shaved since we arrived, and his jaw has filled in with silver scruff making him look rugged in a way he never does in his suits. But it's his eyes that captivate me, the way genuine compassion swims in their ocean depths. He really does care that Jesse's actions have hurt me. He really does care about me.

Even if I'm partially to blame for things falling apart with Jess. Even if I was only minutes away from breaking up with him. But I can't tell Wes that, not after what he said about me being good for his son. I can't bear to see the disappointment in his eyes.

It doesn't matter. What's done is done, and Jess is gone. I should go too, but Weston's right. I have the rest of the week off from work, and I don't fancy heading back to spend extra time with Denise, who's set up her home office in our living room. I'd have to find places to hide out in the city while I figure out what to do next.

That's what unsettles me the most. While I was seeing Jess, I could distract myself from that stuck feeling. At least until I discovered Wes was his father. Now it will be even worse, because not only do I have to go back to my life as it was, I have to do that after spending more time with Wes than ever before. I have to do that knowing how sweet he is, knowing he's *not* married, and knowing—as I always have— that I can't have him.

So yes, I'm eager to delay that, even if it means spending more time with the man I should probably stay away from. The thing is, I can't seem to make myself say no.

"I guess I could stay."

A smile lights his face, and my chest fills with liquid warmth.

"Great. There's a beautiful beach and nature reserve I want to show you, called Sullivan's Cove. I think it would be great to photograph."

I hesitate. After the emotional turmoil of this morning, I'm not sure I'm up for that.

*You should take my Nikon and go shoot something... I have this feeling you'll feel better.*

His words from last night run through my head. He's probably right, as much as I hate to admit it. As much as the thought of picking up a camera to photograph something scares me.

Wes seems to sense my hesitation because he softens. "*I'd* like to shoot it, at least. I'm not asking you to, but it would be nice to have the company, whenever you feel like going for a walk. I think you'd like it."

In spite of everything that's happened this morning, a smile tugs at my mouth. He's probably right about that, too. I was just thinking that I'd like to spend some time outdoors.

"Okay," I relent, finally letting a smile slide onto my lips. Wes mirrors it with a smile of his own, and I have to look away.

He's so sweet. Trying to cheer me up after Jess was a jerk. Trying to make sure I still have a nice vacation.

But it's more than that. He keeps nudging me to get behind the camera despite my resistance, and he's doing it so thoughtfully—so *gently*—that I almost want to give in. It's like he can see past all the masks I wear to cover the pain that hides deep inside, like he won't be content until I take them off.

My chest is a tight knot as I gaze at my ex-boyfriend's father. I'll never have Weston in all the ways I want, and I'm not sure I can deal with that right now.

"Could we go... later?" I ask, sinking onto the edge of the mattress. Exhaustion sweeps over me, and I realize that I want nothing more than to crawl back into bed and not come out for a few days. To not have to face Weston, or think about what happened with Jess, or what awaits me back in the city.

"Of course. Whenever you're ready." He heads for the door, then hesitates, gaze lingering on me. "Let me know if there's anything you need."

"Thanks," I say, smiling faintly. He slips from the room, and I pull the covers over my head, disappearing from the world.

# 14

# WESTON

"I probably should have told you this, but I have a fear of heights." Daisy's gaze moves from me to the rocky cliff face, then back again.

I smile. "It's perfectly safe, I promise. I've walked it many times." Admittedly, I didn't tell her the trail is challenging in places. After she spent two days locked in her room, I was desperate to get her outside. I know she's hurting from Jess's careless actions, and I couldn't bear the thought of her sitting alone in her room for a minute longer. When she finally came out this morning, I threw together some food, stuffed the Nikon and a few towels in my backpack, and casually told her I was going for a walk. I was relieved when it took little to convince her to join me. What she needs is a distraction, something to make her forget Jess, and I know that getting her to shoot is the best way.

She just doesn't know it yet.

"But... I'm not dressed for rock-climbing." Her gaze drops to her sundress, a beautiful, buttery yellow that makes her pale skin glow in the sun, that makes every freckle on her bare shoulders and arms stand out like constellations.

She's right, it's not the ideal outfit for hiking across the rugged shoreline and onto the secluded beach and meadow at Sullivan's Cove, but when she entered the kitchen this morning looking like a golden angel, I couldn't tell her to go change. I could barely take my eyes off her, as inappropriate as it may be. I'm used to seeing her in a plain tee and black jeans at Joe's, hair pulled back from her face, but since we've been away, she's let her hair down—both literally and figuratively. She's always friendly and upbeat at Joe's, but this Daisy is different. More real, more raw. I'm seeing a side to her that I didn't know was there. A side I probably shouldn't see, and yet, I can't make myself look away.

"You'll be fine. We just need to be careful on the rocks." I motion to her sensible Keds. "You're wearing good footwear, and that's all you need. Trust me, it will be worth it for the other side."

She narrows her eyes, a hesitant smile playing on her mouth as if she's considering whether to trust me. "Alright," she says at last. "You lead the way."

That she's smiling at all feels like a win. I grin, hiking the backpack up on my shoulders and stepping around her to begin the journey up the jagged rock face. To our right, the cliff rises steeply to houses above; to our left, the surf pounds the rocks, sending a salty mist over us as we climb. I've walked these rocks so often I know the terrain well, but the surface is unstable and takes some getting used to, and I keep checking over my shoulder to make sure Daisy is okay.

We reach a particularly tricky part as we begin our descent onto the secluded beach, and after stepping off a high rock, I pause and turn to offer a hand to Daisy. She glances at my outstretched palm, then at my face, swallowing. The waves crash loudly below us, but I can't hear anything above the roar of my pulse as her skin comes into contact with mine. Her gaze locks on me as she carefully lowers herself down the rocks, hand tightening in my grip. I should be watching her step, making sure she's steady, but I can't tear my eyes from hers.

This is a mistake, though. She catches her foot on a rough piece of rock and loses her balance, stumbling forward. I catch her just in time, my heart hurling itself against my ribcage as I steady her.

"You okay?" I ask.

She looks up at me, wide-eyed and breathless, nodding. "Yes. Thank you."

I release her and tear myself away, practically jogging down the path onto the sand. Anything to put some distance between us.

Daisy reaches me a moment later, a little out of breath, but smiling. "It's beautiful here."

I follow her gaze across the teal-colored water, shimmering in the midday sun like millions of diamonds scattered from here to the horizon. It laps at our feet, quiet and gentle in this sheltered cove, in contrast to the thundering of the surf against the rocks around the bend.

In contrast to the thundering of my heart.

I tug the backpack off and set it on the sand, near the dunes. There's no one here for miles because there's no direct road here. Most people prefer to swim on the main beach and don't make the trek to this side, which is why I prefer it here. I get the vast expanse of ocean, land, and sky all to myself.

Pulling the camera from the backpack, I busy myself with removing the lens cap and pretending to polish the lens, reminding myself why we're really here. Daisy needs cheering up after what Jess did. I still can't believe my son was stupid enough to bring another woman home. Stupid and thoughtless. And God, when I saw Daisy in a ball on her bed after he left, fighting tears, I didn't think—I just went to her. I was propelled to her side by a need to comfort her. In a way, I feel partly responsible. I mean, it was my idiot son, wasn't it?

But once I'd lowered myself onto the mattress beside her, once I'd let myself touch her arm in an attempt to take back the hurt Jess had caused, I knew I'd gone too far. Because I didn't just want to comfort her, I wanted to pull her close. I wanted to bury my face in her hair and breathe in her sweet, citrusy scent.

I shouldn't have asked her to stay for the rest of the week. Of course I shouldn't. But I can't explain the panic that wound through me when she said she was leaving, and I meant what I said, that she still deserves a vacation. It felt like the least I could do for her after Jess's behavior.

I glance back at Daisy, staring out across the ocean, lost in thought, and shame washes over me like a wave. Here I am, obsessing about my feelings for her, while she's still hurting from my son's actions. It might have been a few days, but that doesn't mean she's over it.

"How are you feeling?" I ask gently. "After... everything?"

She glances back at me. "I'm okay."

I fiddle with the settings on the camera, even though I can't remember how the damn thing works. "You know, it's okay if you need to cry, or... whatever. You're allowed to be upset."

She seems to contemplate this for a moment. "I'm... I'm not, really. Not upset."

My brows draw together. I recall the way she curled on the mattress, the tension in her body as I sat beside her. The fact that she barely left her room for two days. Of course she was upset.

She catches my confused expression, shaking her head. "I mean, it was a crappy thing to do—"

"It *was* a crappy thing to do," I cut in. "You didn't deserve that."

"Maybe I did," she mutters, and indignation burns in my chest. "I wasn't with him for the right reasons," she adds. "And... I probably shouldn't have come away with him."

I'm not sure what she means by this, but I don't press her to explain. "Either way, that doesn't justify—"

"No, it doesn't. But... I'm not really upset, so much as"— she carefully inspects her hands—"embarrassed by what he said about me in front of you."

Ah.

*Sick of you, Miss Uptight, who wants to fucking talk all the time instead of actually fuck...*

Jesse's words replay through my head, as they have since the moment he uttered them. I've tried not to pick them apart, because they're none of my business, but I keep getting stuck on that last part—*instead of actually fuck*. Did they not sleep together? I know they weren't at the house much, but I assumed they'd been at Daisy's place.

I shake my head. Of course they were sleeping together. They're young; they would have been going at it like rabbits. I bet it was more that Jess got sick of the fact that she also wanted to *talk* sometimes, too. God forbid.

I shove the thoughts from my mind. I shouldn't be thinking about this. Their sex life is their business, and Daisy has just said how embarrassed she is that I know more than I should.

"Don't worry about it," I mutter, waving a hand, as if I can somehow wave the entire topic out of my head. "I can barely remember what he said."

She glances at me uncertainly, trying to read my face.

I'm not sure if she believes me, but she seems to accept my answer.

"He shouldn't have spoken to you like that in front of me," I add, furrowing my brow. "Or at all, actually. You did nothing wrong."

Daisy runs her eyes over my face, letting out a long sigh. "That's not... entirely true."

I gaze at her in disbelief. I find it impossible to imagine Daisy could have done anything to justify Jesse's behavior.

She twists her lips to the side. "I..." She grimaces, looking away. "I was planning to end things with him, anyway."

Huh.

I digest this information, refusing to acknowledge the flicker of satisfaction I feel at knowing she didn't want to be with him.

I am the worst father on the planet.

"I'm sorry," she adds quietly.

"Sorry? For what?"

She brings her gaze back to mine, eying me uncertainly. "I know you wanted us to be together, that you thought I was good for him, and I tried to make it work, really I did, but... it wasn't right between us. I'm sorry for letting you down."

My breath comes rushing out in shock. Is that really what she's thinking right now, that she's let *me* down?

"Daisy... I'm so sorry if you thought you couldn't end things because of me. I never meant..." I shake my head. "That wasn't fair that you had to carry that expectation."

"I wanted to help him." She shrugs, looking down at her hands again. "I tried to talk to him about his relationship with you, but he wouldn't let me in. I didn't know what else to do."

"Hey." I set the camera on the backpack and take her gently by the shoulders, forcing her gaze to mine. I know I probably shouldn't touch her again, but it feels imperative that she hears this, that she understands how serious I am. "It's not your job to repair my relationship with my son. It's not your job to make Jesse's life better. I'm sorry if I ever made you feel you had to take on that responsibility."

Her breathing becomes shallow as her dark gaze bores into mine. The beach around us falls away, and I become aware of the softness of her skin under my hands, the heat emanating from her. Her loose hair lifts in the breeze, swirling around us, and for a moment I imagine it becoming a curtain, shielding us from the world, creating a place where we can hide together. A place where I can press my mouth to hers, draw her body close, and let my hands roam across every soft curve of her skin.

A seagull wheels overhead, its piercing cry snapping me back to my senses, and I inhale a shuddering breath, stepping back.

What the hell am I doing? Only a few days ago she was Jesse's girlfriend. Yes, he ruined things, and yes, she wanted to end it too, but that doesn't mean *I* can have her. I can't betray my son by getting together with his ex-girlfriend, despite how hurtful and thoughtless he was. He's still my son after all, and on top of that, I can't be with someone my own son has been with. That's just wrong. It goes against the laws of nature or something.

And even if none of that were true, there are other things standing between us. Daisy is young and full of life. She has her entire future ahead of her. Meanwhile, I come with so much baggage I need my own 747 to fly.

I turn away to stare at the sea, knowing I need to take a moment away from Daisy to get my head straight. The sun beats down on us, making my skin prickle with heat, but I know that's not the only thing affecting me.

"I'm going in," I mutter, tugging my shirt off and striding into the water before I have a chance to hear Daisy's response. I dive into the surf and swim ten yards out, putting as much distance as I possibly can between us without vanishing into the Long Island Sound.

I'm about to swim a few laps to cool off when I glimpse Daisy on the beach. She hesitates before peeling her dress over her head, revealing that damned white string bikini underneath. Then she cautiously wades into the small waves with her head lowered.

I tread water, my gaze riveted on the creamy skin of her bare stomach, her thighs. I feel like a fucking pervert, but I can't tear my gaze from her curves, from the smattering of freckles across her chest, her dark hair cascading to her waist, and the way her breasts perfectly fill out the tiny triangles of fabric. I could untie that bikini in one motion and pull it off. I could grab her by the waist and pull her into me and taste her—

*Stop.*

I tear my gaze from her figure and clench my fists under the water, but it's too late. The image sends blood rushing south, and my cock stiffens in my trunks.

Jesus fucking Christ, I need to get my shit together.

*You can't have her*, I remind myself. *She can never be yours.*

It takes ten minutes of furious swimming for my dick to get the message, and only when she's back on the sand in her dress again do I stalk out of the water and pull my towel from the backpack, unable to look at her. Shame claws at me as I tug my shirt over my damp skin and snatch up the camera again. I'm so fucking irritated, letting myself get distracted from the reason I brought her out here. Today isn't about me. I need to get out of my head and focus on what Daisy needs.

Turning to the ocean, I frame up a shot, trying to capture the way the sun reflects off the surface of the water. I don't really know what I'm doing, but that doesn't matter. I need her to be tempted by the camera. All I want to do today is to get Daisy to shoot one photo. One photo, and I'll be happy.

After playing with the camera for a while, the heat becomes too much, but there's no way I'm getting back in the water with her. I search for shade, spying some trees in the meadow that meets the reserve beyond the low dunes. Maybe we can sit there and get out of the sun for a while.

"Come on," I say, gesturing for Daisy to follow me. I hoist the backpack onto my shoulder as we head through the dunes and into the meadow. The grass is knee high, a vibrant green, filled with white and yellow daisies.

Daisy gasps as we wade into the grass, and I set the backpack down under a gray birch tree.

"Wow. So many daisies," she murmurs, plucking one with a melancholy smile. "They're my favorite." She holds the flower and gazes down at it, her expression so soft and unguarded that I can't help myself. I lift the Nikon and snap a picture of her.

She blinks, glancing up.

"Is that because they're your namesake?" I ask, watching her through the lens. I don't take another picture, not yet, but I get the sense that having something between us might make her feel less exposed.

She breathes out a soft laugh, shaking her head. "No. They're not my namesake."

I'm so busy watching her through the viewfinder that I don't even process her words properly. Not until she adds,

"The truth is... my name isn't Daisy."

# 15

# DAISY

**W**eston lowers the camera, blinking at me in shock. "What?"

"It *is* my name *now*," I say quickly. "I legally changed it, but it wasn't my given name."

His eyebrows shoot up. "What name were you given?"

I hesitate. I haven't said this name aloud for seven years, but there's something about being in this beautiful setting, with Weston's open, curious gaze trained on me, that lets my defenses fall away.

"Dahlia."

"Dahlia," he echoes slowly, as if tasting the name on his tongue. He wrinkles his nose, and it's so cute I have to laugh. "Sorry," he adds, smiling sheepishly. "I just... I can't see you as a *Dahlia*."

I nod in agreement.

"Why did you change it?"

I look down at the daisy in my hand, gently stroking the velvety-white petals. "I changed it when I left home."

"But... why?"

I let my breath out slowly, reluctantly. "It's a long story."

"I'm not going anywhere," he murmurs. I don't dare glance up, but I know he's watching me through the lens of the camera again. I don't know why he took a picture of me a few moments ago, why he might want to take more, but his careful, focused attention makes me feel so... seen. It makes me feel like I could tell him anything, and he'd listen. He'd care.

It's been a long time since it felt like anyone really cared.

I remember what he said about grief a few nights ago—that it can come out of nowhere when you least expect it. I told him I don't think about Beth much, but I do. I think about her all the time. I've never had a friend, never had anyone else in my life I've connected with like her, before or since. I've become a loner over the past few years. If it wasn't for Denise and my regulars at Joe's, people like Violet and Kyle—and, of course, Weston—I wouldn't have anyone to talk to. Most of the time I don't dwell on this. I just live my life. Then I do something stupid like pick up a camera or put on a Steely Dan record, and I remember what's missing from my life. What's been missing since I was seventeen. It hurts a lot to be reminded; it's much easier to work all day until I'm too tired to feel anything, then put on Netflix to drown out my thoughts.

But that's why I've felt so stuck, I realize. I haven't let myself feel things. Not for the past few years, at least. I grieved after Beth died, then I got swept up in life again, and I guess I got afraid to let those feelings back in. It was easier to numb them than feel them. But that's the problem with numbing your feelings; you can't just numb the bad ones, you numb them all.

Talking to Wes the other night, I felt that sharp sting of grief again, but as I gaze down at my daisy, I realize it wasn't a bad thing. Thinking of Beth—letting myself miss her—wasn't a bad thing at all. It felt... real.

I think of my first date with Jess, agreeing to keep things light, and how that, in a way, came to shape our entire relationship. It seems that's how Jess lives his entire life, actually. He focuses on having fun, but he never lets himself feel anything. I didn't realize I'd done the same, but I don't want to live that way anymore. Not when I've been feeling things lately that remind me what it feels like to be alive. Even if they're painful.

"I told you about my friend Beth," I begin, fiddling with the flower in my hand. "But I didn't tell you about her parents, Willow and Sebastian Walker. They were the most wonderful people I've ever known. I felt closer to them than I did to my own parents."

"Why's that?" Wes asks quietly.

I heave a deep sigh. "I was always what my mother would call a 'problem child.' That is, I had emotions, and a huge imagination, neither of which my parents knew what to do with. They were very closed-off, emotionally. Always have been. As a kid, I had so many feelings." I laugh humorlessly. "I'm fairly certain I was born to the wrong parents and should have been born to the Walkers."

"Tell me about them," Wes prompts.

"I was seven when they moved next door, the same age as their daughter, Beth. We became best friends, and her parents treated me like one of their own from day one. They understood me in ways my parents never did."

I frown, thinking back to when I got my first period, at age thirteen. Willow sat me down and explained the birds and the bees. Seriously, I was *thirteen* when I found out how everything worked, because my own mom had never bothered to explain it to me. Thank God for Willow, though. At sixteen, she took me to Planned Parenthood to go on the pill, "just in case." That turned out to be a waste of time, obviously, but it didn't matter. What did matter is that I had someone there for me when my parents refused to be what I needed.

I reach for another daisy, plucking it from the ground, and hear the camera snap as I do so. I glance up to find Weston watching me, the camera pressed to his eye, and quickly look away. Seeing the Nikon reminds me of all that I lost, and I wait for the lump in my throat to soften before I continue speaking.

"The Walkers were photographers. They had a darkroom in their basement, and that's where I learned about photography. They gave me an old camera..." I lift my gaze to the Nikon in Weston's hands. "Just like that. It was my first camera—my *only* camera—and I took it everywhere. I learned everything about how it worked and Willow would spend hours in the darkroom with me, showing me how to get the images to develop just right. She even encouraged me to study photography in college, and I was so excited by the idea. I never felt more like myself than I did in that darkroom."

Weston lowers the camera now, his gaze intense as it roams my face. He says nothing, just waits for me to continue.

"They used to call me Daisy," I say, smiling at the memory. "Willow and Sebastian and Beth—they all called me Daisy. They said I was too wild and free to be a dahlia, that dahlias are fussy, showy flowers, and I was nothing like that." I laugh, remembering how, one afternoon, I told Willow that daisies were my favorite flower as we picked them from her yard and put them in a pretty, handmade vase on her counter. She turned to me, her wild black hair tucked under a scarf, and nodded sagely.

"Would you like to be a Daisy?" she asked me, and I grinned.

"I wish I could be."

"But you can," she said, pulling a daisy from the vase and placing it on each of my shoulders as if she was knighting me. "From now on, as long as you're in this house, you shall be known as Daisy."

I giggled, and Beth threw her arms around me.

"Daisy!" She squeezed me affectionately. "It's perfect."

I didn't dare tell my parents about my new name; I knew they wouldn't understand. They hated the Walkers, my dad especially, calling them "hippie commies." I didn't really know what that meant at the time, I just knew he thought it was bad.

Only, there was nothing bad about them to me. They were kind, and loving, and creative, and made me feel like I had gifts to offer the world.

Until I lost them all.

Tears prick my eyes and I blink them away, looking out at the field of daisies, their cheerful yellow centers reaching toward the sun. I can hear the ocean rolling into shore beyond the dunes, feel the heat of the sun on my skin. The sky feels so expansive and wide above us, and somehow, I know that the Walkers are with me.

"They died in a car accident," I say quietly, gripping the daisies tighter in my hand. "All three of them. Black ice. Semi truck. Head-on collision. You know how it goes."

"Oh, God, Daisy," Wes whispers.

"And then my parents," I continue, my voice shaking, "they said—" A shallow breath shudders through me as I try to rein in the anger bubbling through my veins. "They said it was for the best, and that I needed to get over it. They took my camera away, said it was making me hold on to them, distracting me from real life. Then they told me they wouldn't pay for college unless I studied something 'sensible.'" I blow out my breath, realizing I'm crushing the daisies in my hand, and loosen my grip. "So I left. I left home and moved to the city the minute I finished high school. I cut off contact with them and changed my name. I didn't want to lose who I'd been around the Walkers, even though I'd lost them."

But staring down at the crumpled daisies in my hand, I realize I lost that anyway. I might have changed my name and moved to the city, I might have tried to keep smiling through it all, but I haven't picked up a camera since.

Not until I saw that Nikon on Wes's shelf and found it in my hands before I could stop myself.

My chest hollows at the realization. I lost my friend and the parents I should have had, and I lost myself, too. The feeling is so overwhelming, so painful, that I instinctively push it away, tossing the daisies back into the grass and forcing a smile onto my mouth.

"Anyway—"

"Daisy," Wes says quietly. He sets the camera down on the backpack and, without hesitating, tugs me into his arms. It's so unexpected that I stiffen, unsure, before melting against the solid warmth of him. The tears that threatened earlier spring to my eyes, spilling over my cheeks and soaking his T-shirt.

I forget everything about Wes and Jess and the history between us. All I can focus on is the way someone holds me as pain courses through my body. The way I feel seen. The comfort of being in Wes's arms, finally letting myself feel the ache I've ignored for so long.

"I'm so sorry you didn't have anyone to be there with you as you grieved," Wes murmurs. "I know how painful that is."

I draw away, gazing up at him. His eyes shine with emotion, and a fist wraps around my heart.

"Jess moved out the day after Lydia's funeral."

The fist squeezes, hard. I know I shouldn't, but I can't help myself. I raise a hand to his cheek, gently stroking the scruff on his jaw, needing to give him something from me so he can know I understand. So he can know how much I care.

"I'm so sorry, Wes."

He swallows, his Adam's apple bobbing under the silvery stubble on his neck. His lips part and my gaze falls to them, watching as his breathing becomes uneven. All I want to do is step up onto my toes and press my mouth to his, to take away his pain, but I know I can't.

He knows that too. His arms fall from my sides, my hand drops, and we step apart. Wes stares at me for what feels like an eternity, then turns to the backpack and picks up the Nikon. I take the chance to wipe my cheeks and suck in a deep breath, letting the wave of emotion pass. When I finally feel steady again, Wes holds out the camera.

"Here," he says, his expression gentle.

I hesitate, then reach for it, its curves and edges as familiar as my own hand. He doesn't press me, just gives an encouraging smile, then wanders off to leave me to it.

I think of what he said the other night—that I'd feel better for shooting again—and know in my heart that he's right. My pulse ramps up as I lift the camera, letting my eye adjust to the viewfinder. My line-of-sight lands on Wes, standing at the edge of the meadow, gazing up at a large red maple tree. He's lit perfectly by the sun, the contours of his biceps and shoulders highlighted in his T-shirt as he raises a hand to shield his eyes from the bright light. There's something different about him today, but I can't quite put my finger on what it is.

I take a second to adjust the depth of field, bringing him more sharply into focus and letting the background of trees blur slightly, then I change the aperture to suit the brightly lit setting. With a deep inhale to steady my whipping pulse, I press the shutter. The click echoes through my head as the camera captures the scene, and something in my chest eases.

I've missed that sound.

I press my eyes shut, meeting the onslaught of emotions head-on. The grief, the joy, the relief, the bittersweetness of it all.

When I open them again, Wes gazes at me with a smile that makes warmth pour through me from head to toe. It's not smug or self-satisfied; it's true, genuine happiness, for *me*, for what I'm experiencing. It's a smile I haven't seen anyone wear since the Walkers, and on instinct I raise the camera and press the shutter again, capturing it. I want to look at it every day and remind myself that I deserve to feel good, too.

Weston wades through the meadow toward me, beaming. I laugh, snapping another picture of him, and he laughs too. Then he does something so unexpected it takes my breath away. He picks me up by the waist and twirls me around in the daisies.

"I knew you could do it!" he cheers.

I giggle as he spins me, the sky and meadow little more than a blur. His touch, the beauty of our surroundings, the relief I feel from holding a camera again, all coalesce into a high more potent than anything I've felt before. As Wes spins me, a wide grin splitting his face, I close my eyes and savor the feeling, wishing the moment would never end.

*This is what it's like to feel*, I remind myself. *And it's so good.*

But the moment does end, and Wes sets me back on my feet. I'm breathless and giddy, steadying myself on his arm, smiling so hard my face hurts. It's the simplest thing, taking a photo, and yet it feels monumental.

"Thank you," I breathe, pushing up onto my toes to plant a kiss on his scratchy cheek. He deserves so much more for the gift he's given me, and I realize as I draw away that I want to give it to him.

I want to give it all to him.

Wes's smile is gone when I meet his gaze again, and my stomach drops.

Jesus Christ. What was I thinking, *kissing* him? Sure, it was just a friendly peck on the cheek, but that was too far. He's my ex-boyfriend's father, for God's sake. Talk about getting carried away.

I open my mouth to apologize, but something in his eyes stops me. Heat swirls in their dark depths, as black swallows the familiar blue of his irises. His chest rises and falls with his erratic breathing, and my heart almost collapses in on itself.

I might not have much experience with men, but I could read that look a mile away. I'm not the only one who feels this thing between us. He feels it too.

And in the millisecond it takes to realize that, he pulls away.

"You're welcome," he mutters, turning for the backpack and hoisting it onto his shoulder. "We should head back." He takes the camera from me and shoves it into the bag, then wheels away from me without meeting my gaze.

I wrap my arms around myself, suddenly cold. He starts

off through the meadow without waiting for me, and I scurry along behind, stealing a daisy as I leave to remember today. We walk back over the rocks in silence, keeping our distance, my chest tight with so many feelings I can't even name. When we arrive at the house, Wes tells me he has errands to run, to help myself to the food, then he snatches his car keys off the hall table and disappears.

It's not until he's gone that I realize what was different about him today.

He wasn't wearing his wedding ring.

## 16

## DAISY

I close the door to the guest room, locking it behind me. I'm restless and hot, but it's not from being out in the sun all day. It's from the way Weston looked at me back in that meadow. The way his hands felt on my waist as he spun me around. The way his cheek felt, rough with stubble under my lips.

The fact that he removed his wedding band.

I feel alive and energized in a way I never have, my body pulsing with energy that has nowhere to go, and I know I shouldn't, not when Jess lay in the room beside me only a few days ago, but... I can't help it. I need to. I never felt this need with Jess, not once. But now it's beyond my control.

I lay back on the bed, tugging my dress up and slipping a hand into my panties. I'd rather I had my trusty vibrator, but it's lost in the back of my nightstand at home, untouched for months. It doesn't matter. I'm already wet with need, remembering how dark Weston's eyes were after I pressed my mouth to his cheek. The way his fingertips curled around my waist, digging into my flesh. He might not have realized that's what he was doing, but I felt it. I felt the electric current pass through his hands into my core, sparking life into all the parts of me that have lain dormant recently.

I think again of those hands; the first time I've seen them bare, without that ring, large, strong, firm on my waist. What if, instead of setting me down on my feet, he'd laid me down in that meadow? What if he'd pushed my dress up my trembling thighs and let his fingertips drift between them?

I shiver at the thought, stroking my own fingers through my wetness, wishing it was him instead. Wondering what his kiss would feel like on my mouth, I let the fantasy take over.

"Daisy," he rasps above me, his head obscuring the sun so he's lit from behind like a gift from God. Because that's what he damn well is.

It's only me and him, alone in that meadow, and I reach for him, drawing his mouth down. His lips brush mine, tenderly at first, and heat floods my core when his tongue flicks into my mouth. I moan under his touch as his hand strokes my already-damp panties.

"You want this, don't you?" he murmurs against my lips, hand pushing my panties aside. When his fingertips come into contact with my aching flesh, I arch against his hand.

"I *need* this, Weston. I've needed it since the moment I met you."

He growls, rising to his knees to strip my panties down my legs, parting my thighs to look at me. His dark and dangerous eyes fix on that spot between my legs, and I whimper with need.

"Fuck," I mutter to myself now, my soft curse echoing off the walls of the guest room. The thought of Wes between my thighs almost makes me come right now, but I want to draw this out, because I don't only need him to *look* at me, I need him *inside* me.

Wes strips off his shorts and climbs over me. His thick cock pulses with heat as he drags it through my wetness, and I mimic the motion with my fingertips. When he slowly enters me, I push two fingers inside myself, aching with the need to feel him.

"Fuck, Daisy," he mutters as he sinks into me. "You feel just like I imagined you would."

"Good?" I ask, wrapping my legs around him, inviting him deeper. Every thrust sends ecstasy rocketing through me, and I press my mouth to his neck, sucking on his hot skin.

"So fucking good, babygirl."

*Oh, God.*

I've never wanted to be called "babygirl" in my entire life. It seems so infantilizing, but there's something about hearing that word from Wes's lips... *Fuck.* I'd give anything to hear him call me his babygirl. What is happening to me?

He raises himself to his knees, gripping my hips as he thrusts hard, his eyes watching every sensation play out on my face.

"I want you to come," he grits out. I know he's not bossy like this, but fantasy Wes is a man who knows what he wants, and takes it. "Come for me, Daisy. I want to feel my babygirl come."

*Oh, fuck.*

Pleasure crashes through me, and I writhe on the bed, fingers pressing into my center, riding the wave.

I lie there with my eyes closed as I catch my breath, wishing that hadn't been a fantasy. Wishing it had been Weston making me come, instead of my own hand. Wishing it had been him filling me, instead of leaving me empty.

When I open my eyes to gaze at the ceiling, my heart is heavy, because I know a fantasy is all I can ever have.

———

WESTON AVOIDS me for the next two days, almost as if he knows what I did alone in my room when we returned from the meadow. His car is gone most of the time, and if it wasn't for seeing him in the surf, swimming his laps every morning, I'd think he'd gone back to the city.

Not that he would ever do that. He wouldn't abandon me to figure things out for myself, like Jess did. No matter how uncomfortable he might be.

I know I shouldn't watch him swim. I shouldn't sneak into Jesse's room, where he can't see me, to get a better view of him on the beach as he towels off. And I definitely shouldn't slink back to my room to touch myself, thinking of his solid, wet body and what it might feel like on top of me.

He's gone during the day, though, and I get used to having the place to myself. It's nice, in a way, if a little lonely. I listen to Steely Dan on the record player. I take the Nikon and venture to the meadow to shoot another roll, and it's even more beautiful than the first time we went. Every flower, every butterfly, every tree calls to me. All these details and tiny worlds I missed when I was there before. I shoot an entire roll on the intricacies I find there, when I take the time to look.

And wow, it feels good.

But my vacation has to end. I can't live inside this bubble at Weston's beach house, avoiding my life forever. Wes clearly needs space from me, and I need to go back to the city and figure out how to move forward with my life. I need to figure out what I want.

On our last night, I settle onto the sofa and flick through the TV channels aimlessly. A nature documentary catches my eye, and I set the remote aside, captivated by the cinematography. The close-ups are breathtaking. They remind me, like the daisies and the butterflies, that there's so much beauty out there, if we only stop to look for it. Was it only yesterday that I shot that roll of film in the meadow?

A sound from the kitchen breaks me from my reverie. I'm surprised to see Weston placing pizza boxes on the counter. I didn't even hear him come in.

"Hungry?" he asks, not glancing up. I haven't seen him for two days, and it takes me a moment to realize he's talking to me.

"I... yes."

"I got pizza." He flips the lid open, pulling a couple plates from the cupboard and loading a few slices onto one.

I hover in the living room, wondering if he wants me to wait until he's done, but he finally lifts his gaze to me. His eyes are tired, but when they meet mine, a weary smile touches his mouth. He sighs, turning to the wine rack.

"Red again?"

I blink. Is he asking me to join him?

"Uh, sure."

I head into the kitchen and take the glass he pours for me without letting it breathe, like he usually does. There's a sort of defeated, fuck-it attitude about him tonight. He pours himself a large glass and takes a long drink, before carrying his pizza through to the living room and collapsing onto the sofa. I snatch a couple slices of pizza, then take my glass of wine and join him.

We eat in silence for a while, watching the documentary, and I pretend to care about the details the narrator shares about Loggerhead Sea Turtles, but I'm too distracted by Wes to care. He's here again, beside me, and he seems... off. He's already slugged half his wine, which is unlike him; usually he takes his time, appreciating it.

"Are you okay?" I ask during the commercial break.

Wes blinks over at me as if coming out of a trance. "Sure." The rings under his eyes tell me he's anything but okay.

I swallow, setting my empty plate on the table. It was the kiss, I know it. I crossed a line, and he's so uneasy he can barely look at me now.

I take a deep breath. "If I've done something to make you feel uncomfortable, I'm sorry."

A groove sinks between his brows. "What?"

Heat inches up my neck, but I press on. "The other day, in the meadow. I'm sorry if... if I crossed a line, kissing you. I was just so excited about shooting again."

His eyes soften as they move over my face. "I know you were, and I'm so glad you did." I'm not sure if he means he's glad that I picked up the camera again or that I kissed him. "You have nothing to be sorry for, Daisy."

God, his face is so hard to read. Those blue eyes bore into mine, but something hides in there I can't get to. His scruff has grown into a short beard now, thick and silver with the odd fleck of chestnut brown, lighter than his hair. It suits him, but he doesn't look like the Wes I know. It makes him look a little rough, a little dangerous, and I can't deny the flicker of heat I feel looking at this version of him. Who knew he could get even more attractive?

I drop my gaze to his ring finger again. It's still bare. My heart thuds hopefully, but I tear my eyes away, reaching for my wine.

"I shot another roll, too. I hope that's okay."

Weston's breath rushes out, and when I look back at him, his expression has transformed. "Of course. That's great." He's wearing that smile again, the one I love, the one that tells me how happy he is for me. His gaze lingers on mine for a beat, heavy and filled with all the things he isn't saying, then he drains his wine and rises to grab the bottle from the kitchen. He pours himself another glass, but I've barely touched mine, so I wave him away. Then we settle back in to watch the documentary. The narrator is still talking about Loggerhead Sea Turtles, and I try to be interested.

And then, suddenly, I am.

"The male approaches the female, gently biting her neck and flippers," the male voice-over explains. "This is typical mating behavior for sea turtles."

My face heats as I realize what we're about to see. I itch to reach for the remote, but that will be way too obvious. Instead, Wes and I sit side-by-side, eyes glued to the screen as the narrator continues.

"The male mounts the female, penetrating her roughly."

Jesus. Even the turtles are having more sex than me.

My cheeks blaze as we watch the screen, and I don't dare look at Weston, who's become extremely still. I'm acutely aware of every breath he takes, of how my skin feels hot, the way the air is charged with electricity and neither of us wants to move in case we get shocked.

But that's exactly what I want. I want to know what it would feel like to be shocked by him. What his hands, his mouth—his *passion*—would feel like. His size, his weight, his roughness and tenderness. I want to be shocked back to life by Weston.

The show ends and the credits roll, and Wes rises from the sofa, not meeting my gaze.

"How about some Steely Dan?"

"Sure," I mutter, but really, I'm not in the mood. I push up from the sofa in frustration, grabbing my wineglass and stepping through the open glass sliding door to sit on the deck. The sky is a bruised purple, the first hint of stars winking from the heavens, and as I sink onto an Adirondack chair, my heart twists.

I know what I want. I've wanted it for a year now, and that desire hasn't faded. It's only grown stronger with time.

What I want is Weston, and I think he wants me too. The only question is, will he let himself have that?

# 17

## WESTON

I lower the needle onto the record, watching as Daisy goes onto the deck with her wine. The opening chords of *The Royal Scam* echo through the living room, but I can't enjoy them without her.

I thought getting away from Daisy would be good for me, so I went to work remotely from a coffee shop in town for a few days. I could have gone to the city, but I'd promised she could stay and continue her vacation, and I didn't want to leave her alone at the house. It's not her fault I can't keep my head on straight.

But not seeing her was the opposite of good. I couldn't focus on work. I couldn't sleep. I couldn't stop thinking about the way she looked in that bikini, the way her soft lips felt against my rough skin when she kissed me. It took me entirely by surprise, and I didn't have time to hide my reaction. All I could do was run, because if I hadn't done that, I would have hauled her against me and kissed her back, and not in the chaste way she did.

It's not only the physical attraction I feel for her,

although that's intense enough on its own; it's the way she bared her heart to me, sharing her pain, the way she lit up with that camera in her hand like someone had switched on a light in her soul. I thought she'd been a ray of sunshine before, but this was next level. Her radiance, her sheer joy, was blinding. She was in my arms, spinning through the air before I even knew what I was doing. How could I not celebrate with her? Her exuberance was contagious.

And after that story about her friend's parents, I knew how hard it was for her to get to that point. I went through my own setbacks too, like the fact that it took me a year to even come back to the beach house without Lydia, or that I couldn't swim for months because she and I used to do that together. But we can't let our grief hold us back. We can't hide from it. We have to face it in order to heal, in order to return to who we're meant to be, and to know I played even a tiny part in helping Daisy do that... my chest puffs with pride at the thought.

I shouldn't have come home with dinner tonight. I shouldn't have sat beside her on the sofa to watch TV while we ate, like an old married couple. But the past two days have been unbearable. I knew she was here, alone, and my willpower ran out. I wanted to bring her food, to hear her voice, to see her. I know I shouldn't want that and I'm flooded with guilt every second I'm around her, thinking of what my son would say.

And Lydia... God. I can't even imagine what she'd think. Not because I have feelings for someone new—I know she'd want me to be happy again—but of all the people I could have chosen, it's Jesse's ex.

*She wasn't always Jesse's ex*, a little voice in my head says. *You've known her far longer than he has.*

But that doesn't matter, because she's his ex *now*, and that fact will never change.

Through the glass door, I watch Daisy sitting in the chair, head back, gazing at the darkening sky. I should go to my room, shut the door, and forget she's in the house.

But something compels me out there, and I drop into the chair beside her with my wineglass in hand. I've had more to drink than usual, and the alcohol sends a warm buzz through my veins. It dulls the guilt, so I can let myself be beside her on our last night here.

She doesn't say anything as I join her, just gazes up at the stars, lost in thought. The ocean is a comforting roar in the distance, and I tilt my head back too, thinking of Lydia. She used to love sitting out here, naming the constellations she could never see in the city. My chest burns, wishing she could be here to help me figure everything out. That's who I miss the most: my best friend. The woman who understood me better than anyone.

"You're not wearing your wedding ring," Daisy whispers beside me, so quiet I think I've imagined it. But when I glance over, she motions to my left hand, and I notice I'm absently rubbing the spot. I let out a long, shaky breath.

"It was time," I murmur. I rub the spot again, the groove worn into my skin from the band that was there for over two decades, trying to summon the positivity I felt a few nights ago when I removed it. "I'll always love Lydia," I say, contemplating the best way to phrase it. "But... recently I've felt a shift inside. This seemed like the right thing to do."

Daisy gazes at me with a sad smile. "What brought that on?"

"You." The word is out of my mouth before I even realize what I've said, but I decide to leave it, because it's true, and I'm not sure I have the energy to lie. "I was in a dark place when I met you, Daisy, and you were…" I huff a quiet laugh, thinking of how bubbly she was during those bleak months when my world felt empty and hopeless. "You were this shining light of goodness, going out of your way to make me smile with your wonderful coffee creations. I'm sure you do that for everyone, but—"

"I don't."

Those two words are enough to make my heart trip, but I don't dare meet her gaze. I don't dare let myself consider what that could mean.

"Well, those few moments with you every morning brought hope back into my life. They reminded me that things could be good again." I smile, savoring the feeling of warmth as I take another gulp of my wine. "And lately, we've…" Ahhh, shit. *Stop.* I set my wine down with a shake of my head, aware I'm coming very close to crossing a line I won't be able to uncross. "Never mind," I mumble.

There's a long silence, during which I can feel the heat of Daisy's gaze on the side of my face.

"Lately what?" she asks at last. I try to ignore the breathless note in her voice, but I can't. And I need to be very careful with what I say next.

"Lately…" I shrug, pretending it's no big deal. "It's been nice spending more time with you." I can say that, right? That's not crossing a line. It's perfectly appropriate.

But when I let myself glance at Daisy, it feels anything but appropriate. Her eyes are dark saucers, lit with fire as they pierce mine. The air grows thick with tension as we stare at each other, a thousand unsaid words filling the space between us. A heavy ache starts low in my pelvis, my cock stirring in my shorts, and when she runs her tongue across her bottom lip, I have to shift in my seat.

I think back to the way I felt when I found out she was

dating Jess and the realization she'd never been interested in me, even though I had the nagging sense she was. Watching her squirm restlessly on the chair, watching her eyes fasten on my lips and her breasts shudder with her uneven breathing, I know I was right the first time. She feels this thing between us too, and I'm beginning to think she always has. Even though she was dating Jess.

*Jess.*

My son's name rings through my head, and I yank my gaze away from Daisy, soberness hitting me like a cold bucket of water. It doesn't matter if Daisy feels this. None of it matters. And I need to make that very clear.

"I'm sorry things didn't work out with you and Jess," I begin, trying to segue gently into what I need to say. "And I'm sorry for what he did."

"Me too," she says quietly. "But... I wasn't a very good girlfriend. I have feelings for someone else. I have for a while, and I think..." She hesitates, and I should stop her, but my breath freezes in my lungs as I wait for her next words. "I think he has feelings for me."

Oof. She's not making this easy.

I release a pained, unsteady breath as I look at her. She's so beautiful, her dark hair falling in soft waves over her bare, freckled shoulders, her expression so open and vulnerable that all I want to do is pull her close.

It's excruciating.

"He does," I murmur, despite the rational part of my brain screaming at me to *shut up*. "But he loves his son and doesn't want to hurt him. Even if said son behaved like a total ass."

Her gaze falls to her wineglass, and she gives a tiny, nearly imperceptible nod. "I understand."

Of course she does. Of course she's being perfectly

reasonable. She's young, but she's the most mature twenty-five-year-old I've met. It only makes her more attractive.

I take one last lingering look at her, then force myself to my feet, hardening my resolve. Tomorrow, our vacation ends. We'll drive back to the city, and it might be time for me to find a new coffee shop.

# 18

## WESTON

They say the road to hell is paved with good intentions, so I must be well on my way.

I rap my fist on the solid oak of my neighbor's door, one foot inching toward the steps as if I'm about to change my mind and bolt back to my place. I shouldn't be here, asking my neighbor Kyle—a contractor—if he can help me create a darkroom in my basement. Because as much as I tell myself I'm making the darkroom for me, and me alone, I know damn well that's a lie.

We returned from Greenport last week. The car ride home was torture, with Daisy less than a foot away from me, her sweet scent filling the car, her soft sundress riding up her freckled thighs. I've never had so much trouble focusing on the road in my life.

When I dropped her off outside her building in Bed-Stuy, I tried to tell her I wouldn't be coming to Joe's anymore, but the words wouldn't leave my mouth. I couldn't imagine waking up and getting coffee somewhere else. Sure, she dated my son, but she made me coffee long before that.

So I told her I'd see her in the morning as usual, and her

smile lit the car's interior before fading away. Then she thanked me for the ride and went inside without looking back. I sat on the street for twenty minutes, fighting the urge to press the buzzer to her apartment, before I finally drove myself home.

It didn't surprise me to find Jesse's stuff gone when I returned to the house. I haven't heard from him since he stormed from the beach house, and neither has Daisy, as far as I'm aware. I'm not sure who he's living with, or what his plans are, and despite everything he's done—the way he treated both me and Daisy—I still need to know he's fine. I still care.

Part of me wishes I didn't.

I tried calling him, but it went straight to voicemail. Two messages later and he still hasn't bothered returning my calls. The longer he goes on ignoring me, the more my concern for him morphs into anger.

And the easier it is to justify continuing to see Daisy.

We've spent the week making small talk at Joe's each morning, like the old days. We don't talk about Greenport. We don't talk about Jesse. We don't talk about photography.

But it's not enough for me anymore, not after how close I felt to her on our vacation. Not only that, the light that came on inside her at the beach house has dimmed again, and it hurts me to see it. After knowing how bright she can shine, I can't stand to see her shadow version. Not when I know what's inside her now.

Anyway, after playing with the Nikon at the beach, I had the idea to build a darkroom in my basement. Well, I'll ask my neighbor to build it. I want to learn more about photography after the way Daisy spoke so passionately about it. If she happens to drop by and use the darkroom I'd be okay with that, but mostly I'm building it for me.

At least, that's what I tell myself.

The door in front of me opens, and Kyle appears in the entryway. He's around my age, of a similar height, with a short beard and kind smile. He moved in next door late last year after the place sat empty for years, and while we haven't spent a great deal of time together, we've chatted enough for me to know he runs a company that restores old buildings in New York. In fact, he restored his building before moving in.

His brows rise when he sees me, and he extends a hand, smiling. "Hey, Wes. How are you?"

"Good, good." I give his hand a hearty pump and let it drop, glancing back at the steps. I could turn and leave now, and everything would be fine. I could go back to how my life was before the beach house, before I saw Daisy with that camera in her hand, before she told me she'd never felt more like herself than when she was in that darkroom.

Except I know I won't. I can't.

"Listen," I begin, shifting my weight. "This might be an unusual request, but I've been... experimenting with photography, and I'd like to put a darkroom in my house."

"Right." Kyle lifts a hand to scrub his beard, nodding.

"I was wondering if you might have a few hours free to help me put it together. I'm thinking of using the bathroom in the basement. It only has one small window, which would need to be covered and sealed, and I'd need a table custom-built to fit into the space."

I've spent the past week researching what a darkroom requires, and it's actually pretty straightforward: complete darkness, running water, a table to lay out the trays for the developing process, ventilation, and a line to hang photos to dry. It also helps to have a safelight, which is a special bulb that doesn't affect the photographic material. I figured the downstairs bathroom would be perfect because I never use it. Plus the window is tiny, it has a fan for ventilation, and running water.

Kyle contemplates this for a moment, his brows pulled low in thought. "I'd have to take a look at the space, but I'm sure it would be doable."

I blow out a breath, grinning. "Great. Any chance you could come take a look now?"

He nods. "Sure. I'll just grab a few things."

He pops back inside, and I wait at the open front door, peeking into the interior. Although our townhouses share a continuous matching façade, along with another to the right, inside they couldn't be more different. His place is full of original historic features, while mine has been stripped of its history to showcase everything modern.

He appears at the door again, a measuring tape and notebook in hand. I lead the way down the steps and up the stoop to my place. As I let him into the entry hall, I gauge his reaction with an amused smile. He sweeps his gaze across the minimalist walls, devoid of their crown molding, and grimaces. It makes me laugh. Knowing that he specializes in restoring buildings to their historical roots, this must be killing him.

"Sorry," he mutters, following me as I lead him down to the basement.

I wave his apology away. I have the utmost respect for historical buildings, but this place had already been gutted and modernized when we bought it. Lydia and I simply updated the design.

I lead him into the bathroom, tucked under the stairs at the back of the basement. There's a sink with a toilet to the left, and a bathtub along the far wall. Above the tub sits a small window, and my plan is to fill that, then build a table between the sink and the tub, with a front panel to hide the toilet underneath. We'll use the space over the tub to hang the prints to dry, and we can plug a safety light into the outlet by the sink and mount it to the wall above.

I flick the light switch as we enter the room and catch my reflection in the mirror. Piercing blue eyes stare back at me, daring me to admit that I'm not making this darkroom for myself at all.

I'm making it for her.

I raise a hand to smooth the short silver beard that's filled in along my jawline. Usually I'd tidy myself up when I get back to the city from vacation, but for some reason I resisted this time. Maybe it was the way Daisy stroked my jaw, the way her eyes darkened as her soft fingertips brushed the coarse hair, but something told me to leave it.

Fuck. Here I am thinking about Daisy. Again.

I force thoughts of her from my head and turn to Kyle, talking him through what I want to do with the space. He nods along, measuring things and making notes. After a few minutes he closes his notebook with a smile.

"This won't take much work at all. I could knock this out over a couple of evenings this week."

My mouth stretches into a grin. "That would be great. What's your hourly rate?"

He waves me away. "Forget it. It's a small project and I'm happy to help. I've got more than enough leftover materials to cover what we'll need."

"Thanks," I say, touched by his generosity. "But you at least have to tell me what you drink, so I can buy you a bottle."

He chuckles. "Now *that* I will do."

We shake hands and he heads home with a promise to return tomorrow evening to begin the work, and I spend the rest of the night trying to assure myself I'm not doing anything wrong, making a darkroom for Daisy. My house is huge and I live here alone, with so much space I don't even use. Daisy has a passion she wants to explore, and I can help her do that. She doesn't have anyone else to encourage her, and I tell myself that it's okay for me to be that person. Everyone should have someone like that in their life.

And since my son doesn't want that from me, I can give it to her instead.

With the best smile I can muster, I set the coffee in front of Weston. Today I've crafted a butterfly into the foam of his latte, but my heart wasn't in it.

Things have pretty much gone back to normal since we returned from Greenport. Wes comes into Joe's first thing, and I present him with some sort of coffee creation that makes him smile. Then we talk about the weather, while he pretends he didn't admit to having feelings for me at the beach house.

And I die a little inside.

I know that's dramatic, but it feels like the truth. The Wes I spent time with at the beach was so different from the man who sits in Joe's and says benign things like "It's supposed to get up to eighty-four degrees today." Maybe *he's* able to switch his feelings off, but I'm not. I'm on fire with wanting him, and it's only gotten worse since he admitted to feeling the same.

Weston glances up from the paper to take in the butterfly I've created. Deep creases form around his ocean-blue eyes as he smiles. He lifts his gaze to mine, scrubbing a hand across his short beard. He hasn't shaved since we returned from vacation, and I'm glad. The roughness suits him. It makes him look more rugged, more masculine.

It makes me want to ride his face.

I look away, heat streaking my cheeks, as if he can read my thoughts. When did I become such a little horndog? I hadn't touched my vibrator in months, but during the past couple weeks I've gone through three sets of batteries, imagining the things I want Wes to do to me. Thank God Denise has been out most nights, so I could have the place to myself. Just me and my filthy imagination.

Today, though, I can't bear to look at him. I can't bear the way my chest fills with longing, the way he acts like nothing has changed between us. The way he seems to have taken any feelings he might have had for me and stuffed them away in a box somewhere.

"Daisy—"

I turn for the counter, but Wes catches my hand. My breath stills in my lungs and I freeze, glancing down at him. I don't think he meant to touch me, because he looks at his hand in surprise, quickly releasing his grip, but the heat from the brief contact spreads up my arm and into my veins. I curl my hand into a fist to steady myself.

"Is everything okay?" I ask, using my most polite, customer-friendly voice. Because if I don't, I might actually cry.

This is the problem with letting yourself feel things. They don't always feel so good.

Wes nods. "Of course. I just wanted to ask..." He pauses, rubbing the back of his neck. I follow the movement with my eyes, wanting nothing more than to drag my mouth over the soft olive skin there.

Wrenching my gaze away, I push my mouth into a falsely bright smile. "What's up?"

He swallows. "Could you, uh, stop by the house tonight? Around seven?"

My lips part in surprise. "Your house?"

He nods. I can't read his face, and I'm not sure why he'd want me to come over. Or to use his words, "Stop by," which I'm certain he deliberately chose so I wouldn't read too much into them. Why would he need me to stop by? We haven't said two words to each other outside of Joe's since we returned to the city. Maybe I left something at his place when I last visited Jess, though I can't think what.

"Um..." I blow out a breath. "I guess. Why?"

He shakes his head, reaching for his coffee with a secretive little smile. "I want to show you something."

Okay, now I'm *really* curious.

"What?"

His eyes dance as they move across my face. For a second I'm reminded of the man in the meadow, the man who picked me up and twirled me through the air, jubilant that I'd shot a single photograph. I'd wondered where he'd gone.

Then he schools his expression and pushes to his feet, leaving his coffee half-full. "I... I have to run. Just stop by, okay? I'll see you at seven?"

My breath trickles out. "Yeah, I'll... Yeah. Okay."

And with that, he bolts from the coffee shop, leaving me to get through an agonizingly long day.

———

WESTON ANSWERS the front door on the first knock. He's so prompt that part of me wonders if he was hovering inside the entry hall, waiting.

"Hey." His face warms with a smile when he sees me. "You came."

I huff an awkward laugh. "Well, yeah."

Weston's gaze travels from my face to my feet, drinking me in. My shift finished at three, so I went home and changed into my favorite outfit; a black sundress with a white and yellow daisy print. It has cute little sleeves that swish over my upper arms as I move, a low scoop neck, and a ruffle hemline that cuts mid-thigh. Am I overdressed for "stopping by" at Weston's? Probably, but I wanted to wear something that made me feel good. Made me feel sexy.

Even if I know it's hopeless.

Wes drags his gaze from me, saying nothing. As I step into the foyer, I notice what he's wearing. It's Jesse's Yankees hoodie. Too hot for a New York summer, but with Wes's air conditioning it's actually a little cool in here. The feeling is blissful after being out in the city heat.

I stare at the hoodie, my gut churning. I'd assumed Jess wouldn't be here, but now that I'm back inside the house— now that I'm looking at that sweatshirt—I don't know why I'd made that assumption.

Wes closes the door behind me, catching my expression. "He's not here," he says gently. "He moved out before I got back from the beach."

I feel a cool wash of relief. *Thank God.* But as I take in the sad half-tilt to Weston's mouth, I realize he must be gutted. I know how much it meant to him that Jess was back home, even temporarily, and how hard he was trying to repair things between them.

"I'm sorry," I murmur, and Wes shakes his head firmly.

"You have nothing to be sorry for." A grim chuckle slides from him. "Honestly, I think it was doomed from the start."

I cringe, thinking of my own relationship with Jess. Given how I feel about his father—how I've always felt—I could say the same about us.

"Well…" I laugh humorlessly, trying to lighten the mood. "At least he left you his sweatshirt."

An amused spark flickers in Weston's eyes. "It's not his sweatshirt."

I falter. "What? He wore it all the time."

"He did."

I open and close my mouth, my gaze straying to the hoodie again. I'm so used to seeing it on Jesse's lean, athletic frame, and it looks different on Wes. Or rather, it makes *him* look different. The soft, faded navy-blue fabric contrasts with the rugged silver on his jaw, the olive of his complexion. And it makes the blue of his eyes even more intense.

I think of the day I came to the house when it was pouring with rain, and he gave me that sweatshirt. The way he looked at me wearing it. This entire time it was his.

I swallow, smoothing my hands over my dress. If I do that, I won't be tempted to reach out and stroke the fabric of his sweatshirt, because I know how soft it is, and I want to feel it on him. Actually, I want to peel it *off* him, and—

*Stop.*

I clear my throat. "There was something you wanted to show me?"

"Yes." A grin tugs at his mouth. "Follow me."

He leads me to a set of stairs that go down to the basement, and I follow, intrigued. I've never been down here, and I'm surprised to find a huge entertainment room with a plush sectional sofa and projector facing a huge screen and stereo system. Beyond, a wall of glass doors opens onto the carefully manicured backyard.

But Wes doesn't seem interested in any of that. Instead, he leads me across the room to a door, to what I assume is a closet, or maybe a small bathroom.

He pauses at the door, glancing back at me. His face is a mask of boyish excitement, and I tilt my head, wondering what the hell is going on. I can't help but laugh as I follow him into the cramped space. It's a bathroom, yes, but—

My smile falls away as Wes closes the door. We're standing in pitch darkness, and my heartbeat falters. What's going on? Then I hear a click, and a soft red glow falls over the tiny room. I blink as my eyes adjust to the dim light, and a familiar feeling settles over me.

A feeling like... home.

I glance around, seeing the bathroom properly. There's a sink, but no toilet. Instead, there seems to be some sort of table or counter, and on it sits a stack of wide trays and bottles. Above the bathtub, someone has strung a line with pegs on it. Not someone—Wes. Wes did this. This is what he wanted to show me.

I find him in the half-light, struggling to read his expression. Not because of the dimness of the space, but because he seems a little guarded.

"What... what is this?" I ask.

"A darkroom."

"You made..."

He swallows, the sound loud in the small, quiet space. "I made it. For you."

My breath catches in my throat. He *made* this, for *me*? He made me a *darkroom*?

I blink, trying to make sense of this. "Why?" I ask breathlessly. My heart has taken off at a sprint, staring at the man in front of me. The man who took part of his home and turned it into something... for me. And not just something, a darkroom. He made me the one place that feels like home.

Wes shrugs, as if it's not a big deal, but it is a big deal. It's a huge deal. It's the hugest fucking deal of my life.

"You were so passionate when you spoke about photography, about spending time in the darkroom when you were younger. That's what you should be doing, Daisy. Your passion is wasted at Joe's. I have this big house, and I thought—"

But he doesn't get another word out, because suddenly, my lips are on his.

# 20

## WESTON

Daisy's mouth brushes mine and the rest of the words die on my tongue. I have no need for words when my lips can speak far better like this.

But before I can say all I need to say to her, she pulls away. Her hand, which was firmly on the back of my neck, draws away shakily. Her eyes gleam as she drags in a shuddering breath. There's something so raw and exposed in her expression that my heart burns at the sight.

"I'm sorry," she murmurs, wiping her lips. "I shouldn't have done that, I know. But Wes, you *made me a darkroom.*" She shakes her head in disbelief. "I can't..."

I should be relieved she's stopped. Relieved she's apologized, so we can put it behind us. But I'm not relieved in the slightest. Now that I've felt her soft mouth on mine, my blood pumps furiously through my body. My cock aches, and it was barely the briefest touch of her lips. What would it be like if I had more?

"Oh, shit," Daisy whispers, eyes round as they examine my face.

I don't know what I must look like right now, but if it's

anything like I feel, it's wild and reckless. A little unhinged. And so fucking desperate for her to do it again.

"I'm so sorry." She backs away from me, horror morphing her expression, but I grab her arm and haul her back.

"I'm not." My voice is wrecked, a rough growl that sounds predatory. I don't even recognize it.

Daisy's hands land on my chest, on my thundering heart. She gazes at me, eyes wide and dark, her fingertips hot on my skin even through my sweatshirt.

"You're not?"

"Fuck no."

And before either of us can think better of it, I take her mouth this time. She instantly complies with my touch, turning soft and pliant in my arms. Her lips are sweet and gentle and perfect, and when her tongue nudges my mouth open, I'm all too eager to let her in. Tilting my head, I slide my tongue over hers, and every nerve ending in my body fires with need.

Daisy whimpers at the contact, her hands tightening into fists in my sweatshirt. There's something about that response that sends urgency flooding through my system, and I bend to scoop her into my arms before setting her on the table. She gasps, looking up at me in surprise. I force myself to pause, to make sure I'm not doing anything she's uncomfortable with, but before I can even fully form the thought, she drags my mouth back to hers.

Fuck, she kisses like nothing I've ever known. Like sunshine and rain rolled into one. Like innocence and depravity at the same time. Like a blessing and my biggest mistake all at once.

"Fuck, Daisy." I'm drunk as her mouth devours mine, warm and wet, trailing from my lips, to my jaw, to my neck.

My cock throbs at the way she's trying to consume me because I know the feeling. I tighten my fist in her dark mane and tug her head back, exposing her throat. Then I drag my tongue across the sweet skin, tasting her. Her moan reverberates against my tongue, and she squirms restlessly on the counter.

"God, Weston." She shudders. "I need you so badly."

"You have no fucking idea," I growl in response.

Her legs wind around my waist, and I slide my hands to her ass, drawing her closer. Her hips search for mine until she finds exactly what she's looking for. I groan as she grinds against my rigid cock, the friction so fucking good I grit my teeth to remain in control. My dick hasn't come into contact with anything other than my own hand since Lydia, and it doesn't know what to do with itself.

I suck in a lungful of air, pulling away to gaze at Daisy so I don't explode. She looks up at me with dark, needy eyes, her mouth red and swollen from our kisses. She's never looked more perfect.

"You're so beautiful."

"So are you," she rasps, hands stroking my jaw. "I'm so glad you didn't shave your beard."

A smile tugs at my mouth. "You like it, huh?"

"Fuck yes. I love the way it feels on my skin." She tilts her head, hand palming my jaw. Her eyes are so hooded she looks drunk. "I want to feel it between my legs."

*Jesus Christ.*

My breath rushes out, and I press my eyes shut, because there is nothing I want more right now than to fall to my knees and spread those sweet legs of hers.

But I'm not a casual kind of guy. I don't do one-night stands, or flings, or hookups. I've only ever slept with one woman, and I spent twenty-five years with her. As much as I want to, I know I can't go down that road with Daisy. I shouldn't have even let her kiss me.

What did I think would happen? She kissed me in the meadow when I finally got her using the Nikon. And part of me knew this would have a similar effect.

A dangerous part of me that doesn't care what Jesse would say.

*Jesse.*

The blinding fog of lust parts, and I swallow hard.

I can't let that part win. I can't lose my son. He's all I've got left of my family, and if he found out I'd kissed his ex, he'd never speak to me again. Not to mention how uneasy I feel at the thought of sharing a lover with my son.

"You have no idea how much I want that," I say, dropping my forehead to hers. My hand rests possessively on the back of her neck, and I force myself to let go, to step away. "But I can't, Daisy. I could never do that to Jess. And... I can't be with someone my son has been with. It's... it's not right." *As much as I want that. As much as I fantasize about it.*

Daisy grips the edge of the table, staring at me. "Well, then I should probably tell you—" she breaks off and her cheeks redden, so much so that I can see it even under the dimness of the safety light. "Um..." She shifts her weight uncomfortably. "I was never *with* Jesse. Not... like that."

I blink. She can't be serious.

"I've never been with anyone," she adds, so quiet I almost miss it.

"You've never..." I begin, and she nods in confirmation.

*Sick of you, Miss Uptight, who wants to fucking talk all the time instead of actually fuck...*

Jesse's words come back to me, clear as day. He meant that literally. They never slept together. No wonder she was so embarrassed when he said that. Because she's...

Shit.

*She's a virgin.*

My cock stiffens again at the thought, despite myself, because there's something about knowing no man's fucked her that makes me want to be the one to do it—even more than before.

But that also makes one thing extremely clear: this will never happen.

"Jesus, Daisy."

She stares at the floor, shriveling. "I know. It's ridiculous at my age."

I close the distance between us and take her face into my hands in one swift motion.

"It's not ridiculous. It's..." I try to think of the best word as I stroke my thumb over her soft, freckled cheek. "Lovely." Because it is. Not that I have anything against women with more experience—Lydia had been with someone before me —but there's also something nice about a woman who has waited until it feels right.

But this isn't right.

She's so young, and, *God*, innocent. She has her whole life ahead of her, with so much to learn and discover... and I'm a widowed man nearly nineteen years her senior, with a grown son. Even without the complication of Jess, I shouldn't be pursuing her. I shouldn't even be looking at her.

"It's lovely," I repeat. "But I can't be the one..." I shake my head, lowering my hands. A vise grip tightens around my heart as I step away again, knowing what I need to say. "I don't think we can see each other anymore."

Her face falls. "Wes—"

"It's for the best."

Her brows slash together. "Because I'm a virgin?"

I grimace. "Yes. No. So many reasons. I'm forty-three, about to be forty-four. That's too old for you, Daisy. And Jess..." I trail off because she already knows.

She nods, not meeting my gaze as she slides off the table and adjusts her dress. I hate the way she shrinks and curls in on herself. It's exactly the opposite of what I'd hoped to achieve with this darkroom.

"I want you to come and use the darkroom, though," I add, tugging my keys from my pocket. I slide the front door key off the chain, knowing I have a spare upstairs. "It's for you. I want you to take the Nikon and shoot, and develop your pictures here."

She gives me a frustrated look. "How's that going to work? I appreciate the offer, but—"

"No, I mean it." I press the key into her palm. "I get home late in the evenings. You can come after work, while I'm at the office, or on your days off. I want you to use it."

She looks at the key. "You want me to come into your house when you're not home, and use the darkroom?"

"Yes." And when she looks like she's about to protest again, panic surges through me. "Please," I add, not caring about the pleading note in my voice. "I made it for you. I want you to have it. You need to keep shooting. Please promise me you will."

Her mouth opens and closes as she studies me, then she nods. "Okay. I will."

"And..." I sigh, ignoring the crack through my chest as I say the next words. "I'm going to find somewhere else to have my coffee."

# 21

# DAISY

Weston's front door closes behind me, and I stand on the stoop, the light of summer evening painting the street a pretty gold. My throat is tight as I think about what just happened. How is this fair? That I had a taste of him, only for that to be yanked away?

I never should have told him I'm a virgin. That's what did it. He realized I'm too inexperienced, and it freaked him out. I can't blame him because it's true; I have no idea what I'm doing. No doubt my clumsy kissing in the darkroom made that abundantly clear, and when I said I wanted to feel him between my legs...

My face heats with shame. What came over me? I've never been so brazen in my life.

But that's the way I am with Weston. I don't recognize myself, my thoughts. I don't recognize the way my body reacts around him, the need that pulses through me. The way I want him so badly that I can't think of anything else, can't eat, can't sleep.

And I'll never get to have him.

I knew this all along, but after seeing the darkroom, after the way he pulled me back against him when I pressed my mouth to his... a tiny spark of hope flared to life in my chest. I got greedy and wanted all of him.

But he's worried about the age gap between us.

*I'm forty-three, about to be forty-four...*

Of course he thinks I'm too young. I'm only two years older than his son, for Christ's sake, and nothing in the world will ever change that.

I look down at the Nikon in my hand, my heart thudding hard. I don't want to take his camera and go shoot without him.

But I also don't want to go home right now.

*I'm forty-three, about to be forty-four...*

His words play through my head again as I absently descend the steps. He must have a birthday coming up. I wonder if Jess will do something for him. That seems unlikely, and a knot forms in my chest as I think about him spending his birthday alone.

But I can't let myself think about that. He doesn't want me in his life anymore, and I understand. I hate it, but I understand.

"Daisy?"

I pause on the bottom step, blinking out of my reverie. Violet stands in front of me, her head tilted curiously.

"Oh. Hey." I clear the rust from my voice and paint on a smile.

"What are you doing here?" She motions to Weston's house behind me, and I glance back over my shoulder.

*Nothing, just having my heart broken.*

"Uh, a friend lives here," I say vaguely.

"You know Wes?"

*I did.*

"I..." I look back at her in surprise. "How do you know him?"

Violet laughs. "I live here." She gestures to the building next door, and something on her hand catches my eye. It's a ring.

"Oh my God." I reach for her hand, and she giggles.

"Oh, yeah." She extends her arm so I can see. It's a round cut emerald with tear-drop diamonds on either side, on a tapered white-gold band.

"Holy crap," I breathe. "That's beautiful. Congratulations." I glance up at her beaming face. "When did this happen?"

"When you were out of town. Kyle actually tried to do it at Joe's. He wanted to keep a table by the wall free, but he wasn't counting on you being away. His plan kind of fell apart."

I croak out a laugh. "Shit, I'm sorry."

"Don't be silly! I heard you were off with a rich boyfriend at the beach." She grins, nudging me, and heat crawls up my neck.

"How did you..."

"Jaya told me. At Joe's."

How the hell did *Jaya* know what I was doing? Celine must have blabbed, but she should get her facts straight. It's not Jess who's made all that money. It's his dad.

"I remember you telling me last year you were interested in an older guy who came into Joe's," Violet says, lowering her voice. Her gaze slides back to Weston's house, and her eyes shimmer. "Now it makes sense."

"No—" I grab her arm and usher her away from Weston's stoop, further along the street. "I was dating his son, Jess, but that... didn't work out."

Violet's brows draw together. "Right. I think I saw him a couple times. But what happened to the older guy you mentioned?"

Against my better judgment, my gaze strays back to Wes's. "Oh, it... He... It didn't work out."

Violet follows my gaze, understanding softening her features. "I see. Did you know that Jess was his son?"

"Not until it was too late."

"It's never too late," Violet murmurs.

I straighten my spine. "Well, it doesn't matter because even if Wes could get past that, he told me..." I shake my head, biting down on my tongue. He's her neighbor, for God's sake. An interesting coincidence, sure, but that means I can't really talk to her about him, can I? "Never mind."

Violet leans in closer. "For what it's worth, I respect the girl code. You're a friend and I'd never tell him anything you told me."

I open and close my mouth, desperate to talk to someone about this. Desperate to get it off my chest.

"Okay," I say at last. "He said he's too old for me. I'm not... very experienced." I rub my face, as if I can rub away the embarrassment. "I think he sees me as too young."

"Vi!" a male voice calls from behind me, and I turn to see Kyle approaching. "Oh, hey, Daisy."

"Hi."

I shuffle away from Violet, hoping he didn't catch anything I said. He leans in to press a kiss to her forehead, and Violet waves him away.

"I'm chatting to Daisy. Girl talk. You wouldn't be interested."

Kyle smiles wryly. "Right. Well, I know when I'm not wanted."

He chuckles and ascends their steps before disappearing into the house. When I turn back to Violet, she's looking at the camera in my hand.

"Ah, so you're the photographer."

My brows rise. "What?"

A smile plays on Violet's mouth. "Kyle was over at Wes's every night last week, installing a darkroom in his basement. At first, Wes said it was for him, but then he slipped up and said something that made Kyle think it wasn't for him at all. That it was for a woman."

I press a hand to my hot cheek. "Well, yes. Sort of. He did do that for me."

"That's pretty incredible."

"Then he said we couldn't see each other anymore, so..." I shrug, fiddling with the Nikon. "I don't know what to think."

Violet nods slowly. "You know he lost his wife a few years back, right?"

There's a twinge in my heart. "Yeah."

"Honestly, Daisy..." Violet sighs, twisting her engagement ring on her finger. "I don't know a single guy who would go to the trouble of doing something as generous and thoughtful as making a darkroom for someone if they didn't have feelings for them. Serious feelings."

My heart swells at the thought. I want to believe that. I really do. But the sting of him telling me we can't see each other anymore is still fresh.

"Just give him time," Violet says gently. "He's probably shit scared. Yes, you're young, but look at me and Kyle. Age doesn't stand in the way of love." She gnaws on her lip in thought, before conceding, "It's obviously a little complicated, with his son and all, but I don't think it's about your age, and as for inexperience, I doubt he cares about that. He probably likes it." She chuckles, reaching out to squeeze my hand. "He'll get there when he's ready."

"Maybe," I murmur. I glance along the street, toward the Clark Street subway. The last thing I feel like doing right now is getting on that train and going home. Sitting with the gnawing feeling of rejection from Wes. Dealing with Denise.

Remembering the weight of the camera in my hands, I turn back to Violet. "Is there anywhere around here that would be good to photograph?"

Her eyes widen eagerly. "Uh, yeah. This entire neighborhood is gorgeous. What are you looking for?"

I lift a shoulder, faltering. I liked shooting the meadow and beach at Sullivan's Cove, which is not an option here, obviously. But the light at this time of the evening is so pretty, and Violet's right, the neighborhood is beautiful. Being a historic district, it's full of nineteenth-century brownstones and townhouses that remind me of a different time.

"I have an idea," Violet says before I can answer. "One sec." She dashes up the steps to her place and calls to Kyle that she's heading out for an hour, before appearing back at my side. "Let's go." I let her take me by the arm and tug me along the street. She's so excited I can't help but laugh.

"Where are we going?"

She slides me a mischievous smile. "To a secret little place that you have to photograph. You'll love it."

A giggle escapes me. My chest warms with gratitude at Violet's attempt to distract me from Weston, and for a brief second, it almost works.

We cross the street, continue along for a while, then round a corner into a tiny side street I would have missed.

It's a short, narrow lane with a row of unusual buildings along one side. Buildings that look like garages, or something, but not from this time.

"What is this place?" I ask, curiosity making my fingers flex on the Nikon. The buildings are unique and beautiful, and the urge to capture them on film has me raising the camera to my eye before she's even answered.

"Hunts Lane," Violet says beside me. "These are carriage houses."

"Carriage houses?"

She nods. "Built in the 1860s and used as horse stables. Look at the architectural details, like the brickwork above the arches."

I lower the camera for a moment to take them in more clearly. The first two buildings in the lane are a pair of redbrick two-story homes, with black wooden double-height doors curving into a graceful arch at the top. They look to be used as garages today, but I can imagine where the horses would have entered. The rounded windows and front entryways on each side mirror the large middle arch, their rooflines extending to two points directly over the arches, marking the pair of buildings perfectly symmetrical.

I can't quite explain why, but the photographer in me loves it.

I lift the camera again and find a position that best frames their symmetry in the evening light. A few adjustments of the settings, and I capture their beauty with a press of my finger. It sends a burst of warm, buzzing energy through me, and I turn back to Violet with a grin.

"Look at these," Violet says, leading me further along the lane.

The next row of carriage houses is just as pleasing to the eye. Not as grand as the first two, but understated in their elegance. Two stories of white painted brick with four rows of matching black doors, capped by arched black framed windows with window boxes bursting with greenery. The contrast between the black and white—and the vibrant foliage in the boxes—has me lifting my camera quickly.

I spend a little more time adjusting the settings on the Nikon to get the contrast exactly right, and experiment with capturing the buildings from either end, since they're too long to fit inside the frame head-on. It allows me to play with the perspective and the angles of the flat roofline, and the excitement continues to fizz inside me as I capture the details. I've never photographed buildings before, and definitely nothing so beautiful, with such a unique history.

"There's more," Violet says, motioning behind me.

When I finally drag my gaze from the structures in front of me, I see she's right. There's an entire row of carriage houses extending along the lane. I can hear the hooves on the cobbles as I picture the area bustling with people and carriages a hundred and fifty years ago. One building in particular catches my eye, and I rush ahead, gripping the Nikon. Violet laughs as she follows me.

"It's pretty, isn't it? I love the shutters on the windows."

I nod, lifting the camera to frame the shot. The weathered and worn facade of the brick building is definitely in need of some love, but the patina only makes it more beautiful. The windows and their shutters, as well as the carriage and front doors at the ground level, are painted in a soft cornflower blue. Window boxes spill over with white daisies, their yellow faces hidden as their petals close for the night. I take a few more pictures in the fading light, promising myself I'll return to shoot the house in full sun.

I turn to Violet, feeling fuller than I have in a long time.

"Thank you so much. I never would have thought to come here."

She grins. "I love looking at the carriage houses. It feels like stepping back in time."

I nod vigorously. With a sigh, we meander out of the lane and head back toward Violet's house. The Nikon is warm in my hand, and I look up from the sidewalk to take in my surroundings in a way I never have. My gaze travels across the brownstones, noticing architectural details I've passed over before. When I view the neighborhood from the perspective of a photographer, there's so much to see, so many intricacies to capture. I'll have to come back to shoot the rest of the neighborhood.

I skip along beside Violet, buzzing with energy. I can't wait to develop these shots, and...

My thoughts grind to a halt as the events from earlier in the evening come back to me. The feeling of being in that darkroom, knowing Wes had gone to the trouble of doing that for me.

*Just give him time... he'll get there when he's ready.*

Violet's words come back to me as we weave through the streets of Brooklyn Heights.

Maybe she's right. When I think about the way Wes kissed me this evening, I know he has feelings for me. And he made me a darkroom... Well, I'd even go so far as to say he might have "serious feelings," to use Violet's words.

But... I shake my head as we approach Violet and Weston's building on Fruit Street. He also asked me to keep my distance, and I want to do that, to respect him, but I also don't want to give up on us.

Not yet.

I pull Violet into a hug, thanking her for this evening and congratulating her again on her engagement. Then I head home, an idea formulating in my mind. Weston's birthday is coming up, and I can work with that. I won't push him for something between us when he's clearly not ready, but I won't let him spend his birthday alone, either.

I just have to figure out when it is.

## 22

## WESTON

I never celebrate my birthday anymore. When your wife dies and your son won't talk to you, there's not much to celebrate. And given I haven't seen the only woman I can think about since I lost Lydia, this year is no exception.

I spend the morning throwing myself into work until I'm too numb to notice. And when Pauline, Lydia's best friend, shows up at the office with a bunch of flowers and a cupcake with my name on it, I want to crawl under my desk and hide. But since I'm the boss, and a grown man, I refrain.

How did she slip past my assistant, Nina? She's usually my first line of defense against unplanned visitors, but when I spot her grinning through the glass, I get the sense she might have encouraged this.

"Hello, hello!" Pauline chirps as she enters my office. I don't entirely know what she's doing here; she's never celebrated my birthday before. The first six months after Lydia's death, she took care of me with food and regular house visits. Over time those faded to phone calls, then to texts. So seeing her here in my office is kind of jarring.

"Happy birthday," she sings, thrusting the flowers into my hand and setting the cupcake down in front of my laptop. "It's not Lydia's famous lemon cake," she adds with a wistful smile, "but it will have to do."

My taste buds respond to the mention of lemon cake, anticipating the tang before I can remind myself it's not coming. Lydia used to make me one every year for my birthday, and the past three years haven't been the same without it.

I rise warily from my chair. "Thanks, Pauline."

She rounds the desk, pulling me into a tight hug. I get a face full of blond curls and Chanel No. 5, before she pulls away.

"Let me take you to lunch."

"Uh..." I glance down at my laptop. I've got shitloads of work to do, because I'm still catching up from the time I took away at the beach house.

Besides, I'm really not in the mood.

I'd almost been looking forward to my birthday this year. With Jess back at home and Daisy around, things felt more hopeful. I'd imagined the three of us sitting down to an enjoyable dinner, even if Jess spent the evening sulking. It would have been something, at least.

But the last few weeks have been a whole lot of nothing. Nothing but work, long hours swimming laps in the pool, and fucking average coffee.

"Come on." Pauline slips her arm through mine, tugging me away from the desk. "We'll be an hour, tops. I won't take no for an answer."

I sigh, letting her drag me out of the office. She chats amiably as we ride the elevator, then exit through the glossy lobby of the high-rise onto the bustle of Fifth Avenue, but I barely hear a word she says because my mind has strayed to

Daisy, to that moment we stole together alone in the dark-room. It's all I've been able to think about since it happened.

And I hate myself for it.

The way it felt to have her melt in my arms, her mouth soft and needy as she rubbed herself against me. The moan she made when I kissed her throat, the breathy way she told me she wanted me between her legs.

What is so wrong with me that I'm even *more* turned on by the fact she's a virgin? Knowing that she's never given herself to someone else, that no man has ever been inside her? It makes me want to claim her for myself.

But it's more than that. I haven't been with anyone besides Lydia, and truthfully, I never thought I'd want another woman with any kind of intensity again.

Boy, was I wrong.

I've never felt the kind of pull I feel for Daisy. Don't get me wrong; with Lydia there was attraction, and love—so much love—but I didn't have this animal stir to life inside me, this primal, protective need to possess her, to make her my own. With Daisy, I feel slightly unhinged, and I can't decide if that's a good thing or not. All I know is not acting on this is taking every ounce of my strength. Especially when I know she's at my house most afternoons, using the darkroom.

I know because her prints hang above the bathtub downstairs, and new ones appear on an almost daily basis. There's the shot I took of her in the meadow where she's holding the daisy. One of me gazing at a maple tree. One of me striding through the grass toward her, grinning like mad. And so many others I wasn't aware she'd taken. It makes me happy to know she's doing what she's meant to, but it's bittersweet because I don't get to see her light up.

I don't get to see her at all.

"Wes?" Pauline snaps me from my thoughts as she leads me into an Italian place for lunch. I didn't even notice the four blocks we walked from the office.

"Sorry," I mutter as we take our table. I unfold the napkin and slide it across my lap, forcing a smile onto my mouth. "So how are you, anyway? How are the kids?"

The word "kids" isn't quite right. Hers are a similar age to Jesse. She and Lydia met at a Lamaze class, and our kids grew up together.

"They're good. Julia is interning for a law firm uptown, and Sammy's loving Harvard."

I sigh, trying not to think about my son, ignoring me, somewhere in the city. He hasn't so much as texted to wish me a happy birthday, but that's no surprise. He didn't do it for the previous three years, either. I figured that putting a roof over his head for a few weeks might earn me the tiniest show of gratitude, but apparently not.

We order our food and Pauline turns to me, her brow knitted in concern. "What's going on with you?"

I shrug, taking my glass of merlot from the server. "The usual."

Pauline sips her chardonnay. "I thought things were better lately," she says gently. "Over the past year, you seemed... I don't know. You seemed different, Wes. Like you were finally coming out the other side."

I swallow my wine, not meeting her gaze. She's right. I had been feeling that way, and that was largely thanks to Daisy. She was the one who brought light and hope back into my life.

And now, it's gone.

"Wes." Pauline sets her wine down and reaches across the table to touch my hand. "Talk to me."

Despite myself, I feel a flash of gratitude for her. This

woman was at my side through the worst days of my life, through the worst days of *her* life. We share a bond now that runs deeper than her being my wife's best friend. We share the loss of someone we love. And I'm desperate to unburden myself, to tell her—hell, to tell *someone*—about how tormented I've been ever since Jess brought Daisy home.

"I met someone," I mumble, right as the server sets my fettucine in front of me. I stare at it blankly, my appetite AWOL.

Pauline gives an understanding nod. "And you feel guilty? Because of Lydia?"

I grimace. Maybe I should feel guilty about that, but I don't. Lydia told me before she died that she wanted me to find someone else—that I *would* find someone else, and she would be happy for me.

Of course, I doubt she imagined it would be Jesse's ex.

"No. I know she'd want me to be happy."

"Yes. She would." Pauline nods, reaching for her fork. "So then... why do you look so miserable?"

I twirl my fork through my pasta, my stomach churning. I can't tell Pauline the truth, that I'm falling for my son's ex-girlfriend. Pauline is kind and caring, but even she has her limits.

"It can't..." I blow my breath out slowly. "It can't go anywhere."

Pauline sets her fork down. "Why on earth not?"

I cringe, poking at my food. "She's younger than me."

Her eyes narrow. "How much younger?"

God. I need to generalize.

"Uh... not quite thirty." I glance up. "But she's mature, really mature. And smart, and kind, and so creative. She's a photographer, and she's good." I think back to the prints hanging in the darkroom, the contrast of light, the composition. I'm not a photographer, but with a background in design and advertising, I can tell she knows her stuff. "Really good," I add.

Pauline's mouth twitches with a smile. "Did I tell you Julia is dating an older man? He's in his late thirties."

I frown, stuffing a forkful of pasta into my mouth. "That's not the same thing."

"Not exactly." She pushes her blond curls over her shoulder with a shrug. "But... does it really matter? I haven't heard you talk about a woman like this since Lydia died."

I swallow. I haven't *felt* like this about a woman since then, either.

"You know what I think?" Pauline says. "I think you're making excuses."

I splutter. "I'm sorry?"

She sighs, reaching for my hand again. "It was awful losing Lydia, honey, I know, but you have a chance to be happy again, and you're turning it down? You must be scared, Wes."

"Scared?"

"Of course. Scared of loving someone new and losing them all over again."

I slug back my wine, considering this, because there's a whole other part of the story she doesn't know about Jess and his history with Daisy. And that's something I won't be sharing with her.

"Maybe," I mutter, shoveling more food into my mouth. I'm not hungry, but I know I need to eat. Besides, it would be rude if I didn't, given Pauline dragged me here.

"You like this woman, right?"

I nod. I more than like her.

"I know you, Wes—if you like her, you *really* like her. You're not a casual guy. You must connect deeply with her."

I scrub a hand over my beard, thinking of the Steely Dan records, the hike over the rocks, the long talks about what we've been through. I haven't connected with someone like that in a very long time. In fact, I doubted I ever would again. It's not only sexual, although the chemistry is definitely there; it's the enjoyment I get from her company, the sense that she could be more than simply my lover. She could be my best friend.

I rake my hand through my hair, misery twisting through me. I lose the love of my life, then I meet someone who could be just as great, and I can't have her. This is fucked.

Pauline studies me over her wineglass, compassion swimming in her eyes. "If you like her this much, you need to go for it. You've been through hell, Wes. You deserve something good."

I send her a faint smile as I reach for my wine again. As much as I want to believe her, I know it isn't that simple.

———

BY THE TIME I finally drag myself home from the pool, the sky is a dusky purple, fading into black. I did everything I could to distract myself from Pauline's words, to make myself exhausted and numb, and now I can open a bottle of wine in front of the TV before crawling into bed.

Another year, and I'm no better off than the one before. If anything, I feel worse.

The front door shuts behind me with an ominous thud, and I shuffle into the kitchen, dumping my bag on the floor and placing my pizza on the counter. I don't know why I grabbed dinner on the way home. I still have no appetite. This time of year is always hard without Lydia to greet me at the door, her lemon cake on the counter. My tongue misses the sweet lemony tang of the cake.

And my heart misses having someone to celebrate with.

I eye the pizza box for a moment, then shove it away, deciding to go straight for the wine bottle instead. As I reach for a glass, a throat clears in the living room. I glance toward the noise in fright, my pulse scattering.

And there, holding a cake blazing with candles, stands Daisy.

My heart nearly stops.

"Happy birthday," she says uncertainly.

I stare at her in shock, taking a step forward. "What...?"

"I know you don't want to see me anymore," she adds hastily. "And I'll leave right after this. I just... I wasn't sure if Jess... Well, you know. I wanted to make sure someone celebrated your birthday."

My chest fills with static.

"I was here using the darkroom anyway." She lifts a shoulder. "I figured I'd hang around a little longer. I hope that's okay."

I swallow, my voice thick with emotion as I speak. "How did you know it was my birthday?"

She grimaces, dropping her eyes to the cake. "It said on Facebook. I might have, er, done a little online stalking."

I huff a quiet, knowing laugh, because she's not the only one. She doesn't post a lot online, but that doesn't mean I haven't been on there, looking to see what she's up to. If she might say, in some cryptic way, that she missed me as much as I missed her. She didn't, of course, but that didn't stop me from looking. From hoping.

What truly stuns me, though, is that she's here despite me telling her we couldn't see each other anymore. Even though I pushed her away, she came back.

"I'm not a great baker," Daisy admits, cheeks pink in the glow of the candles. "But there is one recipe I've mastered. I hope you like lemon cake." An awkward laugh slips from her. "You'd better blow these out before I accidentally start a fire."

I ignore her request, my heart snagging on her words. *Lemon cake.* They send goosebumps scattering across my skin, make my heart squeeze in my chest.

In that instant I know, without a doubt, that it's a sign. I've never much believed in God, or the universe, but this is crystal clear.

"I..." I shake my head, my throat so tight it's hard to get the words out. "I can't believe you made this for me."

"Of course." Her eyes move over my face, filled with sadness and something else, something I don't dare acknowledge. "Wes... it's devastating that you lost Lydia, and then to lose your relationship with Jesse on top of that... But you don't have to lose yourself. You deserve to have a day that celebrates what a wonderful man you are."

*Fuck.*

Emotion tangles hot in my chest at the sincerity in her voice. *How* did I push this woman away? *Why* did I tell her I couldn't see her?

"Did Jesse call?" she asks gently. I don't even have to answer; a sardonic grunt of a laugh does that for me.

She frowns, genuinely annoyed on my behalf.

And that's when it hits me. I'm keeping her away to protect my relationship with Jess, but for what? He hasn't called or texted to wish me a happy birthday. He *never* calls. And when I think back to the way he behaved at Greenport, I hardly recognize him. I was there for him when he needed me; gave him food and put a roof over his head when he was more than old enough to do that for himself. I didn't have to, but I did it because he's my son.

And he never once said thanks.

I stare at Daisy, standing in my living room with a home-made lemon cake—a cake she somehow *sensed* I needed. And as I gaze at her face in the flickering yellow of the candles, I feel all my walls crumble. She's here. She cares enough to be here with me, when my son won't even talk to me. I'm desperately trying to protect my relationship with Jesse, but the relationship is nonexistent, and in doing so, I'm sacrificing the potential for something truly wonderful. Something that's right in front of me.

And I'm sick of it.

*You've been through hell, Wes. You deserve something good.*

Pauline's words from lunch come back to me, and resolve straightens my spine. I cross the room to Daisy and, taking a big breath, blow out the dancing yellow flames.

There's only one wish on my mind this year, and it's about damn time I make it come true.

Daisy grins as smoke rises from the candles, carrying the cake through to the kitchen. I follow, watching as she sets it on the counter, then turns back to me, gnawing on her bottom lip.

"I hope you got what you wanted for your birthday," she murmurs, gaze moving over the Yankees hoodie I put on after showering at the pool.

I shake my head, stepping closer. She's less than a foot away from me, and I don't miss the way her eyes darken as she looks up. I swallow, knowing that once I say this, I can't take it back.

But I don't care anymore, because even if she is Jesse's ex, I knew her *long* before he did. I'm not proud of myself for thinking this, but I can't stop the thought that's looped through my head ever since Jess brought Daisy home.

*I saw her first.*

As for her being inexperienced... I'm shocked to realize I don't care about that as much as I thought I did. Maybe I should, but the fact is, I had a child with Lydia before she was even close to Daisy's age. Daisy seems young to me now, but she's old enough to know what she wants, and she wants this as much as I do. That much is clear. Besides, I don't have to sleep with her. Not yet, anyway.

But I also can't keep denying how much I want her.

"Daisy..." I inhale shakily, lifting a hand to her soft cheek. "What I really want for my birthday, more than I've wanted anything in a long time, is you."

# 23

# DAISY

y breath stutters. "What?"

Did he really just say what I think he did? Is it possible I misheard him?

His fingertips trail down to sweep my hair back from my shoulder, his touch igniting fireworks across my skin. Instead of answering right away, he lowers his mouth to my collarbone, brushing his lips over the freckles there, and heat sparks low in my belly.

"I want you," he repeats, drawing back to meet my eyes. Then he slides his hand into my hair to cradle my face, stroking my cheek softly. "Daisy..." My name comes rushing out on an exhale. "I've wanted you for months."

I raise a trembling hand to touch his chest through the Yankees hoodie—*his* Yankees hoodie. It's so much softer than I remember. An image of Jess flashes through my mind, and I hesitate. When I stop to think about it, I know getting together with his father would hurt him, and I don't like that, but he didn't think twice about bringing some random woman home at the beach house, did he?

Still, I'm not the only one who needs to worry about

Jesse here, and I'd hate myself if Wes did something he'd later regret.

"What about Jess?" I ask, almost afraid to say his name. Afraid it will snap Weston out of this and he'll step away again.

"I don't care." His gaze falls away, and he gives a firm shake of his head, as if to emphasize his point.

But I need to be sure. "I don't want to come between—"

"There's nothing to come between. He won't speak to me, no matter how hard I try. He doesn't want a relationship with me. He refuses to grow up, and I'm sick of fighting everything. With him, with you... I won't deny myself a chance at happiness anymore." Weston's gaze comes back to mine, just as the word "happiness" leaves his lips.

That's all the confirmation I need.

I slide my hand around the back of his neck, fingers gliding across his soft, warm skin, and tug his mouth to mine.

When our lips finally meet, every fiber of my being sighs in relief. Every worry, every fear, every reservation evaporates from my mind as our lips touch. It's tentative at first, as if neither of us is sure how to proceed, but that only lasts a second. I feel the moment he gives in, and I melt against his solid form, gripping his sweatshirt. His rich, warm cologne floods my senses, the press of his mouth on mine enough to make me combust.

But I want more. I want so much more of him.

I graze my tongue along his bottom lip, whimpering as he parts his lips to let me in. My body becomes electric, charged with months of longing, with all the things I feel for this man in front of me. And when he meets my tongue with his, his moan makes heat pool hot between my thighs.

"Daisy..." The word is a breathy rasp between kisses as

his mouth trails along my jaw, my neck. "I want to take this further, but I don't want to rush you..."

I take his face in my hands and force him to meet my gaze. "I've wanted you since you first walked through the door at Joe's, Wes. I'm beyond ready. I want all of you. I want everything."

"God," he mutters, his eyes falling closed as if savoring my words. "I want that too."

My heart leaps and cartwheels in my chest, and suddenly, after a lifetime of waiting, I'm so glad I didn't rush this. So glad I get to do this with Weston.

Our lips collide again as he presses himself against me, hands tangling in my hair. The scratch of his beard on my cheek makes me whimper with need. His hips pin me against the kitchen island, and I've never felt so happy to be trapped. He can hold me down and do whatever he wants to me.

My hands stray down his firm torso, sliding around to grip his butt. I need to pull him tight against me, to feel the ridge of his erection on my belly. He's so hard, and I can't believe it's for me.

*Fuck.*

I want to tug his sweats down, to dig my hands into his underwear and take hold of that hardness, but I don't want to stop him from grinding it against the apex of my thighs like that. I don't want to stop shamelessly rubbing myself against him.

His mouth devours mine in a wet, dirty kiss, tongues tangling and teeth crashing as he finally takes what he wants from me, but the way he does it feels more like a *need* than a want. Like I'm oxygen and he's been underwater for too long. Like he'll die if he doesn't get enough.

I know the feeling.

Suddenly Wes's hands grip my waist, hoisting me onto the kitchen counter, and the image of us in the darkroom flashes through my mind. My legs wind around his hips, pulling him between them, right where I want him. I don't care if he wants to have sex here and now on his kitchen counter. I'd let him.

Instead of freeing himself from his sweats so he can bury himself inside me, he works his mouth across my shoulder, sliding the straps of my dress until they fall, exposing my lemon-yellow bra. If I'd known tonight would go this way, I'd have worn something a little sexier, but he doesn't seem to care. His breath rushes out in appreciation as he presses his lips to my collarbone, then my chest, where he hovers, hands gently caressing the sides of my breasts through the lace of my bra. My nipples are stiff, aching peaks against the fabric, begging for his touch, and when he finally slides my bra straps down, they harden even more as they're exposed to the cool air. Weston's eyes are hooded as he draws one into his mouth, gently lapping at the tip with his tongue. A surge of lust rockets through me, right to my toes. It's a heady sensation I'm not used to. I feel like I'm flying.

"Oh, fuck," I murmur, hands threading into the waves of his hair as he works his tongue over my nipple. He cradles my other breast in his hand, thumb stroking the peak. My thighs clamp against him, hips lifting off the counter, restless with need. I've never had a man touch me with such expert precision, had his tongue know just how to flick me right there, to the point that I can feel the heat building between my thighs. He's not touching me below the waist, but somehow the sensation on my nipples shocks me to my core. Is it possible to come just from this?

Before I can find out, he straightens up, arms encircling my bare waist to pull me close, into the heat of his embrace.

He buries his face in my hair and holds me tight, while a deep sigh shudders from his chest. It's like he's forcing himself to slow down, like he's stopping to savor it, and my heart beats harder at the thought.

With another sigh, he pulls away to gaze at me sitting on his kitchen counter, and panic flashes through me at his hesitation. If he stops now, I might cry.

"You are so fucking perfect," he grits out.

Before I can respond, his mouth is on mine again, and his large, warm hands slide up my thighs. I shiver with anticipation, my body throbbing with the need to feel him inside me. I've never been so turned on, felt so needy, so desperate for a man to touch me. I spread my legs wider, inviting him in, as his thumbs nudge the edge of my panties.

"Yes," I whimper helplessly, even though he hasn't done anything yet, because I need him to touch me right there. I'll burn up if he doesn't.

His thumbs advance gently, brushing my clit through the fabric of my panties. The moan I emit is loud enough for the neighbors to hear, but he doesn't care. If anything, his strokes slow, deliberately drawing out the pleasure.

"Jesus Christ," he mutters, drawing back to gaze at me. His eyes are black pools of lust as his thumb brushes my throbbing clit again. "You're fucking soaked."

I squirm on the counter, trying to get more friction from his touch, but he frustratingly refuses to give it to me.

"Because I need this, Wes. I need *you*. I've never needed anyone like I need you."

Fuck, why did I say that? All I'm doing is reminding him of my inexperience.

I brace myself, waiting for him to pull away and tell me we need to stop, but his nostrils flare as he growls in a low voice, "Then let me fucking give it to you."

Oh, God. *Yes, please.*

I reach for the waistband of his sweats, but before I can make contact, he drops to his knees on the kitchen floor. I blink in confusion until he grabs me by the hips and drags me right to the edge of the counter, hooking my legs over his shoulders and shoving my dress up to my waist.

I fall back to my elbows on the cool marble countertop, gazing at his salt-and-pepper head between my legs. His eyes are fastened to my panties, and I watch as he leans forward and drags his nose over my seam, inhaling my scent.

"Fuck," he mutters to himself. The raw, animal edge to his voice makes my heart hammer against my ribs. He wants me just as much as I want him, and I'm dizzy at the thought.

In one swift motion, he tugs my panties aside and swipes his tongue through my slickness. His touch sends a shock-wave of pleasure through me, and I let out a strangled sound that can only be described as a mewl.

How on earth am I going to survive this?

Wes's head pops up from between my legs, concern etched into his brow. "You okay, baby?"

I reach out to stroke his bearded cheek, caressing the coarse hair. "Not really." A breathless laugh escapes me as his brows slash together. He starts to rise, but I hook my heels together behind his head, keeping him in place as I laugh again. "I mean, yes, I'm fine. Good. Better than good." Another awkward laugh. "This is just... the first time a guy has ever... you know."

Goddammit. I grimace as understanding dawns in Weston's eyes. Yet another mark in the "inexperienced" column.

"Daisy, if you don't want—"

"Please don't stop," I beg. "I really want this with you."

His deep, gravelly laugh sends a shiver through me. "Good, because I want to be the first man to do this to *you*."

I breathe a relieved laugh, thinking of Violet's words as we talked about my inexperience: *He probably likes it.* Is it possible she was right?

His tongue meets my center again, flicking over my clit before dipping inside me. "You taste so damn sweet," he murmurs against my swollen flesh, tasting me once more. "So fucking good."

I can hardly hear his words as he works his tongue over me. The way he nips and sucks at my clit sends me to another dimension, and when he gently pushes a finger into me, followed by another, I swear I float off the kitchen island. He has to hold me down, mouth and hands working in tandem as I thrash and buck, gripping his hair, lost in sensation.

He doesn't let up until I'm slack with pleasure, until I'm boneless with release. I stare at the ceiling, blinking the stars from my vision as my pulse slows, my jaw hanging open in disbelief. I had no idea a man could make *that* happen.

When Weston rises from between my thighs, he looks like he's been mauled. His hair sticks up at all angles and his cheeks are flushed, his beard glistening with my arousal, but he looks as satisfied as I feel. There's a glassy sheen to his eyes and his mouth curves in a drowsy smile as he drags the back of his hand across it, cleaning himself up.

I laugh, trying to sit up on the marble, my body still twitching with aftershocks. "Wow. That was…"

"Yeah?" There's a flash of vulnerability in his eyes, like he wants to be sure it was good.

"Uh, *yeah*. I've never, um…" I want to tell him, want him to know what a big deal this is, but I don't want to further underscore my lack of experience. As he studies me, waiting so patiently, I know I can't not tell him. "No one has made me come before," I admit. "Only me."

"Fuck," he mutters quietly. I expect he'll kiss me again, that I'll get to return the favor or we might go to the bedroom, but instead, he sighs and pulls me into his arms, tight against his chest.

I'm too limp to argue. I burrow my head into his shoulder, breathing him in, letting my eyes close. I'm tired after an early start at work, an afternoon of baking, and, I let myself admit as Wes strokes my back, trying to convince myself I wasn't hoping he'd be happy to see me.

Well, I don't have to convince myself anymore.

I go to kiss him, to get back to what we were doing, when my stomach emits a loud rumble.

Wes chuckles, drawing back. "Have you had dinner?"

"No." I smile shyly. "I was too busy baking, and was so nervous about seeing you..."

His fingers brush my cheek, eyes a darker blue than usual. "You never have to be nervous around me, Daisy."

My heart sighs. I could never have imagined how nice it would be to have him look at me this way, to have him touch me with such affection.

And believe me, I've tried.

I lean into his touch, letting my eyes flutter closed, and my stomach protests again.

"Alright." Wes grins, reaching for a pizza box on the counter. "It's probably a little cold now, but I'm more than happy to share my birthday dinner with you."

I rearrange my dress, covering myself up as Wes hoists himself onto the island beside me and lifts the lid on the box. I examine the contents, frowning. He deserves better than cold pizza for his birthday.

"I wish I could cook for you," I say, reaching for a slice and chewing thoughtfully.

Wes is quiet as he downs a slice of pizza and reaches for another, apparently ravenous. "I can't remember the last time someone cooked for me," he murmurs at last.

My chest hurts at this revelation. He's so kind, so caring, so generous. He deserves so much, and there's no one to give it to him.

I really hope he'll let me be the person who can.

"What are you doing tomorrow night?" I ask, polishing off my pizza and wiping my hands on a napkin.

Weston's eyes sparkle as they move over my face. "I don't have any plans."

"Then let me cook for you."

"I'd love that." His hand finds mine on the counter and squeezes.

"Will you come to my place? My roommate is out of town for a couple days visiting her sister." I'd anticipated some quiet time at home alone, binge-watching something on Netflix, but that was before... well... this. "It's not fancy," I add hastily, glancing at the huge, six-burner stove and marble countertops in Weston's kitchen. "And my room isn't—"

"It sounds perfect." The warmth in his eyes tells me he means it. "I can't wait."

I grin, grabbing another slice of pizza, wondering what I'll cook as I chew. Wes wipes his face with a napkin, sliding the pizza box away when we're done. He eyes the lemon cake, and I smile.

"Go on. Have some."

I watch as he removes the candles from the frosting, then cuts us each a slice, but I can't eat until I know he likes it. As his lips close around the cake and he lets out a little moan of satisfaction, I finally let myself take a bite.

"This might be the best lemon cake I've ever had," he murmurs, almost to himself. It feels like there's a meaning to his words I don't quite understand, and I lean my head on his shoulder as he eats. He sighs. "Thank you, Daisy."

"You're welcome."

We finish our cake, then he tugs me into his side, our legs dangling off the kitchen island. I close my eyes, my belly full, my body sleepy and satisfied. I desperately want to continue what we started before dinner, but as I glance at the blackness outside the kitchen windows, a yawn sneaks from my mouth. It must be late.

Wes presses a kiss to my forehead. "Let me order you an Uber."

I furrow my brow, glancing away. He's trying to get rid of me?

"I know you've had a long day," he murmurs, gently tilting my chin back to him. "I have too."

I sigh. He's right, but I can't deny that I'd hoped he'd ask me to stay, that now he's finally given in to this, we'd go up to his bed and make love.

But as Weston removes his arm from me to pull out his phone, I know that won't be happening.

And even though I know it's not logical, a tiny part of me wonders if I did something wrong.

I reluctantly slide from the counter, avoiding his gaze as he walks me to the front door. I'm not sure if I should kiss him goodbye, but he pulls me close and brushes his mouth across mine, lingering.

"Thanks for the pizza," I say when we part.

He smiles sleepily. "Thank *you* for making my birthday

so much better than I could have imagined. I'm looking forward to tomorrow night."

"Me too."

I climb into the Uber and watch the streets pass as it winds through Brooklyn, telling myself that tomorrow night it will happen.

# 24

# DAISY

I don't know what I was thinking, inviting Weston to my apartment. It seemed like the right thing to do in the moment, a gesture to show him how much I care for him, but as I pull our chipped plates from the cupboard and survey the mess I've made in our tiny kitchen, I can't help but think it was a mistake.

The only godsend is that Denise is out of town. If she saw the tomato sauce splattered on the counter, she'd flip her lid. And I'd have to spend the evening arguing with her, instead of losing my V-card to Weston.

The buzzer sounds, and I wipe my hands on a dish towel, removing the stained apron from my waist and quickly checking my hair. I'm wearing my favorite black dress with the white and yellow daisy print, because I always feel confident in it. Plus, I saw the way he looked at me in this last time.

I let Weston into the building, and a moment later there's a knock at the door. My heart flutters wildly as I glance one last time around the apartment, making sure I haven't left dirty underwear on the floor, or tampon wrappers in the bathroom, or something else that might freak him out. But it's not just that; suddenly the entire apartment feels too small, too messy, too run down. I think of Weston's grand house on Fruit Street and grimace. What if he takes one look at this place and leaves?

His knock comes again, and I force a deep breath, shaking the thought from my head.

"Hi," I say, pinning on a smile as I tug open the door.

"Hello." His eyes are a bright blue shimmer as they meet mine, sweeping over my dress before landing back on my face. "You look beautiful."

"Thank you."

I let my gaze drink him in too. Jeans and a white linen button-down, sleeves rolled casually to the elbows. The undone top button exposes a small V at his throat that gives me a peek of salt-and-pepper chest hair, and the sight sends heat zipping through me. If I'm lucky, I'll get to tear that shirt off and kiss every inch of him later.

I swallow, dragging my gaze back to his face. "You look, uh..." *Unbelievably fuckable.* "Nice, too."

The corners of his eyes crinkle, and he pulls a hand from behind his back. "For you."

I glance down to find a bunch of daisies wrapped in cellophane, their happy faces upturned to me. My heart skips at the thoughtful gesture.

"I love them. Thank you."

"I also brought this," Wes says, handing me a bottle of merlot. "I'm not sure what you're cooking, but hopefully..."

"It's perfect." I grin, taking the bottle. Then we stand in the doorway, smiling at each other but not moving, as if neither of us knows what to do next. Is it possible he's nervous too?

I clutch the flowers and wine, unsure of what to say. I

want to kiss him, but I don't have the guts to do it. Less than a day has passed since we last saw each other—since he had his head between my legs, for Christ's sake—but having him here at my apartment makes everything feel different. Maybe I should have—

"I need to kiss you," Weston says thickly, interrupting my thoughts. "Is that okay?"

*Oh, thank fuck.*

"Yes. Please."

His mouth curls in a relieved grin as he steps over the threshold and takes my face in his hands, lowering his mouth to mine. Everything feels right again in the world the moment our lips connect. Warmth melts through me, softening the nervous tension in my body, drawing me closer to him. I still hold the flowers and wine, so I can't press my body to his like I want to, can't grab his ass and grind myself shamelessly against him, but it's probably for the best. I have a meal bubbling on the stove, and I'm not sure how he'd respond if I mauled him before he even got through the doorway.

"Come in," I say, catching my breath as we part.

He closes the door behind himself, letting his gaze wander around the apartment. The living room is a mix of off-white and rose gold, with faux fur on the cushions and a chrome and glass coffee table I'm perpetually terrified I'm going to shatter, making it hard to relax out here. The space is entirely decorated by Denise, despite that I pay half the rent, but I've made my peace with it.

At least, that's what I've told myself over the years, but as I glance around at the space I've never felt quite at home in, I can't help but frown. Why have I put up with her bullshit for so long?

I lead Wes into the kitchen, where I put the daisies in some water, and he slides onto a stool at the breakfast bar.

"This is a great place," Weston says as I open the wine.

I snort a laugh. "It's not really, but it'll do for now." I pour the wine into two mismatched glasses, handing him one. "I can't, um, decant it, or whatever, because I don't have..."

"It's great as it is." His eyes twinkle as he clinks his glass to mine.

I take a long sip of wine, letting the alcohol warm my veins. Weston sips his merlot as I turn the stove off and strain the pasta, trying not to feel self-conscious with him here, watching me. He's so nicely dressed, and I can smell his spicy bergamot cologne. I picture his Audi sitting outside on the street and wonder if he feels as out of place as he looks. I sense his eyes on me as I dish up our food onto chipped plates, wishing I'd had the forethought to at least buy some new dishes for the evening.

Placing a serving of spaghetti in front of Wes, I slide onto the other stool to join him. "I'm sorry the plates aren't great and the wineglasses don't match," I mumble, taking another long sip of wine to calm the anxiety rippling through my stomach. "My roommate—"

"Daisy."

Wes takes my wineglass from my trembling hand and sets it on the counter, scooting closer to me. He tucks a loose strand of hair behind my ear, letting his fingers brush my cheek. It's the lightest touch, but goosebumps dot my skin. His gaze moves slowly over my face, as if mapping every freckle, as if trying to memorize the blush staining my cheeks. His breath comes out on a long sigh, and he leans forward to press his mouth to mine.

"Everything is perfect," he whispers against my lips. "I love seeing where you live."

*You never have to be nervous around me, Daisy.*

I remember his words from last night and touch my mouth to his again. What am I thinking? I *know* Wes, and I know he doesn't care about any of this stuff. He cares about *me*.

I smile as I draw away and return to our meal. Weston picks up his fork with a grin, tucking into the spaghetti.

"Fuck," he mutters around a mouthful of pasta. "This is so good." He slurps up a strand, his eyes closed in pleasure, and, relieved, I finally let myself take a bite. "You'd better be careful, or I'll ask you to cook like this for me every night," Wes jokes.

*Yes, please.*

I huff a laugh as I eat, trying not to let him see how much I want that. To come home to Weston after work and drink wine in the kitchen, listening to his records while I cook for us. I can't think of anything better.

We eat in silence, savoring the food, and when he's finished, Wes turns to me with a huge grin. "That was delicious." He wipes his mouth with his napkin, eyes dancing as they move over my face. "So you're both a photographer and a chef," he muses, and I laugh.

"Hardly."

My gaze falls to a drop of tomato sauce on his shirt and I frown. "Shit. That will stain if we let it."

Weston follows my gaze, chuckling. "Typical. I'm the worst with spaghetti. Lydia always used to tease me about it." He's wistful for a moment, then glances at me, shrugging. "It doesn't matter."

I shake my head, pushing to my feet. "Take it off, and I'll clean it up."

His eyebrows rise playfully. "You want me to take my shirt off?"

Warmth singes my cheeks. "I mean, I can get the sauce out if you do, but if you don't feel comfortable, I understand."

But he's already moving his hands slowly down the buttons, releasing each one, eyes glinting as he does. When the shirt falls open and he tugs it right off, my mouth goes dry.

Oh, fuck. I am not prepared for this.

I mean, I knew he had a good body, because I'd watched him on the beach like the little perv I am, but up close he's *divine*. I could stare at him for hours, taking in his sheer masculine beauty, the solid presence of him. Olive shoulders and pecs, sculpted and firm from hours carving through the water, salt-and-pepper hair dusting his chest, trailing down his trim waist and disappearing into the waistband of his jeans. Heat rolls through me like a wave, starting at my toes and building between my legs. I itch to put my hands on him, to feel every contour of his muscles, to lick my way down his stomach and get into those jeans.

He holds the shirt out to me, amusement flickering in his eyes as I peel my gaze from him and force myself to focus on cleaning the stain. It only takes me a few moments, but I give myself an extra minute to lean over the sink, catching my breath. I'm restless and antsy with need, shifting my weight from one foot to the other, desperate to get him into bed.

I don't notice Weston come up behind me, until his arms slide around my waist, the heat of him pressing to my back.

"Thank you for dinner," he murmurs into my ear, sweeping my hair to one side so he can drag his mouth over my neck.

My knees give way, and I grip the counter harder, the

movement of his lips igniting fire in my belly. I try to play it cool but I can't hold out any longer.

Spinning around, I let my hands land on his pecs as I stare up into his eyes. They're dark pools of desire, the blue swallowed up by the black of his blown-out pupils, and I push up onto my toes to press my lips to his. He eagerly obliges, slanting his mouth across mine. The first lick of his tongue sends lust spiraling to my core, my greedy hands roaming his exposed top half, loving the feel of his hot skin under my fingertips. He groans when I grab his ass and pull him tight against me, aching to feel that hardness I felt last night. The minute it presses into my belly, I lose all sense of reason.

"I need you," I rasp between kisses. "Wes, I need you so badly."

"Fuck," he mutters under his breath, mouth moving along my jaw before he reluctantly draws himself away. He adjusts the erection straining against his zipper, catching his breath. I don't wait for him to say anything more before taking his hand and leading him through the living room into my space. I draw back the curtain to reveal the tiny alcove, my twin bed, the chair where I read and look out over the street. It occurs to me it would probably be far nicer to do this at his house, but I don't have the patience to wait another night.

Weston wanders through the room, taking in every detail, and I drop onto the edge of my bed, my gaze glued to his movements. I've never felt so physically turned on by a man like this before. Interested? Occasionally. Attracted? Sure. But not at his mercy like this, where the low timbre of his voice, his musky, masculine scent, or even just his proximity is enough to make me feel electric. I'm hyper-aware of his every movement, the rhythm of his breath, where his eyes rest.

Wes stands above me at the foot of my bed. I expect he'll climb on beside me, but instead he says, "So this is where you sleep."

I nod, unable to fight the way my gaze strays to his bare torso, at eye-level like this. My hands tingle at my sides, eager to reach out and touch him again.

He takes my chin in his hand, tilting my face up to his. "Have you ever touched yourself here while thinking of me?"

His question sends a bolt of heat through my veins. I've touched myself a hundred times in this bed while thinking of him, but I never imagined I'd actually get him here.

"I..." I glance away, my cheeks hot with embarrassment.

"You have, haven't you?"

I gulp as Weston gently lifts my chin so I'm forced to look at him again. "Yes," I whisper.

His eyes flare with heat, darkening as they move over me, pinning me helplessly to the bed. "Show me."

*What?*

I huff a laugh. "I can't..."

"Show me, Daisy."

*Holy shit.*

I've never heard him so bossy, but it's really working for me. The stern, demanding tone of his voice is the opposite of his usual calm, kind nature. Is this what he'll be like when we have sex? God, I hope so. The thought of taking orders from Weston in bed has me squirming, delirious with need.

And before I know what I'm doing, I answer, "Okay."

# 25

# WESTON

Daisy leans across her bed to her nightstand, digging through the drawer for a moment. When she turns back to me, she's holding a purple vibrator, about five inches long, covered in a soft silicone material.

"I, um, use this," she mumbles, her cheeks streaked pink.

I take the device from her, examining it. When I twist the end, it vibrates in my hand, and the more I twist it, the faster it goes.

I look at Daisy spread out on her back across her bed, and I can't help but toss the toy aside and lower myself over her, taking her mouth again. My hands disappear into her chocolate hair, twisting in the strands, and she lets out a quiet moan as our tongues collide. The sound sends blood rushing to my cock, and I press my hips against her, pinning her to the mattress. This draws a needy whimper from her throat, and her tongue laps more greedily against mine.

I nudge the strap of her dress from her shoulder, trailing my mouth over the freckled skin. Her hands grasp my hair, and I lift myself off her so I can tug her dress over her head, needing to feel more of her. She's wearing red lacy panties with a matching bra, and it takes all my strength not to pull them off, too.

I lower myself down and her legs wrap around me, inviting me closer. When I press my stiff cock into the heat of her core, I release a moan of satisfaction. I'm so fucking desperate to bury myself inside her, but I won't. Not tonight. I don't want to rush, because I know that when Daisy and I do eventually cross that line, there'll be no going back for me. I've thought about this a lot since I nearly devoured her on my kitchen island last night, and I can't let myself get carried away again, as much as I might want to. Daisy is the only woman I've ever wanted—*truly* wanted—besides Lydia, and I need to make sure I'm ready to make that commitment again. More to the point, I need to make sure *Daisy* is ready for that kind of commitment. This will be her first time, and I sure as hell won't take that for granted. I know she says she wants this, but we both need to be sure.

Completely sure.

I force myself to slow down, breaking our kiss as I reach for the vibrator, passing it to her.

"Show me what you'd do if I wasn't here," I grate out, peeling myself from her soft, hot skin with what can only be described as Herculean effort.

She looks up at me with dark eyes, her lips red and raw. Swallowing hard, she reaches behind her back to unhook her bra, not taking her gaze from me.

Fuck, I forgot how perfect her breasts are, her nipples tight rosy buds, begging for my mouth. I stare at them, my cock a rigid pole in my jeans, but I don't touch her.

*Jesus Christ.* I deserve a freaking medal.

"I do this," she whispers, switching on her vibrator and brushing it over her nipple. She jolts at the sensation, a gasp of pleasure escaping her mouth. I ball my fists at my side so I don't take over, watching as she teases her nipples, thighs pressed together.

I need to see more. I need to see her make herself come so that when I get home tonight and furiously jerk off, I can picture her pleasuring herself.

"Take your panties off," I growl. "Show me that pretty pussy."

Her eyebrows spring up her forehead.

Shit, I don't know what's come over me, speaking to her like this. I feel crazed, having her here and trying to hold back. I'm behaving like an animal.

"I'm sorry, Daisy," I mutter, hanging my head in shame. "I shouldn't talk to you like that."

"No," she breathes, cheeks pink as her dark eyes bore into mine. "I... I like it."

Now *my* brows shoot up. "You like me telling you what to do?"

She swallows, nodding. "And... the other thing."

"The other thing?"

"The... dirty talk."

*Oh, fuck.*

I press my eyes shut in agony. How the hell am I going to survive this without jumping her? What if I don't have the strength?

*You do*, I tell myself. *You will, because she deserves for her first time to be meaningful. She deserves better than you losing control.*

Locking my jaw, I force my gaze back to her beautiful naked form spread out on her bed. She's so fucking perfect, dark hair mussed, nipples at attention, freckled skin flushed with arousal. I won't fuck her tonight, but I can still ensure she's satisfied in all the ways that matter.

"Then do as I said," I grit out. "And let me see that sweet little pussy of yours."

She sets the vibrator aside and peels her panties down her legs, kicking them to the floor. Then she leans back on her elbows and stares up at me, but there's something different in her gaze now—a fire that wasn't there before. Her mouth twitches with a naughty smile that makes my cock throb eagerly in my jeans.

*Not tonight, buddy.*

My gaze drifts across Daisy's bare thighs, taking in the dark triangle of hair where they meet. My hands are tight fists at my side, so I'm not tempted to reach out and force her thighs apart.

"Spread your legs."

She bites her lip to hold back her smile, spreading her left leg slightly, then stopping. She's moving agonizingly slow on purpose, and the beast inside me roars with impatience.

"I said spread your fucking legs, Daisy."

Her breath rushes out hard, and she does as I say, eyes wide, chest shuddering. She's right. She fucking loves me taking charge like this, and I can't deny how intoxicating it is to have her at my mercy.

"Touch yourself," I instruct, eyes riveted to her swollen pink opening.

Daisy's fingers drift between her thighs and brush her clit. She gives a little whimper as she begins to stroke herself in a circular motion, and I watch, my cock leaking in my jeans.

This could kill me.

I *should* touch her myself, should use my tongue and hands like I did last night to make her come. Fuck, knowing I'm the first man to make her orgasm is unbelievable. I haven't been able to stop thinking about it—about the way she fell apart on my kitchen island, gripping my hair and riding my mouth. I spent the entire day at work useless, fantasizing about the feel of her, her sweet musky taste, counting down the minutes until I could do it again tonight.

But if I lay another finger on her, I'll lose it. I won't be able to stop myself from thrusting inside her and claiming her for myself.

So instead, I do the next best thing.

I pick the vibrator up from the bed and hand it to her again. "Put this inside you. I want you to pretend it's me."

The flush on her cheeks deepens. "Y-you?"

I nod. "Pretend it's my cock. Imagine it's me fucking you."

Daisy sucks in a deep breath. "On one condition." Her gaze drops to my dick, angrily tenting the front of my jeans. "You join me."

My cock flexes as if it can feel her gaze, can hear her words, and I grind my molars, preparing to say no. But I'm only human, and before I can get the word out, my hands are on my zipper, freeing myself from my boxer briefs. I mean, why shouldn't I join her? I won't lay a finger on her, but still... I can't just fucking watch.

I wrap my fist around the hard heat of my shaft, the pressure bringing me no relief. It knows what it wants, and it's sure as hell not my own hand.

"Oh, shit," Daisy whispers, eyes fastened on where I'm gripping myself. "That is so fucking hot." She twists the end of the vibrator and it springs to life, buzzing in her hand. Then she lowers it between her legs and pushes it inside herself, mouth opening to release a low moan.

Christ. If I'm not careful, I could come right now.

Daisy watches me slowly stroke myself, pumping the

vibrator into herself with one hand, teasing her clit with the other. It's the sexiest thing I've ever seen, this woman pleasuring herself. She knows just how much pressure she needs, just where to touch. I try to take mental notes, to remember exactly what she likes, but I'm dizzy as I climb closer to my release.

"Fuck, Daisy, you're going to make me come."

She breathes out a giggle. "Me? I'm not even touching you."

I grunt as she thrusts the vibrator deeper. "Watching you is enough, baby."

She presses her eyes closed, focusing on her pleasure, on sensation. She writhes on the bed as she works toward her own release, and when her eyes open again, they're wild.

"Then do it," she rasps. "Come on me. I need it, Wes."

God. The way she says my name like that.

She spreads her legs even further, fucking herself with the vibrator as she works her fingers roughly over her clit. "Come on me right here."

*Holy Jesus fucking Christ.*

I explode.

My roar is enough to shake the building as I grip my pulsing cock, watching my seed splatter between Daisy's thighs, her body spasming with her own orgasm. I come harder than I have in forever, painting her freckled skin with my release as she loses herself in sensation.

Our gazes lock as we come down from the high, catching our breath. Then Daisy does something completely unexpected and swipes a finger through my cum, raising it to her lips, sampling it. My heart jumps at the way she sucks it from her finger as if it's melted gourmet chocolate. Her lips kick up on one side, and she lets out a long, satisfied breath.

Is there anything sexier than this woman?

I examine the mess I've made across her lower half, and grimace. "Sorry, that was—"

"So hot," she finishes for me. "I've never done anything like that before."

I chuff a quiet laugh as I tuck myself into my underwear. "Neither have I, actually, and trust me, that's *not* what I had planned for tonight." With a sigh, I turn to find some tissue or a washcloth. "Give me a minute. I'll grab you something to clean up."

"Bathroom is along the hall, to the right," Daisy tells me from the bed.

When I push into the small, tiled room, I spy the bathtub and change my mind, flicking on the tap and letting the tub fill with warm water. There's a bottle of bubble bath on the counter so I add some, and when I spot candles on the windowsill with a box of matches, I light them and place them around the tub. This is far nicer than simply throwing a washcloth at Daisy. She can relax in the water and clean off.

But I'll need to head home. I might have taken the edge off, but I know that given half the chance, I'd climb into bed and make love to her tonight.

"What's taking so... Oh." Daisy appears at the doorway, noticing the candles and bubbles. "You ran the tub?"

I lift a shoulder, trying to play it down. To pretend that it was a practical solution to clean herself up, and not because I wanted to do something nice for her after we were intimate. Not because I want to do so many more things with her, but I'm trying to take it slowly.

"I made a mess all over you," I say, nudging Daisy toward the water. She's still naked, and I need her to submerge herself, to hide under the bubbles so I can forget how exquisite she is.

*Yeah, that's likely*.

She smiles, dipping a toe into the tub. Then she pulls her hair up into a knot on top of her head, before lowering herself into the water with a sigh.

"Thanks for tonight." I inch toward the door. "I had a great—"

Daisy's brows crash together. "You're not joining me?"

I swallow, noting the way the bubbles don't quite conceal her breasts. Her nipples are pink islands floating in the white foam, and my dick twitches to life again.

"I... I really should go."

"Oh." Her face falls. She glances down, picking up a handful of bubbles and blowing at them half-heartedly. "Of course."

Her disappointment is tangible, a thick cloud that descends over the bathroom, and I hate myself for it. She deserves much better than for me to eat her food, come all over her, then leave. I want to tell her how I feel—that she's the only woman I've ever been crazy about besides Lydia, that I never thought I'd feel this way again—but I don't want to scare her, and I don't know how to explain the hesitation tugging at me to take things slowly. I've never been in this position where I've wanted someone so badly, but also feel the need to hold back. It's as new to me as it is to her.

And since I can't find the words, I'll do my best to show her.

"Scoot forward," I say, unzipping my jeans and dropping them on the floor, along with my underwear. Then I step into the warm water behind Daisy, sliding my legs down either side of hers and pulling her back flush against my stomach. She sighs, leaning her weight back into me, resting her head against my chest. My heart melts at the feel of her in my arms, and I make a mental vow that nothing more will happen tonight. That this is the most I'll allow myself to have with her.

"I shot another roll of film today," Daisy murmurs, swirling her fingertips through the bubbles.

"That's great." I knew it was her day off, and it took all my energy not to call in sick to work this morning and spend the day with her instead. "What did you shoot?"

"I went to the West Village and took pictures of the neighborhood. I'd never noticed how pretty the buildings are." She laughs self-consciously. "I don't really know what I'm doing with architecture, but after Violet showed me the carriage houses in Brooklyn Heights, the old buildings in the city have fascinated me."

I smile. It hadn't occurred to me that she might like to shoot the historical buildings of New York, but if anyone can inspire that in her, it would be Violet. She runs the historical restoration business with Kyle.

"I shot more of the carriage houses and other parts of Brooklyn Heights a couple weeks ago," Daisy adds, and I nod, having seen some of those pictures strung up in the darkroom. "I think I want to explore that more. The architectural details of the historical buildings."

My heart presses against my ribcage, hearing her speak excitedly about photography. I'm so damn proud of this woman for reclaiming this part of herself, for taking something that caused her pain and turning it into joy.

I snake my hands around her waist, holding her close as I bury my nose in her hair. The citrusy smell of her shampoo floods my senses, and I press my lips to the shell of her ear. I wonder if she can feel the way I'm growing hard again with her soft, naked body pressed into me. I wonder if she can feel the way my heart beats steadily at the feel of her, the way *I* feel for her. How thoughtful she is, how creative, how sweet and sexy at the same time. Just being around her makes me a better man, and I can't get enough.

"Wes," she murmurs. "I keep thinking about something you said last night."

I stroke her skin softly. "What's that?"

"You said you'd wanted me for months. When I was with Jess..."

"Yeah." I blow my breath out slowly, watching it ruffle a loose wisp of her hair. I could lie to her, but I don't want to. Besides, she's made it clear she wanted me all along, too. "I know I shouldn't have wanted you while you were with my son, but..." My jaw hardens as I shake my head. "I couldn't stop myself. It killed me to see you with him. It killed me to know you were his."

Daisy is quiet.

"I don't feel good about it," I add.

"I don't feel good about having feelings for you while I was with him, either. I tried to make them stop, but..." She shrugs, letting out a little sigh. "I couldn't."

Despite myself, a feeling of satisfaction snakes through me. I shake off any residual guilt at the thought of Jess, telling myself there's no point in thinking about my son when he wants nothing to do with me. When I've got this woman here, right now.

*You're mine*, I want to tell her, but I swallow the words, afraid of what she might think. I pull her closer, letting my hands roam her soft, wet skin. I'll need to leave after this, to stop things from going any further, but for now, I just let myself hold her.

And even after everything I've been through, in this moment, I feel lucky as fuck.

# 26

## DAISY

I'm holding my breath as I let myself into Weston's house after work. I didn't see his Audi out on the street, so I already know he's not home, but that doesn't stop me from hoping.

But the sound of the heavy oak door closing echoes through the empty house, and I release a long breath, turning for the basement. Technically, I'm not here to see Wes, but I'd be lying if I said I wasn't secretly wishing we'd cross paths.

After last night, I'm not entirely sure where I stand with him. I haven't stopped thinking about what happened in my room. Somehow, he made all my inhibitions disappear, made me do something I never imagined I'd do in front of someone else. The way he spoke to me, the dirty words he used, the way he lost control and let me watch him too... Honestly, I didn't know he had that in him. He's always been so sweet and respectful toward me, so careful how he behaves, but that was something else. My body shivers as I replay what he did. If I thought I wanted him before, that was nothing.

And right when I thought he was finally going to give it to me, he left. If I hadn't asked him to join me in the tub, I'm pretty sure he would have left sooner. It was like he couldn't wait to get out of there.

I sigh as I step into the darkroom and drop my bag, pulling out the roll of film I shot yesterday. Flicking on the safety light and making sure the door is firmly closed, I set about developing the film, my mind trying to make sense of the events of the past few days.

Today was my first shift at Joe's since Wes and I... I don't even know what to call it. Got together? Hooked up? When I told him I wanted everything with him, he said he wanted that too, and yet it's almost feeling like after that first night together in his kitchen, he's pulled away. Yes, he came to dinner at my place last night, but he would barely touch me. Don't get me wrong, I enjoyed watching him touch himself, but that's not what I wanted. What I wanted was *him*, close to me. Inside me. I wanted to make love to him.

I still want that, but does he feel the same?

Confusion swirls through me as I sort the film negatives and decide which print to make first. Because yes, he kept his distance and left quickly, but the way he held me in the bathtub... My heart quickens as I remember his hands, so soft on my waist, stroking my skin in the water. The way he tenderly kissed my ear and pulled me into his chest. It felt so intimate, like the way you'd hold someone you loved dearly. Someone you cared for more than anything.

I shake my head as I expose my first print and place it into the tray of developer, because if he felt that way, why would he bolt the minute we got out of the tub? Why would he say something vague like, "I'll text you," then not do it?

And why didn't he come into work today? He kept his distance before, but it's different now. Why not come into

Joe's this morning like he used to? Wouldn't he want to see me?

Because I want to see him. Fuck, do I ever. He's all I've thought about since... well, if I'm being honest, quite a while now.

I move the print through the trays of liquid required to expose the image, then hang it above the bathtub before choosing the next image to expose. I try to focus as I go through the process of developing more images, but it's hard with my mind wandering to Wes, to what he could be thinking. I was so excited when he first said he wanted me, when it looked like things were moving forward with us, but after last night, I'm not sure.

Well, I'm sure of one thing. Despite his mixed signals, I'm falling hard for him. Hell, I fell for him the minute he showed me this darkroom, only I couldn't admit it to myself. Yet after he held me close in the tub last night there was no denying my heart anymore. I'm falling hard and fast for him, and I don't even know how he feels about me.

It's fucking terrifying.

I step back from the row of pictures I've developed, looking at them hanging over the tub. For a moment I forget about Wes, as the thrill of looking at what I've created rushes through me. I've captured some beautiful architectural details of the West Village, like the shots I took of Brooklyn Heights. I don't know what I'll do with them, but just looking at them makes me happy. Just being in this room makes me happy.

With a satisfied smile, I step out of the darkroom and stretch my neck. Even with the ventilation in there, the chemical smell can become too much after a while. I wander to the sliding glass doors that lead out to the manicured backyard, blinking as I step outside into the early evening light. Sucking in a lungful of fresh air, I tell myself not to think about Wes. Even if this thing with him doesn't work out, at least I'm back to doing my photography. I'm back in the darkroom. I'll be forever grateful to him for that.

"Fucking fuck fuck," I hear a familiar female voice mutter from the other side of the fence.

Violet.

I chuckle as I drag one of Weston's outdoor chairs across the yard and climb up to peer over.

"You okay?" I ask, glancing down at Violet. She's on her knees in the dirt, doing something to a rosebush, and glances up in surprise.

"Oh shit, sorry." She rises to her feet, wiping the back of her hand across her forehead, pushing her blond hair back from her face. "I'm fine. Just cut my hand on a thorn." She cocks her head to the side, eying me curiously. "What are you doing over there?"

"I was using the darkroom." I smile, thinking of the first time she realized the darkroom was for me, then took me to see the carriage houses for inspiration. "Actually, wait there for a sec. I want to give you something."

I pop back into the darkroom and shuffle through my stack of prints, choosing my favorites of Brooklyn Heights. Then I head back outside and lean over the fence again, holding out the pictures. Violet pulls a stepladder over, climbing to meet me face to face.

"What are these?"

"Just a few shots from around the neighborhood, to say thanks. I know how much you love the history of this area, and ever since you took me to shoot the carriage houses, I've found my inspiration to explore the historical architecture of the city."

Violet gazes at the images, her lips parted in awe. "Daisy,

these are gorgeous. You've captured such beautiful details." Her eyes are wide as she glances up at me. "Are you sure I can keep these? You should sell them."

A laugh escapes me. "Of course! They're not *that* good. They're just—"

"No, they're that good," Violet interjects, serious. "I'm going to frame these and put them in our living room. I love them."

My heart glows at her kind words. "Really?"

"Really." She nods vigorously, studying the images again. Then her gaze flicks to mine, lit with excitement. "Would you shoot me and Kyle?"

My brows tug together in confusion. "What?"

"I've always wanted to get portraits of us done but never made the time. And now that we're engaged, it's the perfect opportunity."

I hesitate. It was one thing to shoot images of a few old buildings, but to shoot my friends? For their engagement? What if I don't get it right?

"Please?" Violet presses. "We could do it around Brooklyn Heights, so you'd get us in the setting of the neighborhood. It would mean so much to me."

I swallow, studying my hands, because as nervous as it makes me to think about photographing them, there's no way I can say no to that.

"Okay," I say at last. I glance up uncertainly. "But I'm not a professional photographer, so they might not—"

"You will be once we pay you." She grins, bouncing on her toes. The stepladder wobbles beneath her, and she grips the fence, laughing.

"You can't pay me," I say, panic swooping through me. "I'd never accept—"

"Of course we can. And we will. It'll be great." She

glances down at her hand, her brow furrowing. "Shit, this is bleeding. I'd better take care of it before Kyle comes home and realizes I wasn't using gloves." Her eyes lift to the heavens in a dramatic show of exasperation, but her mouth is still fixed in a smile. She waves the photos as she carefully steps from the ladder. "Thanks so much for these. I can't wait to find a place for them. I'll be in touch soon to set up the shoot, okay?"

I nod meekly as she heads into the house. At least *she* has faith in me, because I'm not sure I have what it takes to pull off her vision.

Still, there's no harm in giving it a go, I tell myself firmly, as I climb down and pull Weston's chair back into place. I won't take their money, obviously, and if it doesn't turn out how she hopes, I guess all we've wasted is a few hours, and then she can find a legitimate photographer to do it properly.

I'm nervous all the same as I head back into the darkroom to begin my next round of photos. I look back at the handful of images I took of Weston at Sullivan's Cove, and I have to admit they're not bad. They're candid, and the hasty way in which I took them is obvious by the poor composition, but they capture his excitement in that moment. It's palpable. I stare at the image of him, remembering how genuinely thrilled he was for me when I picked up the camera again, how much he cared about something that to him was probably trivial, but to me was monumental.

And as I set about developing another image, I try to tell myself that things will work out with him—that they have to.

I only hope it's true.

# 27

# WESTON

I close the lid on my laptop and cast my gaze out the window. My office is situated on the fourteenth floor of a Midtown high-rise, and at this time of the evening, the sun slants between the buildings, sending golden light bouncing off surfaces of steel and glass.

The office is empty; everyone's gone home to their families or out to meet friends for drinks, and as I stare down at the bustling city below me, the silence in here suddenly feels suffocating. I rise from my chair and pull my messenger bag from the hook by the door, taking the elevator down to the parking garage.

Usually, I'd drive to the pool and swim laps until it's dark and I'm exhausted enough to collapse into bed, but as I stride across the dimly lit garage and tug my car keys from my pocket, I'm tempted to head straight home.

I tell myself I'm tired. That I could use an early night.

Pulling out into the blazing evening, I head toward the East River and onto FDR Drive. My mind wanders as I follow the traffic along the river, under the Williamsburg

Bridge, curving around the bend as the impressive steel structure of the Manhattan Bridge comes into view. For the past three years, the drive home has been a torturous game of forcing myself to focus on the buildings of Manhattan passing by on my right, instead of dwelling on the bottomless pit of despair that waited for me the minute I walked into my silent, empty home.

But tonight, it's a different kind of torture because it's no longer loneliness and grief tormenting me; it's a woman I can't get out of my head.

I didn't get a lick of work done today, unable to shake off thoughts of Daisy and last night. As soon as we got out of the tub, I left her place, then sat in my car for fifteen minutes convincing myself to drive home, instead of doing what I really wanted to do: walk back inside and pull her close, curl up in that tiny bed and hold her until she fell asleep. I'm trying to do the right thing here—trying to make sure we don't go too far until we're ready.

Hell, I'm fucking ready. I don't care if it feels quick, if she's the absolute last person I should be falling for.

I'm ready.

But I need to make absolutely certain she is, because once we cross that line, I don't think I'll be able to go back. So I've done what feels like the most responsible thing; I've tried to put the brakes on. I didn't go to Joe's this morning, even though there was no reason for me not to. If I so much as saw Daisy, I'd haul her into my arms and touch every inch of her beautiful body. I'd do things that would make her lose her damn job.

What is wrong with me? I've never been like this before; out of my mind with wanting her. I don't know how I kept my hands to myself last night, but the image of her pleasuring herself will live rent-free in my mind forever.

The Brooklyn Bridge comes into view and I take the offramp, idling in traffic as we crawl onto the bridge. The magnificent Gothic stone arches rise before me, and as we inch along above the water, I flick on the stereo to distract myself. Steely Dan's *Any Major Dude Will Tell You* drifts from the speakers, and my grip tightens on the wheel. I glance at my gym bag on the passenger seat, knowing damn well I won't be going to the pool. It'll be a miracle if I make it home instead of driving directly to Daisy's.

I remember her talking about shooting more film yesterday, and wonder if she used the darkroom today. Is it possible she could be there right now?

Despite myself, I grow restless in my seat, itching to pick up the pace. A Chrysler cuts me off and I lean on the horn, gesticulating wildly out the window. Doesn't he realize I have somewhere to be?

It's not until a woman in a Volvo with a backseat full of kids gives me a strange look that I withdraw into my car, shocked at my own behavior.

Jesus Christ. I don't even recognize myself.

By the time I pull up at Fruit Street, my pulse is thrumming. I tell myself I'm eager to get home, to put my feet up and order some food, but as I spring up the front steps and throw open the door, the disappointment at not seeing Daisy's Keds in the entry hall hits me like a bucket of ice.

She's not here. Of course she's not. Why would she be? She's probably wondering why the hell I ran out of her place last night like my ass was on fire. Why I didn't go to Joe's this morning, why I haven't called her, even though I've picked up my phone a hundred times today to do just that.

I toe off my loafers and dump my messenger bag on the counter, then pull a beer from the fridge and pop the top, taking a long swig. Serves me right for rushing home like a lovesick teenager. I should be in the pool, putting in my laps, sticking to my resolve to wait a little, to give this the time it needs to grow.

My nose picks up the faint citrusy notes of Daisy's scent. I set my beer down, telling myself I'm probably imagining it —probably conjuring it out of thin air—but my feet propel me to the basement stairs all the same. Maybe she came earlier and left. Maybe she developed her new roll of film. A smile nudges my lips in anticipation of seeing the new shots she's taken.

I'm completely unprepared when I round the bottom step and come face to face with Daisy. My heart catapults into my throat, and I stumble over my own feet.

"Oh!" Daisy steps back, laughing. "I didn't know you were home, sorry."

*Sorry*? Is she kidding?

"Don't be sorry." I go to reach for her, then hesitate. "I wasn't sure if you were here."

"Yeah." She gestures over her shoulder. "I was just developing that roll I shot yesterday."

My lips lift in a smile. "Anything good?"

"A few good shots, yeah."

I nod, watching as she shifts her weight uncertainly. I want to kiss her. I want to close this distance between us and press my mouth to hers, to touch her.

"And, um, something kind of cool happened," she continues, glancing at the yard and back at me. "Violet asked me to shoot her and Kyle, as a sort of engagement portrait thing."

My heart swells in my chest, pressing against my sternum. "Wow, Daisy—"

"I mean, it probably won't turn into anything," she adds

quickly, huffing a laugh. "I've never done portraits and I'm not a professional, so—"

*Okay, fuck this.*

I cross the few feet between us and pull her into my arms, holding her tight against me.

"That's amazing," I murmur into her hair, breathing in her scent. I can't help myself. I brush my lips over her forehead, and when she glances up at me, my mouth finds hers, warm and soft. "I am so proud of you," I say, then, drawing on whatever dregs of self-restraint I have left, I step away.

"Thank you." Her eyes follow me, watching the way I put space between us again, and her brow dips. "Wes, did I... did I do something wrong?"

My chest tightens. I absolutely hate the way she's looking at me right now.

"No." I rub the back of my neck to keep my hands occupied. "Quite the opposite."

"So you still want this? Us?"

"Yes." I chuff a laugh at her understatement. Want this? I *need* it. Need *her*. "Very much."

Her brown eyes swim with confusion as she looks up at me. "Then why..." She shifts her weight again. "Why did you leave last night? Why... why won't you sleep with me?"

My breath trickles out. I'm an idiot. It's been so long since I've done this that I've forgotten how to behave, how to communicate. It might be hard to find the words, but I need to, for her. She deserves an explanation.

"I like you a lot, but... I won't take that from you until you're sure," I say carefully. "Because once I do, Daisy, there will be no going back. You'll be mine."

Her frown deepens. "First of all, you're not *taking* anything from me. Secondly, did you ever consider that might be exactly what I want, to be yours?" She shakes her head, as if debating whether to go on, then steps closer. Touching my cheek with a shaky hand, she adds, "I'm falling for you, Weston. I have been for a while now."

*Oh, God.*

I drop my forehead to hers, breathing out hard. "I thought it was just me."

"It's not." Her thumb strokes over my beard, feather-soft. "And I want to make love to you."

My heart... fuck, my heart.

She sinks her teeth nervously into her bottom lip. "I want to be your girl, Wes."

I drag my thumb over that lip, my pulse thundering. I want that so fucking badly I can't breathe.

"You want to be my baby?" I ask, my voice rough.

She nods, swallowing, her gaze falling to my mouth. "I want to be your... babygirl."

*Oof.* Why does that turn me on so much?

"Babygirl. I like that."

She rises on her toes, eyes trained on my lips. "Will you please kiss me?"

She doesn't need to ask twice. My mouth falls on hers with so much force she stumbles back, but it only takes her a second to regain her balance. Her arms twine around my neck and she presses her body flush to mine. I respond by sweeping my tongue across hers, and she opens her mouth wide to invite me in. When I press my hips forward, her whimper sends blood rushing straight to my cock.

"Will you please fuck me?" she whispers between kisses.

Christ almighty. I don't know what I did in a past life to deserve having this woman beg me to fuck her, but I'm not wasting another second. We've waited long enough. Too long.

"Fuck yes, baby. Let's go."

I turn and take the steps two at a time, Daisy hot on my heels, giggling as she clambers up behind me. When I reach my bedroom on the second floor, I hesitate in the doorway, gazing at the room. The walls are an eggshell white, contrasting with the dark wooden floor and gold light fixtures. Even though it's not functional, the original white marble fireplace has been preserved, mirrored by the black metal marble-topped nightstands flanking the bed.

Then there's the bed itself, with a king-size mattress and a padded headboard in charcoal gray. I've never been in this bed with anyone besides Lydia. I remember the day we bought it. She picked out the white, waffle-textured comforter, and we argued over the velvet mustard-colored pillows. The same ones I've meticulously placed on the bed every morning just the way she liked, ever since she died. As if doing so would somehow bring her back.

I wait for the wave of grief to crash over me, to fill my lungs like it used to, but it doesn't come. Only a faint swell of sadness that rises and falls, followed by the sense that this is okay. The knowing that it's alright for me to be here with Daisy.

I might buy new pillows, though.

Daisy appears beside me with her bag on her shoulder. She glances from me to the bed, realization settling on her features, then lets her breath out slowly, as if bracing for the worst.

"If you're not ready, Wes, I get it." Her hand is gentle on my arm. "I know it's only been three years, so if you need to wait…"

I take her hand, crossing the threshold into the room with her. It's bittersweet, knowing I'm moving forward from Lydia, but hearing Daisy say it's okay, that she understands, tells me all I need to know.

Daisy is absolutely the right person for me.

And she's finally mine.

"Come here," I murmur, reaching for Daisy. And as I pull her onto my bed and hold her close, I feel my heart finally begin stitching itself back together.

# 28

# DAISY

Weston's hands shake as they slide the straps of my dress down my shoulders. I reach behind my back to help him, unzipping the dress and wriggling out of it. When I turn back to remove his clothes too, he pauses, leaning back.

"I just want to look at you, Daisy." He breathes out on a shaky exhale as his eyes roam over me. "You are so beautiful."

Warmth spreads from my cheeks, down my neck and across my chest, and his gaze follows. It tints my skin the same color as my blush-pink bra and panties, and Weston hums his appreciation at the sight. It's not the first time he's called me beautiful, and while I've never considered myself to be pretty in the conventional sense, with him, I feel like a princess. Every word from him, every look he gives me, makes me feel more beautiful than all the guys I've dated in the past put together.

"I love your freckles," he murmurs, leaning close to trail his mouth along my collarbone. The whiskers from his beard are coarse against the sensitive skin, and goosebumps rush across my bare skin. He notices, and glances up. "Are you cold?"

"No." I smile. "It's the way you touch me. My body goes crazy."

He chuckles, bringing his lips back to my skin as he works his way down my chest, dipping into the valley between my breasts.

"I need to know you're comfortable, okay?" He glances up again. "If you want to stop, or if I do something you don't like, you need to tell me."

I nod, my heart fluttering wildly behind my sternum. This is really happening. I'm going to have sex, and with Weston, of all people. As I watch him tenderly unhook and remove my bra, watch the reverent way he smooths his hands across my stomach and sighs, I can't imagine anyone better to do this with. Anyone I trust more.

I try to tug his shirt off, but he maneuvers to the foot of the bed out of my reach, sliding my panties down my legs until I'm naked. I'm vaguely aware that he's still fully clothed, but my thoughts evaporate the moment his tongue flicks my clit.

"Oh, shit," I blurt, ever the lady. He gives a dark chuckle against my skin, tongue sweeping across me again.

"You're already so wet, baby." His voice is a gravelly rasp as he laps at my slick center, sending heat flooding through me. "I missed the taste of you." His tongue dips inside me, lips closing around my clit to suck. He knows exactly how to make me feel good, and within minutes I've got my hands in his hair, moaning his name.

"Yes, Wes. Fuck, yes..."

Before I can reach my climax, he pulls away, rising to his

feet and unbuttoning his shirt. As he tosses it aside, my gaze falls to the bulge threatening his zipper, and my heart jumps in anticipation. I watch as he slowly removes his pants and boxer briefs, freeing himself.

*Fuck.* I didn't get a good look at his dick last night, because it was so firmly grasped in his hand, but *holy shit*, it is glorious. Not that I've seen all that many in my life. The majority of my experience is from the occasional porn video I've watched, but looking at Weston...

*Wow.*

People always talk about how ugly the penis is, but they're wrong. There is nothing ugly about the way Weston's massive erection juts from his pelvis and curves up his belly. Need shudders through me as I gaze at the red-purple head of it, the veins snaking up its sides. I'm overcome with a primal wave of lust, wet heat soaking my core. I want to crawl across the bed and take him into my mouth, but I've never done that before and don't want anything to ruin the perfection of this moment between us.

Weston climbs onto the bed beside me, leaning in to take my mouth with his. My hand goes to his cheek, touching his beard, but I can't help myself. My other hand strays between us, finding his hardness and circling it. He moans into my mouth as I stroke him, rubbing my thumb over his moist tip and using that to help me stroke. His hips thrust forward into my hand, his mouth devouring mine more greedily, until he pulls away.

"Oh God, Daisy, you have to stop." His eyes are hooded, hazy, and dark. "It feels too good."

I smile, dizzy at the thought that *I'm* making him feel that way. That *I'm* the one doing this to him.

His fingers find my center and he mutters a curse as I

moan for him. He teases my entrance, sliding his fingers through my slickness and over my clit, and my body spasms as he swirls them there, watching my expression.

His fingers are wet with my arousal as he raises them to his mouth. "I can't believe this is for me," he whispers, licking his fingers clean.

*Holy. Shit.*

He returns to his task, pushing his fingers inside me, gently working me open for him, and I lie back on the bed, whimpering in pleasure, desperate for more.

"I need you," I rasp.

"Do you have a condom?"

I nod, stifling a laugh at this, because *yes*, I am very prepared to lose it to Weston. Rifling through my bag on the floor, I pull out a box of condoms and a bottle of lube, setting them on the bed, but something occurs to me, and I turn back to Wes.

"I've never been with anyone," I begin, and he nods.

"I know, babygirl."

*Fuck me.* Hearing that word from his mouth gives me a full-body shiver.

I shake my head, trying to focus. "No, what I mean is... I'm on the pill." I went on it a few months back, when I thought Jess and I were going to sleep together, but I'll spare Wes that little detail. "And I was wondering, when did you last... I mean, have you, since..." I break off, embarrassed. What am I thinking, asking him that?

"Oh." Realization dawns on Weston's face, and he sits up. "I've only ever..." He clears his throat. "Lydia is the only woman I've ever been with."

I stare at him, dumbfounded. He can't be serious.

Wes takes my hand. "Lydia and I met when we were

eighteen. After she died, the last thing I wanted to do was..." He shakes his head. "It's only Lydia, and, if I'm lucky, you."

My heart doesn't know what to do with itself. Here I was thinking *I* was the one doing something big here, but it's a first time of sorts for him, too.

"Oh, Wes." I shuffle forward and brush my lips over his, cradling the back of his head. I have never known a more genuine, wonderful man. "Well, I was going to say, we could use a condom if you want, but if you'd prefer not to, that's okay too."

His eyes fall closed, his jaw tightening. "Christ, Daisy. Yes, I want that. I want that very much." He glances at me, swallowing. "But if we do that, I won't last long."

I smile. "That's okay. I just want..." I take a deep breath, acknowledging the vulnerability that tugs at me and continuing anyway. "I want to be as close as possible to you."

Weston's breath rushes out. He lays me back down, lips touching mine softly. "I want that too. That's all I want."

Emotion is a hot ball in my chest. How did I get so lucky that he wants me as much as I want him?

I spread my legs and motion for him to climb on top of me, but instead, he reaches for the bottle of lube, squirting some into his hand. I watch as he gently applies it between my legs. I don't think I need it, but I love how he's taking care of me. If it's possible, it makes me want him even more.

"Come here." I tug him onto me, the heat of his skin warming me through. His smell washes over me, the bergamot notes of his cologne mixed with just a hint of sweat. It's intoxicating, and the minute I feel his hardness settle at my entrance, I shift my hips to rub myself on the head of his cock.

"Jesus Christ," he bites out, rocking his hips in response.

Our lips crash together as he slides back and forth at my entrance, rubbing my clit into a frenzy.

Fuck, I can't wait anymore.

With a tilt of my hips, I urge him lower until he nudges inside me. I breathe out at the sheer relief of having him, finally, after all this time. The weight of him on top of me, the press of his lips on mine, the scratch of his chest hair on my breasts. It's fucking perfect.

Wes raises himself onto his elbows to watch my face as he slowly enters me. He's much bigger than my vibrator, and my mouth falls open as I feel myself stretch around his cock.

"Okay, baby?" he asks between clenched teeth, easing himself deeper.

I nod, trying to catch my breath at the sensation. It's like nothing I've ever felt; a fullness I never knew I needed, with a whisper of pain. He's not all the way in yet, but having his mouth cover mine, having him stroke my cheek so tenderly, feels like heaven.

He gives a slow, cautious roll of his hips that sends both pleasure and pain coursing through me. I shift my hips, trying to escape the discomfort, and Wes notices.

"Should I stop?" he asks, beginning to pull away.

"No." I wrap my arms around him, holding him closer. I can feel his heart hammering through his chest, against my own shuddering heart. "Please don't stop."

He studies me with concern. "Does it hurt?"

"A little, but I want this, Wes. I want you."

He exhales unsteadily and brings his mouth back to mine, giving another gentle thrust. The pain is a sharp sting, coupled with a faint pleasure, and I groan at the confusing sensation.

"I don't want to hurt you," he murmurs, gently rocking his hips.

"Again," I pant.

Another thrust, deeper this time, and the pain begins to subside.

"That's better." I widen my legs. "I want all of you."

Weston chuckles against my ear. "I'm trying, babygirl. You're so damn tight."

Hearing that name from his tongue again sends heat coursing through me, and I grab his ass, pulling him deeper.

"Fuck," he curses. "How's that?"

"It's good." The pain is little more than a dull ache now. All I can think about is getting Weston's entire dick inside of me. I want it. I *need* it.

"Good," Wes pants, thrusting again, harder. "You're doing so well."

"Yeah?"

He nods, pushing himself back onto his knees so he can watch the place where we join. "Look at you, taking my cock. So good, babygirl."

His filthy words send heat spiraling to my center. "Fuck, Wes, I lose my mind when you talk to me like that."

He grins, licking his thumb and lowering it to stroke my throbbing clit. Sliding slowly out, he pumps back into me, hard. It's deeper this time, and there's more pain, eclipsed by pleasure as he swirls his thumb.

"That's it, baby," he says, watching me stretch around him. "Take all of me. You can do it."

I moan as my body resists the invasion, his thumb working my clit to distract me from the pain. He pinches my nipple with his other hand, thrusting deeper.

"You okay?"

"I'm okay." I watch him above me, the muscles in his torso bunching as he rolls his hips, a wave of salt-and-pepper hair falling across his forehead. I run my hands over his pecs, the definition in his abs, sighing. "I'm more than okay."

His thumb works overtime as he gives another firm thrust. A sharp flash of pain only lasts a second before giving way to pleasure.

"Good girl, there you go." His words make me whimper for him. "You're taking all of me now."

He lowers himself back over me, so his chest is flush with mine, and our mouths come together. He stills his hips for a moment, giving me the chance to adjust to his size. I'm so full with him, and my heart beats double time at the thought.

"I'm so glad I did this with you," I whisper.

"Me too, Daisy." He brushes my hair back from my face with trembling hands, kissing my cheek. "I can't imagine doing it with anyone else."

God, this man. He's making it impossible not to fall in love with him.

I thread my hands into his hair, bringing his mouth back to mine. His lips are so soft, his tongue lapping gently into my mouth, and as we kiss, he rocks his hips again, hitting a spot inside I didn't know was there. It sends ecstasy rippling through my entire body, right down to my toes, which curl into the mattress. A moan tears from my mouth, and he captures it with his, picking up the pace.

"Do you know how hot it is to be the first man inside you, babygirl?" His thrusts are deeper now, nudging me up the bed as he grunts with effort. "How much it means to me?"

"Tell me," I sob, delirious.

"It's amazing. It's everything. It's..." He sits back to watch himself fuck me, gripping my waist tightly as his gaze comes to mine, dark and dangerous. It's like an animal has awoken inside him, and he growls out, "You're mine now. *Mine.*"

My heart squeezes tight at his words, at the possessive way he's holding me. "Yes," I breathe. "That's all I could ever want."

"I need to hear you say it." Weston's jaw is hard as he watches me take his cock, watches me writhe with pleasure. "Say the words."

"I'm yours, Wes. All yours."

His nostrils flare, the beast inside him satisfied by my response. "Good girl."

I whimper, lifting my hips to meet his. He lowers a hand between us, finding my clit as he thrusts again. The sensation of that, coupled with the spot he hits deep inside me, makes my words come out in an incoherent slur. "Yes... right... yes... there..."

"Fuck, Daisy." He grits his teeth, sweat gathering along his brow as he pumps into me, eyes wild. "You feel too good. I can't..."

"I'm close," I rasp, feeling the pressure build in my core.

"Thank God." He kisses along my jaw, the shell of my ear. "Will you come for me?"

"I'm... so..." The words die on my tongue as the pleasure reaches a boiling point.

"Come, babygirl. I need to feel you come on my cock."

*Oh, holy Christ.*

Colors explode through my vision, my body spasming as bliss washes through me. It's like nothing I've ever experienced, no orgasm I've had before. Feeling him so deep inside me, filling me as I clench and grip his cock, my moans echoing off the bedroom walls.

"Fuck, Daisy." He joins me then, his guttural groan shuddering down my spine as he buries himself deep, his body stilling, filling me with his liquid warmth. He's panting in my ear like he's just run a marathon, twitching on top of me with aftershocks. I hold him close, grazing his shoulder with my mouth, across the silver under his jaw, in awe of what we just did, how amazing it felt.

I never knew anything could feel that good. Not just the sex, but being so close to him. Feeling him inside me. Seeing him come undone like that.

When he finally rolls off beside me, I feel hollow at the loss of him. He disappears for a moment but I'm too wrung-out to protest, and when he returns, he's holding a washcloth. Then he does something completely unexpected. He sits between my legs, and gently, carefully, wipes me clean.

A sharp intake of breath has me sitting up on my elbows. "What?"

"There's a little blood," he observes, his brows drawn together.

"I think that's normal." I'm definitely tender down there, and probably will be the next time we do it, too.

Which will hopefully be soon.

"I hate that I did that to you." He sets the washcloth aside, crawling up my body to pull me into his arms and stroke my hair.

I chuckle. "I love what you did to me."

He draws back to examine my face. "You're not too sore?"

I lift a shoulder. "A little, but it was worth it."

"Yeah?" There's that flicker of vulnerability again. I love that about him.

"I'm already counting the minutes until we can do it again."

A warm laugh rumbles from his chest. "I might be too,"

he admits sheepishly. His lips brush softly over mine, and my body tingles in response.

This time, it's Weston's stomach rumbling that interrupts the mood. I laugh, pinching him playfully on the arm, and he groans in frustration.

"I've had no appetite for weeks being away from you, but *now* my body needs to eat." He lifts his gaze to the ceiling, and I laugh again.

"So, let's eat. I'm not going anywhere." I realize how presumptuous that sounds. "I mean, unless you want me—"

"Fuck, no." Weston rolls on top of me, pinning my hands above my head. "I don't want you to leave. I have a spare toothbrush. Will you stay?"

"I'd love to." The grin on my face must make me look giddy, but he doesn't seem to care, pressing his mouth to mine again. And again, his stomach rumbles.

"For fuck's sake," he mutters, rolling off me and sitting up. He wipes a hand down his face, sighing. "I guess it will be good for us to keep our strength up. I have big plans for you later." He wiggles his eyebrows comically, and a laugh erupts from me. Playful Weston might be my favorite.

"What about Thai?" I suggest.

His eyes sparkle as they move over me, still naked on his bed. "I was thinking the exact same thing."

He reluctantly climbs from the bed and tugs on some sweatpants, and my eyes follow his ass as he pads from the room. This man is so fucking sexy—and so much more than that, too. I think of the way he carefully applied the lube, the way he checked I was okay throughout, the way he cleaned me afterward. I could never have imagined how caring and sweet he'd be, and my heart is complete mush about it. And now he's going to order my favorite food.

He couldn't be any more perfect. This night couldn't be any more perfect.

I tug my dress on with a sigh, reaching for my bag. My phone catches my eye, an unread text flashing on the screen, and I pull it out. As I read the message, my stomach falls through the floor.

**Jesse: Are you free tomorrow? We need to talk.**

# 29

# DAISY

My heart is in my throat as I step into the dark bar. I'm not sure why Jesse asked me to meet him here—a bar in the East Village, called Bounce—at four in the afternoon, but I was too chicken to question it.

I've reread his text a hundred times since last night, dissecting his words, looking for clues.

*We need to talk.*

Does he somehow know about me and Weston? Does he want to call me out in public, make a scene? That doesn't really seem like his style, but then I never really knew him that well, did I?

I slide onto a barstool, my gaze drifting around the interior, looking for Jess. It's dimly lit, one wall lined with vinyl booths, the other lined with the bar itself, tables dotted between. At least one small mercy is that it's not too busy.

"Daisy."

I almost jump out of my skin when a familiar voice utters my name. I whip my gaze back to the bar where Jess leans on the other side.

Wait. What? Does he *work* here?

"Uh, hi." I smooth my hair, try to paste on a smile. I know it's ridiculous, but part of me wonders if he can tell I'm no longer a virgin. If there's something different about me, some kind of vibe or clue that I've had sex.

With his father. Jesus.

I grimace, pushing the thought from my head. "New job?"

He nods, wiping his hands on a rag and walking out from behind the bar to join me on the next stool.

"How's it going?"

"Good. My boss is really cool. He owns a few bars, but spends most of his time here." Jess chuffs a quiet laugh. "We're a lot alike. I mean, he has a wife and kids, so not totally, but he gets me."

I lift my eyebrows, uncertain about what that might mean, but not wanting to ask.

An uncomfortable sensation prickles my skin as Jesse's gaze drifts over me, slowly absorbing my figure from head to toe. I changed out of my work clothes into a summery dress because no one wants to meet their ex looking like trash, but as Jesse's eyes drink me in, I wonder if that was a mistake.

"You look good, Daisy."

I swallow, nervous energy fluttering in my belly. "Thanks." Shit, he's not going to ask me out again, is he? That's not why he wanted to meet me? What the hell would I say?

*Sorry, I'm fucking your dad instead.*

The thought makes me cringe, but Jess doesn't seem to notice. He leans back on one elbow on the bar, exhaling long and slow as he brings his gaze to mine.

"So, uh, I wanted to apologize for the way everything

went down at the beach house. I've had a lot of time to think, and I was a complete douche. You didn't deserve that."

I blink, unsure of what to say.

"And I want you to know, nothing happened with that chick. But... it was a shitty thing to do, and I'm sorry."

I swallow, processing this. "I... thanks, Jess. I appreciate that." I think back to the part I played in our relationship and sigh. I can't tell him I had—*have*—feelings for Wes, obviously, but I also want to apologize for my role in things. "I'm sorry, too."

He shakes his head, gaze falling to his hands. "Nah, you don't have anything to be sorry for. I should have been more patient." His gaze lifts back to mine. "I'll always regret fucking things up between us, Daisy." He draws breath to say something more, and panic pierces my chest at the possibility that he might be about to say we should give things another shot.

"How's your dad?" I blurt. Inexplicably. Because I know how his dad is—he's good. We made love again after dinner last night, slowly, tenderly, and then fell asleep in each other's arms. So if Wes is feeling anything like I am—and I think he is—then he's pretty damn good indeed.

Apart from things with Jess. Wes doesn't talk about his son much, and that's not because he doesn't want to mention him around me. It's because he doesn't want to think about him. He doesn't want to think about what he's lost. And that breaks my heart.

A frown creases Jesse's forehead. "No idea," he mutters. And just like that, he's back to being the same sullen guy I wanted to break up with in Greenport.

Well, not quite. That guy wouldn't have apologized to me so sincerely, would never have admitted he was wrong, and regretted his actions. It's funny how time can make a person reflect on things. Why can't he do the same with Weston?

Still, I can tell he's grown in the short time we've been apart, even if just a little. Maybe I can work with that.

"Are you really sorry about what happened at the beach house?" I ask carefully.

Jesse's gaze flies to mine. "Of course. I was an asshole."

I nod, deciding to try my luck. "I'll accept your apology on one condition."

His brow knits. "Okay... What's that?"

"You make up with your dad."

Jess scoffs, leaning back. "No way."

"Look." I lean forward, hazarding a hand on his arm. He glances down in surprise, softening. "I know you never wanted to talk about this with me, and I'm sorry for pushing you, but your dad..." How do I say this without giving anything away? "He's a good man, Jess. He cares about you so much, and—"

"You don't know what he did," Jess interrupts.

"I do." I squeeze Jesse's arm gently. "He told me what happened, why you're so mad at him."

Jesse's eyes widen. "He did? When?"

I roll my lips to the side, wondering how much to share. I don't want to lie, but I need Jess to believe me. "I... spent a little time with him while you were out partying in Green-port." That, at least, isn't a lie.

It seems to pluck at the string of guilt Jess feels about our time away, because he sighs, slumping against the bar. "It's complicated," he mutters. "I don't want to talk to him."

Maybe I should just accept this and walk away. After all, if he does get back in touch with his dad—if they repair their relationship—what would that mean for *my* relationship with Wes? How would we continue to see each other with Jess back in his life? We wouldn't be able to, would we?

But I also know how important Jesse is to Weston, despite what he says about not caring anymore, and if I can help them fix things, then I will. I'll do that for Wes, regardless of what it means for us, because it matters to him.

"I know you want to blame him for what happened with your mom," I begin tentatively, well aware I'm inserting myself into a delicate family matter, but Wes feels like family to me in a way now, too, and I can't let this go. "I know what it's like to lose someone you love. I did too. And when that happens, it's all too easy to feel anger instead of dealing with it. I felt that way for years."

Jesse sighs, fiddling with a cardboard coaster on the bar, not meeting my gaze.

"Anger is easy to feel," I continue gently. "But grief is harder. It's so much more painful. And I wonder..." I give Jesse's arm another squeeze. "I wonder if you've been trying to avoid feeling that pain, Jess. I don't blame you, because it's awful."

I think of the anger I still feel toward my parents for their heartless response to the death of the Walkers, and how I let that overshadow my grief for months afterward. They were not who I needed them to be and they never have been. They haven't once reached out to me since I moved to the city, and therein lies the difference between Jess's situation and mine. He had a loving relationship with his parents before Lydia's death. I've never had that kind of relationship with my own family. I'd give anything to have parents who care as much as Weston cares for Jesse.

"It's devastating that you lost your mom, Jess, but you don't have to lose your dad, too."

When Jesse finally brings his gaze back to mine, his eyes

are sad. "Maybe you're right," he mumbles, and surprise trickles through me.

Wow. I'm actually getting through to him.

"I know it's hard to see now, but you really are lucky to have a father who cares about you as much as Wes does."

Jesse's eyebrows rise curiously. "*Wes*?"

Shit.

I cough, glancing away. "Please, Jess. Please think about it, for me. If you really are sorry about your behavior while we were away, then it's not just me you need to apologize to. It's your dad, too."

He studies me for a long moment, and I think he's going to press me again on the overly familiar name I used for his father, but instead, a sound at the door catches his attention.

"Ah shit, my boss is here."

I follow his gaze to where a tall, good-looking guy with dirty-blond hair and a tidy beard steps inside. When I say tall, I mean *tall*—easily six-foot-six. I'd place him close to Weston's age, and as he approaches the bar, I notice threads of silver in his beard and fine creases beside his friendly hazel eyes. His muscular shoulders fill out his T-shirt nicely, his height and build creating an air of confidence that commands the room, and a group of women who've been quietly chatting in a booth over a bottle of chardonnay abandon their conversation to watch him stride across the room.

I don't blame them.

"Hey, Jess," the guy says as he slips behind the bar. His eyes move to me, shimmering with a smile that no doubt gets him a shitload of tips when he's serving drinks.

"Hey. This is my... friend, Daisy." Jess motions to me. "My boss, Cory."

"Hi." I smile at Cory, unable to stop my gaze from

straying to the gold band on his left hand. That's hardly surprising. Whoever she is, she's one lucky lady.

Jess turns back to me, and as I fix my attention on him again, he lets out a heavy breath. "Okay. I'll... I'll think about what you said."

"I'm glad." I give his arm a final squeeze before pulling my hand away and rising to go, a bittersweet feeling twisting in my chest. If he really does reach out to his dad, then that will make things unbelievably complicated for me and Weston.

But if it means Weston gets his son back... I'd never stand in the way of that.

# 30

## WESTON

"Mr. Abbott?" My assistant, Nina, pokes her head into the door. "You have a visitor."

I look up from my laptop, where I've been staring blankly for the past thirty minutes, doing nothing. I've been useless at work all week. Daisy has spent the last three nights at my place, and each evening we follow the same routine—sex, dinner, more sex, before finally giving in to the need for sleep. It's the absolute highlight of my day, being with Daisy, spending our evenings talking and laughing, and, of course, naked. I thought the first time we had sex was freaking amazing, but somehow, it's only gotten better. When I don't have my hands on her, it's all I can think about. I haven't been to the pool in days, but I don't care. This is better than any workout. Honestly, I feel like I'm twenty years younger.

I push the thought of Daisy's soft curves from my mind and focus on my assistant. I don't have any meetings scheduled for today, and I could really use some uninterrupted time to actually get some work done. Whoever this is, they can come back later.

Unless, of course, it's Daisy. Would she surprise me at work? I have the sudden image of closing my office blinds and bending Daisy over my desk, and my dick twitches in my pants.

*So much for not thinking about her.*

"Who is it?" I ask Nina, both hoping it's her and knowing it probably won't be.

"Your son."

My heart stops cold.

"My *son*?"

She nods, sensing my shock. I've tried not to air my dirty laundry in the office, but everyone knows things have been a little strained since Lydia's death.

"Should I tell him it's not a good time?"

"Uh, no." I close my laptop, trying to keep my hands from shaking. "No, send him in."

What the hell is Jess doing here? Does he somehow know about me and Daisy?

*Don't be ridiculous*, I tell myself. *How would he know?*

I suck in a breath, trying to calm my whipping pulse as Jess enters my office. And despite how panicked I am, despite how angry I still feel after what he did to Daisy and how he behaved at the beach house, my heart softens at the sight of him. I've missed him.

"Hey, Dad," Jesse mumbles, glancing around my office. He examines the bookcase stuffed with graphic design books and awards, my diploma framed on the wall, even the coffee machine in the corner, before finally letting his gaze settle on me.

I breathe out in relief. He doesn't look like he's here to pick a fight, quite the opposite. His shoulders are curled inward, his expression vulnerable. He looks like the kid who found out he was losing his mom, and emotion wells up in my chest.

My voice is hoarse when I say, "Hey, Jess. It's good to see you."

He nods, eying the chair in front of my desk, and I motion for him to sit. He seems relieved at this and sinks down into the leather.

"I, uh, wasn't sure if you'd want to see me."

I swallow down the emotion clogging my throat. "Of course I want to see you. I always want to see you. You're my son."

Jess balls up his fists and rubs them into his eyes. They're red when he finally looks at me again. He hasn't shaved for a while, so his jaw has filled in with stubble. I don't know if that's a choice, or a sign he's not looking after himself. Either way, I can sense his uncertainty, so I try to break the ice.

"How's work?"

The minute the question leaves my mouth, I wince. Last time we spoke it was to fight about his job, among other things. I half expect he's going to roll his eyes and storm out the door, but instead a smile whispers across his lips.

"It's good, actually. I got a new job at a bar in the East Village. Good pay, good hours. The owner is really nice; he's already got me closing up two nights a week."

Warmth suffuses my chest. He's got a job. He's happy and doing well there.

He's *talking* to me.

"That's great, son." I'm trying not to be too enthusiastic, but I can't help it. "Sounds like you get on well with your boss."

Jess nods, chuffing a laugh as he looks down at his

hands. "Yeah. That's actually why I'm here. I mean, uh..." He shakes his head, his smile fading. "We had a long chat the other day before the rush started, and ended up talking about you."

I blink in surprise. "Me?"

Jess nods, picking up a paperweight from my desk and examining it. "We started talking about family and stuff. He asked about my parents and I told him about Mom." Jesse passes the paperweight from one hand to the next as he speaks, careful not to look at me. "And when he asked about you... Well, I'd been thinking about calling, but Cory really put things into perspective. He told me about his own father, who was..." Jess grunts a laugh. "Not great. And the more I thought about what you'd done for me, the more I realized... I don't know. That I should apologize, or something."

I gape at him. He's here to *apologize*? To *me*? Who is this kid?

"I had time to think after Greenport," Jess continues, setting the paperweight down and looking at me. "I'm sorry for the way I acted. Not just then, for the other stuff, too. I don't think I ever said thanks for letting me crash at the house."

"I..." I open and close my mouth in shock, searching for the words I need. "It's your home, Jess. You're always welcome there."

"I'm grateful for what you've done for me," he mumbles.

"I know." Though I'm not entirely sure I did, until now.

"And I feel bad for storming off at the beach house and moving out while you were away." Jess drops his gaze. "I'm sorry I missed your birthday."

I draw breath to tell him that actually my birthday turned out okay, then catch myself. I can't tell him that, can

I? I can't tell him I've met an amazing woman and I'm falling hard for her.

I'll never be able to tell him.

Even if he treated Daisy badly. Even if he didn't deserve her.

"I'm not the person you need to apologize to about the beach house, Jess." I fiddle with the cuff of my shirt, lowering my gaze as I say her name. "It's Daisy you need to speak to."

"I did."

I can't stop my eyes from whipping up to his. "You did? When?"

"A couple days back. She met me at work and we talked."

My pulse trips unexpectedly. Daisy went to see Jess and didn't tell me?

"She's the one who first got me thinking about talking to you," Jess adds. His breath trickles out slowly as he leans back in the chair. "She was always pushing me to fix things with you. I just didn't want to hear it."

I think about Daisy telling me at Sullivan's Cove how she tried to talk to Jess, how he wouldn't let her in. How bad I felt that she took it upon herself to try to repair things with us.

"I really screwed up with her," Jesse mutters, scraping his hands down his face. "She's so great, and I messed it all up."

I press my eyes shut, my insides twisting.

"I really liked her, too." Jess puffs out a breath, and when I glance at him again, he's shaking his head. "I got mad because she didn't want to sleep with me. She was a virgin. Did you know that?"

I can feel color coming into my cheeks as I shrug

absently, praying he doesn't notice.

"Of course you didn't. Why would you?" Jess gives a rueful laugh. "I should have been more patient." He drags a hand through his hair. "Anyway. What's done is done."

I study my son, slumped in the chair opposite my desk. Of course he liked Daisy. She's incredible. I don't blame him one bit for regretting that he let her get away, but based on what she's told me, they never stood a chance. Guilt tugs at me, knowing she wanted me while she was with my son, that I wanted her just as much, that it only took us a month to act on it after they broke up. But the feeling fades as I think about how freaking amazing it's felt being with her. It's hard to tell myself it's wrong, when it feels so right.

I pick up a pen from my desk and roll it between my fingers to dispel some of the nervous energy running through me. "Where are you living?" I ask, hoping he doesn't notice my awkward segue.

He cringes, glancing away. "I'm... between places right now. I've been crashing on Rex's couch, but he's subletting his place while he's out of town for a couple weeks."

I set the pen down, frowning. That's hardly an ideal situation, and not only because I don't want him spending any more time with Rex than is absolutely necessary.

"Come home, Jess." The words leave my mouth before I've thought them through, more as a reflex than anything. Inviting him home is the last thing I should do. How will I explain the darkroom in the basement? More pressingly, how will I continue to see Daisy?

He shakes his head, setting his jaw. "No. I'm not going to use you anymore, Dad. That's not why I came here."

I should leave it here, should let it go, but he's still my son and I still love him. I still want to provide for him, despite everything that's happened. I'll just have to figure out how to do that without him learning the truth.

And without losing Daisy.

"You're not using me, Jesse." I sigh. "It's your home."

Jess grimaces, picking at lint on his jeans. "Are you sure? It won't be for long, just until I find my own place. I want to stand on my own two feet."

If I wasn't so preoccupied with my own racing thoughts, I'd be proud to hear those words come from my son's mouth. I force my gaze to his, promising myself I'll figure out the details later.

"You can stay as long as you need, Jess. I mean it."

Gratitude flashes in his eyes. "Thanks. I work late most nights, so I'll be out of your hair."

I shake my head, softening. "I don't want you out of my hair."

"Well... I'll help out more, I swear." A sheepish smile touches his mouth. "I'd offer to cook, but we both know I'll only end up poisoning one of us."

A laugh shakes out of me, the sound completely at odds with the roiling in my stomach. I look at my son, smiling at me for the first time in years. If he needs a roof over his head, then that's what I'll give him, despite how torn I feel.

"Can I come after work tonight?" Jess asks hopefully. "I finish up at midnight."

"Of course."

"Thanks, Dad." He rises from the chair and stands there awkwardly, looking at me. It takes me a moment to realize he wants to hug me.

Shit.

I stand too, pulling my boy into my arms. Not a boy anymore; a grown man. I can't remember the last time I held him, and my throat closes with emotion. He's come to me to apologize, to repair things, and it's all I could ask for. It's all I've wanted for three years.

But it's bittersweet, finally mending this rift between us. Because I might have Jess back, but now I have something else I care about—something so precious I still can't believe it's real.

Something I'm not sure I'm willing to sacrifice.

# 31

# WESTON

My heart is heavy as I plod down the stairs to the basement that evening. Jess will be home later tonight, and I have to tell Daisy things are about to get way more complicated. A better man would end the relationship to focus on his son, but it turns out I'm not the man I thought I was.

She's not in the basement when I enter, but her bag sits on the coffee table with the Nikon poking out of the zipper, and the door to the darkroom is open. I step inside, glancing around at the space I created for her, the space she's made her own, only to find it empty. There are stacks of prints on the table, with more pinned over the tub, drying. I let my gaze wander over the images, some familiar, like the surrounding neighborhood, and some I haven't seen yet.

I stop short when I see an image of me, asleep in bed. Not just one, but several. I'm not used to seeing myself like this, and the details are incredible; the landscape of sheets across my stomach, the prickly whiskers on my jaw contrasting with the soft cotton on the pillowcase, the blissful look of slumber on my face as I no doubt dream of her. She must have taken these the other night, after we made love.

Fuck, she is so talented. Somehow she's captured the texture of the room, the mood of the moment, the way I feel.

My heart clenches as I turn from the images. I don't even want to think about how I feel, because it's too much. It's too much, too soon.

I drag both hands down my face, my insides churning. How will we make this work with Jess home? What was I thinking, letting this go so far?

The moment I step out of the darkroom and spy Daisy on the lounger outside in the yard, I know exactly what I was thinking. She saved me from the depths of my pain with her smile and her heart. She reminded me how good it feels to laugh. How good it feels to be alive. And I sure as hell don't want to give that up.

Even if Jess will be home in a few hours.

*Goddammit.*

Daisy spots me through the glass door and saunters across with a grin, sliding the door open and stepping inside.

"Hey, you." Rising onto her toes, she brushes a kiss over my mouth, and I let her. I let her circle her arms around my neck and pull me close, her bright, sweet smell washing over me. I let her tongue dart out and greet mine, let her hands roam my back.

And I'm utterly miserable when she pulls away, glancing at me uncertainly.

"Everything okay?"

*No. No, it's not fucking okay.*

"Jesse came to see me today."

"He did?" She clasps her hands together, eyes lighting with a surprised smile. "I was hoping he would."

"He mentioned you'd spoken." My brows draw together involuntarily. "Why didn't you tell me?"

She gnaws on her lip, dropping her gaze. "I'm sorry. I wanted to, but I wasn't sure if he would reach out to you, and I didn't want to get your hopes up."

I give a slow nod. That makes sense, I guess.

"He said you encouraged him to talk to me," I murmur.

"Of course."

"Why would you do that, Daisy?"

Her eyes fly up to mine. "Are you mad?"

"Mad?" I stare at her, incredulous. "Why on earth would I be mad?"

She lifts a shoulder. "I know you told me it wasn't my responsibility to fix things, but I had to try, Wes."

"Why?" I press. Surely she must have known that if Jess came back into my life, it would make things nearly impossible for us. As grateful as I am to have my son back, a tiny part of me wishes things could have stayed as they were. That she and I could be happy in our little bubble without worrying about anything or anyone else.

I hate myself for being so damn selfish.

"Because..." She gives me a strange look. "Because he's your son. Because I know you want him in your life."

I heave out a breath, raking my hand through my hair. "And what about us?"

"Well..." She shifts her weight. "Look, I don't want things to end. I feel like we're just starting something... something big. But if being with me means you lose your son, that's too high a price to pay. If I have to give you up so you can have him in your life... that's more important."

There it is. The thing I'd suspected ever since Jess mentioned his conversation with her this morning, but wouldn't let myself acknowledge. She put my relationship with Jess above my relationship with her. She was prepared to sacrifice what we have, even though she doesn't want that any more than I do.

She cares about me that much.

And suddenly, I am irrationally angry.

"This is so fucking unfair," I growl. I spent three years grieving the loss of my beautiful wife, convinced I'd never meet another woman I could feel that way about again. Then, by some mercy of God, I was lucky enough to do just that, only to have her snatched away.

Again.

I sink onto the sofa, letting my head fall into my hands. How have I ended up here? Why is this so fucking complicated? I don't want to lose Daisy. I want the complete opposite.

"It's okay," she says quietly. "I know it's a difficult situation. I'll... I'll go." She steps past me to grab her bag off the coffee table, but I reach out and tug her onto my lap, heat pressing at the back of my eyes.

"No, you won't. I should be able to have the woman I'm crazy about *and* my son. I shouldn't have to choose." *Crazy about* is an understatement. Just thinking about what Daisy did for me, fuck...

I can't deny it anymore. I'm in love with her.

And that thought terrifies me more than losing my son.

Shit, Pauline was right. Losing Lydia was the worst thing that ever happened to me, and I can't lose another woman I love.

"Wes—"

I capture her mouth with mine, plunging my hands into her hair. She doesn't hesitate, swinging her leg over my lap so she straddles me. Her hands find my face, thumbs stroking my cheek as her tongue laps at mine, her hips rocking on my stiffening cock.

"You're not going anywhere," I rasp, untangling one hand from her mane to slide it up her thigh. I can feel the heat pouring out of her, and my other hand tightens in her hair, making her whimper.

"Are you sure? What about Jess? How will we—"

"I don't want to think about that now." I don't want to think about Jess, about my feelings for Daisy, about this mess we're in. I don't want to think about anything other than burying myself inside her.

But I'm also painfully aware that if I make love to her now, I will no doubt blurt out my feelings, and after everything today, that doesn't feel like the right thing to do.

So when Daisy gives me a dirty grin and says, "Do you want me to distract you?" I can't help but nod.

"Yes. Take your panties off."

Heat flares in her eyes and she climbs from my lap, reaching under her dress to wriggle her underwear down her legs. My cock flexes at the sight, at the way she steps out of the pink lace, looking at me expectantly, awaiting my next words.

"What else do you want?"

She loves me bossing her around when it comes to sex. At first I thought it was because she was inexperienced and wanted instructions, but I see now it's a kink. She gets so turned on when I take charge, and honestly, I'm all too happy to oblige. I didn't realize I was into that, but the way this woman responds to my commands makes me harder than steel.

"I want you to ride my face."

Her breath stutters. "Really?"

"Fuck yes. Get over here."

I slide down from the sofa onto the floor, my head leaning back at just the right angle for her to sit over me and hold the back of the couch.

Daisy looks nervous as she stands above me, her lemon-yellow dress obscuring the parts I want to see. I grab her hips and nudge her onto the sofa, her knees falling on either side of my head. Her dress covers my face, so it's just me and her sweet, wet center. Her musky scent fills my nostrils, and I suck it deep into my lungs.

As much as I want to hide under here forever, I lift her dress away so I can breathe, and look up at her. She's gripping the back of the couch, her eyes dark and wide as she stares down at my head between her legs. She frees a hand to hold her dress out of the way as I lift my tongue to meet her slickness.

"Fuck," she whimpers, her body spasming over me as I give a long, slow lick, savoring her taste. "I've fantasized about this."

"Yeah?" Another agonizingly slow swipe of my tongue.

"Y-yes."

"Tell me, babygirl." I scrape my beard across the tender skin of her inner thighs, making her quiver.

"I can't..."

Withdrawing my tongue, I send her a stern look. "Tell me, Daisy." When I give a tiny nip on her clit, she sucks in a sharp breath.

"It was on my bed," she confesses, her cheeks streaking with pink.

I reward her by hooking my arms around her thighs and tugging her firmly onto my mouth, sliding my tongue inside her.

"Oh—God—"

"More," I demand into her swollen flesh. "Tell me more."

"I..." She bucks her hips as I suck her clit into my mouth. "I put a pillow between my legs and pretended it was you."

*Fuck.* My dick pulses as I imagine Daisy in her room, rubbing her needy little pussy against her pillow and picturing my face. My hands tighten on her thighs, tongue and lips working over her throbbing clit.

"It was wet when I was done," she pants, hips rocking against my mouth now.

I growl into her pussy, my own hips instinctively lifting, my cock raging at the lack of friction. I hadn't known my babygirl was such a filthy little minx, but every time we fuck, I learn something new that turns me on even more.

"You're such a dirty girl." My fingers dig into her flesh possessively. "*My* dirty girl. All mine."

"Yes," she rasps. "All yours." She grips the back of the couch, riding my face with abandon now, her wetness all over my beard, my chin. I fucking love it, love the way she's getting exactly what she wants and isn't holding back.

Her eyes meet mine, half-lidded and dark with passion, and one final long suck on her clit pushes her over the edge. She pants my name as she grinds herself on my mouth, wringing every last drop of pleasure from her body. When she finally stops quivering, she climbs off and collapses onto the sofa. I wipe my mouth, rising to sit beside her.

"That was amazing." She slumps against my side, sighing with pleasure, but my cock is still thick and hard in my pants, her taste warm on my tongue, and even though I should probably stop, should force myself to figure out what we're going to do about Jess, I'm still not ready to face it.

"I'm not done with you yet, babygirl."

Her eyes are glassy as she leans away to meet my gaze.

"I want you on your knees for me."

A filthy grin slowly curls along her mouth, and she

climbs off my lap, kneeling on the floor between my parted legs.

"Unzip my pants."

She bites her lip, leaning forward to unbuckle my belt and slowly slide my zipper down. Her hands brush my erection as she passes, and it twitches eagerly, sending heat sizzling through me. She hasn't wrapped those pretty little lips around me yet, and now seems like the perfect time.

"Take my cock out."

A shudder moves through her at my words, legs pressing together on the rug. Before she can complete her task, I lean forward to tuck her loose hair back over her shoulder, then tug her dress and bra down, freeing her breasts.

"Perfect," I say thickly, motioning for her to continue.

She reaches into my boxer briefs, her hand circling my shaft and pulling it out. It throbs the instant she touches it, hot and aching against the cool skin of her palm.

"Is it weird to say I love your dick?" she murmurs, gazing at it reverently as she begins to stroke.

I give a dark chuckle, caressing her hair. "Not at all, baby. I love every part of your body."

"Oh, well, if I'm allowed to list *all* the parts I love..." She grins, reaching one hand up to unbutton my shirt. Then she runs her fingertips across my beard, my chest, my stomach, rising to her knees to kiss me as she jerks me slowly.

Honestly, the way this woman worships me... I feel like a god.

Her mouth moves lower, and when her teeth find my nipple and bite gently, heat sparks through my abdomen. Christ, I didn't even know I liked that.

I reach out to touch her breasts, cradling them in my hands, rubbing my thumbs over their rosy peaks. "I absolutely love your tits."

*For fuck's sake.* I mentally roll my eyes at myself. Seriously, *tits*? I sound like a freaking caveman.

"I like you calling them that," she purrs, arching into my hands. "It sounds so dirty."

I shake my head as she lowers herself between my knees, focusing on my cock. "You never stop surprising me, Daisy. Everything about you turns me on."

She gives a grunt of arousal, looking up at me from under heavy lids as she rubs her thumb over my tip, collecting the bead of precum and bringing it to her mouth, sucking her thumb clean.

Jesus Christ.

"Everything about *you* turns me on, too. I mean it, Weston. Everything."

God, the way she says my name in that husky voice. She's so fucking perfect, face flushed and lips moist, my taste on her tongue and my cock in her hand. I want to capture her like this forever.

"Is there any film left in that camera?" I ask roughly, motioning to the Nikon sitting in her bag on the table behind her.

She glances over her shoulder. "A few shots. Why?"

"Pass it here, baby." She hands me the camera, and I raise it to my eye, watching her through the viewfinder. "These are just for me." I press the shutter, watching as it captures her dark gaze, her fingers curled around my length. Her mouth hooks into a naughty grin, and I press the shutter again, needing to record that image forever.

Needing *her* forever.

Fuck. I can't think that. I don't know how I can have that.

The moment she takes me into her mouth, all thoughts evaporate from my head. My entire existence narrows to this moment, to the sight of Daisy's lips wrapped around me, the feel of her soft, warm mouth.

My breath hisses out as she sucks, fingers flexing around my base. She bobs up and down, the heat of her mouth making my balls draw up tight. Nothing has ever felt so good.

Then she pops off, looking up at me uncertainly as she licks her lips. "Tell me what you like. I've never done this before and I want to do it properly."

A disbelieving laugh rumbles out of me. "You could have fooled me, babygirl. You're doing fucking great."

The smile that breaks across her face makes my heart pull taut. She's so happy with my praise.

"Keep going," I tell her, threading my hand into her hair and winding it around my fist. "Just like that."

She takes me back into her mouth, squirming as she does, clearly still aroused.

"Touch yourself while you suck me, baby. Make yourself come with my dick in your mouth."

Her moan reverberates down my shaft as she lowers a hand between her thighs, reaching under her dress. She looks so fucking depraved like this, with her lips wrapped around my cock and a hand between her legs, and I have to take one last photo. Then I toss the camera aside and give in to the pleasure, watching her work.

"That feels so good."

She whimpers, hand moving faster under her dress, legs shifting restlessly.

"Look at you, sucking my cock like such a good girl."

She grips my base tighter, trying to draw more of me into her mouth. It makes pleasure wash through me, brings me closer to the edge, and my fist tightens in her hair.

"Yes, like that," I grate out, voice shredded as I feel

myself losing control. I reach down to touch her breast, tweaking her tight nipple with my fingers. "Take all of me, baby."

Another moan vibrates down my shaft as she draws me back into her throat, gagging on my size. Heat bolts through me, and when she reaches down to tug on my balls, I explode.

"Fuck, Daisy—"

I'm dimly aware of her writhing and groaning on the floor as I spill down her throat, one hand tight in her hair, a bestial moan tearing from my mouth. It takes me a few minutes to blink the haze from my vision, and when I finally look down at Daisy again, she's licking my shaft clean, smiling at me like a fucking porn star.

Christ.

She lets me go with a sigh, pulling her dress up and rising to her knees to flop onto the sofa beside me. I tug my still-throbbing dick back into my pants and pull Daisy into my side. She's so soft and pliant in my arms, letting her head fall onto my exposed chest. I can't imagine sending her home, telling her she can't use the darkroom anymore after all the progress she's made.

"Daisy... I want nothing more than to take you up to my bed, to sleep beside you, but Jess is coming home after work later, and..."

"I understand." She sits up, adjusting her dress. "I'll go."

"I'm not ending things," I say hastily, needing to make that crystal clear. "I don't want to lose you, baby. I just need to figure this out."

My mind works overtime, trying to come up with a solution to this mess. Jess said he works late into the night, so I could still see Daisy in the evenings before then. She could still use the darkroom when Jess is at work, as long as she's careful not to leave any of her belongings lying around the house. Not that she would—she's too considerate for that. I could put a lock on the darkroom. It's unlikely Jess would go down to the basement anyway; he lives his entire life in his room on the top floor. Daisy couldn't sleep over, of course, that would be too risky, but I could go to her place when her roommate is out of town, and if we ever wanted to get more time alone we could go to the beach house. In fact...

"When do you next have a day off?"

She glances back at me. "Um, I'm not working next weekend. Why?"

"I want to go to the beach house with you. On purpose this time."

Her brown eyes sparkle. "I'd love that."

I grin, ignoring the unease that snakes through me. I'll make this work. It's not ideal, but it means I don't have to lose her. Of course, it also means lying to Jess, but as I pull Daisy against my chest, that feels like a small price to pay.

I press my lips to her forehead, my heart pummeling my ribcage, and not because she just gave me the blowjob of a fucking lifetime. It's not about sex at all, actually. It's about *her*. It's the way I spend all day looking forward to seeing her. The lengths she goes to to care for me, from the simple act of creating coffee just to make me smile, to bringing me a birthday cake despite me telling her I couldn't see her anymore. The fact that she was willing to sacrifice whatever this is between us, so I could have my son back in my life.

*You've been through hell, Wes. You deserve something good.*

I think of Pauline's words from my birthday lunch, and my arms tighten around Daisy protectively. She might be prepared to sacrifice us, but I'm not. I won't let go of this woman now that I've found her. I can't.

Not even for my son.

# 32

## DAISY

Weston grins as we step from his car. I stretch, my back stiff after the drive and a ten-hour shift at Joe's. When I try to grab my duffel bag from the trunk, Wes nudges me aside and carries both our bags, leaving me trailing behind him up the path empty-handed, but grinning with anticipation.

I run my eyes over the weathered cedar siding, burnished by the evening light, and I'm immediately taken back to the night Jess and I arrived, and how hesitant I felt with him. Guilt swirls through me as Wes and I step inside, thinking about Jesse's apology last week, and that he made up with his dad. He's not a bad guy, and he doesn't deserve us sneaking around on him like this.

But as Wes drops our bags and turns to me with a sinful smile, any guilt I feel melts away. Weston is worth everything.

"Hi," I say, which is ridiculous after we just spent an entire car ride together. But we didn't say much; instead, we enjoyed each other's company.

Wes and I have hardly seen one another since the day he reconciled with Jess. He's popped into Joe's each morning for coffee like the old days, and when no one else is around, I'm able to steal a quick kiss, even though what I've really wanted is for him to lock the door and bend me over the counter. Ever since that moment in his basement, I haven't stopped thinking about the taste of him, the feel of him in my mouth. I'd always assumed giving head was a chore, something you did for the other person, and I'd never expected to enjoy it myself, but being on my knees, watching him slowly lose his mind as I pleasured him, made me feel powerful. I've been horny as fuck ever since, and I know I'm not alone in that because Wes spent the entire car ride here stroking my thigh, touching my hair, gripping my hand. I was electric and restless in my seat, hoping that once we got inside he'd rip my clothes off and reward me for waiting.

But as Wes steps back from me, my brows collide in frustration. What's he doing? That car ride was like two hours of foreplay, and I'm more than ready to go.

"Let's eat," Wes says, his voice husky as he turns away from me, dragging a hand through his hair.

I suppress an impatient groan. "Fine," I reluctantly agree. The sooner we get that out of the way, the sooner I can get his clothes off. "What do they have in the way of takeout around here?"

He shakes his head, eyes shimmering. "We're not eating in. I want to take you out."

"Out?"

He nods, reaching a hand for me, then letting it fall away, taking another step back. "If we don't, we'll just spend the entire weekend in bed."

A laugh escapes me. "So what if we do?"

He chuckles too. "I want to take you out, babygirl. You deserve to be spoiled."

My reluctance softens. That's so sweet. I've spent the past few days worried he would cancel our trip, that he'd come to his senses about us and call it off. I can't imagine how difficult it must be for him to hide this from Jess, especially since they've finally reconnected. I've found it hard to fathom how he could think it's worth the risk—that *I'm* worth the risk.

"What if we run into someone you know?" I ask.

He scrubs a hand over his beard. "I think we'll be okay. I hardly know anyone around here, and we'll go to the next town. I just... I want to go on a date with you, Daisy. A proper date. All we've done is eat takeout in my kitchen and have sex. Don't get me wrong"—his lips tilt into a wicked smile—"it's fucking awesome. But you deserve more. I want more with you."

Warmth radiates through my chest. I want that too, and I was beginning to wonder if it would ever be possible.

"That sounds really lovely," I whisper, wishing he were closer so I could kiss him, but he's being very intentional about keeping physical distance between us right now, and I want to respect that.

A grin breaks over his face. "Good. I've made reservations at a restaurant in Mattituck, so we'd better get ready."

He reaches for our bags again, turning to pass through the kitchen, and I follow him, feeling weird at not heading to the room I stayed in last time, which makes no sense. Why would I stay anywhere other than in his bed?

And what a glorious bed it is; huge king mattress, frame and headboard upholstered in a cream, bouclé fabric, draped in a soft, seafoam-colored linen comforter, adorned with throw pillows. The room itself is an off-white, with simple wooden nightstands, intentionally distressed to give them a rustic look.

Weston sets our bags in front of a pair of matching dressers, topped with various photo frames. My gaze drifts across them—pictures of the beach, of Jess as a kid, playing in the sand—and comes to rest on one of a beautiful blond woman. She's around late thirties, with hazel eyes, and the kind of smile that lights up an entire room. There are more pictures, too. One of her with Wes and Jess on the beach, one of her with Weston, laughing. They're a lot younger in that one, and I don't have to ask to know it's his late wife, Lydia. She's beautiful, and even though I never got to meet her, my heart snags a little, thinking of what Weston and Jess lost.

I glance at Wes, but he's too busy looking through the closet to notice, and I force myself to rummage through my bag for something to wear.

"You can shower in here if you like." He motions to the ensuite I hadn't noticed, and pulls a dress shirt from the closet. "I'll get ready in the main bathroom."

"Thanks," I murmur, watching him leave.

I head into the bathroom and turn on the shower, letting the hot water flow over me. My mind wanders to the pictures of Lydia again, and it occurs to me, as I scrub the day of work from my body, that I've never seen a picture of her before. Weston has a huge house in the city, but there's not a single picture—or item that appears to belong to a woman—anywhere. Not in the living room, not in the entertainment room in the basement, not in the ensuite bathroom—not even in his bedroom.

And that makes my heart break a little for him.

I step from the shower and towel off, wiping the fog from the mirror. When I pull on my new dress, I take a moment to admire my reflection. I splurged a little and went shopping, knowing we were going away for a couple days. Tonight I'm wearing a mustard-yellow dress, printed with large, white daisies and green leaves. It's got buttons from the sweetheart neckline to the hem, which falls to just below my knees, and thin spaghetti straps. It's probably more suited to the beach than a fancy restaurant, but it's all I've got, so it will have to do.

I pin my long hair back in a low bun, letting a few loose strands fall around my face, and paint my lips with a soft, blush-colored lipstick. Then I slide my feet into my navy peep-toe sling-back wedges, hoping I look okay for wherever Weston is taking me.

"You ready, baby?" Wes calls from the entry hall, and there's an anxious ripple through my belly. I grab my purse and head out, smiling shyly.

I don't know why I feel nervous all of a sudden. He's seen me completely naked, seen me with no inhibitions, with nothing to hide behind, but somehow, walking into the foyer to meet Weston for a proper date, I feel more exposed than ever.

I needn't have worried, though, because the minute I meet him at the front door, his jaw falls open.

"Holy shit, Daisy. You look..." He finishes the sentence with an audibly rough exhale instead of actual words, and I take that to mean I look alright.

"Thanks," I say, smoothing a hand down my dress. "I didn't know we were going out, so I only had this, but—"

Weston strides across the foyer and slides his hand around the back of my neck, crushing his mouth to mine.

"You are so beautiful," he rasps, walking me backward until I hit the door. "Fuck, babygirl, you're killing me."

His mouth lands on mine again, hot and urgent, and I

hook a leg over his hip. He responds by sliding his hand under my dress and up my thigh to grip my ass, palm warm on my skin. When I feel his hardness dig into my belly, I moan into his mouth.

He draws away with a low growl, adjusting himself, dark eyes pinning me to the spot. "I want to fuck you up against this door."

Heat shudders through me. I *love* it when he says filthy things like that to me.

"But we have a reservation..."

I give a whimper of disbelief as he reaches for his wallet and keys, a grim expression on his face. My dress falls back down my thighs, and I scowl in frustration. What kind of torture is this, to get me all riled up and then just *stop*?

He notices my agitation and takes my hand with a chuckle. "Let's go have a lovely meal together, and afterward I'll make sure it was worth your while."

My impatience dissolves, and I lift his hand to brush a kiss over the back of it. I don't need sex from him to make it worthwhile—just being with him is enough.

"Sounds good," I say, tipping my mouth into a smile. I glance at my reflection in the large mirror in the entry hall and laugh.

I'll need to reapply my lipstick.

———

I'M COMPLETELY under-dressed for the restaurant—an upscale place with linen tablecloths that overlooks the harbor—but Weston doesn't seem to notice. He keeps reaching out to touch me, his gaze straying from my face to sweep over me from head to toe. More than once I catch him looking at me instead of his menu, and it makes my chest bubbly and fizzy, makes me feel like I'm living inside some kind of dream instead of reality.

How did I end up here, with this man who can't keep his eyes off me, can't keep his hands to himself? This man who wants to make me smile, who cares about me in ways I could never have imagined possible, who knows exactly how to make my body feel good?

I don't know, but I'm going to appreciate every damn second of it.

The menu is almost too fancy for me to understand, but Wes makes a few suggestions that sound good, and when he orders us a bottle of wine, I try not to balk at the price. I tell him that a bottle of expensive wine like that is wasted on me, but he waves my words away, insisting I'm wrong. I've never had a man spend money on me like this before, and I'm not going to lie, it's good to be spoiled.

"Tell me about your week," he asks as the waiter pours our drinks. His gaze is warm, focused on me as I take my first sip of wine, savoring the notes of cherry and chocolate that are somehow infused into the dark red liquid.

So, he was right. This wine is to die for.

A happy sigh escapes me as I set my glass down. "My week was good. I had that shoot with Kyle and Violet."

Weston nods. He must have seen the photos I snuck in to develop while he and Jess were at work. Thankfully, he gave me a key to the basement entry, so it's been easier to slip in unnoticed, but I'd be lying if I said I didn't feel a little sick with dread each time I did.

"The prints looked fantastic, Daisy. Did Violet and Kyle like them?"

I nod, unable to suppress the excitement that surges through me because they didn't just *like* the prints, they were thrilled. So thrilled, in fact, that Violet begged me to shoot their wedding. They're having a small, quiet ceremony in their yard a few weeks from now, and I was honored by her request. It's a little intimidating, shooting someone's wedding—there's a lot of pressure to capture the magic of the most special day of their life—but I couldn't say no. Not when she's supported me so much.

I tell Weston about her request and he beams at me, reaching for my hand across the table. Creases form beside his ocean-blue eyes as they move over my face. It's that look from the meadow, the one where he's so happy and proud of me, where my achievement means the world to him.

It's a look that, if I'm being really hopeful, is filled with love.

But I'm too afraid to let myself want that from him.

"You know, I'm not at all surprised," Wes murmurs, lifting my hand to his lips. "You're so talented, baby. You have a knack for capturing the mood of a moment so well."

I'm not the only one who can capture that; I also developed those pictures he took of me while I was on my knees for him last week, and *holy crap*, I couldn't believe them. The look of pure lust in my eyes, the hunger on my face as I wrapped my fist around him. I've never seen myself like that before—as a powerful, sexual woman—but it showed me another side of myself. It showed me the woman that Weston sees, and it helped me to see that there might be more to me than I give myself credit for. That I'm more powerful than I realized.

"I got an invite to their wedding," Wes adds, during our starter of locally sourced oysters.

"Well, I'll see you there." I smile, but only to disguise the uncertainty rippling through me. I'm not sure if he wants to tell Violet and Kyle about us, given they're so close to his home and probably see Jess around.

"I'd love to have you as my date," Weston adds quietly, as if sensing my unease. "But I'm not sure if that's a good idea just yet. Not until we figure out what to do about Jess."

"I get it," I murmur. The waiter sets my entrée down in front of me, and I poke at it absently, wondering how we're going to make this work. How it's even possible for us to be a couple.

Why does it have to be so complicated?

"How was it having Jess home?" I ask, taking a bite of salad.

Wes nods, chewing thoughtfully but saying nothing, and my brows pinch together in concern.

"Did you argue?"

"No." He reaches for his wineglass and takes a long sip. "No, it was good. I wasn't sure if I should... if you wanted me to talk about him."

"Oh." I set my fork down. "Why wouldn't I?"

He lifts a shoulder, going to set his wine down, then changing his mind and taking another gulp. "He's your ex-boyfriend, Daisy."

"Who also happens to be your son," I point out.

Weston's gaze flits to mine. "Exactly. I guess... I don't know the protocol for this situation."

I reach for his hand where it rests on the stem of his wineglass, and squeeze. "We only dated for a few months, and I never felt for him anything close to what I feel for you. Besides, I knew you first."

Wes chuffs a small, quiet laugh. "That's true."

I withdraw my hand, reaching for my wine. "The protocol is whatever we want it to be. Yeah, it's a little weird, but I want to hear about your relationship with your son. I want to hear about how things are going for you guys. It's important to me."

His eyes move between mine, as if trying to read me. Finally, he exhales, giving in to a smile as he picks up his fork again. "Things are going well. He had a night off work and we hung out and watched a game, had a few beers. It was really nice."

My heart swells as I listen to Wes talk about spending time with his son. Not just for him, but for Jesse too. For the relationship they both so clearly need.

And when we finish our meals and Wes rises to use the restroom, I force myself not to think about how much worse this makes it for me and him. How it could, very possibly, spell the end of whatever is blossoming between us.

I drain my wine and place my napkin on the table, a sigh of satisfaction slipping from my lips. The food, the wine, the company—this has been an absolutely perfect evening.

"Daisy?"

My head jerks up in surprise at hearing my name in such an unfamiliar setting. I glance over my shoulder, and my blood turns to ice in my veins.

# 33

# DAISY

Rex weaves between the tables, gaze intent on me. His auburn hair has been cut and styled neatly with gel, and he wears a button-down shirt tucked into his dress pants. He's smiling broadly as he approaches, but my pulse races so fast I can barely compute what's happening.

How is Rex *here*? Why?

More importantly, did he see me with Weston?

"I thought that was you." He reaches the table and takes my hand, raising it to his lips for a kiss, as if I'm a princess in a Disney film. Everything about this moment feels out of character, and I blink, trying to make sense of the situation.

"Um, hi, Rex."

"You know, that's so strange." He laughs, gesturing over his shoulder. "I swear I just saw Mr. Abbott in the bathroom."

My breath freezes in my lungs. Somehow, I manage to coax my mouth into a bemused smile.

"That's weird." I choke out a laugh. "Are you sure it was him? I doubt he's out of the city." Rex opens his mouth to say something, and my pulse spirals. "Who are you here with? You look..." I wave a hand at his clothing, taking a moment to really look at him. He's like a different guy, dressed up like this; if he hadn't called out to me, I'm not sure I would have recognized him. "Fancy," I finish at last.

Rex laughs, raking a hand through his hair, pink washing his fair complexion. "I'm, uh, on a date."

He motions to a woman across the restaurant, and when I turn to see, she gives me a shy little wave. I return her wave, glancing back at Rex. He's dressed up, on a date at a *very* expensive restaurant, and he looks almost... nervous. I've never seen him like this.

His expression turns serious. "I'm sorry it didn't work out with you and Jess."

"Oh." I fold my hands in my lap. "Yeah, that wasn't... it wasn't meant to be."

"Still, he has you to thank for figuring things out with his dad," Rex adds warmly. He gives my shoulder a squeeze, but it's not the kind of touch from him that, in the past, would have made me flinch; it's a sincere gesture.

I smile tentatively, flicking my gaze over his shoulder to make sure Wes is still in the bathroom. "Oh, I don't know if I'm the reason—"

"You are," Rex assures me. "You, and his boss. If it weren't for the two of you, he wouldn't have gone back home. I think it's good he did."

I nod. "They need each other."

"For sure." Rex nods in agreement, rocking on his heels. "And no doubt therapy is helping him to work through everything."

My lips part in shock. "Jess is in therapy?"

Rex tilts his head to the side. "He didn't tell you?"

"I... no."

He cringes. "Shit, I probably shouldn't have mentioned it then. He's been going for about a month now, after I drove him back from the beach. I could tell he was in a really bad place, and I pushed him to go see someone my shrink recommended."

I reach for my near empty glass to cover my shock, draining the last dregs of wine. *Rex* is in therapy? Somehow, that's almost harder to believe than Jess.

"I think it's really helping," Rex adds. "I felt bad about kicking him out last week, but I'd already agreed to the sublet at my place. Anyway, I was hoping it would make him reach out to his dad. He's lucky to have a father who cares as much as Mr. Abbott."

I set my glass down and assess him carefully. My mind flashes back to that moment in his car when Jess used the restroom, leaving me alone with Rex. He'd told me he was worried about Jess's partying, worried he might lose his job if Jess didn't settle down. In that moment he'd seemed like a completely different guy, but I'd dismissed it.

I think of Weston's disdain for him, for how I've felt every other time I've been around him. But it dawns on me now that's when he was with his friends, when he was "one of the boys." If that's all Weston has seen of him too, no wonder he doesn't like him.

It's clear now, though, that we've been missing another side to him—the side he showed me briefly on that car ride. The side who has his buddy's back, who wants to make sure his best friend is okay. The side who goes to therapy and dresses up to take his dates to fancy restaurants.

Is it possible that Rex is... mature? That he only acts like a dickhead around his friends, because *they're* dickheads? Because the guy standing in front of me now is nothing like the guy I thought I knew.

Realization flashes through me as I recall the way my parents spoke so poorly of Beth and her family, because they didn't really know them. Because they didn't *want* to know them.

And I bet, if Weston saw this side to Rex, if he knew the lengths Rex had gone to, to take care of Jess, he'd feel differently.

I see a flash of salt-and-pepper hair behind Rex, and my stomach capsizes. If I'm not careful, that moment could come about a lot sooner than I'd like.

"Well, it's been great to see you, Rex," I say, my voice coming out in a ridiculously high pitch. I try to signal with my eyes to Wes over Rex's shoulder, but he turns and heads to the hostess to settle the bill, buying me another moment.

Thank God.

Rex makes no move to leave, so I rise from the table, grabbing my purse. "I should be off..."

"Who are you here with, anyway?"

"Just, um, a girlfriend." It's a blatant lie, because it's really not that kind of restaurant, and I pray my scarlet complexion doesn't give me away. "And I should, uh, go now."

His forehead wrinkles with amusement. "Where are you rushing off to?"

Over Rex's shoulder I see Wes head in our direction, and my insides plunge. *Look at me, Weston!* I silently plead. *Do not come this way! Abort!* I try to surreptitiously catch his eye, but he's gazing down as he walks, smiling to himself, lost in thought. Panic floods through me as Rex begins to turn, as if to follow my gaze.

"I need the bathroom," I blurt, and Rex's eyes swing back to mine. "I, um, have a *feminine* problem." I touch my lower belly and grimace, knowing this is the one thing that will make any guy freak out.

It works like a charm, and just in time; Wes glances up as he approaches the table, his gaze landing on Rex, and his eyes widen in alarm. He glances about frantically, looking for somewhere to hide, before ducking behind a large ficus.

"Oh." Rex seems to catch my drift, raising his hands and taking a step back, as if whatever is plaguing my womanly parts is somehow contagious. "I'll leave you to it."

"Thanks," I say, turning toward the bathroom, but as soon as his back is turned, I scurry across the restaurant and slip out into the parking lot, my heart jackhammering in my throat.

That was *way* too close.

I slink behind Wes's Audi, peering over the roof into the restaurant. From here I can see Rex with his date, pouring her a glass of water from the pitcher on the table, taking her hand and listening intently as she speaks. I really had the wrong idea about him.

Weston's car bleep-bleeps as he unlocks it from across the parking lot, and I slip into the passenger seat, keeping my head down. A moment later he joins me, his mouth set in a thin line as the car roars to life and we peel out of the parking lot.

"I'm sorry," I blurt, guilt gnawing at me. "I tried to get rid of him, but he was talking about—"

"It's okay." Wes reaches for my hand, holding it in his over the gearshift. "I don't think he saw me."

*I swear I just saw Mr. Abbott in the bathroom...*

I shake Rex's words from my head. The most important thing is that he didn't see us *together*. He can't draw any conclusions without that.

"It was close, though," I say, and Wes gives a silent nod. I want to tell him what I realized about Rex, how I think he might be a better guy than we've given him credit for, but now isn't the time.

All I can think about is the huge risk Weston is taking by being with me, and whether I'm worth it.

# 34

## WESTON

Daisy is quiet on the drive back from the restaurant. I think we're both a little shaken after almost getting caught by Rex. I mean, what the fuck was he doing *there*, of all places?

"Thanks for dinner," Daisy murmurs as I pull the car into the driveway and shut off the engine.

"You're welcome, babygirl."

I press a kiss to the back of her hand, and she gives me a faint smile before letting herself out of the car and silently walking up the path. I follow suit, opening the front door to toe off my loafers. We head to the bedroom where she perches on the end of the bed, looking pensive. I wander to the sliding glass door, gazing out to the pool below. The moon hangs high and bright in the sky, making the pool water shimmer with silver. The night air is hot and sticky, and I'm restless as I unbutton my shirt and cast it aside.

"Let's swim," I say, glancing back at Daisy.

She blinks as she surfaces from her thoughts. "In the ocean?"

"The pool." I fish my swimming trunks out of the dresser. "It's nice at night."

A smile brushes her lips. "Okay."

I turn away as she changes, knowing that if I see her naked we won't make it to the pool, but when I find her in that white string bikini, it's still a battle to head outside. I have to march ahead of her, straight to the pool's edge, without looking back.

I dive head-first into the water, the cold doing little to ease my agitation. Daisy gingerly lowers herself down the pool ladder, and I begin to swim a few laps, attempting to settle my whirling thoughts.

The way Daisy asked about Jess at dinner made my heart clench. It's been great to spend time with him that doesn't involve eye-rolls and strained silences. The night we watched the game was just like old times, and it felt so good to hang out with him again. As much as I wanted to share that with Daisy, I have to remember they used to date. Not only that, he didn't treat her well. I wasn't sure if she would want to hear about how I'm enjoying spending time with the guy who was a jerk to her. That she does shows how much she cares, and knowing I can talk to her about my son, even with their history, means the world to me.

What I didn't say is that it's also been impossibly hard to be away from her all week. My bed somehow feels even emptier now, and while I love spending time with my son, his presence in the house has come at the cost of having her there. I'm beginning to wonder if that's too high a price to pay.

Almost running into Rex tonight was a wakeup call. When I saw him standing at the table with Daisy, my stomach dissolved. I'm fucking lucky he didn't see me, but even him seeing Daisy was bad enough. He might be a pain in the ass but he's not stupid, and he could put two and two together. I can only pray his date distracted him enough to not give much thought to Daisy's presence at an upscale restaurant only ten minutes from my beach house.

What we're doing isn't sustainable. I know that. It's not fair to keep this from Jess, to make Daisy feel like we have to hide. It's not fair on myself, seesawing between the guilt at lying to my son and the longing for Daisy when she can't be with me. I believe what Pauline said, that I deserve something good, and I know that something, or rather *someone*, is Daisy. She's the light in my life, the one who brought me back from the brink, who helped me reconnect with my son, who made me remember how good it feels to be alive. She's more than I could possibly have dreamed of.

I just don't know how to keep her without losing Jess.

When I surface from my laps, I lean back against the tiled edge of the pool, watching Daisy paddle through the dark water. Her pale skin glows in the moonlight, giving her the look of a mythical creature from another world. For all the magic she's brought into my life, she may as well be.

She swims across to rest beside me, smiling as she leans her head back to gaze at the moon. "It's so beautiful here."

I hum in agreement, but I'm not looking at the scenery. I'm looking at the woman next to me. Beautiful doesn't even begin to describe her.

"Why don't you have any pictures of Lydia up at home?"

Her words take me by surprise, and I falter, dragging my gaze away as she turns to look at me.

"You don't have any family pictures, or anything that looks like it belongs to a woman," Daisy adds gently. "I didn't realize until I saw the picture of Lydia on your dresser here."

"I..." My breath trickles out. I can feel Daisy's eyes on the side of my face as I try to find the words to explain why I hid everything that reminded me of Lydia. "I did, for a while, but it was too hard, seeing her face all the time, seeing her stuff everywhere. I guess it was an act of self-preservation." I chuff a grim laugh. "Maybe not the best approach, but it made it easier."

"I get that," Daisy murmurs, circling her hands through the water. "What about now?"

I lower my gaze to meet hers. "What do you mean?"

"It's been three years. I'm not saying it would be easy to be reminded of her more, but maybe it wouldn't be quite so hard now."

I nod. She's probably right. I'll always miss Lydia, but the feeling doesn't crush me like it used to.

"You should put some pictures up." Daisy gives me a tentative, encouraging smile. "You should see her and remember her every day."

My brows tug together curiously. Though I don't disagree with her, it seems odd that my new girlfriend would want me to cling to memories of my late wife.

"Would you be comfortable with that?" I ask.

Daisy gives me a strange look. "Of course. Why wouldn't I be?"

"Well, I haven't thought about it all that much, but... I guess I figured you'd want me to focus on you. That you wouldn't want pictures of another woman in my house."

"*Another woman*?" Daisy twists in the water to face me, her expression incredulous. "She's not some other woman, Weston. She's Jesse's mom. You were a family." Her voice thickens, eyes shining with emotion in the moonlight. "I know she'll always hold a special place in your heart. You should acknowledge that. *We* should acknowledge that. Don't hide her away because of me. It's not right."

I stare at Daisy in disbelief, my heart a hot ember in my chest.

Holy shit, I am so in love with her. How could I not be? She can't stand the thought of me not honoring Lydia's memory. She's actually *upset* at the notion of me not keeping Lydia in my home, in my heart. I never dreamed I could meet someone who would understand the fine line I have to walk between loving my late wife while also moving on with someone new. But that's Daisy; mature and thoughtful and so fucking selfless it hurts.

I reach for her hand, the feeling of love mingling with grief in my ribcage. I'd never considered how much the two emotions fit together, but they do. They have to. There's love in grief—love that has nowhere to go when you lose someone—but there's grief in love, too, knowing that one day you could lose the person you love. That you *will* lose them, eventually, because nothing in this world is permanent.

And if losing Lydia taught me anything, it's not to hold back a second of love.

"Come here," I say, my voice raw as I tug Daisy roughly into my arms. She gasps in surprise, then settles against me with a little sigh. Her legs wind around my waist, arms around my neck, and I capture her mouth with mine. I only mean to kiss her, to hold her close, but she's warm and slippery against my chest, and I can feel the heat of her center against my thickening cock through her thin bathing suit. Before I can stop myself, I tug at the ties on her bikini top, just like I imagined doing the last time I saw her in this, at Sullivan's Cove. It slips from her chest and floats away, her perky breasts floating on the silvery surface of the water.

I dip my head to take one in my mouth, and Daisy moans into the night air. Her hands go to my trunks, and I help, kicking them off under the water. When her warm fingertips wrap around my length, stroking eagerly, I let out a low growl. I spin us so her back is against the tiled wall of the pool, sliding a knee between her parted legs. My mouth devours hers as she tugs on my cock, the heat of her core on my thigh. I lift my leg, loving the way she grinds herself on me, thinking about what she told me the last time we were together, that she fucked a pillow on her bed and imagined it was me. I've jerked off more than once since that night, picturing her in her room, horny and desperate as she rubbed herself on her pillow. Now she's rubbing against my thigh, whimpering as I lift it to meet her rocking hips, the water lapping at her tits as she moves. There's nothing sexier than this woman owning her sexuality, giving in to the things that make her feel good.

But I need to be inside her. It's been too fucking long.

I untie the strings of her bikini bottom, wrenching it from her body. Then I wrap her legs around my waist, taking her mouth in a deep, hungry kiss as I push into the heat of her. Her breath comes out on a long, tortured moan, fingernails digging into my shoulders as I pin her to the wall of the pool, burying myself inside her.

"Fuck, Weston." Her voice is a throaty whisper. "You're so deep."

"You like it deep, baby?"

She nods, wide-eyed as I withdraw and slam back into her, pool water sloshing out onto the tiles. I'm desperate to tell her I love her, that she's turned my entire world upside down and I can't imagine my life without her, but after our conversation about Jess, after everything with Rex tonight, I'm not sure if it's the right time.

And if I'm being really honest, I'm fucking terrified. I know she cares a great deal for me, that much is clear, but *love*? She's only twenty-five. I'm the first guy she's ever been intimate with, and our situation is beyond complicated. I don't want to rush her into something she's not ready for, pressure her to say something she's not sure about. And once I say it, I can't take it back.

So, no, I won't tell her I love her. Not tonight.

But I can fuck her like there's no tomorrow.

"Yes," she breathes as I thrust deep inside her again. "Harder."

"Fuck yes, babygirl." My voice is a savage rasp as I press her into the tiles. "You want my cock?"

"Yes."

"Tell me."

"I want your cock. I need it." Her mouth finds my neck and sucks. "More, Wes. Please."

I grasp her thighs and drive myself deeper, her tight heat gripping me with every thrust. I want to fuck her so hard she feels it tomorrow, fuck her so good she'll never dream of being with another man. I want her to know she was built for my cock, that she's the only woman I can imagine being with now. I want to show her all the things I can't bring myself to say.

"Tell me who you belong to," I choke out, unable to stop myself. I need to hear her say it, need to know she understands. "Tell me, Daisy."

"I'm yours, Wes. I'll always be yours."

*Damn right, baby.*

Under the bright moonlight, we cling to each other in the pool, our bodies moving in a frenzied, primal rhythm, the only sounds our grunts and the sloshing pool water. And as we both reach our limit and fall apart in each other's arms, I make a vow to myself.

I'll do whatever it takes to make sure I keep Daisy.

# 35

# DAISY

I wake early on Sunday morning. The room is silent, apart from the distant roar of the waves and Weston's soft snores beside me. I'm not used to waking up to so much quiet; usually I'm woken by the sound of Denise crashing about in the kitchen at 5 a.m. as she gets ready for her early morning spin class. It's especially annoying on my days off.

I roll onto my side and let my gaze travel over the sleeping man beside me, knowing I will never tire of waking up next to Weston, seeing his eyelashes flutter as he chases the last remnants of a dream, listening to his rhythmic breath, feeling his warmth in the sheets.

I don't want to go home today. This has easily been the most blissful weekend of my entire life, and I don't know what awaits us in the city. I know Wes can't keep lying to Jess, and I don't want him to. How can he truly heal things between them if he's keeping our relationship a secret? How can he be close with his son like he wants to, if there's a huge lie standing between them?

I don't have the answers. All I have is this man beside me, and the silent wish that I won't have to let him go.

---

WE SPEND the day in bed, only climbing into the car to come home in the late afternoon when we can't put it off any longer. Then we ride most of the way back to the city in silence. Well, not complete silence. Steely Dan keeps us company, along with a little Fleetwood Mac and Creedence Clearwater Revival. More of the music the Walkers loved, the music I haven't let myself listen to in so long, but with Wes, it feels safe to listen, to let myself hurt a little as I remember the time I spent with the people who loved me, the people I lost. It's the same with my photography. Somehow Wes anchors me, makes me feel like the pain won't hurt too much. Maybe it's because he's felt it too. Or maybe it's because I just feel so good when I'm around him, that letting in a little sadness every now and then is okay. Good, even.

We pull onto the Brooklyn-Queens Expressway, and Weston slides a glance my way. "You okay?" he asks.

I nod, chewing on the inside of my lip. I might be unsure about what will happen for me and Wes back in New York, but I can't deny the anticipation I feel about shooting Violet and Kyle's wedding in a few weeks. My plan is to spend some time studying wedding photography, to get a few books from the library and find some good websites and pour over the images—the lighting, composition, the details they capture. I'm not a professional, but both Violet and Wes have told me I have a natural talent, a good eye. Willow used to tell me that all the time. Hopefully, with a little research, I'll be able to capture the magic of Violet and

Kyle's special day. In the past I would never have considered taking on a project like this. I wouldn't have believed I could do it, but again, it comes back to Wes, to the self-belief he's instilled in me, the strength I find inside myself when he's by my side.

I think of my old life, the one where I'd work all day at Joe's so I could catch a glimpse of Weston, where I wouldn't date because I was scared of guys judging me for being so inexperienced, where I couldn't even admit to myself that I wanted to do photography again. The life where I'd go home to Netflix every night and numb myself to my feelings. That life was easier, less risky. My heart wasn't on the line like it is now, and there was no threat of Weston losing his son for good because of me.

But it sure as hell didn't feel like this.

It didn't feel like living at all.

"You're quiet," Wes murmurs beside me.

I send him a secret little smile. "Just thinking about you."

Tiny creases form beside his eyes. His hand finds mine over the gearshift and holds it tight. "I'm always thinking about you, Daisy. I can't seem to stop."

A quiet laugh slips from me. A year ago I would have given anything to hear him say that, but as we speed toward his house—to the life where he has to hide me away from the world, from his son—it's harder to enjoy those words.

I stroke my hand over Weston's upturned palm, letting it rest on the inside of his wrist. His pulse thuds reassuringly under my fingertips, and I close my eyes, feeling the life force move through his body. It feels so precious, and a jagged shard of fear slices through me as I hold my hand there. My pulse spikes, but I force myself to breathe deeply and try to figure out what, exactly, it is I'm afraid of.

It's the fear of losing him, I realize.

And just like that, everything becomes clear. I haven't been stuck because of my job, or my apartment, or my lack of experience with men. I've been stuck because I closed myself off from the world, from life. It's been eight years since I really cared about anyone, and that person—those people—were taken from me. I never realized, but I've been too afraid to care about anything or anyone since.

Until Weston. He cracked my heart open and made me fall in love with life again. He saw something in me that I'd forgotten was there, and he brought it into the light.

I open my eyes, letting my gaze rest on him as he drives, focused on the road. I've never met a man who made me feel like this—like who I am, what I want, how I feel matters. But that's Wes in a nutshell, isn't it? He cares so much. He took Jess in when he needed somewhere to stay, he put that camera into my hand when I was too scared to pick it up myself, and then he built me a freaking darkroom in his house, so I'd have no excuse not to develop my photos. When he loves someone, there are no limits to what he'll do for them. That's just who he is.

A good, kind, generous man.

I swallow, glancing away. Does Wes love me? I can't be sure, but I know without a shred of doubt that I love him. And if I truly loved him, I wouldn't let him lose his son.

If we can't find a way to work this out, if us being together jeopardizes his relationship with Jess...

I can't let that happen. I can't let him give that up for me.

We pull onto Fruit Street and Wes finds a place to park, easing his Audi into the spot.

"Are you sure it's okay for me to be here?" I ask, scanning the street for any signs of Jess, my middle churning with unease.

Weston nods, turning to look at me as he shuts off the

engine. "Jess closes the bar on a Sunday, so he won't be home until after two in the morning. At least come in and have dinner." Wes leans back on the headrest, gazing at me with a soft sigh. "I'm not ready for you to go home yet."

I smile faintly. I'm not ready to go home yet either, and not only because my roommate is a nightmare. I don't want to be away from Wes. I want to move into his beautiful house and wake up to him every morning, to greet him when he comes home from work. I want to build a life with this man, and I don't think I'll ever be able to have that.

"I don't have a plan," Wes says, reaching out to tuck a strand of hair behind my ear. "I don't know what we're going to do about Jess. But... we'll figure something out. We have to. This weekend was..."

"I know." I lean across the center console to press my mouth to his. "For me too."

His eyes are deep blue in the darkening evening light, but he looks tired. Weary. Like he's carrying too much. Carrying something he shouldn't have to.

"We'll figure it out," he says again, and I'm not sure if he's saying that to reassure me, or himself.

We climb from the car, Weston fetching our bags from the trunk before we ascend the steps to his house. I know he says Jess isn't home, but I can't ignore the quiver in my gut as we enter the foyer. Every second Wes and I spend together is another step closer to things imploding with him and Jess, and I can't stand the guilt that gouges my heart. He's risking too much.

"What do you feel like for dinner?" Wes asks as we kick off our shoes.

"I don't know," I mumble. Food is the last thing on my mind.

I follow him into the kitchen absently, colliding with the

back of him as he comes to an abrupt stop. The bags fall from his hands, landing in the middle of the kitchen floor with an ominous thud. The air in the room tightens and shrinks.

I step around Wes to see what's halted his steps, and my gaze lands on a stack of photos scattered across the kitchen island.

My photos.

There are the ones I took of Brooklyn Heights. The ones of the West Village. Some of Violet and Kyle from the shoot we did.

But that's not all.

There's the ones of Wes in bed, half-naked, asleep.

The ones he took of me, on my knees, in the basement.

I stare at the photos in shock, my stomach plummeting.

What are they doing on the kitchen island? How did they get here?

When I glance at Wes, his expression shifts from confusion to panic, and my insides follow. There's a sound from the living room, and we turn to find Jess glaring at us.

My lungs seize.

"Oh, good," he snarls, glancing from me to his father. "You're both here." He steps into the kitchen, his frame rigid, his expression stony. "It seems we have a few things to discuss."

# 36

## WESTON

Fear washes cold over me.

I glance from my son to the pictures on the counter, my pulse ringing in my ears. How did he find those? There's a lock on the darkroom door. I know, because I installed it myself. Besides, Jesse *never* goes down there.

But none of that matters. He's found the pictures. He's seen them.

He knows.

My gaze swings to Daisy. The color drains from her face, eyes wide and startled. Her hands shake at her sides, and it takes everything in me not to reach for them. Before I can soothe her, I need to face my son. I need to tell him what's been going on and take responsibility for what I've done. No more lies.

I press my eyes shut, sucking in a fortifying breath. "Jess—"

"Tell me this isn't what I think it is," he growls. I expect he's talking to me, but when I open my eyes, he's glaring at

Daisy, holding up one of the photos. The one of her, on the floor between my knees.

The one *I* took.

Like an idiot.

Shame and mortification flood through me, stealing the air from my lungs. How could I have been so *stupid*?

"It's—" Daisy begins, but Jess continues to speak right over her.

"Tell me"—his voice vibrates with rage—"that this is *not* a picture of you with my father."

Daisy raises a trembling hand to cover her face, which is somehow both translucently pale and bright red at the same time. She doesn't answer Jesse's question, but the way she hides her face in shame is enough.

"I don't believe it." He flings the photo onto the floor with sudden revulsion, as if it's turned into a dead rat in his hands. "I figured I had to be wrong. That it wasn't what I thought. But this..."

"We didn't mean for anything to happen," I say, but Jess acts like I'm not even here, his furious gaze trained on Daisy.

"*Him*?" he spits in outrage. "You wouldn't fuck me, but you'll fuck my *dad*? Do you know how old he is, Daisy?"

She studies the floor, her voice wobbling as she says, "He's not that old."

"He's fucking ancient!" Jesse throws up his hands in disbelief, and I take a step forward. Anger comes off him in waves, his gestures become jerky and agitated, and my first instinct is to protect Daisy.

"Jess—"

"Don't you fucking come near me!" he spits, hands raised in my face as he finally acknowledges my presence.

I sigh, knowing there's no way to get through to him when he's this irate. "Please calm down," I urge, trying to keep my voice steady. "I didn't mean for this to happen, and we—"

"Calm down?!" he bellows incredulously. "How could you do this? You *knew* I liked her."

I open and close my mouth, faltering, because that's not entirely true; it wasn't until he came to see me at work that I realized how much he liked Daisy.

By then, it was too late.

How could I have known, though? He'd brought home another girl, then stormed out of both our lives, and while that doesn't justify us getting together, it does show how little he cared for her at that point.

How little he cared for both of us.

"Don't blame your dad," Daisy says, shaking her head. "He was very clear that nothing would happen between us, but I—"

"Stop." I place a hand on her arm. Jesse's gaze follows the motion, and I quickly pull it away. "It's not your fault."

"Wes—"

"No, Daisy." I turn back to Jess. There's no way I'm letting her take the fall for this. It's time to come clean. "I've known Daisy for a while. She'd been making my coffee at Joe's for a year when you brought her home as your girl-friend. I had intended to ask her out, and I was shocked as I didn't know she was seeing anyone, let alone my own son. I did my best to act like I had no interest in her, but I couldn't help how I felt. I know it was wrong. Then after things with you, we... We didn't mean for it to happen, Jess."

He barks a cold laugh. "Of course you didn't." His gaze swings to Daisy, lips curled in disgust. "You want me to call you *Mommy* now?"

She recoils in horror. "No!"

"You'll never replace my mom. *Never.*"

My blood heats with irritation. This kid fucking disappeared after his mother died, leaving me to pick up the pieces alone. He has no idea what it's taken for me to get to the point where I could consider spending my life with anyone else, and while he's allowed to hate me for moving on with Daisy, I'll be damned if I let him take his resentment out on her.

"Don't you dare speak to her like that."

"What are you going to do about it?" He steps forward, hands colliding with my chest, eyes wild with fury. His obstinate attitude throws gasoline on my own anger, until it's a raging fire inside me.

"Let me remind you, Jesse, that you didn't treat Daisy well. You behaved like a child. You partied without her, leaving her alone. You brought another woman home, for fuck's sake!"

"That doesn't—"

"I'm not finished," I growl, fists flexing at my sides. "It wasn't only her you walked all over. It was me too. You've treated me like shit ever since your mom died, and I've allowed it. I've tiptoed around you, bending over backward to try to make things better between us."

There's a flash of shame on Jesse's face, and I continue.

"I didn't want to act on my feelings for Daisy. I knew that wasn't okay, but then you stormed out of the beach house. You moved out without telling me. You wouldn't take any of my calls. You missed my birthday, just like you have for the past three years. And you know what? I snapped. I decided that if you didn't care, then why should I?"

My chest shudders with my jerky breaths as I confront my son, and behind me, I feel Daisy's hand brush my lower back. It's a tiny gesture of solidarity, giving me the strength to go on.

"Do you realize how fucking painful the past three years have been for me? How hard it's been going through this on my own?" My eyes are hot and I swallow hard as I continue. "You weren't around, Jess. You took off, and I had to deal with everything alone. I never thought I'd meet someone who would help me heal from what happened, another woman who would make me smile, but I did. I met a barista who went out of her way to make my day better. You're right, she won't replace your mom. No one can. But she can make my life a hell of a lot better just by being in it."

My words hang in the air, and I stand there, breathless, hands on my hips as I stare at my son. I hadn't planned to let all that out, but I've been holding in my frustration with Jess for so long that once I start, I can't stop.

"I'm sorry that the woman I met was someone you also liked. I didn't plan for that to happen, and if I could make it be anyone else, then I would, but I can't. I can't choose who I fall for. None of us can." My voice cracks, and I won't let myself look at Daisy in case she can see right through me. "Daisy and I are together, and you need to come to terms with that."

But Jesse hasn't heard a word I've said. With his face twisted in a scowl, he's fixed his gaze on Daisy's hand as it rests on my lower back. And I realize that telling him what's on my mind hasn't made me feel any better. If anything, I feel worse because while all of it is true, it doesn't justify acting on my feelings for Daisy behind his back, and even if it did, it doesn't explain why I didn't tell him when we reconciled a week ago. Why I acted as if nothing had changed.

Jess shakes his head as he regards me bitterly. "So you've just spent the past week lying to me? Acting like things are all good with us, then sneaking off to fuck my ex-girlfriend?"

I can *feel* Daisy's grimace beside me.

"You're right." I shake my head with remorse. "I haven't been honest with you since you got back, and I regret that, but I didn't sneak off to—"

"Where have you been all weekend?"

Now it's my turn to grimace. He's got me there.

I square my shoulders, forcing myself to answer honestly. "We were at the beach house."

"I knew something was off," he mutters. "I could just tell. You were way too happy to get out of town, even though I was home. Now I know why."

We both glance at the photos strewn across the kitchen island, and my gut twists with nausea as I imagine him finding them, imagine the shock and horror he must have felt.

"I'm sorry, Jess."

His eyes are sad when they come back to mine. "I should have known better than to trust you."

His words land like a grenade in my chest.

Because he's right.

I might have been able to excuse what happened with Daisy after his behavior at the beach, but I sure as hell can't excuse it now that he's home.

"I'm sorry," I say again. "I should have told you. It hasn't been easy keeping this from you."

He spins on his heel and stalks into the living room, returning with a bag stuffed full of his clothes, and my heart plummets.

"Well, you don't have to worry anymore," he says, pausing in front of us both. When he hoists the bag onto his shoulder, anxiety clenches my stomach. "I'm leaving."

"Please, Jess," Daisy begs beside me. "Don't do that. I'll go."

The anxiety transforms into full-blown panic. "No, you

won't." I reach for Daisy's hand, grasping it tightly, before turning back to Jess. "Let's talk about this."

He stares at our clasped hands, his jaw hard. "There's nothing to talk about."

I release Daisy's hand, taking a step toward my son. "There's everything to talk about. Please don't run away again. I want you in my life, Jess. I don't want to lose you again."

He swallows, his eyes cold as they move over my face. "Well, you should have thought about that before you got together with my ex." And with that, he stomps out of the kitchen.

I stare at the photos scattered across the kitchen island, waiting for my shuddering pulse to settle. Daisy holds her breath beside me, and when I eventually glance at her, she looks stricken.

"Wes..." Her voice trembles, just like her hands as she wrings them in front of herself. "I'm so sorry—"

"Shh." I reach for her, relieved to finally be able to pull her into my arms again. "It's not your fault."

"But—"

"No, baby. He was bound to find out." I breathe in the smell of her, letting it calm me. Letting it soothe the sting in my chest from Jesse's parting words. From knowing I've lost my son for good now.

"But not like this," Daisy whispers against my chest. The front of my shirt feels wet, and when I look down, I notice she's crying.

"I'm sorry he spoke so harshly to you." I wipe her cheek, and she shakes her head.

"It's not that," she sniffles. "It's... you've lost him again, Wes. After he came back."

I sigh, fighting the tightness in my throat. Trying not to let myself think about what this means for me and Jess.

"It's all my fault." She tries to step away from me, but I hold her shoulders firmly.

"Don't you dare say that. None of this is your fault."

"They're my photos," she protests.

"Not all of them. Not..." I cringe, once again mentally cursing myself. "Not the most incriminating ones."

"But if I wasn't with you, none of this would have happened," she presses.

"Daisy..." I take her face gently in my hands, forcing her gaze to mine. "If you weren't with me, he never would have spoken to me. The only reason I even had him again to lose is because of you."

But as I say these words, I have to wonder. If I'd spent the short time we had together lying to him, did I ever really have him back at all?

I glance at the dark street beyond the windows, thinking of my son, heading into the city alone. My heart crumbles at the thought of him hurting, but I shove the feeling away.

I still have Daisy, and I can't let her see how losing Jess hurts. That's not fair to her.

Clearing the emotion from my voice, I take a step back, trying to regain some semblance of normality for us. "We should eat," I murmur, but Daisy shakes her head.

"I'm not hungry."

"Me neither," I admit.

We exchange a somber glance, and it drives a wedge into my chest. I wrench my gaze away, picking up our bags, and trudge up the stairs to the bedroom. Daisy follows me wearily, and we're silent as we brush our teeth and climb into bed. It's not late, but we're exhausted and emotionally wrung-out.

We don't make love tonight. Instead, I hold her tight, savoring her warmth, the comfort of her breath fanning over my chest, the gentle caress of her fingertips on my skin.

But I'd be lying if I said I wasn't heartbroken over my son's words.

Over knowing I'll never get him back now.

# 37

# DAISY

I hardly sleep, despite trying. I have an early shift at Joe's, but there's no way I can deal with going to work after what happened tonight. After tossing and turning for hours, I send Dave a text telling him I have a stomach bug and that I won't be in. It's a lame excuse, but he's such a good guy that he instantly replies, telling me to rest up and get better. I should feel bad about that, but I already have too much to feel bad about.

Jess has left, and it should have been me.

Beside me, Wes rolls over, trying to get comfortable, and I hold my breath. A few minutes later his soft snores assure me he's asleep, and I breathe out slowly.

I can't stand it. I can't stand that I'm here in his bed while Jess is gone. I knew this was too much of a risk, and now I have the proof. He's lost his son because of me.

Seeing those photos on the kitchen island... I've never felt so sick to my stomach. How did Jess get his hands on them? I must have left the darkroom unlocked when I last went in there. I'll never forgive myself for my carelessness.

I glance at Wes, sleeping beside me. His face is the

epitome of peace: eyelashes fanning out over his cheeks, the whiskers of his beard smushed into the pillowcase, lips parted slightly as his breaths come slow and even. But it hides the turmoil he feels underneath. I know it. He might have done his best to hide it from me after Jess left last night, but I know him better. He's hurting.

I'll never forgive myself for causing that. And I don't think I can live with the guilt of coming between him and his son.

At some point I must drift off because I'm woken by Weston gently touching my shoulder.

"You're going to be late for work," he murmurs sleepily.

"Called in sick," I mumble in response. I burrow back into the pillow, mostly unconscious, but vaguely aware of how thoughtful it is of him to worry about me, even after everything.

That's the last thing I remember before drifting off again. The next time I wake, sunlight presses at the blinds, and Wes sits in the chair by the window nursing a cup of coffee, one hand scrubbing absently over his beard in thought.

I reach for my phone, shocked to see it's nearly ten. "Shit, sorry," I say, bolting up in bed. "Don't you have to be at work?"

"I called in sick too."

"Oh." I rub my eyes, the events of last night coming back as my brain reboots. They bring a sour taste to my mouth, and I contemplate crawling back under the covers and never coming out again.

"How did you sleep?" he asks, setting his coffee down.

"Not great." I stifle a yawn. "You?"

"Fine." His face is lined and tired, his complexion

drained of its natural color, eyes missing their usual spark. My heart is a tight ball of misery at the sight.

"I'm sorry," I begin again, but he shakes his head.

"It's okay."

"No, it's not." I swallow, guilt clawing at my throat. "It's not okay, Wes."

"Daisy." He wipes both hands down his face, and that's when I realize he's wearing the same shirt he wore yesterday. He must have just pulled it on this morning, which is unlike him. It's wrinkled and not buttoned properly, the chaos of his appearance belying how unsettled he feels inside.

I can't stand it. This isn't my Weston. This is a man who's broken.

A man *I've* broken.

"We can't keep worrying about this. What's done is done." He rises from the chair with a weary sigh, lowering himself onto the bed beside me, but when he reaches to tuck my hair behind my ear, smiling in a way that doesn't reach his eyes, my heart cracks.

"I don't think I can do this, Wes."

He hesitates, letting his hand fall. "What?"

"I can't be responsible for you losing Jess."

His eyebrows sink into a frown. "You're not—"

"I am." My voice breaks as tears press at my eyes. "He left because of me. And I can't—"

"He left because of *me*," Wes corrects. Up close I can see the dark circles under his eyes, suggesting he didn't sleep nearly as well as he said.

"No." I rub my temples, frustration bubbling up inside me. "You can't blame yourself. Everything was fine between you until he found those photos. Until he realized I was—"

"Daisy, stop." He reaches for me, and the tears brimming in my eyes fall. "Come here."

I shake my head. "I can't, Wes. I can't live with myself, knowing I've come between you and your son."

"But you haven't—"

"I can't," I repeat, wiping my cheek. "You need to fix things with him, and you can't do that as long as I'm around."

"What are you saying?" Weston asks, his eyes wild with alarm as I push the sheets off my legs and tug my clothes on with unsteady hands. He springs to his feet. "I want to be with you, Daisy, and if Jess can't understand that, then I don't care."

"But you *do*." The words nearly lodge in my throat as I turn to gaze at him. I touch his cheek with a shaky hand. "I can't let you give him up for me."

"I'm not giving him up. It's Jess's choice."

"If I wasn't here, he wouldn't have left. It's as simple as that." I take a deep breath and reach for my bag. "I think... I think we need to take some time apart until you can fix things with him."

"Please don't do this, baby." Wes's voice cracks. "I can't lose you."

My heart curls in on itself. "You're not losing me, but we can't carry on as if nothing has happened. We could pretend for a while, but you'd resent me for making you choose. And I can't live with the guilt."

"Daisy—"

"We're just taking some time apart," I reassure him, but even I'm not sure if it's the truth. What if he can't fix things with Jess? Could I live with that, or would it spell the end of us for good?

I push the thought from my mind. We have to at least try.

"You need to focus on fixing things with Jess," I say firmly. I step onto my tiptoes to press a kiss to his cheek, and when I pull away, his expression is agonized. "Promise me you'll try."

I turn for the door, and Wes grabs my hand. "Where are you going?"

"I..." I don't know how to answer. I should go home, but I'm in no mood to deal with Denise's shit. Work is out of the question, and there are very few other places in the city I feel like being. Maybe I could try to find Jess, try to explain my side, but I'm sure I'm the last person he wants to see right now. And I don't know if I could even face him.

Wes examines me worriedly, and I open my mouth to tell him I'm not sure.

But instead, I shock myself completely when I say, "I'm going to visit my parents for a while."

# 38

# DAISY

I t's a four-hour ride from the city to my parents' house in Hartford, Connecticut, and at least five times I almost get off the bus.

But each time I gather my things to leave, something stops me. I haven't felt the need to return home in seven years, but for reasons I don't understand, I'm propelled there now. It's not until the bus pulls into the station in downtown Hartford that I wonder if it's because Jess left, if some part of me subconsciously identifies with him. I walked out on my parents, too. Jess is hurt, but I know Wes still cares about him deeply, even if he can't see that. Maybe part of me hopes for the same with my parents.

I get an Uber from the bus station out to West Hartford because it's fast, and I'm worried if I wait too long I might lose my nerve. I don't know how my parents will respond to me showing up unannounced. We didn't end on great terms, much like Jess and Weston. I never forgave them for the way they responded to the death of the Walkers, to them taking my camera away. And when I finished high school, and I announced that I wanted to move to New York, we argued about why I wasn't going to college. They couldn't understand that I was still grieving the loss of my friends, that I didn't *want* to study to become an accountant like my father and brother. I left for the city three days later, and haven't spoken to them since. They haven't so much as sent a birthday card, and while that was hard the first year, in the years that followed, it was a relief. It meant I was free from any obligation to them. Free to get on with my life.

It wasn't until the morning that Dave handed me my celebration cupcake and praised me for seven straight years at Joe's that I realized I hadn't gotten on with my life at all. I'd gotten stuck.

And it wasn't until I got close to Weston that I finally became unstuck.

But I can't think about that now.

I step from the car and thank the driver, turning to look up at my parents' house, set back from the pretty, tree-lined street. It looks the same as it did when I left; a two-story colonial style house with white siding, much like every other house on the block. Every other house, apart from the Walkers'. Their house had been painted in a faint lilac color with dark lavender trim, but as I glance to my left now, I see those colors have long since been replaced with the same boring white. My throat tightens as I look away, forcing my feet up the front path.

My parents could barely afford this house when they bought it, but more important than the practical aspects of living within our means was convincing everyone we were doing well as a family. My parents have always been about keeping up appearances, despite what might go on behind closed doors.

It takes three attempts for me to ring the doorbell because my hands tremble so much. When it finally trills there's no answer, and I hike my duffel bag further onto my shoulder, wondering whether I should feel relieved. I'm turning to leave when the door opens, and my mother blinks at me.

"Dahlia."

There's a name I haven't heard in a long time. It hits me like a punch to the stomach, and I suck in a breath.

What am I doing here?

"Er, hi... Mom." I consider correcting her—telling her that's no longer my name—but I can't get the words out.

She blinks again, fussing with the collar of her shirt. My mother has always worn immaculate button-down shirts, despite never having a job. In the seven years I've been away, she hasn't changed. Her shoulder-length hair is still dyed a dark brown—it started going gray years ago, but she'd never admit that to anyone—and her brown eyes have a few more creases around them, but she's the same woman I remember.

The same woman who could never be the mom I needed her to be.

"What are you doing here?" she asks, clearly flummoxed.

That's understandable. I'm a little flummoxed myself.

"I, uh, I've taken a few days off work. Thought I'd... visit."

"Right." She glances over her shoulder, then back at me. "Your father isn't home from work yet."

I nod. Of course—it's late afternoon on a Monday. He'll be home in an hour or so.

"That's okay," I say, shifting the weight of my bag. "I can see him later."

Her thin brows snap together in a frown. "You're not

wanting to stay for dinner, are you? I wasn't expecting guests, and I have book club tonight."

*Guests.*

I press my eyes shut in frustration.

Seven years. It's been *seven years* since I've said two words to this woman, and all she can think about is whether I'm going to mess with her evening plans.

"I'm not hungry," I mumble, wondering if it's too late to get a bus back to the city. What was I thinking, coming here? Did I really believe things would be different?

"Well..." Mom wrings her hands, as if someone's put her in a difficult position. "I guess you'd better come in."

I follow her inside, noting how the interior of the house hasn't changed at all. The wallpaper looks tired and dated, but as we enter the kitchen, I notice they've redone the countertops. My mother glances around the kitchen, hands fluttering anxiously as if she doesn't know what to do with them, then she snatches her cellphone from the counter.

"I have to make a quick call," she tells me, pulling her lips into a tight smile. She waves vaguely at nothing in particular. "Make yourself at home."

I try not to laugh at the irony of this as she heads out of the room.

Dumping my bag on the counter, I sink onto a stool. I glance at my own phone and notice a missed call from Weston, but shove it back into my pocket with a sigh. Mom's voice drifts down the hall and I lean closer to the door, trying to catch her words.

"...completely out of the blue... no idea what she... home... yes, now please..."

My head drops into my hands and I blow out a long breath. I don't know what I was expecting from my mother.

A smile, maybe? Some pleasure at seeing me? Would it be so ridiculous as to go so far as to expect a hug, even?

Clearly.

"That was your father," Mom says, breezing back into the kitchen. "He's on his way."

"Oh." I shift my weight. "You didn't have to..."

"Nonsense." She waves a hand. "I didn't know how long you were staying, and he'd hate to miss you."

I find that hard to believe.

Mom sets her phone down, eying me. "How long *are* you staying?" she asks casually.

I fight the urge to roll my eyes. "I'm not sure. Maybe a few days."

"Right. Okay. I'll make up your bed." And with that, she's off again, as if she can't bear to be alone in a room with me for five minutes.

I push up from the stool and go to the fridge, hesitating before pulling out a soda. This might be the house where I grew up, but it doesn't feel like home. I feel more at home in Weston's house.

I shake the thought off and take a long pull of cola, studying the photos pinned to the fridge door. My parents on a cruise. My parents in Florida. My brother, Brad, and some woman I assume to be his girlfriend, Anne. I've never met her, but on the rare occasion we've emailed, Brad has mentioned her.

I turn and wander through the living room, looking out at the backyard. It's weird being back here. So much has changed for me, not in the years since I left, but in the time that I've been with Weston. That's why I have the courage to be here right now. If you'd told me a few months ago I'd be coming back here voluntarily, I'd have laughed, and not in a funny way. But with the inner strength Wes has given me, I know I can face this. I can face *them*.

My heart slumps thinking about Wes, and my eyes sting. I don't want to give him up. I don't want to think about what will happen if he can't make it right with Jess.

"Dahlia."

My father's voice interrupts my thoughts, and I turn around, blinking from my reverie. I must have stood there for some time, because the shadows have moved across the yard, and the half-drunk soda is warm in my hand.

"Hi, Dad."

He sets his briefcase on the coffee table and gives me a once-over that makes me break out in a cold sweat.

"How's big city life treating you?"

My grip tightens on the soda can. "Good."

He grunts as he loosens his tie. His mustache is almost entirely white now, and his dark eyes are beady as they appraise me. I forgot how intimidating my father can be, and just like that, I'm right back to feeling like a kid in trouble.

"How's the career?"

I swallow, shrinking into myself. "It's... coming along."

I'm almost relieved when my mom enters the room again.

"Oh, good. I see you two are getting reacquainted."

Dad nods, saying nothing, his eyes still assessing me, and somewhere inside, a small voice reminds me that I'm not the same kid they let down all those years ago. I'm an adult now.

I think of all the times Weston tried to talk to Jess, all the times he wished his son would sit down and work through the things that stand between them. And while it should probably come from my parents first, I know that's not going to happen. It's up to me to repair things.

In that moment, the childlike, hopeful part of me truly believes it's possible.

I take a deep breath, facing my parents squarely. "I was hoping we could talk."

They exchange a frown.

"About what?" Mom asks, issuing a nervous laugh.

Is that a joke?

"About... everything. The Walkers. The fight we had after I graduated. My life since I left—"

"Dahlia." My father pinches the bridge of his nose, releasing a long-suffering sigh. "Is that why you've come here? To dredge up the past?"

The balloon of hope inside my chest bursts.

I glance between my parents, fighting the sting in the back of my throat as reality settles back in. As much as I want what Wes has with Jess—what he desperately *wants* with Jess—I can't have that. It's not the same, and it never will be.

"I..." I shake my head, the notion of having a healthy, healing conversation with these people suddenly striking me as preposterous. "No," I mumble. "Never mind."

"Anyway, your mother has her book club tonight," my father says, apropos of nothing.

A weary sigh gusts out of me. "I know."

"And as for dinner—"

"It's fine." I set my soda can down, wanting nothing more than to get away from the people in front of me. "I'm actually quite tired," I say, despite it being no later than 5 p.m. "I might head up to bed."

Dad just grunts again, and Mom looks relieved.

I direct a tight smile their way and scoop my duffel bag from the floor, turning to go. "Goodnight."

"Night," Mom calls, and as I begin up the stairs, I hear her mutter to Dad, "I don't know what she's doing here. It's very odd."

I pass my brother's room, untouched since high school, like a time capsule designed to preserve every aspect of my brother's life, but when I come to my room, they're cleared it completely; my photo wall has been taken down, my bed moved to a different corner, with a different comforter. My desk is gone, my dresser replaced with an elliptical machine. My books, my clothes, my knick-knacks... Every trace of my existence erased, as if I'd never lived here at all.

As if they couldn't wait for me to be gone.

I know I'm the one who left. I know we fought. But they've kept every scrap of Brad's room intact. I might not be perfect, but I'm still their *child*.

Except, it never really felt like that, did it? I always felt like I belonged more with the Walkers; that's why it hit me so hard when they died. And maybe my parents knew that. Maybe they resented it and wanted to punish me for it.

I shove the door closed and collapse onto the guest bed as tears flood my cheeks. If I've ever had any doubt about my decision to cut off contact with my parents and move to the city all those years ago, it's gone now. They can't even muster the *pretense* of enthusiasm at my being here. And while I'm not surprised, I can't say it doesn't hurt.

It doesn't matter how old you get, how independent, every child wants their parents to love them. To care about them. To be happy to see them.

My mind flashes on Weston, on the way his face lit up when he talked about how great it was to reconnect with Jess. What must it be like, I wonder, to have a father who is that delighted to have you in his life? A mother who would do almost anything for you?

I don't know. But I do know that I can't be the thing that comes between Jess and his father. I can't live with the guilt that eats away at me, knowing I'm what drove them apart.

I curl into the mattress, letting the tears fall freely, suddenly exhausted after the confrontation with Jess last night, after hardly sleeping since, after spending hours on the bus. Then that cold reception from my parents...

I'm so worn down, so disheartened by the unfairness of my life. Finally, I find a man who makes me feel loved in ways I could never have thought possible, a man who helps me reconnect with the thing that brings me more joy than anything.

And what happens? I fuck it all up. Jess finds my photos and my life implodes. What was I thinking, even developing those photos?

Hell, what was I thinking even picking up a camera again? Photography has done nothing but get me into trouble, every single time. I should have known better than to chase that dream again.

And when I think about that, my mind returns to the Walkers, to the people who believed in me and encouraged me. To the family I had, for such a short time, and lost.

I wriggle under the comforter and pull it over my head, letting the pillow soak up my tears. I'm not welcome in this house, and yet I can't imagine going back to my life in the city; my job at Joe's, my shitty bedroom in Denise's apartment.

A life without the man I love.

All I can do is cry, and hope I sleep through the night.

———

IT'S EARLY when I wake. My head hurts, my eyes puffy and sore from my crying jag last night. I peel myself from the bed, tiptoe along the hall to the bathroom, and splash water on my face. I can't bring myself to look at my reflection.

In the kitchen, I switch on the coffee machine and listen to it drip while looking out over the backyard. The sun peeks through the hedge that borders what used to be the Walkers' yard and ours, and after pouring my coffee, I take my cup and step into the cool morning air. The leaves of the red maple tree glow burgundy in the early morning light, and I pick one up from the grass, twirling it in my hand. When I look up at the branches, the sun pours through in beautiful shafts of light, and the photographer in me aches to pick up my camera and capture it.

I shove the thought away, looking into the dark steaming liquid in my mug. I don't know what I'm doing here, why I was drawn back here. What did I possibly hope to achieve?

But when I glance up and spy the Walkers' old backyard through the fence, realization dawns inside me like the sun rising through the trees.

I didn't come back here to see my parents. I came back to reconnect with the Walkers. With the person I was back then.

With *Daisy*.

I peek over the hedge into their old yard. It's early enough that whoever lives there is probably still asleep, and I push through an opening in the hedge to their side. The garden is nothing like I remember; the wildflowers that Willow had so lovingly nurtured are gone. In their place sit neatly boxed rows of roses, tulips, and other flowers that are far too fancy for themselves. They've even taken down the huge oak tree that Beth and I used to climb.

My heart falls and I turn to go, when my gaze snags on a

profusion of large daisies clustered along the back fence. The very same ones that Willow named me for. They're far enough back from the house that the new owners probably don't bother taming them, and I couldn't be more glad. I set my coffee down and kneel among them, my heart brimming with joy.

"Hi, guys," I whisper, gathering their smiling faces in my hands, but I'm not talking to the flowers, I'm talking to the Walkers, and I swear, on the whisper of the wind, I hear them say hello back.

My eyes well with tears as I press my nose into the flowers, wishing with all my heart that I could see Beth and Willow and Sebastian again. That they were here to help me figure this whole mess out, to encourage me to keep going.

*Keep going.*

The words ring through my head, as if someone else has said them. As if Willow herself is kneeling beside me, her curls sneaking out from her colorful headscarf as she smiles, telling me to keep going.

*Keep going.*

I dash my hand across my cheek, letting myself believe it's her. Letting myself believe that's what she'd say.

Because it is, isn't it? She'd tell me that I've come so far, that I can't possibly give up now. She'd tell me that she's always believed in me, that she's proud of me, that I deserve all the good things in my life.

And I would believe her.

I *do* believe her.

I tug a daisy from the soil and rise to my feet, clasping it in my hands. It reminds me of the meadow at Sullivan's Cove, the first time I picked up that camera and raised it to my eye, and how damn right it felt. I think of how proud

Weston was to see me shoot again, and resolve hardens my spine.

I'm not giving up.

Picking up my coffee mug, I head back into the house. Then I go up to my room—to what was once my room, but is now no more than a guest room—and grab my things. I dash off a quick note to my parents to say goodbye, letting myself cry as I do, because this time it really is goodbye. There is nothing for me here, with them, and I know for certain that moving on is the right thing for me.

I need to go back to the city. Back to my life. I'm not sure what will happen with Weston, but I owe it to him to keep shooting.

And I owe it to us to try to fix things.

# 39

# WESTON

I pace the lobby of the Midtown building, raking a hand through my hair.

It's been almost a week since Daisy left, telling me we needed time apart so I could focus on Jess. A week of me calling him and trying to track him down, so we can talk it through like adults.

So I can get Daisy back with me, back where she belongs.

But either Jess has his phone off, or has my number blocked, and I can't blame him. I got so angry with the way he attacked me when we walked through the door. Daisy and I had just had such a wonderful weekend together, and it was a reality check that took me by surprise. I was angry with Jess, as I have been for a long time, but I was also angry at the universe for putting me in such an unreasonable position. For giving me a woman to love, at the cost of my son. And in that moment, I let all that rage pour out onto Jess.

But now that I've had time alone to reflect, time to toss and turn, miserably missing Daisy, I realize that wasn't fair. He'd obviously suspected something was going on with us, because he'd pried open the lock on the darkroom. Either that or he'd gotten curious, and then discovered the photos.

Either way, I can't begin to imagine the horror he must have felt at finding them. The betrayal at seeing Daisy with *me*, of all people.

*I really liked her... She's so great, and I messed it all up.*

His words have played through my head on a loop, torturing me. Why didn't I just tell him? Why didn't I come clean then and there, and tell him that something had developed between us? I was so shocked to see him when he came to my office that day, let alone have him talk to me, and I was terrified if I told him the truth, he'd turn around and never speak to me again.

Turns out that was bound to happen either way, wasn't it?

I shake my head, trying to focus. That's what happened, and I can't change it. All I can do now is find a way to repair the damage.

Properly, this time.

The elevator doors ping open and a group of men in suits flood out into the lobby. I spot a flash of auburn hair and step forward. This is nothing like I expected, if I'm honest. I did a little research on LinkedIn and found out where Rex works, knowing that if I couldn't track Jess down myself, he could help. Not exactly my first choice, but I'm out of options.

Still, I never expected the weed-smoking, video-game playing friend of my son to be at a midtown office building in a neat suit. I half expected he'd be working at a Chipotle or something, up to his elbows in guacamole. When I followed the address to this building, part of me wondered if it was a joke.

But here he is, crossing the lobby, heading home for the day.

I clear my throat and call his name. He looks my way, his eyebrows springing up in surprise.

"Mr. Abbott?" He turns in my direction, threading through the crowd to appear at my side. "What are you..."

"Do you have a moment?"

Confusion passes over his fair features. "Uh, sure. What's up?"

"I thought we could grab a beer, if that's okay? There's something I want to discuss."

His expression morphs into something that suggests he might know what I'm referring to. He motions for me to lead the way, and we head into the fading evening light. We cross Broadway and find a bar with standing outdoor tables. They're crammed full of people, but one clears as we arrive, and Rex snags it. I head to the bar to grab us a couple of beers and return to find him playing with a cocktail straw, looking pensive.

When I hand him his beer, he clinks it to mine with a grim smile.

"So... what's up?" he asks, shifting uncomfortably. I guess it must be odd that the father of his best friend—who has only ever glared at him—is now inviting him out for a beer.

"Have you heard from Jess lately?"

Rex swallows, averting his gaze. "Not since... the weekend."

There's something about his answer that makes the hairs on the back of my neck stand on end.

"What do you mean?" I ask carefully.

He grimaces, flicking his gaze up to mine, then back to

his beer. "I'm really sorry. I didn't mean to cause problems, I just—"

"Rex." I'm trying to keep my voice calm, but it comes out as an irritated growl. "What are you talking about?"

He puffs up his cheeks, then exhales slowly. "I saw you and Daisy in Mattituck. I didn't know you were together!" he adds hastily. "I just thought it was odd that you were both there at the same time, and when I mentioned it to Jess—"

"Jesus Christ." I slap a hand to my forehead in disbelief. So he *did* see me. "Did it ever occur to you," I begin menacingly, "that it might not be the best idea to—"

"It wasn't intentional." He lifts his hands to placate me. "I swear. I had no idea you and Daisy were…"

I slam a fist on the table, rattling our beer bottles. I've had about enough of this kid and his shit.

"It's none of your business what Daisy and I were doing there!"

His face pales. "I know, I know," he babbles urgently. "And I never meant to cause problems with Jess. You'd finally gotten to a good place and the last thing I wanted to do was ruin that."

I stare at him, surprised. "What?"

"Well…" His fingers flex nervously on the beer bottle. "I know how difficult things have been between you two. He wouldn't admit to himself that he needed you, and when he finally did, I wasn't going to fuck that up." Rex cringes, as if I'm going to tell him off for cursing like he's ten years old, and I wave it away with an irritated roll of my eyes.

"So you *wanted* him to move back home," I say, trying to make sense of this.

"Of course." Rex looks confused. "He's been struggling for ages."

There's a concerned note in his voice that makes the irritation slowly seep out of me.

"He has?"

Rex nods, twisting his lips to the side as if he's not sure how much to share. "Ever since... I mean, the past few years have been hard."

Ah. It's not that Rex doesn't want to share—it's that he doesn't know how to phrase it. To say that Jess has been struggling since his mom died.

"All he's wanted to do is party, or smoke weed and play video games," Rex adds. "He's found it hard to hold down a job."

My chest tightens. I'd always known Jess didn't want anything to do with me, but I hadn't known how much he'd been struggling outside of that. And as I sit in the middle of bustling Midtown with a warm beer in my hand, absorbing that knowledge, it suddenly occurs to me... how could he *not* be?

He lost his mom when he was nineteen.

And then he lost me too. It might have been his choice, but it couldn't have been easy to go through that without me. Without someone who understood.

But... why did he push me away? If he was so lost, why not lean on me instead?

The answer hits me with such blinding clarity that I wonder how I didn't see it earlier.

Because if he could focus on being mad at me, he wouldn't have to grieve the death of his mom. I was too wrapped up in my own pain to see it—that forgiving me meant having to face what happened. And then he did forgive me—he tried—but right when he started to do that, I all too easily gave him another reason to push me away. I sent him back to the start.

I drop my head into my hands. This whole time I've blamed Jess for putting distance between us, when I haven't been the father he needed. I haven't been there for him.

As if reading my thoughts, Rex speaks quietly.

"I tried to support him. I don't know much about... you know... losing someone, but I tried to help, and when he came back from Greenport, he... It felt like it was getting worse. I was really glad when he agreed to see someone."

I glance up in shock. "*See* someone?"

Rex nods. "She's good, I swear. My shrink recommended her."

"Your..." I think my head might explode. "I'm sorry—both you and Jess are seeing a therapist?"

"Well, not *together*," Rex says with an awkward laugh. "But I think it's helping him."

I blink, processing this. Jess had certainly seemed more calm when he was home last week. A little less angry.

Until I fucked it all up.

"Is he still seeing her?" I ask, and Rex nods.

I blow out a long, weary breath. If Jess is ever going to need a shrink, it will be now. Now that the father he finally decided to forgive betrayed him.

"Argh." I drag my hands over my face. "Did he tell you..." I trail off, letting my words hang in the air, hoping Rex knows what I'm referring to. His grimace tells me all I need to know.

"Not in detail. I called to ask him for a favor while I was out of town, and mentioned seeing you guys"—another grimace—"then I heard him tearing through the house, a shitload of banging, and he said... uh, just that he'd discovered something, and that you and Daisy..." Now it's Rex's turn to trail off, the tips of his ears turning crimson. "Next thing he'd texted to tell me he'd moved out."

"Yeah," I mumble. I probably shouldn't be talking to my son's best friend about this, but he's the only line I have left to Jess. "You need to know... we didn't..." Shit, I have no idea how to phrase this. All I can think of is what I want to say to Jess, and hope he'll pass it on. "It wasn't something we planned, and I didn't know Jess truly liked her. Did he tell you what he did at the beach house?"

Rex winces and nods.

"So I figured... and he'd made it clear that he had no plans to ever speak to me again, no matter what I did." I rake a hand through my hair. "It's been so hard since Lydia—Jess's mom..." God, I'm rambling. "Daisy and I, it's not just casual. I'm... I'm in love with her." I haven't said that out loud yet, but hearing the words from my mouth reinforces them in my heart.

I'm in love with her.

*And she's not here.*

Rex softens. "Have you told Jess?"

"I tried. He didn't want to hear it, and I don't blame him, honestly."

"But you and Daisy..." Rex hesitates, as if wondering how much he can say to me, then seems to decide *fuck it*. "You want a future with her? It's real?"

"It's real. It's very real. I want to build a life with her."

A melancholy smile passes over Rex's mouth. "I'm sure if Jess could understand that, he'd want you to be happy."

I lift a shoulder, because I'm not so sure myself.

"Has she moved into your place?"

I give a sad shake of my head. "She left. Said she can't come between me and Jess, and that I needed to fix things with him first."

"Fuck," Rex mutters in dismay. "So now you don't even have her."

I nod miserably. *Now I don't even have her.*

I must look absolutely pitiful, because Rex straightens up in his seat with determination. "Okay. I'll help."

"What?"

"I'll try to track down Jess. I haven't seen him since he was last at my place, but I know where he works and I'll see if he's there, if he'll listen to me. It might take some time, but I'm sure we can get him to come around."

I stare at Rex in disbelief. This is the kid I thought was derailing my son's life, the guy I've always considered a bad influence, but as he lifts his beer to clink it against mine in an attempt to cheer me up, to give me some hope, I realize how wrong I was.

It wasn't Rex who was a bad influence.

It was Jess.

And it's my fault.

I take a long pull from my beer, finding it hard to swallow. "Thanks," I mumble through a chest full of emotion. "For everything, Rex." And I can't believe I'm saying this, but I sure am grateful Jess has a friend like him.

He won't listen to me, but he might listen to Rex.

# 40

# DAISY

I f there's one place on this planet I really don't feel like being right now, it's the bar where Jess works.

I push through the crowded doorway, my pulse ramping up as I enter the dimly lit setting. It's quitting time on a Friday evening, and the dive bar is swarming with people enjoying that end-of-the-week buzz. Jess will be busy, but that's intentional. I've waited all week for this moment, both to give him time to cool off, and to come when it would be busiest. I figured if I approached Jess when the place was packed, he'd be less likely to yell at me and storm off.

I still can't completely rule that out, though.

This week has been torture without Wes. On Wednesday I went back to work, and have spent the past three days doing everything possible to keep myself busy. I deep cleaned the espresso machine. I scraped gum off the underside of every table in Joe's. I cleaned out and reorganized the food cabinet.

But there are only so many things you can do in a coffee shop to pass the time, especially when it's unusually quiet, like it has been this past week. Wes has mercifully respected my wishes for us to take some space and hasn't come into Joe's. He texted to check that I was okay, but that's all. I replied that I was fine, and I hoped he was okay too, but it did nothing to soothe me. I desperately wanted to tell him about the disaster with my parents, to tell him I miss him like I've never missed anyone in my life.

I never knew it was possible to miss someone like this, that missing them could be a whole-body experience. My heart aches without him. My bones feel hollow. My limbs are heavy, and I have to drag myself around. But after that fiasco with my parents, I know I'm doing the right thing by putting his relationship with Jess first. It only reinforced how important that is.

I'll have to see him at the wedding next weekend, though. I'll just... have to keep my distance, I guess. Besides, I'll be busy with the photography, and it's not like we were going to be all over each other anyway. He didn't want Violet and Kyle to know about us.

And I'll have to pretend I'm okay with all of that.

Of course, I'll have to find somewhere else to develop the photos from the wedding, but I've already done some research and discovered there are several darkroom spaces you can rent in Brooklyn. And while I'd rather be ensconced in my own private, custom-built darkroom at Weston's house, I know that's not the best idea right now. It would be all too easy to sneak upstairs to Wes's bed, to fall into his arms and tell him I'm in love with him, to tell him I can't stand to be apart.

Anyway. Enough thinking about him. It's all I've done since I left, and it's not helping one bit.

I elbow through the crowd, making my way to the bar where Jess is pouring a glass of Prosecco for a woman. She tucks a generous tip into his hand and saunters away, and it occurs to me that this is probably a pretty lucrative job for a good-looking guy like him.

He turns to the next customer, listening to their request, then I watch as he chats animatedly to the bartender next to him, a woman who looks to be mid-twenties, with long black braids, a wide smile, and warm brown skin. Jess says something as he mixes a cocktail, and she throws her head back, laughing and touching him on the arm. It makes me smile.

Until his gaze lifts to find me waiting at the bar, and his brows slam down. For a second I think he'll ignore me, but he leans forward, the tendons flexing in his forearms as he grips the edge of the bar hard.

"What do *you* want?"

"Can we talk, Jess?" My heart rattles against my ribcage at the anger swirling in his gaze. "Please?"

"I'm busy, Daisy. Find someone else to talk to." And with that, he turns to the next customer in line.

I let my breath out in a long stream, telling myself that's a fair response. I'd probably behave exactly the same way if I were in his shoes.

But I have nowhere to be and nothing to lose.

I slide onto a barstool and watch him work, acutely aware of the other bartender—the woman who laughed uproariously at Jesse's earlier words—eying me the entire time.

Eventually, she comes over, her pretty face scrunched in a frown. "You can't sit here if you're not going to drink," she says pointedly.

I pull my purse out with a sigh. "Can I get a glass of merlot, please?"

She fetches my drink and takes my money, then hovers

near me behind the bar when there's a lull in the crowd, letting Jess and the other bartenders serve.

"He's taken," she tells me as I watch Jess pour a line of shots.

I glance at her. "What?"

"The guy you keep staring at." She motions toward Jess. "He's mine."

Despite her frosty tone, I fight the urge to smile. Jess is dating her? Good for him.

"I'm not interested in Jess," I say, and her eyebrows lift at my use of his name. "So... I'm happy for you two."

"You know him?"

I take a long sip of wine, deciding how to answer. "Yeah. We're... friends."

She glances from me to Jess, who's restocking the cocktail napkins on the counter and studiously ignoring me, her expression doubtful.

"I mean, we were," I clarify. "I let him down recently, and... I need to apologize."

Her face softens. "So *that's* why he's been weird all week."

I give her a curious look. "He didn't tell you? I thought you were together."

"Uh..." She smiles sheepishly, picking up a rag to wipe at an invisible stain on the bar. "We're not *technically* dating... yet." Her mahogany eyes flash to mine, full of fire. "But we will be."

I can't help but grin. Gotta love a woman who knows what she wants.

"Maybe you can put in a good word for me," she adds, looking hopeful.

I sigh. "Hard to do that when he won't talk to me."

She taps her index finger to her lip for a moment, looking thoughtful. Then, sweeping her long braids over one shoulder, she says, "Leave it with me." She walks away to speak quietly into Jess's ear, and he shakes his head, frowning at me. Another word from her, a huge eye-roll from him, and he stalks out from behind the bar, shoving through the crowd to my side. I'm astonished when he bends down to say,

"You have five minutes. Make it good."

Christ. I don't need to put in a good word for her. She's already got him wrapped around her finger.

"Can we go somewhere less crowded?" I ask, knowing I'm pushing my luck.

He glowers at me, then looks over to my new friend—I'll need to get her name—motioning that he's popping outside. Relief trickles through me as I follow him out of the bar and onto the sidewalk, into the soft apricot light of late evening. It's cooler out now that summer is slipping into fall, and I pull my thin sweater tighter around me.

"Thanks, Jess," I say as we wander slowly along the bustling pavement toward Tompkins Square Park.

"I'm not doing this for you," he mutters, hands shoved into his pockets. "I'm doing it for Simone."

*Simone.* So that's her name.

"I like her." I try to smile at Jess, but he's kicking his sneakers angrily along the sidewalk, refusing to meet my gaze. "And I think she likes you."

He shakes his head, looking across the street. "What do you care?"

"I do care." I reach out to touch his arm, then think better of it.

We cross Avenue A, entering Tompkins Square Park, and I motion for us to sit on a bench. Jess hesitates for a long moment, then eventually joins me, facing a statue of some guy I don't recognize.

"Jess..." I take a deep breath, hoping he'll stay long enough to hear me out. Hoping he'll listen. "I'm so sorry."

He folds his arms stubbornly across his chest, saying nothing. I give him a moment to absorb my apology, then draw breath to speak again, when he finally says, "I don't get it, Daisy." His ocean-blue eyes, identical to his father's, express hurt when they meet mine. "I know things didn't end well—"

"Things didn't just *not end well*," I say, knowing this is not the reason I'm here, but struggling to let that go. "You brought someone else home, then yelled at me for not sleeping with you, in front of your dad, before vanishing. It was humiliating."

Regret flickers in Jesse's eyes, but it quickly passes. "Yeah, but my *dad*? Of all the people to—"

"I know." I look down at my hands. "But you have to understand, we... There was already something there, before I even met you. It's not like I went after him out of revenge, or something."

"But..." Jess rubs his eyes. "This is what I don't get. If you two liked each other—which is still something I'm struggling with, by the way—but if you did, then why didn't something happen before you met me?"

"Because..." How do I explain this? "I thought he was married. He still wore his ring."

Jess picks up a red oak leaf that falls onto his lap, the edges rimmed in gold, heralding the start of fall. He folds it between his fingers, his jaw tight, saying nothing.

"You know things weren't great between us," I murmur. "We weren't a good fit."

He huffs, tearing the leaf in two.

"I didn't hold back with you because of We—" I cringe. "Because of your dad. I did that because it didn't feel right, and I think you knew that too. That we weren't a good match."

He shrugs, still refusing to speak.

"Honestly, Jess..." I sigh, picking up a leaf of my own and smoothing it between my palms. "I'm not sure you were even ready for a relationship. I'm not sure you'd... dealt with what happened with your mom. You wouldn't let me in. You wouldn't talk."

"For fuck's sake." He flings the leaf onto the ground and goes to launch to his feet, but I grab his arm.

"This is what I mean," I say gently. "I'm trying to talk to you about this, but you won't let me." I remember what Rex said about Jess speaking to a therapist, and wonder if I should mention that, then think better of it. I can only hope he's still seeing them.

"So that makes it okay?" He wheels to face me, eyes dark with fury. "I wouldn't talk to you about my dead mom, so you thought it was okay to fuck my dad?"

"Jesus." I press a hand to my forehead. "Of course not. It wasn't like that."

"What was it like, then?" he spits. "Tell me how it happened. I need to know."

"Jess—"

"Tell me."

I exhale slowly. "I spent a lot of time with him while you were out with friends at the beach. Mostly I think he felt sorry for me, being left there alone. And it was nice to have the company. Then when you took off, we..." Ugh, this part doesn't make either of us look good. "I stuck around for a few days, and we went for a walk to Sullivan's Cove. We both knew at that point that we had feelings for each other, but we agreed not to act on them." I pause, wondering whether I should mention the darkroom, then decide to be honest. Jess has already seen it, anyway. "While we were away, your dad really encouraged me to get back into my photography. He was quite insistent." I chuff a tiny laugh at the memory, and Jess glances at me, puzzled.

"You do photography?"

I nod. "This is what I mean about us not being a good match. You should have known this about me."

Realization dawns on his face. "The darkroom... the photographs... those were yours? You took those?"

"Yes. Well... most of them," I add, my cheeks heating at the memory of the ones Wes took. The ones Jess found.

He must be remembering that too because his brows crash together again and he turns away.

"Your dad built me the darkroom to encourage me. It's..." I shake my head, still partially in disbelief about his actions. "It's the nicest thing anyone has ever done for me."

There's a crack in Jesse's anger for a split second, but he quickly hides it, snapping, "So you slept with him?"

"Of course not. We actually agreed not to see each other because of you. We decided it was for the best. I only used the darkroom when he wasn't there. But then it was his birthday, and..." I shake my head, pulling my hair over one shoulder and fiddling with a split end. "I made him a lemon cake, and he—"

"Lemon cake?" Jesse's tone is a knife-edge of sadness and hostility. "My mom used to make those."

"I know. I mean, I didn't know that until after. It was a coincidence. But... I think your dad was having a hard time on his birthday, not hearing from you. I was going to give him the cake and leave, but I didn't. You need to know"—I touch Jesse's arm so he looks at me—"it's not his fault. He was very clear that nothing could happen between us. If I hadn't showed up with that cake..." I trail off here, because I want to believe Wes and I would have gotten together anyway. I can't let myself imagine a world where we didn't.

Jess leans his elbows onto his knees, heaving out a long breath, absorbing everything.

"I'm sorry we kept it from you, and I'm really sorry you found out the way you did." I grimace, remembering the photos strewn across the kitchen island, the disgust on Jesse's face. "That must have been awful."

He grunts a sardonic laugh.

"But I'm not sorry I fell in love with him. It's probably hard for you to imagine, but he and I are a good fit. I'd never dream of replacing your mom," I add quickly. "But I think... I think I make him happy. And doesn't he deserve that, after everything he's been through?"

Jess digs his hands into his hair, staring at the ground. There's a moment where I think he's coming around, but when he finally sits up to look at me, his eyes are dark with misery and red-rimmed.

"I can't do this," he mutters, shoving to his feet.

Panic flares in my chest. What happened? It felt like we were making progress.

"Jess, please—"

"Look, I might be able to forgive *you*, but my dad..."

I grab Jesse's arm, desperate for him to hear me. "It wasn't his fault. I was the one who—"

"The one who lied to my face for a whole week after I moved home?" Jess snaps, shaking my hand off. "Who pretended everything between us was fine?"

"He was scared to lose you again. You have to understand—"

"I don't, actually." Jess stares at me hard for a long

moment, grinding his jaw, then shakes his head, turning away. "I have to get back to work."

"Jess—" I call desperately, but he doesn't so much as turn around.

I know there's no point in following him. I've said all I wanted to say, and I can only hope that in time, he'll come around.

With a leaden heart I watch him stalk away from me, then I head home to another lonely night without Weston.

# 41

## WESTON

I wake early on Sunday, my heart bright and full at the knowledge that I'll see Daisy at the wedding today. The two weeks since I last saw her have been unbearable. I've fought every day not to pick up the phone and call her, to hear her voice and beg her to change her mind. I know she's doing the noble thing by putting my relationship with Jess first, but we can't control how he feels. We can't force him to forgive us—forgive *me*. And so, we're sacrificing our own happiness.

I spend the morning at the pool, swimming laps for over two hours. The only good thing to come out of the time I've spent away from Daisy is the improvement of my swimming times. I never used to pay much attention to my time, but it's given me something to focus on while we're apart. Something to pretend to care about.

The ceremony doesn't start until five, so I still have the entire afternoon to kill before it's time to get ready. I spend the time in the attic, going through some of Lydia's stuff, choosing a few framed pictures to put around the house. It's good to see her again, if a little painful. But Daisy was right

—it's easier now than it used to be, and I'm glad to be reminded of her. I still can't believe Daisy encouraged me to do that, and it makes me love her even more.

After that, I set about fixing the busted handle on the door to the darkroom, so it's ready for Daisy when she's ready to use it again. I have to believe she will, that this isn't it for us. Otherwise, what was the point? We found each other only to give each other up, and for what?

I push these thoughts from my mind as I dress for the wedding, pulling on a light-gray suit over a crisp white dress shirt, knotting a navy-blue tie at my throat. Then I pick up the gift I chose for my neighbors—a set of Le Creuset cast-iron cookware wrapped in gold paper—and head next door.

Violet and Kyle have decorated their stoop with white ribbons and flower garlands. I climb the steps and knock on their front door, and a moment later a vivacious redhead in a floor-length, emerald-green dress with russet-colored curls spilling over her shoulders greets me. She shoots me a wide, beaming smile.

"Hello! I'm Sadie, the maid of honor." Her gaze drifts over me appreciatively, drinking in my suit, and I stifle a chuckle.

"Weston. I live next door."

"Weston, of course. Please, come in."

I follow her across the entry hall and into the living room, where she finds me somewhere to deposit the heavy gift I'm carrying. Then she hands me a glass of champagne, and we head downstairs.

It's fascinating to see the interior of Kyle's house, completely different from mine. Where I've got gleaming chrome and modern fixtures, he's got rustic wood and warm, historical elements. His kitchen is situated in the basement, unlike mine, and it opens out onto a beautiful yard, where they've set up a white wooden arch underneath a large, blooming magnolia tree. On the lawn sit a handful of folding chairs, and above, string lights zig zag across the garden, which will no doubt glow golden over the yard later in the evening. It's a beautiful setting for a wedding.

My eyes scour the yard for Daisy, but while I spot a few small groups of people I don't recognize, there's no sign of her. Violet isn't here either, and as Sadie disappears, I realize they're probably upstairs. Maybe Daisy is photographing Violet as she gets ready.

As I step out into the yard, I spy a familiar face among the crowd. Wyatt, our other neighbor, to the right of me. He's a landscaper, responsible for my beautiful garden and, from what I can tell, Kyle and Violet's, too.

He wanders across, taking my hand to shake. "Wes. It's been a while."

"Sure has." I release his hand, motioning around the yard. "Is this your work?"

He nods, lifting his champagne glass to his mouth, tattoos snaking out from the cuff of his suit jacket, across his knuckles. The guy's covered in them.

"Looks good," I say. Even though we've lived beside each other for years, I haven't spoken to Wyatt much recently as we're usually both so busy. "Been out on the bike lately?" I ask, thinking of the motorcycle he keeps in front of his place under a cover. I've seen him work on it a few times, but never ride it. From what I can tell, it only seems to gather dust.

"Nah." His eyes go distant as he scrubs a hand over his tidy salt-and-pepper beard. "Haven't taken it out in a while." He blinks, as if coming to, and looks back at me. "How's the boy? Jesse, isn't it?"

My grip tightens involuntarily on the champagne glass.

"Ah, he's..." Shit, I don't know. *He hates me. I've let him down. We're not speaking.* None of these seem like appropriate answers. "Busy," I add at last, because it's probably true. "How's Bailey?"

Wyatt's eyes light up. "Good. Graduating soon." He's a single father, and from what I understand, he was never actually together with Bailey's mom. In fact, I don't think his daughter was in his life until she was twelve. Despite every-thing, they've managed to build a solid relationship. I have to admire him for that.

"You must be proud," I murmur.

He shrugs. "It's all Bailey. I can't take the credit." His gaze snags on something across the garden and his face clouds. "Hey, watch out for the roses," he calls. He shakes his head at a woman accidentally trampling a rosebush. "I'll talk to you later," he mutters, before going to check on the plant.

I stifle a laugh, turning to grin at Kyle as he approaches.

"Wes! Glad you could make it," he says, looking sharp in a black suit. A sprig of pine and a single, purple violet sit in his buttonhole.

"Of course." I take his hand and give it a hearty pump. "After all you did for me with the darkroom, I wouldn't miss it."

He scrubs a hand over his tidy beard. "How's the dark-room working out?"

"It's been great," I say, leaving out the part about my son breaking into it to discover photos of me and Daisy.

"Good to hear. You know... Daisy is our photographer today. Violet suggested her, and she's great. She gave us some stunning pictures of the neighborhood." His eyes shimmer. "Have you seen her work?"

It occurs to me that Daisy has probably told Violet all about us, and there's every chance she's told Kyle. Why didn't I think of that before? Either way, there's no reason to hide anything anymore. Not now that Jess knows.

Still, with my future with Daisy feeling so uncertain right now, I'm not sure I want to get into all that. So I simply raise my champagne glass to my lips and say "Mmm," before taking a long sip.

Thankfully, Kyle doesn't push it. He turns to a guy a few years older than us and smiles.

"Rich, this is our neighbor, Wes." He glances back at me as I take Rich's hand. "This is Violet's father, and my best friend."

I smile, processing this. I must look a little perplexed, because Kyle laughs, and Rich joins him with a hearty chuckle.

"It's a long story," Kyle says. "Vi and I fell in love while working on this house, and"—he elbows Rich with a sly grin—"Rich here did *not* approve. Especially since I've known him for years and Vi is a little younger than me."

My eyebrows lift. I'd certainly noticed the age gap between those two. It must be similar to the gap between Daisy and me.

Rich snorts into his champagne glass. "Try eighteen years," he says good-naturedly.

"Hey, you can't help who you fall for, can you?" Kyle chuckles, and I give a grim laugh in response.

*No, you can't.*

"So, you've obviously forgiven him," I say to Rich, intrigued. While not quite the same, their situation isn't completely unlike what's happening with Jess. Hiding their relationship from someone they loved, and no doubt wishing they had his blessing.

Rich rubs his chin thoughtfully. "I have. It took time for

me to come around, believe me. But, they're happy. That's what matters."

I nod wistfully, letting my gaze wander around for Daisy again. If Rich can forgive his best friend for getting together with his daughter, is it possible Jess could ever forgive me for falling for his ex-girlfriend?

A blond woman appears in the yard, stepping into Rich's side.

"This is my wife, Diana."

She smiles at me, then turns to Kyle. "Violet's ready, honey."

He inhales, laughing nervously. "About damn time," he jokes, then asks everyone to take their seats.

There's still no sign of Daisy. I drain my champagne and settle on a chair, waiting for the ceremony to begin, telling myself to focus on the real reason I'm here; Violet and Kyle, not Daisy.

But when Violet walks down the makeshift aisle, followed by Daisy with the camera pressed to her eye, I can't look away. It's Violet I should watch, looking stunning in a long white gown, but Daisy is the one who steals my breath. She's dressed in a pale yellow silk dress that reaches the ground, skimming her hips and draping in soft folds across her breasts, exposing just the faintest hint of cleavage. The color would make anyone else look washed out, but it suits Daisy perfectly, making her skin glow, making the constellation of dark freckles across her collarbone and shoulders stand out.

Fuck, she is so beautiful.

I'm relieved that she's too busy trying to capture Violet and Kyle to notice the way I'm captivated by her. My heart swells in my chest as I watch her work, so fucking proud I could cry. A few months ago this woman would barely touch a camera, and now she's here, doing what she's meant to do.

It's not until the couple begin to say their vows that I realize I've been staring at Daisy the entire time, and I force my gaze to them. As I watch them pledge their love, I'm reminded of my wedding to Lydia, over two decades ago. We didn't have much money then, so it was a small ceremony at her parents' place. I'd never felt happier than I did that day, holding Lydia's hands in mine, knowing I was going to grow old with her.

Turns out God had other plans.

My eyes prick with tears as I think of the woman I lost, the love we shared, and the family we had. I have to swallow them down, letting the grief pass. As Violet and Kyle exchange rings and kiss, I look at Daisy again. I could never have imagined I'd meet someone I'd want to do it all over again with, and even after everything I had to go through with Lydia, I feel lucky.

Lucky that I've been given a second chance at love. At happiness.

And there's no way in hell I'm going to let her get away.

# 42

## DAISY

"**A**re you sure?" I ask Violet, lowering the camera from my eye.

I look down at my new toy, smiling. I decided to treat myself by investing in a new SLR film camera of my own. It's a symbol of my commitment to my photography, plus it has a bunch of cool features I can't wait to explore.

Besides, I can't keep using Weston's.

"I'm sure." Violet holds out a glass of champagne, grinning. "You've captured the most important parts, and I'm sure you'll grab a few candids throughout the night. Please relax. Enjoy yourself."

I let the camera hang around my neck, secured by the strap I bought for it. It's much easier to use this way. Then I take the glass from Violet's outstretched hand with a smile.

"Thanks."

We clink glasses and she sighs, leaning against the wall as we watch people dancing in the yard. The ceremony was beautiful—romantic and heartfelt—and I might have shed a few tears as I watched my friends declare their love. Thankfully, it was easy to hide behind the camera. Now, after dinner and speeches, we're enjoying a few drinks while the guests dance.

"How does it feel to be married?" I ask Violet, sipping the sweet bubbly liquid.

"Amazing." Her gaze follows Kyle as he dances with her mom, Diana. Violet's entire face is lit with affection and joy, and I can't help it—I lift the camera to snap a picture before letting it fall again. Kyle motions for her to join him, and she saunters over.

I hover near the wall, clutching the champagne glass in my hand. I feel naked without the camera pressed to my eye, and despite my best intentions, my gaze finds Weston across the yard, nursing his own glass of champagne. He looks unbelievably handsome, in a suit that makes me weak at the knees.

Seeing him again knocked the wind out of me. I've spent two weeks convincing myself that I could live without him, that he needs to focus on repairing things with Jess, but being here now, with him only a few feet away... my heart burns with longing.

His gaze meets mine across the yard, and a tingle starts in my toes, rippling through my entire body. We haven't said two words to each other all evening, but the way he's been looking at me could set the room on fire. I've tried to focus on Violet and Kyle, really I have, but I could feel Weston's gaze with every move I made. What I wouldn't give to have his hands on me, too.

He lifts his champagne glass, sending me a melancholy smile. I know he's trying to do the right thing by keeping his distance, but it physically hurts me to see him and not be able to speak to him. Not be able to touch him.

I tear my gaze away, my chest tight, and escape upstairs

under the guise of changing my camera battery. I need a moment to center myself.

*You're not here for Weston*, I remind myself, pacing the quiet living room. The sound of music and laughter drifts up from downstairs, and I square my shoulders resolutely. *You're here to do a job.*

With a deep breath, I turn to head back down, just as Kyle appears at the top of the stairs.

"Hey, Daisy!" He grins, clearly a little looser than usual after a few glasses of champagne. Either that or he's drunk on love. "You having a good time?"

"Yep." I paste on a smile and move to step around him, but he stops me.

"You sure?" He peers at my face, then gives a shake of his head. "You're not. What's going on?"

"Nothing." As if I'll ruin his wedding by blabbing to him about my problems with Wes. I try harder to make the smile seem genuine, but he's not buying it.

"Hey," he says gently, motioning for us to take a seat in the living room. "Talk to me."

"It's nothing," I repeat, forcing a light laugh, hovering by the stairs even though he's settled in for a chat.

"It's Wes, isn't it?"

That's all it takes for me to sink into the chair beside him. "How did you know?"

His green eyes sparkle. "Violet filled me in on a few details, but even if she hadn't... it's hard to miss the way he's looking at you."

"How's he looking at me?" I ask, in spite of myself. Has it really been that obvious to everyone else?

"Like a lovesick puppy." Kyle chuckles. "And based on all the looks I've seen you send his way, I'd guess you feel the same."

*Busted*. Shit, I am so unprofessional.

"I swear, I've got so many good pictures—"

Kyle's laugh cuts me off. "I know you have. That's not what I'm saying. I'm saying you should be down there dancing with him. We don't mind."

"Oh." My cheeks warm. "It's not... it's a little complicated."

Kyle strokes his beard, eying me thoughtfully. "Wait here." He disappears down the stairs, then returns with two fresh glasses of champagne, handing me one. "Now, tell me what the problem is."

I take the glass gratefully. "That's very kind, but this is your wedding. I'm not going to—"

"Exactly." He gives me a smug look. "It's *my* wedding, so you have to do what I say. Now, tell me why you're up here talking with me and not down there with Wes."

I open and close my mouth, hesitating. I really don't want to dump my problems on the groom, but he's gazing at me expectantly, waiting for an answer. And it's not like Kyle doesn't know about us, despite Weston's intentions to keep things discreet.

At my hesitation, Kyle softens. "Do you remember that early morning I came into Joe's last year, and you listened to me talk about what was going on with Violet?"

"Of course."

"This is me returning the favor." He smiles gently, and I sigh.

"Fine. Five minutes, then you go back downstairs."

"Deal." He clinks his glass to mine. "Now, go."

I take a deep breath and begin, finding it surprisingly easy to spill everything to Kyle. I haven't spoken to anyone about this, and the words come tumbling out. I tell him about meeting Weston at Joe's over a year ago, slowly getting to know him, thinking he was married, getting together with Jess, things imploding with Jess, then eventually getting together with Wes. His encouragement for my photography, falling for him, then Jess discovering our relationship. My decision to step back, and how hard it's been.

Kyle listens intently, cradling his glass, his face kind. When I finish, he exhales long and slow. "That's... a lot."

I nod, staring morosely into my glass.

"I understand why you want him to fix things with his son," Kyle says. "But... you staying away from Wes isn't making that happen. You can't control what his son is going to do, how he's going to feel."

"I know," I mumble.

"And you're just hurting yourself in the process."

He's not wrong there, because this totally fucking hurts.

"Not only because you're refusing to be with the person you love," he continues, "but because you're letting the guilt win."

I glance up. Is that really what I'm doing?

"Trust me." Kyle gives me a knowing look. "I did it myself when Rich found out about me and Vi. And really, there's no point. Guilt is a useless emotion, especially when you've done all you can do. At that point, you need to forgive yourself."

I blink at him. "Forgive myself?"

He nods. "Forgive yourself for being human, for making a mistake. Yes, Wes's son moved out and won't speak to him, but from what you've just told me, it sounds like their relationship was incredibly rocky before you came into the picture. If anything, Daisy, it sounds like you're the one who helped them."

I look down at my hands. That's true, but...

"Anyway," Kyle adds, "you've done your best to fix their

relationship, but ultimately, it's beyond your control. The only thing you can control is deciding to be with Wes, but you won't allow it. It's like you're punishing yourself."

My lips part in shock. Is he right? Am I staying away from Wes because I feel guilty, because I want to punish myself? I'm about to respond when Violet arrives at the top of the stairs.

"There you are!" Her gaze lands on me and Kyle, and her smile fades. "Why the long faces?"

Kyle looks at me, indicating that it's up to me to explain, and I offer her a faint smile.

"Your husband is giving me some very sound relationship advice."

Her lips curve in a dreamy smile. "*My husband.* I love how that sounds." She crosses the room and lowers herself onto Kyle's lap, wrapping her arms around his neck and looking at me. "Is this about Wes? He's like a lost puppy down there without you."

Kyle chuckles, squeezing his bride. "That's what I said."

I gaze at my friends, my heart aching at how happy they look. I want that.

"I hope *my husband* was helpful," Violet adds, giving Kyle a playful nudge.

"He was very helpful." I rise to my feet. "Thanks, Kyle. You've given me plenty to think about." Then I head downstairs, leaving the happy couple to steal a moment alone.

The party is in full swing when I reach the yard again, and no one seems to notice the bride and groom are missing. Instinctively, I lift my camera and wander around, capturing some candid shots of couples dancing, drinking, laughing. I try not to think about Kyle's words as I work, but they ring through my head.

*You're punishing yourself.*

*You're letting the guilt win.*

*You need to forgive yourself.*

I finish my round of pictures and wander to the back of the yard, by the brick wall of a neighboring building that backs onto the section. Here, behind the magnolia tree, I can hide in the shadows to gather my thoughts.

When I spot a familiar silhouette in the darkness, I realize I'm not the only one looking for somewhere away from the crowd.

"Daisy." Weston's voice is quiet above the music, but even as my eyes adjust to the shadows, I can't make out his expression.

"Oh." My stomach flutters with nerves. "Hi. I didn't see you there."

He gives a deep, weighted sigh. "I just... needed a moment."

I fiddle with the camera, my anxious fingers needing something to do.

"New camera," he murmurs.

"Yeah. I wanted to get one of my own to, I don't know, prove to myself I'm taking this seriously."

"That's..." There's a pause, and when he speaks again, his voice has a raw edge to it. "That's great."

I swallow. "How've you been?"

He shoves his hands into his suit pockets. "Not great."

My heart presses against my ribs. I'm reminded of the man who first came into Joe's last year. The one who would barely look at me. The man who was broken.

"I tried to speak to Jess," I blurt. "I went to his work, and we talked, but he's still so angry. I tried..." I trail off helplessly.

Wes is quiet, and I strain my eyes, wishing I could see him more clearly, could read his face. I open my mouth to say... honestly, I don't even know what, but he looks at me and asks, "Would you like to dance?"

It takes me completely by surprise. I should say no, because if he so much as touches me, I'll crumble in his arms, but I don't have the strength to be anything other than honest.

"Yes. I'd really like that."

I can't see his expression, but he turns for the dance floor, and I follow, my heart beating in my throat. Violet and Kyle are back outside, swaying closely to a slow, romantic song. I set the camera aside, catching Kyle's eye as I join Wes on the dance floor, and he sends me a hopeful smile.

Maybe he's right. Maybe I've been punishing myself, and it's time to stop.

Weston looks uncertain when we face each other, but I step forward and slide my arms around his neck, so we're closer. When his hands land on my waist, the nerves in my stomach settle, because this is where I'm meant to be. In Weston's arms.

He draws me close as we sway, lowering his mouth beside my ear. "You look absolutely beautiful, Daisy. I haven't been able to keep my eyes off you."

His words make my pulse jump. "Thank you." I run a hand down the front of his suit, tugging gently on the lapel. "You look good too." That's an understatement if there ever was one.

"I don't feel good." His thumbs draw gentle circles on my back, sending a shiver across my skin. "I can't eat. I can't sleep. I miss you too much."

I let out a shuddering breath. "Me too. It's been... it's been hard."

He's quiet as we move together, slowly drawing closer,

until our chests are touching. My skin buzzes with electricity. My heart hurts.

"I'm sorry," I whisper, and Wes draws back to look at me from under low brows.

"For what?"

"For leaving."

He lifts a hand to tuck a loose tendril of hair behind my ear. "You don't have to apologize. I know your heart is in the right place. You want me to be happy."

I nod, my throat tight. "I really do."

"But what you don't realize is that I'm happiest when I'm with you." His thumb brushes my cheek tenderly. "*You* are the person who makes me happy." He takes my face in both hands, his ocean-blue eyes searching mine. "I love you, Daisy."

My breath catches in my lungs. "You do?"

"I do." His eyes glisten in the light of the bulbs strung above the yard. "I never dreamed I could feel this way again, but I do, and I don't want to lose what we have. I don't want to lose you. I've lost enough."

I press my eyes shut, his words piercing something in my chest. But it's still there, that guilt, the knowledge that I drove his son away.

"But Jess—"

"Jess will do whatever he wants," Wes says, lowering his hands to my waist again. "We can't control that, and there's no point in us being apart for his sake."

"But…"

"No." The sharp tone of Weston's voice forces my gaze to his. "If you want to end this because you don't want to be with me, I'll respect that, and let you go."

I open my mouth to protest because that is not and has never been the case.

"But if you're only walking away because of my relationship with Jess," Wes continues, "then I won't let you."

"But you need to—"

"*No*," he repeats firmly, fingertips tightening on my waist. "You don't get to throw this away because of my son. You don't get to make that choice for me."

I gaze at Wes, my eyes stinging. My heart is tight, wrung out at the expression on Wes's face. At his refusal to give up on us.

"It's not your fault," he murmurs, thumbs caressing my waist again. "I know you blame yourself, but it's not your fault. My relationship with Jess has been rocky for years. I should have been honest with him when he came back home, and I have to own that. I won't let you keep beating yourself up."

*You're punishing yourself.*

*You're letting the guilt win.*

*You need to forgive yourself.*

Tears spill from my eyes, and Weston's thumb is there to brush them away in an instant.

"Do you love me, Daisy?"

"So much," I whisper.

The relief in his gaze is like the first light of dawn after the longest night. Like finding land when you're lost at sea.

"Then come home," he says, his eyes moist. "Come home to me, baby."

My heart caves in. I swallow, letting the word *home* wash over me, because it's always felt like home at Weston's house, and if he wants me there, then that's where I'll be.

"Okay," I breathe, gripping the lapels of his suit jacket.

He doesn't wait to lower his mouth to mine, and when our lips connect, everything else fades away. The music, the people...

"Wait." I draw away, casting a furtive glance around the dance floor. "Are you sure we should do this here?"

Weston's hands tighten on my back and pull me closer, his lips finding mine again, tongue sweeping hungrily into my mouth. "I want everyone to know you're mine," he murmurs, warm breath fanning across my lips. "I'm never going to hide what we have from anyone again." Then he captures my mouth once more, and I sink into his kiss. His touch is a healing balm on my heart, and it only takes a few seconds before I ache to be alone with him, to make love to him, to make up for the time we've lost.

I glance around the dance floor only to find Violet and Kyle watching us with massive grins. My cheeks heat at the fact that I was openly making out with their neighbor at their wedding, but Violet dances our way.

"You can go if you like," she whispers, winking. "We've got more than enough pictures."

I blush even harder. "But—"

"I'm the bride," Violet reminds me, "and I'm sending you home. Now." She nudges me playfully, then spins away back to Kyle.

I glance back at Wes, who obviously heard every word.

"What do you say, babygirl?" He lifts my hand to his lips, pressing a kiss to the back of it. "Want to go home?"

This time, I don't hesitate. "Yes, please."

I grab my camera, and we pause to thank Violet and Kyle, before racing through their house, back to Weston's. He struggles to get the key in the front door, mostly because he's got one arm around me and his face nuzzled into my neck, but I don't mind. It's amazing to have him touch me like this, hold me close, out on the stoop where anyone could see us. Knowing he wants the real deal with me, wants everyone to know, makes my head spin. By the time we get up to his bedroom, I'm dizzy with the knowledge that this is really happening. I'm back here, and it's right.

"I missed you," I say between kisses, as Wes lays me back on the bed. His hands are everywhere at once: my hair, my face, my stomach, my breasts.

"I was going crazy without you, baby." His mouth moves across my jaw, my neck, down to my chest, while his hand slides my dress up my thighs. "I missed the way you feel, the way you smell." Then his eyes flick up to mine, dark and hungry, as he slides my panties down my legs. "The way you taste."

His head disappears between my thighs, and a second later pleasure surges through me as his tongue finds my most sensitive spot.

"Fuck, babygirl," he rasps, devouring me greedily. "You taste so good. Like you're mine."

"All yours," I whimper in response, inching closer to my release, but I don't get there because he rises to his feet, urgently unbuttoning his pants.

"I need to be inside you," he says, eyes wild. "Now." He shucks his pants and boxer briefs, then slips his suit jacket off, until he's only in his shirt and tie, his erection straining toward me. When he starts to loosen the tie, I bat his hands away, taking hold of it and tugging him close.

"Leave this on. It's sexy." My hands find his cock and take hold of him, so hot and hard in my palm. I guide him to my entrance, already soaked with need for him, and when he thrusts hard into me, I throw my head back and moan.

We lie like that for a few beats, Weston buried to the hilt inside me, savoring the feel of us finally being one again. I can feel his heart drumming against mine, and tears blur my eyes. How could I have walked away from this man?

"I love you, Weston," I whisper, and when he brings his gaze to mine, his eyes are wet too.

"Daisy..." He peppers kisses across my cheek. "I love you so much. I'm never letting you go, you got that?"

My heart fills my chest, pressing against my ribcage. "Good." I hold him tighter. "Because I wouldn't let you."

He rolls us onto our sides, wrapping his arms around my back, holding me tight into his chest as we rock together, hands traversing each other's skin, mouths fused. It only lasts a few more minutes before we both reach our breaking point, falling apart in each other's arms. Then we lie there, clutching each other tight for what feels like an hour. When we finally part, Weston searches my eyes, his expression serious.

"I know it's not good with Jess," he murmurs, stroking my cheek, "and I can only hope that one day he'll come around, but we can't put our life on hold for him anymore. We can't only be together when life is good. We need each other when it's hard, too. I need you always."

*Always.*

God, how did I get lucky enough to end up here, with this man?

"I need you always too," I whisper, turning my face into his palm.

"I meant it when I told you to come home. I want you here with me, baby. I *need* you here." He tilts my face back, so I meet his gaze as he swallows hard. "Will you move in with me? Make this house feel like a home again?"

I try to fight off the grin tugging at my mouth, but it's hopeless because there is nothing I want more.

Snuggling in close, I bury my nose in his shirt, letting out the softest, happiest sigh.

"I can't imagine being anywhere else."

## 43

### WESTON
THREE AND A HALF MONTHS LATER

"Will you stop being so impatient?"

Daisy pulls the turkey from the oven and sets it on the counter, shaking her head at me in mock irritation. I know she's only pretending because of the way she's biting back a smile. The way she's looking at me, with love in her eyes. It's what this house had been missing for years, and finally, it's overflowing with love again. So much love.

"I can't help it," I say, sliding my arms around her apron-clad waist from behind. "It smells delicious."

She gives me a quick peck over her shoulder, then elbows me away so she can stir the gravy bubbling on the stove, throwing in some fresh parsley. I offered to help her—hell, I offered to cook the entire thing myself, it's the least she deserves—but she insisted on cooking a full Christmas dinner for us. I can't say I don't love it. She looks so damn good in here, so comfortable, so at home. Right where she belongs, with me. Not a day goes by that I don't thank God for this woman. Everything about her makes me a better man, and I like to think I make her better too.

Daisy has been busy with her photography since the wedding and was even booked for another paid gig. I've never been more proud. She's considering enrolling in the photography program at the New York Film Academy, but I'm still talking her into letting me pay for it. Why shouldn't I? I have the money, and I'll do anything to support her dream. I'll do anything for her.

I want to do a lot more than pay for her tuition—I want to ask her to marry me. I never dreamed I would feel this way about a woman again, and I know without a doubt that she's who I want to spend the rest of my life with. I'm quite certain she feels the same.

But without Jess in our lives, it doesn't feel right. It's one thing for Daisy and I to be together, but to get married without my son? Without him helping me celebrate what I know will be one of the best days of my life? The thought makes my chest ache.

I've tried for months to get in touch with him—sending emails, reaching out again to Rex—but I've come to terms with the fact that Jess isn't ready to forgive me, and there's a chance he never will be. If that's the case... then I'll have to find a way to live with it.

I shake off the thought of my son and focus on Daisy, on all the good in front of me. All the happiness that's here, right now.

"You know this is way too much food for just us," I point out as I slide back onto the stool at the kitchen island and pick up my wineglass again.

She lifts a shoulder, serving up the mashed potato. "We'll give some leftovers to Kyle and Vi."

I smile. We've spent a lot more time with our neighbors lately, since Daisy moved in. She and Violet get on well, and it's been great getting to know Kyle better. Great to feel like I'm part of something again, part of a community, and not just sad and alone in my big house.

My gaze drifts to the Christmas tree in the living room, lights twinkling in the dark, and a bittersweet sensation weaves through me. It's the first year I've bothered to get a tree since losing Lydia, but it was a no-brainer. With Daisy here, filling the house with her photos and her laughter and her love, I knew we needed a tree. It's sad to celebrate without Lydia, but I couldn't be more grateful for the chance at a new beginning.

Daisy wipes her hands on her apron, surveying the spread on the kitchen island. "I think that's everything."

"Not everything," I say, rising and rounding the island to her side. I take her face in my hands, tenderly brushing flour from her cheek, and press my mouth to hers in a soft kiss. Her hands stroke my chest, settling over my heart. We share another lingering kiss before she playfully pushes me away.

"I did not spend the entire day cooking just so it could go cold." She smacks me playfully on the butt as she passes. "You'll get your dessert after."

I chuckle, helping Daisy carry the food through to the dining room. I haven't eaten at this table in years, but it feels good to use it again. Daisy lights two candlesticks in the center of the table and lays out the plates while I begin to carve the turkey, trying to ignore the pain tugging at me. The last meal I ate in here was with Lydia and Jess, and I taught Jesse how to carve the turkey. The memory makes my eyes sting, and my throat is thick when I swallow. Will there ever be three plates at this table again? Will I ever get the future I want with Daisy, with my son's blessing?

A sound at the front door interrupts us, and Daisy's gaze meets mine, curious.

"What was—"

The sound comes again, clearer this time. A knock.

Her brows draw together in confusion. "Were you expecting someone?"

I shake my head, setting the carving knife down. Daisy trails behind me as I wander to the front door, wiping my hands on a dishtowel. Without looking through the peephole I swing the door open, expecting to see Kyle or Wyatt, maybe carolers.

I'm completely unprepared to find my son, standing beside a woman with long dark braids over one shoulder.

My heart jams in my throat. Has he come here to get the rest of his stuff from his room? To tell me again what a fucking terrible father I am? Has he—

"Hi, Dad." His voice wobbles, and the woman beside him slides her hand into his. When I glance up again into my son's stormy blue eyes, I notice they're not as stormy as I remember them. And despite myself, hope balloons in my chest.

"Jess," I say on an exhale. "What are you..." I trail off, not totally wanting to ask the question in case I'm wrong. In case I'm kidding myself.

The woman beside him extends her hand. She's a foot shorter than Jess, with a broad smile and warm umber skin. "I'm Simone. It's nice to finally meet you, Mr. Abbott."

To finally meet me? What's happening?

I glance at Daisy for clues, but she looks just as lost as me.

"Uh..." I clear my throat, finding my voice. "Nice to meet you, Simone. Please, call me Weston." My gaze drifts to Jess, his breath puffing out in the cold December air. His eyes reflect my uncertainty back at me.

"I hope it's okay we just showed up," he mutters, kicking his sneakers against the door frame absently. "Simone thought we should stop by."

"Of course it's okay." The tight ball in my stomach eases. "It's always okay." Daisy nudges me gently, and I step back, motioning for them to enter. "Come in out of the cold."

Simone grins, leading Jesse inside by the hand. I don't know who this young woman is, but I like her already.

"It's nice to see you again," Daisy says, reaching for Simone's coat with a broad smile. She leans in and murmurs something to her that I don't catch, but Simone nods, and the girls share a giggle. It makes me smile. How do these two know each other?

Jess shucks his coat and hangs it on the hook by the door, shifting his weight. I'm not sure how much he wants to be here, how much of this was Simone's idea.

But he's here. That's what matters.

"Have you eaten?" Daisy asks, finally peeling the apron from her waist as she leads Simone and Jess into the kitchen. I trail along behind them, half afraid that Jess is going to bolt out the front door at the first opportunity.

"Not yet," Simone says. "We were going to grab something on the way home."

"No way." Daisy reaches for the wine bottle and wordlessly asks if Simone would like some. She nods her response, and Daisy pours a generous glass. "You should eat with us. We made way too much food."

I love watching Daisy, making Simone feel at home. I can tell she's really trying to make her comfortable, and hopefully if Simone is comfortable, Jess will find a way to be, too.

"*Daisy* made way too much food," I correct, sending her a teasing smile. She gives a good-natured roll of her eyes.

"Well, now it won't go to waste." Her gaze flits to Jess, who's standing stiffly at the end of the kitchen island. She seems to debate something for a moment, then pulls a beer from the fridge and pops the top, handing it to him. "It's really good to see you, Jess."

He takes the beer, lifting his eyes to hers. After studying her face for a long moment, he seems to soften. "It's good to see you, too."

It's not until he finally answers that I realize I've been holding my breath. Maybe Jess isn't glad to see me, and I can't blame him for that, but just hearing him say that to Daisy makes my heart settle.

"Dinner's getting cold," Daisy says, gathering more plates and cutlery. She motions toward the dining room. "Let's eat."

The carving knife is still where I left it on the table, beside the turkey. I pick it up, then pause, glancing at Jess. I'm probably asking for too much too soon, but I hold the handle of the knife out to Jess hopefully.

He hesitates, looking from the knife to my face, then sets his beer down. When he takes the knife from my hand and turns to the turkey, I have to blink tears of relief from my eyes.

Jess is here. He's carving the turkey for Christmas dinner, and he's here.

Daisy beams at me as I sink into my seat beside her. Her hand finds mine under the table, and she links our fingers together. Her touch steadies my trembling hand, calms my jangled nerves.

We fill our plates quietly, then Simone raises her wineglass, glancing around the table. "I'd like to propose a toast." She clears her throat uncertainly, and her gaze flicks to Jess, then back to the room. "To family."

I steal a glance at Jess as I raise my own glass, tension twisting my chest, but his eyes meet mine, and he raises his beer with a quiet nod. There's something so different about him tonight, and I have no doubt it's because of the woman by his side. I watch her with interest, the way she silently encourages him, smiling as she eats and touching his arm on the table. The way he responds with a smile of his own, a warmth in his eyes I haven't seen in years. It truly is amazing how finding the right woman can help a man heal, and relief floods me at knowing my son has her in his life.

"How long have you two known each other?" I ask.

"We met at Bounce when Jess started," Simone answers. "But we only started dating a month ago."

"Because I was an idiot," Jess mumbles into a mouthful of turkey, and she laughs.

"You weren't ready." She leans over to press a kiss to Jesse's clean-shaven cheek. "I didn't mind waiting."

He sighs, kissing her forehead and letting his eyes close for a moment. I haven't seen my son like this with anyone since his high school girlfriend. Even with Daisy, he didn't have this ease, this... love. That's what it is. The thought makes me smile, makes me wonder if there could be hope for my son and me after all. I mean, I never expected he'd be here, on Christmas Day, carving the turkey, eating dinner with us. I could never have predicted this turn of events. But has he forgiven me? Has he accepted me and Daisy?

We finish our meals as the questions swim through my head, and Daisy rises to clear our plates. I push to my feet with a shake of my head.

"I'll clean up. You did all the cooking."

But Daisy puts a firm hand on my shoulder and nudges me back into my seat. "I'm on it." She glances at Simone. "Would you mind helping me clean up?" She doesn't say it aloud, but I know what she's doing. Giving me and Jess a moment alone.

"Of course."

Simone gathers our dishes and the two women head into the kitchen, leaving me and Jess in silence. The only sound is the ticking of the large, gold-rimmed clock on the wall behind me, counting down the minutes until... Until what? Jess leaves again?

"I'm sorry," I begin, right at the same time Jess says, "That was good."

Our eyes lock, and we both issue an uncomfortable laugh. It seems neither of us is sure how to navigate this.

"Yeah, Daisy is a great cook," I murmur, and Jess nods slowly.

"Yet another thing I didn't know about her."

I swallow. "Jess, I am so sorry for what happened. For what I did. I should never have gone behind your back to get together with Daisy, and when you moved back home, I should have been honest. I should've come clean."

Jess scrapes his palm over his jaw. "Yeah. You should have." I wait for the yelling, the storming out, but it doesn't come. In fact, he's surprisingly calm. "It was not fun to find those pictures of you two."

I grimace in shame. "God, I know," I mutter, screwing the heels of my hands into my eyes. "If I could go back and do it over, I'd change everything." I reconsider my words. "Well, not everything. Not falling for Daisy. I'm sorry, I know I should probably say that I wouldn't have fallen for her if I could have helped it, but... I don't regret that part."

"Good."

My gaze flies to Jess, confused. "What?"

He lifts a shoulder, fiddling with his napkin. "I'm glad you two found each other," he murmurs. "I mean, sure, I wish you hadn't done it behind my back. And I wish I hadn't found out the way I did. But..." He shakes his head, lifting his gaze to mine. "I'm glad you're happy."

I splutter. "You are?"

"Of course. I want you to be happy, Dad. I didn't realize how much you needed that."

Holy Christ. Who is this kid?

I must have a look of utter incredulity on my face because Jess gives a grim laugh.

"It's taken a lot for me to get to this point, believe me. And"—he wrinkles his nose—"I'm still not entirely happy about you being with my ex. That's going to take some getting used to."

"But?" I ask hopefully.

"But..." He lets his breath out in a long stream. "But Simone has helped me to see— Well, Simone and..."

"A therapist?" I prompt gently.

Jess looks at me, surprised. "How did you know?"

"Rex mentioned something."

"Oh, yeah. He said you'd spoken." Jess sticks out his chin. "Well, yes. I've been seeing a therapist, and Simone says there's no shame in it."

"There isn't," I assure him. I move to reach for his hand, then think better of it. "I saw someone for the first two years after your mom died."

Jesse's jaw hardens for a split second, then softens. "It's helped me deal with some stuff. I realized..." He sets the napkin back on the table and faces me squarely, his eyes swimming with remorse. "I've been a selfish asshole the past few years, and I'm sorry."

"Oh, Jess." This time I put my hand over his, and squeeze. "You haven't. You've been dealing with the loss of your mom. I wish I'd been a better father, wish I'd been there for you more."

"I'm the one who left," Jess says, his voice cracking. "I shouldn't—"

"Hey." I push to my feet and tug my son into my arms. "You were dealing with it the only way you knew how. I wish I'd realized you were pushing me away to avoid your pain. Maybe I could have helped more. I was so lost in my own grief I didn't see it."

He shakes in my arms, crying softly into my sweater, and I hold him. He lets me hold him. He lets me soothe him, and it stitches every last piece of my heart back together.

"You're here now, Jess. That's what matters."

When he finally draws away, he wipes his cheek and gives me a sad smile. "I've missed a lot and I don't want to miss anymore. Mom wouldn't want us to be apart."

My eyes burn as I settle back into my seat. "No, she wouldn't."

"And she wouldn't want me to stay mad at you." Jess sniffs, and a watery smile comes onto his face as laughter drifts from the kitchen. "She would have loved Daisy," he adds quietly, and my throat constricts with emotion.

"Yeah." I can't say anything more than that or I'll break down. It's too much.

"I'm still a little angry," Jess admits, his eyes clearing as he looks back at me. "Mostly that you lied. But I understand why you chose Daisy. She wasn't right for me, but I can see now she's right for you. And it's nice to see you happy again."

"It's nice to see you happy, Jess." I nod my head toward Simone before turning back to him. "No more secrets between us, okay? No more running away. I want you in my life. I know I need to earn your trust again, but I'll do that. I'll do whatever it takes to have you back in my life."

"I just..." Jesse's voice catches and he shrugs, fiddling with the napkin again. "I just need you to be my dad."

My chest floods with emotion, and it makes breathing difficult. I nod, focusing on my wineglass to give us both the space we need to compose ourselves. "That's all I want. If you'll let me."

Jess nods too. "Yeah. I can do that."

Daisy appears in the room, a steaming apple pie in her oven-mitted hands. "Ready for dessert?"

Both Jess and I sniff, straightening in our seats as Simone follows with a tub of ice cream.

"I am," Jess declares, and as Daisy heaps apple pie onto his plate and tops it with a scoop of vanilla ice cream, he sends her a grin. She smiles back and squeezes his shoulder, Simone watching them fondly. I must remember to thank that woman for helping my son, for bringing him home to me. Knowing he's here to stay makes my heart sigh with relief. We have a long way to go to repair everything between us, but I'll work on that every day. I will be the father Jesse needs.

And when the time feels right, with Jesse's blessing, I will ask Daisy to be my wife.

My chest is full of warmth as I watch the three of them chat while they eat their dessert, their voices and laughter filling my home. Simone, the person who helped my son find it in his heart to forgive me. Jess, finally back in my life after too much time apart. And Daisy, the woman who brought light back into my life, who helped me find happiness again when every part of me felt broken.

As I look around the table, the atmosphere noticeably lighter since Jess and I talked, I can't help but feel immensely grateful. Grateful for all I have, for the people here right now, but more than anything, grateful for Daisy.

For the woman I met in Joe's, at just the right time, who knew exactly what I needed to heal.

# EPILOGUE

Head to:
www.jenmorrisauthor.com/ishf-epilogue
to read an exclusive *I Saw Her First* epilogue!

———

Did you enjoy *I Saw Her First*? Reviews help indie authors get our books noticed!

If you liked this book, please leave a review on Amazon. Or you can leave a review on Goodreads. It doesn't have to be much—even a single sentence helps! Thank you.

# ACKNOWLEDGMENTS

I'd like to thank the following people:

Carl and Baxter, first and foremost, always. You're my favourites.

Katie Wyrill, Samara Reyne, Sarah Side, and Ellowyn Gretton. Thank you for always encouraging and believing in me.

Rachel Collins, thanks for not only your fantastic editing skills, but for mopping up my tears when my brain chooses to only see the bad stuff. You always remind me I can do this, and you help me to keep pushing forward when I feel like I should give up.

Melanie A. Smith, Eve Kasey, and Alicia Crofton, for critiques and proof-reading. Enni Amanda for always helping me with my blurbs.

Kira Slaughter, Emma Grocott, Tammy Eyre, Michele Voss, and Leigh-Ann Jordan for beta reading and encouraging me.

Elle Maxwell for her beautiful cover design and illustration, as always.

Dahné Nyboer at Bookblossom PA for all the help with this release. And for putting up with me in general.

All my ARC readers and reviewers. There are way too many to name, but you all help me so much. Thank you for your time and energy and enthusiasm.

And to all readers who've taken a chance on this story. Thank you.

Note: If you're struggling with grief, there's no shame in seeking help. Reach out to friends and family, or find a therapist who can support you. You don't have to go through it alone.

# ABOUT THE AUTHOR

Jen Morris writes sexy escapist romance set in New York. She believes that almost anything can be fixed with a good laugh, a good book, or a plane ticket to NYC.

Her books follow people with big dreams as they navigate life and love in the city. Her characters don't just find love—they find themselves, too.

Jen lives with her partner and son, in a tiny house on wheels in New Zealand. She spends her days writing, dreaming about New York, and finding space for her ever-growing book collection.

*I Saw Her First* is her sixth novel, and the second book in the *Forbidden on Fruit Street* series.

## ALSO BY JEN MORRIS

If you enjoyed *I Saw Her First,* you might also like Violet and Kyle's story: *She Was Made for Me*. It's book one in the Forbidden on Fruit Street Series.

If you liked the sound of Jesse's boss Cory, you can read his story in *The Love You Deserve*. It's book four in the *Love in the City* series. You might also like *Outrageously in Love*, book three in that series. Both are forbidden romances, with The Love You Deserve also being age gap (my fave trope!), and both can be read as standalones.

**Stay in touch so you don't miss anything:**

Find me on Instagram, TikTok, Threads, and Facebook: @jenmorrisauthor

Subscribe to my newsletter for updates, release info, and cover reveals: www.jenmorrisauthor.com

www.ingramcontent.com/pod-product-compliance
Lightning Source LLC
Chambersburg PA
CBHW051319250626
47155CB00007B/2383